REALM

OF

LORE

AND

LIES

CLAIRE WRIGHT

Realm of Lore and Lies

Published by Leannán Press

www.leannanpress.com

Cover Design Art and Design by Tairelei

www.tairelei.com

Copy Editor: Second Pass Editing

Proofread by Sara Starbuck

Identifiers

ISBN: 978-1-7397320-0-4 (eBook)

ISBN: 978-1-7397320-1-1 (Paperback)

ISBN: 978-1-7397320-2-8 (Hardback)

authorclairewright.com

CONTENT WARNING

Contains some scenes not suitable for younger audiences, including expletive language, violence, death and sexual references . . . so all the fun stuff.

CONTENTS

For Michaela, look at what you made me do.

To my family with love.

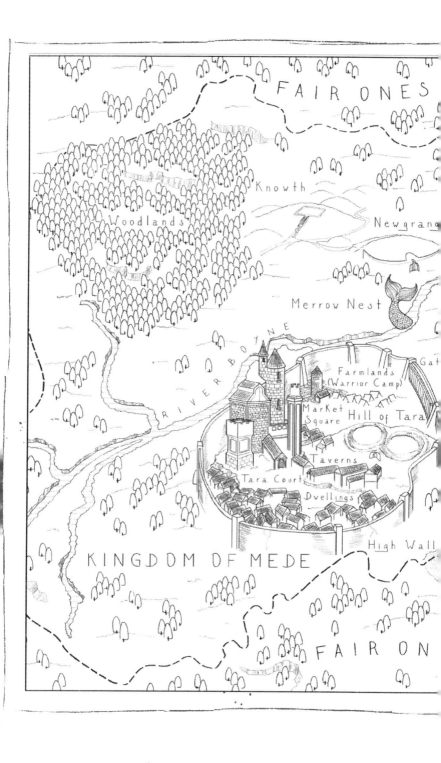

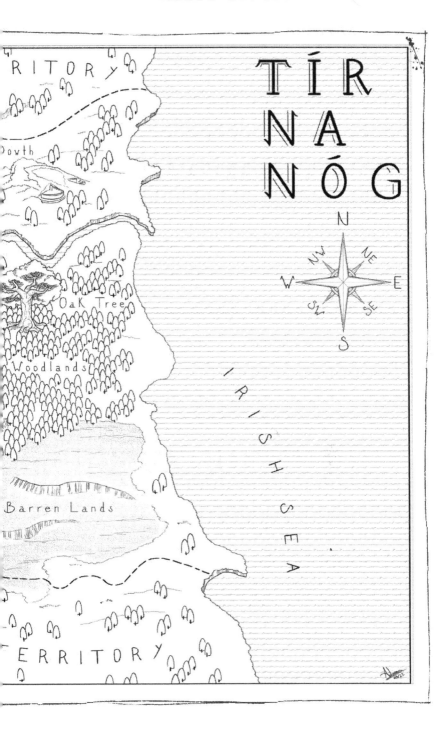

CHAPTER 1

AISLING

A púca had broken the espresso machine, again.

It was the third one this month, and Ash knew she would get the blame. Again. Huffing a wisp of black hair from her face, she squinted at the 'cat'. Its tawny eyes stared back at her, a knowing look of mischief on its face. To everyone else, a striped ginger cat sat on the floor, blocking the narrow hallway leading to the 'staff only' area.

To everyone except Ash. She stuck her tongue out at the creature as its tail flicked lazily across the uneven terracotta tiles. Windows stretched across the expanse of one side of the room, the only modern addition to the renovated cottage, but the autumn sun did little more than cast a faint glow across the closest line of tables. The interior looked more like a Victorian tea room than the trendy cafes and bars its patrons would be used to, but the quirk of makeshift furnishings and crowded aisles brought a charm in its own right.

Over the long hedge across the carpark, Ash could make out the grass roof of the ancient monument enticing tourists. It wasn't only sightseers that were drawn to Newgrange, however, and her gaze met the púca once more with a scowl.

Its glamour flickered like a badly set television channel and the hairless creature switched to its true form for only a

1

moment. Similar in size to a cat, it reminded her of a four-legged goblin, its smile full of needle-sharp teeth surrounded by translucent green skin. She could make out veins and muscle, and jagged edges of bone as she found herself in a staring contest with the small fae. It continued to taunt her, silently daring her to acknowledge it as she scooped coffee beans from the floor and into the rubbish bin.

"Why are you making faces at a cat?" Brian's voice rumbled across the counter, an obvious hint of laughter matching the crinkle of his blue eyes.

Ash adjusted her hairband as she stood, her straight black hair falling heavily, some sticking to her nape. It was uncomfortably warm thanks to the working ovens from the nearby kitchen and a crowded room full of patrons trying to warm themselves after braving the frigid weather.

"They'll start deducting my salary from all the breakages at this rate. It always happens on my shift."

Brian lifted his cup towards the animal. Not an animal; a beast. "And it's the cat's fault?"

"Well, it's not mine," Ash retorted as she washed her hands, the stain of the beans darkening her pale skin. She didn't mind smelling like coffee and baked pastries for the day. It beat chopping onions in the kitchen. She grimaced as it occurred to her that Mary may punish her with exactly that when she discovered the broken machine, but smiled as new customers arrived at her counter.

"Welcome to Newgrange Coffee and Gift Shop. What can I get you?" Ash tried and failed to keep her customer service smile as the couple greeted her, a baby bundled in a wool playsuit in the woman's arms.

"Do you realise how impossible it is to manoeuvre a pram in here?" the young mother said, the barely concealed annoyance as clear in her tone as on her face. "I can understand the passageway"—she pointed towards the window—"but not here."

Ash didn't mention that the clustered cafe was strategically designed for this purpose.

"Let me help you," Ash offered, coming from around the small counter that held an array of pastries and fruit-filled tarts. She rolled her eyes at Brian, who grinned as she passed, before following the woman to where she'd abandoned her pushchair at the door.

Ash pointed for the couple to take the seat closest to the window by the entrance, and only had to ask two tables full of patrons to vacate their seats while she steered the bulky wheeled contraption to its destination. After listening to the woman complain about the poorly run layout of the cafe not being 'family friendly' and taking their order, she returned once more to the counter where Brian was still sitting, shoulders shaking with laughter. As she made tea and prepared scones for her new customers, she kept her gaze trained in their direction, their baby now laid in the pram she'd just manhandled.

"Why are you staring at them?" Brian asked, his six foot lumbering profile in no way subtle as he perched on a barstool beside her till.

But Ash didn't turn to look at him.

There was something off about today, a sense she'd learned to pay close attention to; like the prickling of skin when she felt as if someone was watching her, or the hair on her arms rising when an icy, malevolent presence passed. She was almost always right.

"You said you had notes for me," Ash said, her gaze flicking between her task and the table in the farthest corner.

Brian set his cup down and reached for his backpack. "Lecture notes from this morning's class. Professor Mathews was as dull as ever, but you should have been there. He questioned everyone about our destination choices for next semester's excavation site. Ash, hand yours in."

She set a teapot and saucers on her tray beside the warm scones. Reaching into the glass fridge that sat underneath the counter, she pulled out jars filled with butter, jam and fresh cream. She sensed the púca shift closer, probably hoping it could snatch something from her when she passed it.

"Ash, are you listening?"

There. Ash's fingers halted above the tray, nearly knocking over the butter dish. A shadow crept along the floor underneath tables, weaving its way between discarded bags and weary feet, sweeping closer to the couple waiting for the tray by her hands.

"I have to get this order delivered," Ash murmured, not before loosening the lid of a glass salt shaker and positioning it at the edge of her tray. She took a deep breath and zigzagged between patrons over to the table, racing to reach the shadow's target before it was too late.

"Here you go," Ash said, slamming the tray down and knocking the salt shaker with the back of her hand. Loose salt spilled like quicksand, the glass container landing with a light thud on the fleeced bundle within the cot.

"What are you doing?" the mother cried out before pulling the pram closer in a jerking motion; it banged against the table and a loud wail came from within.

"So sorry, how clumsy of me," Ash said, reaching in and brushing the salt in every direction. The pink flesh of the newborn was spotted in white granules and Ash sighed in relief. Her eyes darted to the dense shadows now pulsing at the mother's feet, swirling around as if it was composed of tadpoles in a pond.

She stared it down, almost able to make out a pair of black eyes glaring back. But she would not cower. A jerk to the pram made her jump, and she swallowed as the mother lifted her baby close to her chest, swiping at the salt. There was enough on his skin to ensure he would remain safe.

"Tom, do you think he swallowed any?" the mother asked; her husband now stood behind her seat as they inspected their baby.

"He'll be okay, love." The man patted her shoulder. "Only a bit of salt."

The woman glared up at Ash before standing. The baby continued to wail, and Ash suspected it was more to do with being woken than anything else. "I want to speak to your manager."

Ash nodded solemnly before escorting her to the narrow hallway, shooing the púca away with her booted foot. She called to Mary, who stood over a large pot in the kitchen, the smell of baking bread filling the air.

When Mary approached them, Ash let the woman give her version of events, but her gaze continuously flickered to the dining room. Shadows filled the area, but none as black and ominous as before. Ash murmured an apology when Mary coaxed her and left to attend the counter, only half listening to the woman complain about the ordeal she and her now sleeping baby had endured.

Brian watched her with raised brows as she wiped the counter and righted already straightened jars. The other patrons had noticed and had either remained quiet or murmured during the scene, but now they were back to ignoring her, deep in their own conversations once more.

"Why do you work here?" Brian eventually asked, setting his empty cup before him. "You could work in a cafe close to Trinity. That way, you could make your lectures, too. And maybe we'd get to spend more time together."

"This is my home, Brian. You know that," Ash said, finally looking at him. His short brown hair was styled like most college

5

boys, and his rugby jumper stretched over his large frame. Brian's smile was wide enough to show his dimples and she knew she was supposed to get flutters when she looked at him. Those feelings had been there when they'd first started dating, but now she wasn't so sure. Sighing, she pointed towards the other end of the cottage where the living quarters were. "I work here in order to pay rent, and they also let me give tours of Newgrange. They were short-staffed today, so I had to skip lectures."

"Ash, come on."

"What?" She turned back around, fiddling with the broken machine, her shoulders stiffening at his tone.

"You're choosing to spend more time at your job than your final year at college? What's more important? I don't want to sound like your father or anything but—" Brian winced as the steamer nozzle Ash had been trying to fix came loose and she threw it on the counter. A group sitting nearby looked at them, scowls on their faces. Ash snatched his notes from the counter.

"Sorry, Ash—"

"Just leave."

Brian's jaw clenched. "That's a little harsh, don't you think? I didn't mean it like that and you know it. I've come all the way from town to be—"

"Nobody asked you to." Ash hated the way he said 'town' as if there was only one in all of Ireland. She reached under the counter, and avoiding his gaze, stuffed his notes unceremoniously into her backpack. "Shit."

Taking them out again, she realised she'd shoved them into the section where her letters were. With shaking fingers, she took the now creased letter from the top of the pile and carefully straightened it. Ash had opened, read and placed it back within its envelope so many times that the new crease looked obstinate and wrong against the soft, aged folds. The silence from above her was louder than the chatter echoing around the room. She looked up, surprised to see Brian was still there, looking at her with the expression she hated more than anything in the world.

His face wrinkled up as he cleared his throat. "Have you got any new ones lately?"

She knew he was going for sympathy, but she needed his pity like she needed the púca at her feet.

"No." Ash regretted ever sharing that piece of her life with him. She shouldn't have told him about her brother's letters, she saw that now. "You should go."

He opened his mouth but closed it. As he gathered his belongings, he opened his mouth again and closed it just as quickly. She expected him to leave, saying nothing, but grimaced when he finally stared down at her and spoke. "And so, I'm the next guy on your list to be discarded? I lasted longer than the others, at least."

Ash scowled at him but didn't answer. It seemed to goad Brian further. Pointing his finger towards the bag by her feet, he raised his voice. "I came here because I care about you. You're going to fail your final year, and for what?"

Ash noticed the room had become quieter as the other customers stared. She was really giving them a show today. She gritted her teeth as heat rose to her cheeks. "Enough."

"How can you look to the future when you're clinging to the past?"

"Thanks for the psychoanalysis, Dr Dick, but we're both taking archaeology, not psychology. Now, leave."

Murmurs filled the cafe once more as the door rattled on its hinges. Ash's vision blurred as she raised her clammy hand to her cheek, willing it to cool her temper. She knew her reaction was over the top, caused by her own issues rather than his good intentions, but their relationship would never have lasted, and she only had herself to blame for trying. She laughed without humour. Another one bites the dust.

Unlike Brian's unwarranted advice about clinging to the past, she'd learned long ago how to move on. Even if that meant she'd unintentionally left her brother behind.

Staring down at the púca, she cast a glance around the cafe. Straddling the line between 'normal' and her old Fianna life, she was destined to be alone. Perhaps once she graduated, she'd end up living in a one bed apartment with ten púca wannabe cats for company. A shiver that had nothing to do with the weather had her scanning for that shadowy wicked fae once more. Ash wouldn't make it to graduation if a Fair One like that ensnared her for their wicked games, but she'd always known that protecting humanity came at a deadly price.

CHAPTER 2

AISLING

A feline body pressed against her leg and as Ash looked down at the púca, it had the gall to meow at her. Ash rubbed behind its ear despite herself and reached for the bowl they kept for such occasions. She poured full fat milk into it and saw the creature's face light up with excitement as she grabbed two butter sticks and dumped them in.

"Come on. You really are going to be the death of my job, Fluffy," Ash said as she led it through the staff hallway, where she could still hear Mary and the woman, and then made her way outside to the gravel car park beside Newgrange.

If anyone saw the contents of the bowl that she placed in front of the beast, they'd surely tell her cats were dairy intolerant and should not consume any. What she couldn't tell them was that púca were certainly not intolerant to it. The only way to keep peace with this species of fae was to gift them with as much of it as possible. If only all Fair Ones were as easily pleased. The ancient fae stalking the room in shadows earlier was evidence of that.

The púca devoured its meal in slurping delight. Clearly, peace with this faerie fecker did not entail it staying away from tinkering with coffee machines, but hopefully it would stay quiet about her interference with a changeling attempt.

9

As Ash's cheeks reddened with the stark temperature change of the stuffy cafe to outside, her thoughts swept to Brian's departure. Stuffing her hands into her apron, she noted his car was nowhere in sight. It was inevitable. It was difficult to maintain a relationship with a human with no knowledge she had Faerie Sight, but it was downright impossible for Ash. She knew it, of course. But sometimes she forgot her resolve to avoid relationships; especially when they looked like Brian.

She sighed and watched her warm breath rise in the cold air as her gaze drifted towards Newgrange. A hedge roughly her height obscured most of it so she could only see the grass covered roof from where she stood. The sun hung low, continuing to provide little light, barely visible through thick grey clouds.

A tour bus ambled towards the car park as a familiar voice startled her from behind. "There you are, Aisling. You left a cafe full of thirsty customers."

Ash knew before she turned towards the plump older woman, she would have her short arms crossed across her ample bosom. Ash didn't call breasts 'bosoms', but it always seemed appropriate with Mary. She couldn't suppress her smile as her suspicions were proven right. "Sorry, I had to deal with *that*."

Mary uncrossed her arms, only to prop them on her wide hips as she eyed the creature between them. It didn't raise its head as its distinctly non-cat like noises emanated from the ground between their feet. "I suppose I'd better call our distributor again. Honestly, at this rate I may dock your wages."

Ash huffed, stomping her foot and feeling every bit like the teenager she no longer was, but not caring. "It's not my fault!"

She knew Mary didn't mean it. After taking her in, feeding and clothing her, all those years ago, Mary and Dom insisted she lived as good as rent-free in their cottage. Even though they paid her a fair wage, they'd covered her university bills and supported her financially. The only payback they said they ever wanted was to see her thrive. She'd find a way to return the favour, she was indebted to them in more ways than financially. They'd given her love and security when she'd lost it at the side of a road where her clan had once been.

"What do I see when I look at this creature?" Mary asked, her freckled pale face frowning towards the púca.

"A cat." Ash grumbled, knowing where this argument would lead.

"And what do you, dear?"

"In my defence, I'm not even supposed to be here this morning."

"When you see it's . . . not a cat, you're supposed to get it away from my coffee machine. I'm so well acquainted with our maintenance guy that I may invite him round for dinner. Roll your eyes again and I'll offer him a full board in your room." Before Ash could retaliate, Mary's gaze drifted towards the bus. "I'll tell you how you can make it up to me. Paul up at the visitor centre called to say we're down a guide. Cover this tour and all will be forgiven."

Mary's voice sounded stern, but Ash could see amusement behind her foster mother's eyes. It was an unofficial term. Ash had been seventeen when she'd moved in with the couple that owned the Newgrange farm and cafe. They also liaised with the Office of Public Works with running tours for the ancient monuments in Boyne Valley. They hadn't contacted the authorities, and it wasn't as if social services could keep track of the travelling Fianna clans to note a runaway teenager. Her family certainly wouldn't have had outsiders involved.

They both knew that guiding a tour was never a punishment. Ash's face cracked into a wide smile as she untied her apron and threw it at Mary. "Really?"

"Really," Mary said, disappearing inside only to retrieve a tour guide jacket and microphone headset, which she handed to Ash's already outstretched hands.

Even though Ash wore a knitted jumper, the cold air made her shiver, and she was thankful for the lined fleece Mary offered.

As she put on the extra layer that had 'tour guide' stitched on the chest, she frowned toward the door. "But I'm already covering the cafe. How can you manage both kitchen and serving duties?"

"Oh, I think I can manage. Dom will be back soon after tending to the animals. Anyway, you were doing such a stand up job of it, out here pampering a púca." Mary laughed, but the sound quickly cut. She stepped closer to Ash, her voice lowering. "Was it a changeling?"

Ash looked beyond Mary, but she couldn't see the parents or their baby from here. "Yes."

Mary didn't answer for the longest time, and Ash knew her thoughts were elsewhere, with her own painful history. Eventually, she smoothed down her flour crusted apron and smiled at Ash. "Thank you. I know it's difficult for you to defy their rules." Mary sneered at the mention of the ancient agreement between Ash's kind and the Fair Ones. "But you've saved an innocent life today."

Ash smiled at the woman but didn't answer, knowing there wasn't a good enough response to console her. What could she say to soothe a mother who'd been robbed of the chance to care for her child before he was snatched away?

"Hopefully, Fluffy will keep quiet, too." Ash kicked the now empty bowl, and the púca glowered at her with an unnatural sounding hiss. "Or else no more dairy offerings."

"A letter came for you this morning," Mary said, and Ash's attention snapped to the other woman. "I've kept it safe for you, don't worry. Go on." Mary jerked her head toward the bus that was now idling across the car park nearer to the monument. "I'll cover the cafe while you impress all the Yanks with what a ridiculous amount of knowledge you have for such a young girl."

"I'm hardly young," Ash said, straightening as she placed her headset on and zipped up her fleece.

She swallowed the reprimand on her tongue at Mary for not telling her a letter had come. It could only be from her brother Conor. He was the one person from her past who had kept in touch. His letters were a tenuous link tethering her to the life she walked away from. It was a torture she looked forward to every month. Reading about his life, absorbing guilt at every word, knowing she'd left her only brother without saying goodbye.

If he ever stopped writing, she'd never know why. So every month, she waited to see if this would be the time his letter didn't arrive. His last one had been full of sketches of recent tattoos he'd drawn for a girl he'd met. Her chest burned, imagining Conor moving on with his life without her. It was a selfish thought she would never voice. Of course she wanted her brother to be happy. He was a young adult now, and she'd left a child.

Looking at the woman who had replaced her mother for the past seven years, she knew she probably saw the angry teenager she had been. In truth, still was.

"I know." Mary's eyes filled with that look Ash hated, but only for a second before a wistful smile replaced it. "You've come a long way since the day you crashed into our lives, dear."

Ash would have responded if she'd known the right words, but the tourists began their descent from the bus, so she only smiled and jogged to greet them.

"Hello, folks. Welcome to Newgrange. My name is Aisling, and I'll be your guide as we walk around the three ancient tombs in Boyne Valley. We start with this glorious monument to our left." Ash gestured for the small group to follow her and smirked at the bemused looks on some of them.

She knew what they saw. What kind of tour could she give in such a historic place? A nose piercing and tight fitted jeans with black glitter ankle boots gave the impression that she didn't belong in front of this crowd. Ash revelled in the exact moment their expressions transitioned from prejudiced condemnation of her contoured make up to grudging admiration of her vast knowledge. Ash knew everything there was to know about Newgrange, and as she led this group towards the steps leading to the narrow opening, past the engraved boulders that guarded it, she recited it with such enthusiasm, she already had the attention of every tourist trailing behind her.

Ash was shit at making coffee and holding on to relationships, but this was where she shone. Not only because she lived and breathed archaeology, it was in her blood. She was Fianna, whether that community recognised her as one of them or not. She spent most of her life pretending. Seeing Fair Ones around her, averting her eyes when they played with their food. It had once been easy, before she saw just how vicious they could be.

Fair Ones, gods, fae—whatever you wanted to call them. Those mythical bastards were real and very much alive.

Ash continued her lesson before inviting the first set of tourists to enter the dark passageway in single file to walk to the antechamber within. She traced the spirals engraved on the stone at the entrance, picturing the lone triskele engraved in the ancient wall of the head recess hidden beyond. She loved pointing out that feature, the exact likening of the tattoo she had inked on her inner arm on her eighteenth birthday. Mary had been furious, but luckily Dom had been the ever-present buffer between them. He was the long suffering man amongst the two most stubborn women in Ireland, apparently.

Where would she have ended up if she hadn't stumbled into their cafe? Her families' caravan camp had been stationed not too far when she'd run away, only taking a small bag of clothes before storming off with no direction in her mind. Ash shook her head and forced a smile at the passing tourists before ducking low and following them into the narrow tunnel. She refused to think of that day. The guilt of leaving Conor ate away at her, and the fact her clan had left camp before she'd had time to calm down and return had stung more than she cared to admit.

Three hours later, and a fleece pocket full of tips that outdid any amount of money she could make in a full day serving coffee, Ash entered the cafe once more.

"Go on and take your break, love. There's soup and bread waiting for you on the stove." Mary patted her shoulder as the tourists who had just finished with her filed into the almost full cafe.

Ash's stomach gurgled at the mention of lunch. "Tomato and basil?"

"You know it. I also placed your letter in your bag."

"You're a star." Ash bumped shoulders with Mary before grabbing her backpack and disappearing to the kitchen. Hoisting her bag securely on her shoulder, she wiped her sweaty palms against her thighs. What news would her younger brother's letter bring this time? She silently thanked Mary for allowing her to take her break even when the cafe was so full.

She couldn't help the appreciative groan at the smell of soup and freshly baked bread that greeted her, but she ignored it in favour of perching on a barstool and placing her bag on her lap. It wasn't as bulky as it should be, and she frowned. Ash, through a mixture of sentimentality and sadism, kept a year's worth of letters from her brother in her bag. Conor's letters may come only once a month, or two in the space of a few weeks, and the anticipation in between them was something Ash had never gotten used to. She often re-read them before realising she'd even opened one. It had become a habit she couldn't shake.

Jostling the bag, she retrieved her laptop and set it aside before spilling the remaining contents across the counter. Brian's lecture notes were still there, a few notebooks, her purse, makeup bag, pens, a broken pencil, and random knick-knacks. As she looked inside the section that mattered more than any amount of tips in her pocket, her mouth went dry.

All of her letters were gone.

CHAPTER 3

AISLING

"And you're sure Brian didn't come back into the cafe yesterday when I gave that tour?"

"Honestly, love. I'm sure." Mary's voice was less patient than the first twenty times Ash had asked her the same question that morning, all the way to lunchtime, but to her credit, she still answered.

Ash watched her in momentary silence, kneading dough, Dom's jovial voice floating back to them as he served customers out front. Saturdays were normally their busiest day, and today was no exception. The morning had brought rain, but the sun was finally peeking through the ever present clouds, and Ash was grateful she wouldn't have to spend the impending tour herding a group of rain sodden tourists. They never tipped her as well.

Tearing off a lump of dough from the floured counter, she twisted it in her fingers, her brows furrowed as a headache threatened. She had searched the entire cafe after hours, but couldn't find her letters anywhere. She'd always taken such good care of them. Conor was the only one who had bothered to contact her over the years. It was one-sided, which annoyed her, but she understood. Fianna clans never stayed in one place for too long so Conor couldn't give her a forwarding address. She'd often wondered how he knew she was at the cafe, but decided it was a blessing she wouldn't question.

Mary hummed while Ash silently spiralled beside her, the dough turning tight and overworked, breaking into clumps. Dropping it, she cleaned her hands on a towel, dusting flour from her grey cashmere jumper and black shiny leggings. Turning her back to the counter, she let out a weary sigh. She had tried to keep tabs on her clan's movements at first, but it was futile. Unlike other clans, like the McQuillan's, her mother didn't advertise where they visited next. They hadn't performed in this area since the day she'd left them, and she hadn't heard of their fairgrounds showing up anywhere in recent years.

Where was her mother leading their clan? Not theirs; it hadn't been her clan since she left. Ash was no longer a matriarch in training. Conor's letters never gave much information about what their mother was doing. He hinted at places they visited, but it didn't matter. By the time the letter arrived at the cafe, they were already long gone.

Her studies were more important, as reluctant as she was to admit, her now ex-boyfriend Brian had been right. With another heavy sigh, she retreated to the other side of the warm kitchen where Mary's office was and sat at the desk where she'd abandoned her laptop. In between tours, she would spend the weekend studying and catching up on her missed lectures, starting fresh on Monday. Logging into her email account, a prompt popped up, reminding her to change her password, but she clicked out of it, opening the last email from her lecturer, requesting her late assignment.

A few minutes into staring at a blank screen where she'd made no progress, she reached for her phone, clicking into her social accounts and getting lost in scrolling. Ash pivoted in her chair, pasting a smile on her face as she took a selfie, showing Mary's row of intricately knotted dough rolls in the background, ready to go into the oven. Her smile faded as soon as she snapped, but her followers didn't need to know how miserable she really was. Sharing it to her stories, she waited to see if Brian viewed it.

"Your tour has pulled up, dear." Mary gestured without looking towards the open doorway as a bus idled across the parking lot.

Stuffing her phone into her pocket, Ash donned her beanie and gloves before muttering a farewell to Mary and jogging outside towards the new set of tourists. Her forehead continued to pulse with the foreboding of a headache, and Ash hoped this tour would be quick. Switching her microphone on, she began her introduction, the repetition of her rehearsed speech flowing even without her full attention. This group was larger than yesterday's and had a lot more questions, so she smiled through the haze of her turbulent mind, shaking herself to pay attention.

After they'd walked inside and around the Newgrange passage tomb, Ash herded them on the bus to head to the mound at Knowth. The old bus jostled on the potholed roads, the sky turning overcast. Condensation already obscured the windows, the many bodies crammed together causing a temporary heat that would make them even colder when they arrived at their next destination.

"What does 'Sam-hane' mean?" one of the Germans asked, notebook in hand.

It took a moment for Ash to register what he had meant, but she smiled when it clicked. The bus had been decorated for the holiday and stickers saying 'Samhain Blessings Ye Old Witches' were scattered throughout the bus.

"*Sow-in* is the Irish celebration of the division between the light and dark halves of the year. It predates Halloween and many traditions stem from our customs."

"Go on. But talk slower please."

Ash smirked as the German scribbled furiously before his fingers poised above the page.

"Many years ago, people believed that at Samhain, the veil between this world and Tír na nÓg—that's the Otherworld—was at its thinnest. They dressed up in order to trick harmful spirits into leaving them alone. Hence the tradition of dressing up as witches and ghouls at Halloween."

"Is that when the passageway in Newgrange lights up?" a voice from the back of the bus called out.

"Not quite. That is the Winter Solstice on December twenty-first." Ash refrained from adding she had already told them about this in Newgrange. She also ignored the throbbing in her head that would surely cause her to be tetchy and lose out on tips. "On that morning only, light fills the passageway in the tomb we just visited, through a strategically placed opening in the roof above the entrance. Nobody knows the true significance of why it's there, but our ancestors from five thousand years ago must have had a pretty impressive reason." Ash smiled through her lies. Fianna knew the real reason behind it. It had nothing to do with sacrificial offerings, and it wasn't a burial site. "Samhain is associated with two hills close by. Let me check with the bus driver to see if we can include them on our tour."

Hoping this would earn her serious tips, and ignoring the now fully present headache, she convinced the driver to include the extra stops after they traipsed across the Knowth and Dowth passageways. She would have to share half her earnings with the driver—even though the greedy bastard earned way more than she did in the first place—so she needed to make sure it was worth her while. Ash impressed her tour with tales of how the hills were used for a Great Fire Festival to celebrate Lugh, king to the mythical Tuatha Dé. Even though the tourists seemed to want more, she stopped herself from talking too much about the Fair One, as if Lugh himself would appear and condemn her for exposing his existence.

Ash always trod a fine line during these types of tours and her head wasn't fully in it today, so she was afraid. She knew the consequences if she blabbered and a Fair One, even one as lowly as the mangy púca, was within earshot. Reciting widely known mythology was fine, but if she wasn't careful and became engrossed in her storytelling, she could let one of the heavily guarded secrets slip. Lugh hadn't been seen by any Fianna in years, but Fair Ones lived for several millennia, longer than the monuments Ash gave tours for.

She could make some serious tips if she told this group the Fianna were the guardians of Ireland's true history. Unknown to everyone else, Fianna kept the peace between the fae and the rest of the unsuspecting humankind through a treaty forged thousands of years ago. Ash would not allow the fact that technically she was no longer part of the club be the reason to spill the beans on all things fae. Smirking, she imagined the tourists' reactions. As if anyone would truly have believed her, anyway.

She tried not to think about what would happen to her foster parents if word got out that they knew the truth. They hadn't found out from her, but that wouldn't matter. They were unfortunate to discover the truth with a changeling baby long before she'd entered their cafe.

Ash told her group to walk around to take photos and explore while she stood near the boulder at the top of the hill of Tara, taking in the rolling green hills around her. Filling her lungs with a deep breath of fresh air, she allowed herself to think about that day seven years ago. After she'd walked away from the only life she'd known over a stupid argument with her overprotective mother, Mary and Dom took her in. Whether it was fate, or she stumbled upon the only humans outside the

Fianna community that knew of the existence of fae, Ash didn't know.

Mary and Dom had been all she'd needed ever since. She'd never replace the baby they'd lost. The act of changeling was forbidden, but it didn't stop some ancient fae from performing it. It was a cruelty Ash couldn't think about without feeling sick to her stomach. Stealing a newborn and abandoning them in the other realm, the old, dying fae would take their place, being cared for by unsuspecting humans. They often blamed cot death when the fae eventually died. Mary and Dom had somehow realised the truth before they buried their baby.

Ash's breath hitched at the memory of how upset Mary had been when she first told Ash. Even years after it had happened, the mourning mother seemed to break her heart every time she talked about what had occurred. Ash couldn't imagine the pain, and felt useless when she was unable to console Mary with any further knowledge about what happened to babies who were taken. It was something even the Fianna didn't know.

She didn't know why her presence seemed to bring them comfort. Living with a deeply hurt and sarcastic teenager didn't sound appealing. At twenty-three, she was still those things but was much better at hiding it.

"Can you tell us more about these hills and the tombs?"

Ash jumped at the heavily accented German behind her as she came back from her reverie. She smiled as she gestured for them to walk around the spire at the top of the hill. "The Hill of Tara used to be where the High Kings of Ireland lived."

She didn't add that the latest High King lived there, in the other realm. Ash wondered what Tír na nÓg looked like. She'd never been, and if she'd stayed with her clan, she might have one day been permitted to go.

"And what about the warriors? The Fee-a-na?"

Ash turned to the voice behind the question, but she could see that the tourist had no malice and didn't seem to know her heritage.

Licking her lips, chapped by the icy wind, she said, "Fianna warriors long served the High Kings of Ireland. They were his personal guard and travelled across the country on his orders. They encountered many mythical creatures along the way, or so the legends say."

More of her group gathered, and she switched her microphone on so they could hear her over the wind that had picked up. "Nowadays, Fianna are still a travelling community and if you ever come by one of their fairgrounds, I'd encourage you to visit. They hold performances in individual tents with all manner of entertainment for you to enjoy. In fact, one of the most popular Fianna clans is holding a fairground not too far from here. The McQuillans are renowned for their dancing and singing."

"Have you been to many shows?"

"Yes, you could say that." Ash smiled and fought the urge to mention that she was once a part of an equally notorious travelling clan.

She remembered attending one of the McQuillan's shows as a young girl and had been in awe of the beauty of their matriarch. Her twins were Ash's age, but she had been far too intimidated to talk to either. The McQuillans were distinctive in appearance. Where her family were dark-haired and fair skinned, the McQuillans were blonde. The men were towering blocks of broad shoulders and strong jawlines. The women had thick curves and high cheekbones. They were the closest thing to Nordic warriors Ash had ever encountered.

She often wondered if the other clans knew about her. Why would they care? She was just a runaway nuisance, not fit to belong to the great Breen clan.

By the time they made it back from the extended tour, the carpark beside Newgrange was cast in darkening shadows and Ash no longer had the mildly annoying headache but a full-blown migraine. A keening rang in her ears and at first she believed it was her pounding temples, but then she saw it. Long, streaming red hair spilled out of a hood; the cloaked figure shadowed in the dark, on the lone road the bus had just driven on. It was a spectral; it had to be. But as Ash stared wide-eyed, it came into focus. The longer she watched, the louder the banshee's cry sounded.

Chapter 4

Tiernan

"We've royally fucked up," Tiernan said in greeting to the huddled group around the campfire, ignoring the glares he received at ambushing the elder's early morning meeting.

If their matriarch had been there, she would have invited him, but it was clear most of them didn't approve. Since joining their clan almost seven years ago, Cara had taken a shine to him, especially when she'd found out he could hack into just about anywhere. Something the elders seemed to forget, and how he'd learned of this meeting. The reason he'd decided to attend, uninvited, was because Cara had been missing for three days longer than she normally would. He hadn't slept the previous night, his mind zinging with different reasons his matriarch hadn't returned yet; with each passing hour, his theories became as dark as the autumn sky.

She'd recently allowed him to become an advisor, much to the elders' collective disapproval. They muttered about being cursed with a foul-mouthed brat as Emer sighed. Tiernan's cousin was slightly older than him and her tone never let him forget it. His jaw clenched as he noted they had invited her.

"It'll be grand." Emer shrugged her shoulders, although the gesture was lost in her heavily padded coat. Looking at him with a grim smile, she added, "Isn't it always? She's gone on loads of . . . excursions before."

"Never for this long," he replied, but it was as if he hadn't spoken, for all he got in return was blank stares.

It was a wintry morning, frost coating the short grass beside the black rushing river; the sun had yet to rise. The Breen clan had pitched camp in a location between the Hill of Tara and Newgrange monument before Cara's departure, and Tiernan wondered, not for the first time, why their matriarch had decided on this particular spot after years of avoiding it.

He regarded his elders—and Emer—as they huddled by the campfire in the bite of early morning. When all he saw was indifference and wrinkles, his gaze went beyond to the surrounding countryside. Their caravans dotted the bank, the lone road yards away, already busy with traffic as the Gluttons commuted to work. He wondered what it would be like to live in a house, going to a mundane job, blissfully ignorant to the existence of the otherworld cloaked around them. Fianna didn't have the luxury of this, and the thanks they had for this knowledge was being glorified watchdogs to the Fair Ones.

Although it seemed like the Breens were a big clan, it was nothing compared to his previous one, where his family name had been painted boldly across their caravans. Now, his Cassidy kin was dispersed amongst the remaining clans, his cousin and he deciding to join this one, along with a small collection of others. They had all blended in seamlessly, while he hadn't.

The elders continued in their soft-spoken conversation, ignoring Tiernan completely. Emer joined in when prompted, clearly in favour over him. She had joined through marriage, and he was the unwanted addition. The Breens no longer provided entertainment through travelling fairgrounds, so their camp was not as impressive as it once had been. It was clear that's what this morning's meeting was about. Without their matriarch's knowledge, he noted with a grimace.

He shouldn't have let her go.

"She took Conor with her this time," Tiernan interrupted once more, and when no one acknowledged him, he pressed on, raising his voice. "She's dragging him down this path and he's too young for it."

Another sigh from Emer and a shake of her head, causing her long dark plaits to sway. "She's his mother, Tier, so it's up to her. She's also our matriarch so—"

"Don't give me that. I know who she is. Cara took us in when our clan was . . . when we parted ways." Tiernan flinched, knowing that wasn't the right way to say it, but he couldn't find the appropriate words.

Emer didn't answer for once, and her gaze seemed to say she knew he hadn't meant it like that. Seven years on and he found speaking in a factual, impartial sense kept the demons at bay. Clenching his hands into fists, he stepped closer to the fire, bumping shoulders to widen the closed group. What if it was the other way around? Would he want his mother to speak of him without feeling? But it wasn't him. She was the one to disappear, and it had left him behind to deal with a barrel of shite.

His next words came out low, directed at his cousin alone. "Cara is as close to a mother as I have. I'm just worried. All of these years, she's searched for my mother. You know I want to find out what happened as much as she does."

"She decides our quest," Mrs O'Malley said before Emer could open her mouth to reply.

The Breen second in command threw another log into the fire, and Tiernan took it as a sign to give up. For now. Mrs O'Malley wasn't the type of woman who suffered fools gladly, and he knew he'd already pushed his luck by showing up uninvited. Pinks, orange and indigo painted the horizon as the sun made its ascent, silhouetting the trees and hills, along with a sporadic cluster of houses. He rubbed his hands together and stretched his long fingers as close as he dared to the flames, illuminating his brown skin.

The elders moved back to the worrying topic of money. Or lack of it. It had been so long since they'd hosted a fairground show, he wasn't sure if they were up to it anymore. Tiernan groaned internally, but kept it to himself. Even though he continuously proved his loyalty to the Breen clan by following his matriarch's orders, hacking into places he had no business being, he knew the elders would expect him to perform in their shows if they reopened.

He'd always hated it. Performing tricks and wooing crowds during their fairground days, but they were Fianna, that was how they made legitimate money. Even though he'd suggested other ways they could make a substantial income, they always shot his ideas down. So what if his suggestions fell between the web of almost illegal? Cara had warmed to the idea, but she'd been completely distracted in recent months, and now she was missing.

Looking towards his cousin, who was mid-flow in sharing her much more acceptable suggestion, he envied her. Perhaps it would have been the same for him if he stopped 'tinkering with screens' as Emer had put it. *"Get your head out of your phone and into the real worlds,"* was another way she not so subtly cajoled him. Even she didn't understand just what he could do while tinkering on screens. What made his suggestions illegal was his ability to hack into anywhere. If it had a digital fingerprint, he could pry the full hand open in a matter of keystrokes.

Emer finished whatever brilliant idea she'd had and huddled close to her wife. Another reminder of how she belonged more than he ever could. Even though she was only two years older than he was, she was married. He couldn't imagine getting hitched at twenty-five, but Emer knew her own mind and had found the perfect partner in Niamh.

"What do you think, Tier?" Emer's voice broke through his thoughts, and he started when he looked up to find everyone's face turned towards him.

"I think we shouldn't be discussing reopening the Breen fairground without the matriarch present."

Mrs O'Malley raised her hood as a light speckle of rain descended, glaring at him as she spoke. "We are the elders, boy. We decide in the absence of our matriarch."

"Funds are low. There's no time to wait any longer," Niamh said, and Tiernan noted the nod of approval from the elder, who only cast disdain toward him.

Emer looked at Tiernan pointedly, as if he was failing some test of hers. He probably was.

"What my cousin means is we need to come up with a solid plan to bring to Cara when she returns. It's important to prepare now."

That's not what Tiernan had meant, and everyone knew it. When the elders discussed the different performances they could do, and how the Breen warriors could practice swordplay and combat on stage, he had to fight the urge to roll his eyes. Another Brehon law meant all young clan members had to train as warriors for their High King in case he called upon them. Although Tiernan trained, he wasn't as enthusiastic as most. He could see the excitement on both Emer's and Niamh's faces at the mention of it. The newlyweds shared a blanket on a log beside him and their happiness made his throat tighten. She was the only family he was close to. It was a pity she was such a pain in the ass.

It was highly unusual for clans to merge. But after the caillte, nothing normal had happened for Tiernan. The media had

29

named them 'the lost clan', showing just how ignorant Gluttons were to the Fianna community. His people called them the caillte, or *the lost*, but the group who'd gone missing seven years ago had belonged to different clans.

His mother, his former matriarch, had been one of the five clansmen who'd gone missing. If it had been his father instead . . . his cheeks flushed with guilt for thinking it but he also felt a tang of truth in it. It wasn't like he saw much of the legendary Bradan Cassidy, Rígfennid of Leinster, anyway. Both of his parents held prominent positions within the community, and here he was, a hacker who had to gatecrash an elder meeting. How would his father react to seeing him now?

Tiernan would never know.

Bradan wasn't part of this clan; he was too important, ruling over one of the provinces and licking the High King's arse. At least if his mother, the Cassidy matriarch, were still around, their clan would have remained intact and he wouldn't be in a field in Meath, freezing his balls off and waiting for his current matriarch to come back from her own disappearing act.

Would Cara ever stop looking?

At the start, he'd been grateful the Breen matriarch continued to search for the caillte, but with every obscure location, he got the sense she'd been lying for quite some time. What if she wasn't looking for what he thought she was? Tiernan worried at his chapped lips with his teeth and felt a warm trickle. He tried to lick the blood away, but the keen eyed elder beside him who gripped his arm until it hurt had caught him.

"Ne'er shed a drop, or bubble's pop. Keep your blood within."

"I know."

"Blood spilt on Samhain is an invitation for all manner of evil to befall you."

"Aye," Tiernan replied, licking the evidence of his indiscretion from his lips.

He shouldn't be so flippant, but sometimes it was hard to know which of their laws were just mere superstition. Fianna clans travelled to different countries, but Ireland was home. The laws of the land were followed, but clans also adhered to the ancient Brehon laws enforced upon them by the human High King of Fianna. It was hard to remember they had a ruling human king, little more than a watchdog to the ancient fae.

When he was a child, his nightmares often included the High King coming to punish him for breaking an ancient law he hadn't yet learned. He'd wake up drenched in sweat and tears, his parents unable to console him. But now, the king was only a passing thought. Tiernan knew the true enemy: the Fair Ones.

CHAPTER 5

AISLING

The blood drained from Ash's face, and through a tight-lipped smile, she thanked her tourists as they dumped coins and notes into her tip bucket. The banshee continued her lament, reaching for Ash with her bone white hands. She was nowhere near, but Ash felt the urge to approach as if the banshee had grabbed hold of her arms and pulled.

This type of encounter screeched bodings of ill will, and she checked herself for any cuts. She *could not* bleed on this day. Menstrual cycles were the only exception, which were apparently considered a gift from the goddess of spring and fertility, Brigid. Ash had always wondered why the female thought to add cramps to that particular monthly souvenir, but in this moment, as her heart thrummed in her throat, her feet moved toward the creature before her mind caught on. A frigid breeze clawed her skin and her attention immediately snagged on familiar envelopes drifting at the feet of the deathly pale fae. Her breath caught in her throat as she tried to come up with a reason they would be at the feet of this terrifying creature. She was ten feet away, and even despite the darkened sky, Ash could see the red-rimmed eyes of the constantly weeping female. She would not harm Ash, but she was a sign that death was close by, and no matter how much she recited under her breath that the fae would not touch her, she fought with the urge to turn and flee.

As the wind picked up, she cursed, ducking low to grab her lost letters before they flew away. When she looked up, the banshee's face was millimetres away and she froze, unable to breathe. Her piercing wail was so loud Ash covered her ears, not caring that she was crumpling her already battered letters. Her cry went on for so long, so close to Ash's face, that she could see the fae's eyes bleed, her breath hot and putrid. And then she slipped away, gone before her eyes could adjust.

Her heart thrummed loudly in her ears as deafening silence replaced the banshee's cries and she noticed more envelopes discarded along the path towards the ancient monument, paper breadcrumbs to something Ash wasn't sure she was ready for, but she found herself walking cautiously down the midnight black passageway, anyway.

The wind howling at her back, she was on high alert as she made her way blindly down the tomb. It didn't smell like it normally did—cold stone and even colder air. This smelled metallic and sweet but also brought the memory of when she had opened the refrigerator at Brian's dorm and someone had left an uncooked two-week-old burger rotting inside.

A soft buzzing became incessantly louder as she picked up each discarded envelope. With every step, her breath deepened and a few lumps lodged at the back of her throat, so quickly that she spluttered. Wiping her mouth, she realised flies were swarming around her. Disgusting. She stood just before the antechamber that fed into three smaller enclaves, pitched in deep shadows. Realising that her phone was in her pocket, she blindly retrieved it. Memory over vision allowed her to eventually unlock it, turning on the torch app.

Swatting away flies, she looked back towards the entryway and almost gasped, but covered her mouth to avoid swallowing another fly. Through the long corridor, she could see large clouds lumbering overhead but it wasn't the fact they were there, it was the colour of them. The heavy clouds were black in their entirety, rimmed with red lining. She had never seen clouds that looked like they would bleed, not rain, but blood. If the banshee hadn't already spooked her, seeing a blood omen on Samhain would. Brehon law, the ancient rules all Fianna lived by, was very clear about blood spilt on this day. It was prohibited, and your matriarch decided the penalty for such an act. Though Ash didn't have to worry about that, years of warnings were hard to ignore.

Ash's breath was loud in the otherwise quiet chambers, her light bouncing from the various stone walls, until her attention snagged on the discarded envelopes to her left. Ducking down, she reached through the roped-off section to retrieve them. Her breath caught as she noticed splotches of red staining the otherwise white paper and the grip on her phone tightened as she stood abruptly, knocking into the barrier. Light bounced in her hand as she pressed a finger to the stain. It was dry.

She swivelled then, her torch light not doing enough to show her the pitch black chambers. The buzzing of flies heightened her unease as she noticed the chamber to the right of where she stood. A noise came from her she'd never heard before, something between a shriek and a moan, but she couldn't look away, even when her mind begged her to. Where a small stone basin stood low on the ground lay a body. A corpse.

Her breaths came out in ragged chokes as her heart kicked into a frantic beat. Ash's flashlight darted around the room, looking for and fearing the prospect that she may not be alone. Realising nobody else was in the other chambers, she ran to the narrow passageway, willing herself to move quickly. Halfway down the stone antechamber, she halted, warring with herself.

Aiming her torchlight back to the tomb, her ears still rang with the echo of the banshee's cry.

The fae had appeared before *her*; it was no accident she was led here. Steeling her nerve, she forced one step in front of the other, keeping her torch trained on her feet, until she stood before the basin. Through shallow breaths, she looked. It was a woman, but Ash couldn't force herself to study anything beyond her legs, sprawled over the shallow stone. It was called a basin, but it was more like a carved dip in the slab of granite, just over one metre in diameter. The glimpses she'd already seen of the body, and the reason she knew the woman was dead, was something her eyes wouldn't focus on. Her actions became alien to her, as if she'd shifted into autopilot.

Stuffing the envelopes into her fleece, she forced her gaze to follow along the woman's pale, slim limbs, but she stopped before they reached any further. A familiar tattoo was etched against one of those overhanging arms near her wrist. The paleness of the woman's skin made the tattoo even more visible as Ash's light trained on it. She was close enough to see it was almost identical to the one she wore on her own wrist, and she fought back another sob. She'd told Mary she'd chosen the triquetra because it was popular amongst clansmen, which was true, but it wasn't why she'd had it inked on her skin.

Moving her torch light, she trained it on the woman's torso, forcing herself to look. The light bounced back and forth erratically, and it was only when she gripped it with two hands, could she control her shaking. The woman's face—no, she couldn't look yet. It could be anyone. Why she didn't just run out of there, she didn't know at that moment. The banshee's cry, the blood cloud omen, were all reasons Ash should leave, but she knew she had to look. A gash, deep and wide, went from her navel to neck, as if someone had gutted her and pulled her apart. She wasn't an expert, but she knew this didn't feel right.

The body didn't appear decomposed, but something didn't add up.

Saliva pooled in Ash's mouth as her knees weakened, but she forced herself to continue looking, internally convincing herself that this was just like the crime investigation programs she loved watching. It could be anyone. Her world was not about to fall apart. She continued this mantra, over and over, gazing at the tattoo. She couldn't look at that symbol and not remember the comforting scent of vanilla and pine as her mother wrapped her arms around her as a young girl. Ash had traced the intricate spirals countless times while listening to her mother hum a lullaby, patiently waiting for her to fall asleep.

But, this could be anyone. Gritting her teeth, she forced herself to continue her assessment; she wasn't leaving until she finished. Although there was dried blood on the woman, it was nothing compared to how it should be, considering the wounds inflicted on her. As she looked around the body to the shallow dip of the stone she lay on, there was no blood pooled underneath, just specks like the ones on her letters.

Ash still hadn't found the courage to aim her light higher, so she followed one arm that hung awkwardly to the side. Her fist was bunched with a crumpled page within.

Her letter. Conor always used the same paper, yellowed parchment with a gold border, and even in the darkness and stains, she knew.

Dread so fierce that she couldn't see, Ash willed her brain to slow down before she was ready to acknowledge familiarity in the woman lying dead before her. For a solitary second, she debated turning around and calling for help without finding out the truth for herself.

But those letters. Why were they here? Why had the banshee cried to her? Her heart shrunk as if someone gripped it from within, squeezing, eliciting pain. She knew, but needed proof.

Blinking several times, she finally angled her phone and looked upon the woman's face, a sob of recognition burning her throat.

She was so battered that both eye sockets were swollen and bruised. Dark hair hung over the basin, chunks of it clinging to her bloodied face that was painfully familiar, even in this gruesome state.

Ash couldn't breathe. She couldn't move. She couldn't see.

Hunkering as close as she dared, she aimed her light along the basin ground, but again, no blood. She moved before she'd time to realise how stupid it was. Trying desperately not to touch her mother, she clutched her letter, but the death grip was so tight Ash had to use both hands to clasp the precious paper. After an eternity that was probably only seconds, she finally felt a slip to her advantage.

Getting too cocky or eager to get it over with, she grazed her mother's cold skin, almost passing out and vomiting. She never wanted to feel that type of cold again. Letting out a wretched cry of both triumph and hysteria, Ash pried her letter free, only to hear a tear too late to stop her momentum. Staring dumbly at the torn paper, she saw the other half still secured in her mother's hand.

She was going to be sick. Filled with an icy dread, so strong it took her breath away, Ash blindly stuffed the letter into her fleece before stumbling back the way she had come.

Half falling down the steel ladder that protected the boulders outside, she cried out as she collided with the kerbstone at the front of the tomb.

Tomb.

It certainly was a tomb today.

CHAPTER 6

TIERNAN

It had been a long day. After the sham of a meeting earlier, Tiernan had retreated to his caravan, even though the elders were still discussing their next move. As if all their talk would make any difference; Cara would decide and they would follow. He'd spent the day brooding and scheming, his fingers dancing across his laptop keys in a quick and reassuring speed. All the clansmen had the day off from training to avoid spilling any unnecessary blood on Samhain. He relished in the downtime.

As the sun shifted to give way to the moon, Tiernan's stomach growled in protest and he stretched. When allowed to lose himself in his screen, he'd often forget to eat. A pang ached in his gut and it had nothing to do with hunger. Conor would have called on him by now, ensuring he'd have eaten. Even though the matriarch's son was six years younger, he'd taken on the role of being Tiernan's keeper. *Where was he?*

Lighting the small stove, he moved around the kitchenette with soothing familiarity, making the only thing he knew how: porridge. Seeing as it was Samhain, and he was worried about his matriarch and Conor, he stacked his porridge with berries and syrup. Emer would say he was eating his feelings.

He returned to his laptop as he stuffed a spoonful into his mouth, savouring the quiet of his small home. The soothing sound of electronics whirring to life and the splatter of rain against his window eased his harried mind. For the tenth time that day, he checked the usual spots first. Hacking into An Garda Síochána was so easy he could do it in his sleep. He typed in the same keywords as he had hours ago, 'Fianna', 'Meath open cases', but nothing new showed up. He moved on to hospitals, scanning through their patient files to make sure there were no 'Cara Breen' or 'Conor Breen' or 'unknown patients' admitted that morning.

Sighing, his fingers flexed as they hovered over his worn keyboard. Typing in another set of words, he searched the archives from seven years ago in all his usual haunts. Why did he bother? It was not as if anything new had been added to any detective files, newspaper articles or even the journalists' personal drives he always hacked into. Perhaps Emer was right; he needed to stop tinkering with screens and get his hands on physical files. Maybe there was more information he didn't have stuffed in some discarded boxes in the gardai station.

As the moon shone beyond the winding river, his stomach hurt. He pushed his bowl aside even though he knew the pain had nothing to do with his supper. Something wicked was afoot, and he feared his bleeding lip would not be the only blood spilled on this day of magic and mayhem.

Another idea struck him and his fingers whirled across the keyboard once more. This time he was more hesitant, as the guilt that always greeted him for what he was about to do unsettled his stomach. Cara had convinced Tiernan it was for her safety, and after several attempts to refuse, he'd eventually given in to his matriarch's request. Typing in the words 'Aisling Breen', he went to work on hacking into all of Cara's daughter's social accounts.

From a quick peruse of her DMs, he noted she must have recently broken up with her latest boyfriend. Not surprising, although this one seemed to have lasted longer than the others.

Next, he went into her university profile. She had a late assignment but otherwise her last year studying archaeology was going well. He squinted at her calendar and noted she still had too many hobbies. How could she keep up with these sports and social clubs? By just looking at what she had scheduled that week alone exhausted him. Her bank account showed that she still worked at Newgrange Coffee and Gift Shop, but he already knew that as it was also her address. One that Conor had convinced him to give so that he could write to her.

With weary eyes, he logged into her email. Tutting, he silently reprimanded her for not having changed her password since the last time he'd hacked her. With a few keystrokes, he prompted a reminder to show up the next time she logged on. Scrolling through, he noted that she and Conor still hadn't reunited. The thought had crossed his mind that perhaps that's where they had gone. Why else would Cara stop here, so close to her daughter? He wondered how Aisling felt about her family. Her brother missed her terribly, so much to the point he had expected Conor to sneak out and find her years ago.

Tiernan logged into her online journal, again with the same password. It rarely contained personal notes. It was more a log of Fair One sightings, their appearance, where and when she'd seen them, and sometimes an account of how she'd interfered with their malevolent actions. Thankfully, that didn't occur often, and somehow Aisling had gotten away with it until now.

When he'd told Cara about her log, the matriarch had gone deathly pale, asking him to give her daily updates on it. He had faithfully done so, noting a pattern of only interfering with changeling attempts. He thought it was admirable, and had made the mistake of sharing his views with Cara. It had been the one time she'd lost her temper with him, lecturing him on what would happen to her daughter if she was ever caught. Brehon law was clear on the matter. Fianna caught breaking the treaty were brought before the High King. Punishments recorded in history included being enslaved to the Tuatha Dé, who lived and ruled in the other realm. Tiernan often wondered what the High King's role truly was. He was crowned a king, but lived to serve the Fair Ones.

He scanned the latest entry, only from yesterday. His brows raised as he read, eyes widening as they flickered left to right. Whistling, once again, he marvelled at her bravery, but he couldn't get a sense of how she felt about her heritage . . . and he'd never spoken to her before.

"Fuck this," Tiernan muttered, angry with himself for snooping into a woman's personal life.

He hadn't even met Aisling Breen. She'd left a month before he'd joined the clan, but he felt as if they were friends. Which made him a creep. Donning his coat and boots, he exited his caravan and strode towards Conor's, reaching it in a matter of seconds. Few people were around so he slipped inside through the unlocked door. Most of his clansmen kept their doors unlocked. No outsiders dared infiltrate their camp, and a mere locked door wouldn't keep any Fair Ones out if they chose to . . . visit.

The stuffy caravan was a mess. Dirty dishes were piled in the small sink facing him, along with random socks and sheets of paper full of Conor's drawings. None of that was concerning, as Tiernan had never seen this place clean. Even at twenty-three, his own home looked a lot like this except instead of sketch pads, charcoal and pencils scattered everywhere, deconstructed computers and devices lay about. Tiernan headed towards the only room Conor kept semi-tidy, deciding to start his search there.

Slanted shutters on the lone small window let some light from the neighbouring caravans, and as he entered Conor's tattoo parlour-bedroom, he didn't bother turning the light on. He stooped to all fours, glancing under the bed, but all he found were more discarded socks and who knows how many months' worth of dust. Seeing as Conor had furnished his room with a tattoo station, there wasn't any space to fit more than his bed and an overhead storage.

After opening the high door and being greeted by a cascade of clothes in the face, he found nothing out of the ordinary. Conor's laptop lay on the small table in the kitchenette, and lifting it up, he cursed when he spotted the black device underneath. No wonder he couldn't track him.

Pocketing the powered off phone and laptop, he stowed them in his own caravan before turning towards his matriarch's. More people were milling about now, so sneaking in would be difficult, though necessary. If he had been caught in Conor's, nobody would have questioned him, seeing as they were like brothers. When the matriarch's son wasn't sketching or inking one of the clan's skin, he was with Tiernan. But sneaking into Cara's caravan was a significant risk, and one he couldn't easily talk his way out of.

It didn't matter. He was the only one who seemed to realise something was wrong. She was never away this long. He hated prying into her personal space and if she'd have gone by herself, he'd be more patient and wait for her return. But if something had happened to Conor . . . He couldn't think that way. Tiernan preferred technology over what he considered Fianna superstition, but he couldn't shake the feeling that something was wrong.

Taking the long way around the perimeter of their camp, Tiernan slowed his pace when he spotted Emer and Niamh ambling arm in arm close by the largest caravan. Leaning against one of the other homes, he huffed his breath into his stiff hands, rubbing them together. When the space looked clear, he hurried forward and let out a curse when he realised Cara's door was locked. *So much for all clansmen trusting one another*, he thought as he took out his pick lock set from his pocket.

Children tore past him, laughing and jostling one another as he worked, but luckily, they hadn't seemed to notice him or what he was doing. Letting out a triumphant chuckle, he opened the door within seconds. While other Fianna men thrived on wielding blades, he found satisfaction in more subtle accomplishments; picking locks was a trick he'd mastered, but one he couldn't perform on stage.

Gently clicking shut the door behind him and taking off his muddied boots, he went to work, searching through Cara's long, multi-roomed caravan. Circling the conference table the elders held their meetings at, he entered a room to discover storage boxes towering to ceiling height. Rummaging through a few, he realised these must have been Aisling's old belongings. He moved past the bathroom and into Cara's office. Though he'd hacked into Aisling's online accounts, it felt wrong to rifle through her physical belongings. He decided not to dwell on the contradiction. A man had to have some fibre of moral code.

In the office, his heart skipped as he opened a locked drawer with his tools. It soon steadied into a disappointed thrum when what had looked promising turned into endless paperwork and ledgers of the clans' comings and goings and financial records. Seeing as Cara was off the grid—something that made his eye twitch whenever he thought of it—the clan had no bank or digital footprint of any kind. Turning to the latest page, Tiernan took in a sharp breath. Their finances were worse than he'd thought. No wonder the elders wanted to perform again. He still wouldn't take part if he could help it, though.

Tucking the book back under the files it had been lodged between, he turned towards Cara's bedroom and the last room of the caravan. Worrying his bottom lip once more, he moved before he could talk himself out of it. He'd realised after Aisling's boxes, hacking into files in the comfort of his home didn't feel as intrusive as physically rummaging through someone else's belongings. The door was locked and Tiernan almost turned around, but it had been nearly two weeks since they'd left and a deep worry had taken root inside of him, urging him forward. Unlocking this door took even less time than the others, but he didn't smile as he pushed it open.

Scanning the neatly made bed, he went around it to the bedside table, opening and closing drawers full of his matriarch's underwear. A blush crept to his dark cheeks, but he gritted his teeth as he opened the bottom drawer. *Bingo*. A dark leather journal sat underneath what looked like letters in his matriarch's handwriting. Glancing at the intended recipient, his pulse quickened.

Dear Aisling . . .

A noise outside the shuttered window caused him to jump. Closing the drawer as quietly as possible, he stuffed the journal and letters into the inside pocket of his coat then, bending over, he walked underneath the window, hoping his tall frame was low enough whoever was outside couldn't see his shadowed form creeping past. Exiting the caravan took more time, but he had to make sure nobody spotted him.

As soon as he got home, he read the unsent letters to Aisling. Frowning as he scanned the paragraphs, he set them down with frustration seeping in his blood. What a load of nonsense. For years, Cara hadn't spoken to her daughter, and the letters were full of old fairy tales: ones he hadn't heard before. Why would those be the words she wanted to say to her estranged daughter?

A string of expletives left his mouth as soon as he opened the first page of Cara's journal. All this time, he had thought his matriarch was looking for his mother and the other caillte. He'd had his suspicions, but had still hoped that she shared the same

44

drive he had in finding out what had happened to the Fianna who had vanished overnight.

It had all been one big lie.

CHAPTER 7

AISLING

"I told you. I was going back into the passage because I thought I heard a noise and wanted to make sure nobody from my tour was sneaking back in."

"And when did you see the body?"

The body. As if it were just *any* body.

"I already said. When I went into the . . . tomb."

Ash shivered as she sat facing the detective in the draughty interview room at the gardai station. The building was old, weathered, with thin glass panes that did very little to keep out the battering winds. Raindrops splattered through onto the chipped window sill, even though the window was shut. Clearly, the government had bestowed no funding to the local gardai station. Bare plaster covered most of the walls with the odd patch of yellow paint and the only furniture in the room was the two chairs they sat on, and the steel table between them.

The tomb. She had always secretly mocked historians who had referred to it as that. It turned out they had been right, just not in the way they had thought. Ash hugged her arms tightly around herself, finding no warmth as the detective stared at her, his expression unreadable.

"Not before?"

"How could I see the body—her, before?" Ash's throat burned with pent up *everything* and she shifted in her uncomfortable chair. "How many times do we need to talk about this?"

She felt nothing and everything at the same time, and refused to say 'the body' again. She'd lost count how many times she already had.

It wasn't just *any* body.

The detective ignored her, his dark cropped hair matching his narrowed eyes. "When was the last time you saw your mother?"

Ash hated everything about the man in front of her. She had been here hours, days, years. It wasn't always him, but it mostly was. She knew his face and the uncovered hairy forearms so intimately through staring at them for so long. He was slimly built, wiry and his gaze never faltered. When his eyes were trained on her, Ash immediately felt guilty. He was the detective Ash would have chosen to solve the murder of her mother. But not when she was inconceivably his number one suspect. She hated him so much she refused to remember his name.

"It's been years."

"So you haven't spoken to her recently?"

"No."

"What about your father?"

"Is that supposed to be funny?" Ash grit out.

Her father had gone missing seven years ago, along with a group of other Fianna, and the detective was pretending he didn't know?

The detective's smile was asinine. "Nothing about this is funny, Ms Breen."

"Ash. I've told you already. Call me Ash."

"What about your brother?" The detective looked at the file in front of him, even though they both knew he didn't need to. "Conor. Have you spoken to him recently?"

"No."

Ash was acutely aware of the torn, bloodied letter stuffed in her closet back home. She hadn't had time to think of a better hiding place for her letters before the gardai arrived at the crime scene. If this detective decided she seemed guilty enough to arrest, her room would be searched and then she'd be in serious shit.

Technically, she wasn't lying. She hadn't spoken to Conor. He had sent her letters. She'd read them until they were imprinted in her brain. Until she saw the words scrawled behind closed lids. And then she waited for the next letter. On and on, this was their one sided cycle. Until the last one disappeared and she'd found it grasped in the hand of her murdered mother.

"What about the blood?"

Ash's heart stuttered into an erratic beat. Did he know about the letters already? When she didn't answer, he asked again.

"What?"

He repeated the question.

"I don't understand." Ash could hear the lie in her voice.

"Isn't it strange that you find the body of your estranged mother?" The detective thrummed his hairy fingers on his closed file.

"Yes," Ash replied. Because it was.

"Did you touch her?"

"What?"

"Ms Breen, did you touch your mother when you found her?"

"I . . . no. Yes." Ash's throat tightened as she wrapped her hand gently around it. She lowered her face so her collarbone length black hair gave a minor form of protection from the detective's penetrating stare. "I did. To see if she was alive."

"I think it was pretty clear she wasn't. Where did you touch?"

Ash glared at the man, refraining from the urge to punch his unshaven, smug face.

"Her hand."

"Did you see anything unusual with her hand?"

"I . . . no."

"Ms Breen, did you remove anything from her hand?"

"What? No, of course not. It was dark. I couldn't see a lot."

"What about the blood?"

They stared at each other for an eternity before a knock forced the detective from his chair. Ash could tell he was annoyed and had probably thought he was getting somewhere with her. He was having fun. With a shuddering intake of air, she tasted soured sugar and reached for the glass of water that had been placed on the metal table hours ago. As she swallowed the lukewarm water, she chalked this certainty of his emotions down to one of those things she was just good at doing. Reading people was a talent she'd always had.

The detective re-emerged with another file. Sitting down, he fixed his tie before resting his elbows on the table. "Do you think she looked staged?"

Ash squinted at him, wondering why he would ask that. "I don't think so?"

"It's the blood."

"Why do you keep saying that?" Ash's voice became weakened with every syllable, but she forced it down, refusing to give in to the emotions clawing their way up her throat.

"Preliminary reports state that your mother died in the exact location you found her." He tapped the files underneath his hand. "But the problem is there's a lack of blood evidence to corroborate this finding."

The detective seemed to expect something from Ash; a response? Her gaze returned to his hairy arms.

"I know to an untrained eye it looked like there was a lot of blood on your mother." He paused and when Ash met his gaze, for once he looked uncomfortable before continuing, "From your mother—"

"Stop saying that. Call her by her name."

His jaw tightened, and any trace of sympathy disappeared. But he obliged. "From Cara's wounds, we can deduce that there should be more blood at the crime scene."

"So what do you think happened to her?"

They sat in silence as the clock above the door ticked for the fourth incessant hour they had cooped her up in there. Someone had taken the time to scratch obscenities into the surface of the table, and Ash, despite herself, found her eyes drawn to one particular phrase, *Pigs lies, lies with pigs*, had been written multiple times and Ash wondered how long the author had to have been in this room to have accomplished it. She'd been here for hours, and the only thing she wanted to scratch was at the detective's eyes.

"You tell me what happened to her, Ms Breen."

Enough. Ash sat forward, her words tripping through her clenched teeth. "Why am I being questioned like this?"

"Like what, Ms Breen?"

"My. Name. Is. Ash. Am I . . . a suspect?" Ash hated that word almost as much as she hated this man. "I haven't seen my family in seven years. I'm . . . I'm . . ."

Ash hated the break in her voice. She hated everyone and everything. She needed to get out of this room and away from this detective, along with every other damned gardai in this horrible station. It was impossible to process what she'd seen in front of him. "I want to go home."

"And where is home again?"

"Like I said the first twenty times. I live with Mary and Dominic Tully who run the Newgrange Coffee and Gift Shop. We live in a cottage beside it."

"And how did *you* come about living with the Tullys?"

Ash slammed her fist against the metal table. Chains securing it to the floor rattled as she raised her voice. "I fucking told you. They took me in when I was a teen. Now, let me the fuck out of here or else."

"There she is. Finally." The detective leaned back with a knowing smile. "You're all the same. Fianna, I mean. I've had so many in this room and you all reduce to this."

"To what?" Ash asked, even though she knew where this was going.

He gestured to her still tightly grasped fists. "Animals."

A knock on the door stopped Ash from retorting with the array of expletives she had lined up. The detective disappeared for less than a minute before returning with a grim expression. "You're free to leave, Ms Breen."

He had said 'Ms Breen' the same way he had said 'animals'. Ash hugged her chest as she silently left the brightly lit interview room. He shoved a card in her face as she walked past.

"If you think of anything, call me," he said. She made it ten steps before he called after her. "Sorry for your loss."

When Ash reached the waiting room, her legs buckled as Mary and Dom enveloped her. She breathed in their soothing familiarity and somehow felt a mixture of sorrow, worry and love. *She* didn't feel it, but she somehow knew it was coming from them. Tucking this new level of weird away for a time when her head wasn't so muddled, she asked them to take her home. It had been jarring enough to read the detective so clearly, but the idea she was sensing, no *smelling,* their emotions was too much.

The journey home was filled with the silence only death could create. The welcoming lights of the small cottage were like a beacon. Ash wordlessly walked down the long, narrow corridor until she came to the bend that led to her room. She turned to find both of her foster parents still huddled by the front door, watching her departure.

"How about I check in on you after I make tea," Mary said.

It wasn't a question.

Ash shrugged and made the last few steps to her bedroom. It was only when the door clicked shut that she carefully retrieved the stolen evidence. At the sight of blood splotches, Ash choked on her wail. She had to hold it together for a little longer. She could see that the blood was dry, but she was afraid to open the folded torn pages. From quick inspection, it looked like she'd retrieved all of her missing letters, along with the new letter she hadn't had the chance to read. That was the one that'd been gripped in Cara's hand. The one that lay torn in half on the ground in front of her. Why had her mother taken these from her bag? What was so important that she'd broken into the cafe to steal them, and then gone on to the Newgrange passageway to meet her gruesome death?

Rummaging under her bed, Ash grasped an old handbag that she'd probably only used once and forgotten about. As she placed the letters inside, her conscience screamed at her for wilfully withholding evidence from An Garda Siochana. Animals. That's what the detective had called her people. Her mother was Fianna. Would he even care about solving this case? She had always known how prejudiced outsiders viewed their community, but it hadn't bothered her when she was safely cocooned within its caravans. Each fairground was filled by people who bought tickets to both scorn and admire them. She had only realised how bad it was when she'd moved in with Mary and Dom.

Lifting the torn half of her unread letter, she unfolded it with care. It had the most blood; the others had only a splattering. Her mother's blood. The realisation of this one fact caused her eyes to fill with tears. She blinked, and a few escaped. Turning it over, she tried to make sense of the cramped handwriting underneath the darkened stains. Squinting, she could make out one line, 'Teamhair holds the answer.' *The Hill of Tara*. The original, Gaelic name given to the ancient mound floated in her head, fluttering out of reach to any reasonable explanation. Hearing the faint noises of Mary and Dom outside, she quickly hid the letter with the others. What would they think if they found out what she'd taken from the scene?

As she sat on the edge of her bed in borrowed clothing that the detectives had given her, she'd never felt more tired. Her last words to her mother seven years ago were a stupid argument. And now she wouldn't have the chance to change that. She couldn't remember the exact conversation, but the nuances and tone remained the same each time she tried to. Ash had replayed the conversation so many times and daydreamed she'd said something different, argued or didn't. Cried or didn't. Begged, screamed, had the best, most sarcastic and hurtful retorts, or had the most loving and emotionally exposed conversations with her mother. She had so many variations that the real account was long since smudged and lost in the recesses of her mind.

She'd been a seventeen-year-old with a bad attitude and even worse communication skills. No wonder her mother hadn't waited for her to return. Ash somehow always forgot to think about her dad's involvement. It was probably because he'd done his own disappearing act soon after. That and the fact he hadn't exactly been a present father, even when she was young. The detective had brought up Lorcan Breen, as if he believed the Breen matriarch's second in command hadn't disappeared like the other caillte seven years ago. What a bastard.

Lorcan had been a good second to the clan leader as far as Ash could remember and had been a popular warrior and talented swordsman during their performances. He'd also been more doting with Conor when they were little, but Ash chalked that to the fact he was a boy, and perhaps their father hadn't wanted a girl. It was also very hard not to dote on her brother.

A knock on the door startled her, and she only had enough time to ensure she'd hidden everything before Mary's full frame towered over her. She set a tray packed with a pot of tea and biscuits on Ash's single bed.

"I've started a bath for you. Why don't you have this," she said, gesturing to the tray. "And then have a soak."

Again, it wasn't a question.

Ash remained hunched over, staring at Mary's feet. "I didn't realise. You know. I didn't realise it was her. Maybe I did. But she looked . . ."

Ash didn't know her own voice, and she didn't like where her train of thought was going. She leaned against Mary's legs. Instantly, soft hands patted her head.

"It'll be all right."

Mary said this like a question, Ash thought.

CHAPTER 8

SETANTA

S et woke in a breath between sweet oblivion and wretched consciousness. It took a moment for him to realise he was chained to a bed. He tried to scream, but couldn't open his mouth. Blood pumped so quickly through his broken body it was all he could hear, until a feral sound rumbled from the back of his throat. Everything fucking hurt.

"Hello, my sweet boy." A female's voice floated from somewhere close by, and his head snapped in that direction, only to face darkness.

He was blind. *No.* Someone had bandaged his eyes.

Temporarily. A word recited so many times he wasn't sure whether they'd been uttered in that moment, or it was a memory. It was always temporary. The female was his mother. He picked up her scent in between the overpowering cleaning supplies recently used in the room, his blindness allowing his other senses to kick in. A faint whiff of her floral fragrance and a note of wariness. It took several minutes for Set to piece his mind back together enough to visualise what she looked like. Blonde hair and a soft smile, but cold eyes.

Remembering the meaning of words taken for granted by everyone else was his initial challenge. The unafflicted knew things like 'hello' and 'sweet boy', but they did not register when he first woke. Then, he was always a wordless but noisy . . . animal. Counting—when he remembered what that was—helped his focus and when he made it past one hundred, reality set in.

He inhaled, but pain splintered his lungs. With shallow breaths, he willed his mind to calm—to shift from beast to man once more. He uselessly jerked his head back and forth, but his bandages didn't budge, and he remained blind. His pulse rushed in his ears as a hardness settled in his gut. Freaking out only prolonged his episode to last longer. Once again, he tried to form words but realised his jaw was wired shut.

"Try not to move, you'll tear your stitches."

Set grunted that he wanted a mirror and because they'd been through this too many times, Imogen knew what he had asked for.

"You know that's not possible."

The panic that was never too far away banged against his already battered chest, waiting to be invited in. What he looked like was left to his imagination. Imogen wouldn't allow her precious son to witness the damage he did to himself.

His tanned skin, blond hair and grey eyes were the only similarities he shared with her. His physique and natural height meant he would tower over her if he could stand. Restraints notwithstanding, he wouldn't have the energy to attempt it. So he remained where he was, lying on his back, blindfolded and held together with bandages and despair. Calming breaths were impossible. He had no way to fight against the waves of self-loathing as they crashed through him.

More gargled grunts foamed at his clenched mouth as he recalled the night before.

"Don't worry about that. Nobody was . . . badly hurt. I've already cleaned it up."

He had hurt people. Again. His chains rattled against the bed Imogen had secured in the caravan of horrors. That's what he called it. From the outside, it looked like one of their small storage caravans. *The McQuillan Travelling Clan* sticker wrapped on the vehicle's body. Most people assumed it held props for their shows, if they thought of it at all. Only Imogen's select few knew what it really housed. She had it kitted out with everything they would need: a hospital bed, restraints, operating lights, sedation station. Everything needed to imprison and subdue a beast.

Caravan of horrors. He was that horror.

Abomination. Monster. Freak. His chains rattled louder this time as he berated himself for his lack of control, the tension of the leather wristbands against the metal chains ready to snap. He could break them. Just a little more pull and—

"Now, dear. Don't strain yourself." Imogen's voice came closer. "Here. Drink this. The straw is in front of you. Don't turn away, Setanta; you know it heals you faster."

Set's aching limbs went limp as he obeyed. It smelled like shit wrapped in sweaty socks and tasted worse. As the druid's concoction took him back to the brink of oblivion, he remembered Orla Corrigan pinned against a caravan just before he turned. Was she okay?

"Hush, dear. You'll feel better after sleep."

His mother's words did little to soothe him. As he drifted into a fitful nightmare, he welcomed the torture of it. It was what he deserved.

CHAPTER 9

MAEBH

"Gods, I hate everyone." Maebh tipped her whiskey glass back to let the last of the warm liquid trail down her throat.

The tent walls kept most of the stiff wind outside, but she could hear it beating against the heavy canvas as she sat at her dressing table, watching the other dancers finish their hair and makeup before their performance. Costume filled racks dotted the crowded room, lighted mirrors and tables full of cosmetics, bras, and lace lined every wall. Floral and spiced fragrances mixed with hairspray and pre-show nerves were almost ruining Maebh's buzz.

"You've mentioned that once or twice," one dancer said under her breath.

Maebh squinted towards her kin, smirking as she saluted whomever had answered back. She admired anyone who dared try, but none would outright say it to her face, of course. Not when she could retaliate with more than words. Imogen forbade her from using her gift in that way, but Maebh rarely did what she was told. If she really wanted to, she could sniff out the feelings behind the snide remark, but instead she poured another drink.

"Slainte," Maebh said, raising her glass to no one in particular before downing another finger of amber liquid.

Reaching into her bag, she doused herself with her favourite perfume—it was expensive, but a necessity. Its scent-laden odour helped mask the smell of the surrounding emotions of her clansmen. No matter where she went, she couldn't hide from the scents that rammed into her with no regard for the headache they induced. In truth, it wasn't that she hated everyone. She detested the onslaught of their feelings.

The band was warming up out of sight as she poured another drink; the sound of random instruments, along with the merriment of a full audience, floating towards her through the thin wall separating the main tent. Theirs was the biggest tent, always at the centre of the fairground they pitched in every location they visited.

"Show begins in two minutes, ladies."

A tall and elegantly poised figure appeared at the tent entrance, the light radiating behind her shadowing her features, her many curves accentuated. The opening of the dressing room curtain caused a waft of booze, sweat and merriment to trickle in and Maebh raised her glass in order to shield her nostrils.

Imogen's next words were barely audible against a loud chorus of laughter from the main tent at her back. "It's a lively crowd tonight. Stag Do up front. Groom-to-be is all hands. Maebh, behave."

Before Maebh could retaliate, the matriarch disappeared, and dancers bustled towards the exit. She set down her tumbler and joined the end of the line.

Malachy's booming voice sounded from the unseen stage as the musicians and crowd quietened. "Ladies, gents and all that's in between, welcome to the McQuillan Clan festival. We hope you've enjoyed our many attractions. I see a few of you have spent some time at our ale and mead tent."

A raucous cheer responded and a wave of abandonment and glee that only came with consumption of too much alcohol swept towards her. She was half-way there herself. She attempted to smooth her short skirt but stumbled into the dancer in front of her. "Soz." She patted her without really seeing who muttered under their breath.

"You've made it to the right tent now, as we have a special treat for you. As you know, Fianna clans are fiercely traditional and we instil into our girls the importance of learning our oldest dances."

Several catcalls and wolf whistles ensued, and Maebh gritted her teeth as she listened to the rest of Malachy's speech. It was always the same. Every country and every town their shows ended with a 'never seen before special performance' from the McQuillan clan girls.

They started their performance in a traditional Irish jig, until halfway through, one girl would get bored and feisty, stopping the band and demanding the stage to herself. She would command the floor in utter silence, her footwork the only sound against the wooden stage. As the crowd ate it up, two by two, the other dancers would pick up the new routine in perfect synchrony until all kicked back into a seductive, crowd-pleasing spectacle. Maebh was that one feisty girl. *Of course*. She rolled her eyes. She was by far the best dancer within the clan and had choreographed the routine into perfection at thirteen. Back then, she was nearly as tall as she was now, already with the shape of a woman, and when her mother watched the dance for the first time, the only feedback Maebh received was to make it more flirtatious.

The lights flickered, signalling the dancers to move towards the stage. The main tent was in darkness except on the wooden platform, and as Maebh followed behind the others through the crowded room, chatter and laughter came in sporadic bursts, but it was the smell of foolish men's thoughts that penetrated her senses. It was woodsy, sweaty and sweet, to the point her teeth ached. She hurried by the group up front and a meaty hand grabbed under her skirt. Maebh stumbled into the dancer in front as jeering laughter came from the group, whose faces were barely visible from the stage lights. She spun around, ready to confront the drunken sleazebag, but stopped short when she noticed the lone female amongst the group of men.

Dressed in a red satin slip, her pale skin emanated an ethereal glow as her red lips parted to show a hint of sharp canines. She stared back at Maebh, her dark brow arched as one man whispered in her pointed ear, his hands roaming her body possessively. She chuckled at whatever he said, her perfect face angled towards him, but her eyes never leaving Maebh's. The female's glamour wavered and her smile widened as Maebh saw her other form. Decaying flesh and sunken, white filmed eyes stared back as the female lifted her bony hand to the man who had assaulted Maebh, pulling him toward her so he was flush against her. She kissed his neck as the other man continued to touch her, his eyes hazed with lust. If these men knew what was amongst them, they'd cower like babes at their mother's skirts.

"Get it together, McQuillan."

One of the Corrigan twins hissed down at Maebh, and she pivoted towards the stage. She could never tell the sisters apart—which was pretty shitty considering she had a twin brother. She could sense her fellow dancer's retort brimmed with rotten eggs and soured apples. Her hot, angry breath almost caused Maebh to gag as they took their places on stage. With a peppermint-filled exhale, she aimed her contentment towards the Corrigan twin but let the feeling drop before it reached the crowd, lest the Fair One discover her secret gift. All around, she could see her fellow dancers' shoulders droop momentarily before stiffening into position. They never ratted her out when she made them feel good, but hopefully, the fae or her mother hadn't spotted the subtle change.

The band started up and lights flared overhead and Maebh plastered on a smile, beginning the routine without missing a step. As the mindless movements progressed, the dancers altered positions, so that she ended up centre stage. Right on cue, she outstretched her hands and shook her head, signalling for the band to stop. She opened her mouth to speak—

"Are your tits too heavy to dance any more, love?"

Another torrent of laughter, followed by a chorus of their own with a stomping of beer-fuelled feet. "Get your tits out, get your tits out, get your tits out for the lads! Get your tits out for the lads."

How original.

Malachy took a step towards the stage, but Maebh gestured for him to stop. Smiling down at the group of idiots, she wrinkled her nose and made her eyes shine. The Fair One, a dearg due, eyed her with obvious delight, sensing mischief afoot.

With a breathy laugh, Maebh gestured towards the men. "I hear we have a stag in our tent." The group of men guffawed as they pushed and punched the drunkest one forward, the bloodsucker giving him another kiss before winking at Maebh. She ignored the female, placing a hand on her supple hip, and beckoning him closer with her finger. "I have a special dance for you, Mr Stag. Stand right there, in front of me."

"You can see up her skirt from there, Mick. Is she wearing any knickers?"

Maebh winked at the laughing group before beginning her solo, her eyes steadfast on her prey. As the tempo of her footwork quickened and the entire crowd cheered, she sensed the man in front of her. She could smell it radiating off of him, the vile taste of lust, drunkenness, and something more sinister. The dearg due emanated an allure, much like Maebh's gift of sensing and manipulating emotions of those around her, but the Fair One didn't create the added hidden rage in this man. A terrible combination for an already warped mind. He was perhaps in his mid-thirties, attractive in that posh, past boarding school pupil kind of way. He was used to getting what he wanted, and Maebh knew he intended to pursue her tonight, after he had his way with what he thought was a beautiful, seductive woman in a red slip. His wife-to-be would have been in for a treat shackled to this lump of meat. The wedding would never happen, the dearg due would see to that.

Just before the music started back, Maebh twirled in front of him, breaking routine. She spun and spun until the crowd became a blur. On her last rotation, she kicked her foot outward and felt the crunch of bone vibrate from her heeled shoes right up to her thighs. She finished spinning with a flourish, her hands splayed above her head. Ignoring the cries of outrage as the group of men swarmed to their fallen comrade, Maebh bowed to a murmuring crowd and stormed off stage. Not before noting the dearg due nodding her head in approval before circling the men once more, intent on catching her own prey.

She had just made it back to the sanctuary of the dressing room when sharp nails dug into her arm. "I told you to behave."

Maebh shirked out of her mother's grasp and plopped down on a sofa, ignoring the pile of fabric she sat on. Her blonde hair was pinned painfully tight to her scalp, causing a headache to form, her curls cascading around her. Or maybe her hangover had already begun.

"Yes, well, why break the habit of a lifetime, Imogen?"

As Maebh unbuckled her shoes, the matriarch of the clan paced in front of her. "You never think beyond yourself, do you? Your clan sisters will have to entertain that man and his drunken party all night to reverse the harm you've done."

Maebh's smile was all teeth as she retorted. "Don't act like you weren't already planning on whoring out your kin before I kicked that shitebag in the face."

The sting of her mother's hand across her cheek was the only sign that it had happened. If Imogen was surprised by her outburst, or felt a tang of remorse, Maebh couldn't smell it.

"You will do well to remember your place and *mine*, darling daughter."

Maebh clasped her delicate looking fingers in front of her. They looked soft and pretty, permanently sun-kissed, like all McQuillan's; one of the few traits Maebh shared with her mother. Even though those hands looked completely harmless, they both knew there was nothing delicate about them. Maebh refused to place a hand on her cheek, even though a cooling touch was all she yearned for right then. She wouldn't react.

"He groped me before I went on stage."

"Yes, well. Look at you." Imogen gestured towards Maebh as if that was answer enough. They both seemed to study Maebh's short, revealing costume, displaying her voluptuous figure. It didn't seem to matter that it was Imogen who forced her to wear it. "You harp on endlessly about being treated unfairly. But honestly, dear. How will people look at you the way you want them to when you can't accept who you truly are?"

When Maebh didn't answer, Imogen began pacing in front of her once more. "You know, there were a hundred ways you could have dealt with that better."

"But my way was so much fun." Maebh smirked as she stood and brushed past the woman who'd raised her. "You may not have time to make any money from that group. A dearg due has set her sights on feeding on them. Imogen looked towards the main tent, her expression unreadable, so Maebh continued, "The fae have become bolder. That's the third encounter within our fairground in the past month."

"It's not our place to question." Imogen turned back to Maebh, her chin raised. "Or to intervene. They have been exiled to this land, our only task is to ensure they remain here."

Maebh snorted in disgust. The Fair Ones were divided into two species, and after The Great Battle, the ruling Tuatha Dé cast their enemy, the Fomorians, to the human realm. Maebh's kind were given the responsibility of making sure the wicked fae stayed here, forbidden to return to Tír na nÓg. Apparently, their exile didn't mean they couldn't prey on innocent humans while the Fianna were forced to watch. Shaking her head at her mother's unquestioning obedience to the ancient Brehon law, she headed towards her dressing table. Something rattled within her shoe, and as she tipped it over, she caught a small lump; a glint of white shining under the overhead light.

Without looking back, she tossed it over her shoulder towards her mother. "Here, have one of your girls give the perv his tooth back. I'm sure he'll forgive all and you'll make the money you wanted before that fae slaughters them all."

Maebh tensed as she felt a whoosh of air behind her, but before her mother could lay her hands on her, a deep voice sounded from within the tent. "Imogen, give me a minute with her, please."

Without another word, Imogen's footsteps retreated. Sagging into her seat, Maebh grabbed a jar of coconut oil and began removing her makeup. Glancing upwards between strokes, she caught Malachy's frowning expression in the mirror as he stood behind her. "If you're going to take her side, don't waste your breath."

The large man sighed before placing his hands on her shoulders and giving a gentle squeeze. "Since when do I ever take her side over yours?"

"How bad is it out there? Did you see the dearg due?"

"Never mind that," Malachy said, but she noted his troubled expression as he radiated frustration. She felt it too. The inability to intervene when humans were in danger. He squeezed her shoulders again. "How are you?"

Maebh huffed a laugh, concentrating on gently wiping under her eyes that had blackened from the oil. "Did you see that kick? And my finish? I didn't miss a beat."

A chuckle was his only response. He was waiting; Maebh knew it. The matriarch's second in their clan, he towered over everyone except her brother. Most Fianna men favoured long hair and scruffy beards, imaging themselves like the Vikings, but Malachy was clean shaven with his light red hair cropped short; a modern soldier. He had always known how to handle Maebh. When to give her space, and when to tell her off. There had been heavy doses of both over the years. He'd replaced her father in some ways. Maebh winced as her face tightened, her vigorous cleansing tugging at her skin too tightly. That thought was wrong. Nobody could replace him.

"He groped me." Maebh's voice didn't come out with the nonchalance she had hoped for. She spun and gripped his arm as the smell of sulphur filled the small space. "No, Mal. Imogen will punish you as well as me. Besides, look at me. I deserved it, apparently."

Several seconds passed by as Maebh sensed Malachy's rage ebb into a tentative calm. She wouldn't manipulate his emotions, having promised to never do so. He was a cool headed man, but one thing he wouldn't tolerate was a lack of control. As she waited, life from the outer tent trickled in. Cheers erupted from the crowd as the band played. Heeled shoes stomped across the wooden stage as the dancers performed without her. The space between them didn't fill with lavender or even camomile, but at least the sulphurous anger disappeared. Only when Maebh was sure he wasn't about to go out and pummel the stag party did she release his arm. They both looked at the oily handprint she'd left on his once pristine white shirt.

Cracking his neck in a way that would intimidate any smart man, he lifted his fingers to Maebh's face, but she looked away. "She marked you this time."

"Yeah. Well."

"I could have a word with—"

"Don't you dare."

"What about your brother?"

Maebh pivoted in her chair. "Don't be an idiot. You know he's just been through fucking hell—"

"Language, please."

"I can't believe you'd suggest breaking him out of his 'recuperation time'.

Malachy only nodded once, clear displeasure on his face. They both knew her brother would be in no fit state to intervene. Not that she needed him to. She'd fight her own battle with her mother, her way.

Maebh busied herself by wiping her face with a muslin cloth, hoping Malachy didn't push for finding her brother. She hoped he was okay. He always tortured himself after an episode. Imogen forbade Maebh from seeing him after she found out what had happened. That bitch wanted to be his only comfort, hating the closeness the twins shared with each other. Their mother didn't know Setanta found her pampering and preening unbearable. Malachy nodded before heading back towards the entrance and Maebh reached for a whiskey, her face pink from scrubbing. She needed another drink, especially if they would have to clean up after the dearg due's mess.

Before disappearing, Malachy turned. "Maebh. I'm looking at you. And you didn't deserve it. Not any of it."

CHAPTER 10

SETANTA

He was no longer chained, but he might as well have been. Set's skin was on fire as it stitched itself back together, and he found it hard to remain still on the bed. Although one half of his face was now free from bandages, his vision still impaired, he could make out the ceiling window covered with metal shutters through a weeping eye. He had no way of knowing whether it was night or day. How long had he been out? Was it still the same day as his turning?

Sweat beaded his face and body as he lurched sideways, spilling the contents of his stomach all over the floor. After the violent spasms turned into pitiful heaves, his head collapsed on his pillow. The smell of spoiled milk and that dreaded potion stung his nostrils, but as his sweat turned cold and his body shook, he didn't have the energy to do anything about it.

After what seemed like hours, Set could form thoughts, and his first one was unwelcome. Had his eyeball come out this time? If only he could see himself after an episode. Paul had described it once, but Set never knew whether to believe Imogen's lackey. How could one eye move inward, lodging itself in his throat and the other grow five times larger, along with the rest of him? Paul had a tendency to exaggerate, but he'd seemed uncharacteristically solemn as he described it.

Set was a big man by normal standards, but when he turned, it was into some kind of giant creature. Paul had told him, "Think Hulk's bigger, meaner and uglier brother."

He'd been sixteen then. Seven years later, and he still found it difficult to sleep without imagining it first. He hadn't asked Paul to describe it again. Laying as still as he could in the dark room, blinking through tears, he replayed his nightmare.

Orla moaned his name as he kissed her neck, one hand under her dress. It had been a frosty night, rain pelting down on their half-naked bodies, but it hadn't deterred either of them, choosing to create their own heat with ravenous kisses and feverish touches. The sound of the dancers' tent vibrated towards them. The live band was in full swing and the mixture of tap shoes on the wooden stage and the roaring crowd was deafening. It was always the last show in the main tent. There was never any point in telling Orla to be quiet when they sneaked off. He had pinned her against one of the outer caravans after his performance.

They'd finally made it back to Ireland after spending months travelling around the U.K., and being in the homeland was like a tonic, as if something finally tethered him to his source of self. His show had been electric, pushing his limits with every stunt he pulled.

Swallowing fire-lit swords, throwing axes and performing his one-man warrior act was like foreplay. He always ached with an inferno of searing urgency after being on stage, and Orla liked being with him outside with the thrill of getting caught. So when he sought release afterwards, Orla was side stage and ready for him. It wasn't like they were anything more than those stolen moments. She'd made that clear the first night she lifted her skirt for him.

Shifting in the bed, he tried to sit upright, but whatever remained in his stomach threatened to crawl up his throat and he lay down again. Was Orla okay? He pictured her, face flushed with swollen lips and hazy dark eyes, her brown hair dishevelled from the low bun she favoured while working in the bar tent. His mother, and clan matriarch, had the infamous McQuillan clan tents arranged in their travelling fairground to allure and satisfy even the most prejudiced to their kind. No location they chose ever left them without full capacity.

During the day, if they ventured to the towns or villages nearby, they were met with suspicion and distrust. Fianna clans were a mystery to non-travellers and it was something Set had grown up with. At night, in their fairground, the same people came and left with awe on their faces. The matriarch had designed each tent to intrigue and entertain, and every clan member had a role to play and a costume to wear. Orla played the role of flirting bar wench, and it seemed to work her up as much as his performance did him.

Before her, he'd always fooled around with an admiring fan. It had been perfectly uncomplicated. They'd have some fun, and the next day he moved on and nobody got hurt. They both knew it was a one night deal, and he'd go back on stage, in front of another crowd. But then Orla had started showing up after his performances, intimidating anyone who'd tried to talk to him. When he'd confronted her about it, she had convinced him to fool around with her instead. She had pinned *him* against a wall that night. Orla insisted she wanted nothing more from him other than her own release, and he was happy to go along with it.

Until last night.

He'd felt it shifting inside him. The demon. The thing that made him turn from man to monster. A thing that didn't know—or care—who it maimed. Usually, he had more time before turning. None of the normal signs had shown until it was too late. He'd had just enough time to push her as far away as he could, telling her to run as he fled to the caravan of horrors.

He hadn't made it in time.

Flashes of visions were the only thing that pieced together the rest. His warped claws flung and ravaged his clansmen. His yowling and lashing out as they stunned and gassed him into unconsciousness. Thankfully, nobody outside of their clan witnessed him. How had Imogen dealt with them? No doubt she had another druid's concoction on hand, ready to steal memories. Her avoidance of revealing what, exactly, was in that drink she forced him to take made it even more difficult to swallow each time he did. He was uncontrollable when his demon surfaced; helpless when the savage within him appeared. Blaming his helplessness did nothing to ease his guilt, it only made him hate himself more.

"You're awake." Imogen appeared in the doorway, adorning a sterile medical gown and gloves.

She switched on a lamp, illuminating the stainless steel trolley and glass cabinet along the opposite wall. They both looked at the mess on the floor and, as his cheeks reddened, she wordlessly retrieved a bucket and mop from the corner and began cleaning it up.

"It's happening too much." Setanta's voice was barely audible through his wired jaw.

His throat was raw, burning as he swallowed. He couldn't remember the last time he drank anything other than that liquid shit.

"It's going to be okay," she said when she'd finished cleaning. Standing by his bedside, she removed some of the gauze covering his face. The smell of her latex gloves and antiseptic cream filled his nostrils, and he gagged, afraid he'd vomit again. She smiled at him. "You're healing nicely. All will be right again tomorrow."

He glared at her through his one unfocused eye. "How can you say that?"

"We have it under control. You've killed no one."

"That you know of."

Imogen looked at her son with such unrelenting love that he had to turn away. "Don't say that."

He couldn't even clench his wired jaw. He wanted to punch the wall, scream and rage, but would only wake the beast. "You know it's true. If I killed my own father—"

"Enough." Imogen moved closer, her gaze as stern as her tone. "You need to let it go, honey. That was seven years ago. You can't control who you are, only embrace it."

"You want me to embrace this . . . this curse?" Set tried to gesture towards himself, but the paltry amount he could lift his arm was only enough to cause him to grunt out in excruciating pain.

"Your condition is not a curse. Far from it. Here, drink this."

"I want no more healing potions."

"Setanta." Her voice left no room for argument.

He let her ease the straw into his broken mouth. She'd force it down his throat. He had tried to refuse before, had planned to die from his self-inflicted injuries, but she wouldn't allow that.

Tears stung his face as he drank and sleep stole him once more.

The next time Set woke, the ceiling window overhead was shutterless and he could make out a clear sky. He lifted his arm to his face and tentatively traced his newly set jaw. The wire contraption was now lying on the steel bedside table. Imogen must have removed it while he was unconscious. Listening for any sign she was still there, his own ragged breathing filled the otherwise quiet room.

Deciding it was safe, he sat up with a groan and swung his legs over the side of the hospital bed. Bunching his shoulders, he thanked the heavens his limbs had rotated back to their original position. Along with 'hulking out', another one of his monster's tricks was to rearrange the positioning of his arms and legs. Healing physically was one thing, but he found it hard to walk properly for days after an episode. He wasn't allowed to hobble in public. Walking as if nothing was wrong was worse than waking up with the jumbled senses of the beast still present.

Counting to ten, he eased his feet to the floor and pushed up to an unsteady stance. He'd been asleep long enough for the mopped floor to dry. Set inhaled and exhaled five more long breaths before the room stopped spinning and he could step away from the bed. Moving towards the narrow ensuite, he relieved himself before leaning against the basin and psyching himself to look up. He hadn't turned the light on, and although he'd asked for and been denied a mirror earlier, it was several minutes before he could force himself to raise his gaze to the small circular mirror above the sink. Shadows etched across his wide jaw and under his eyes. He looked haunted, but he was a man once more.

Laughter and music trickled in from outside and Set realised the McQuillan fairground was in full swing. They always parked the caravan of horrors on the outskirts, never near to the unsuspecting public. Just in case.

He knew without trying that the doors and windows were locked. The glass was reinforced and bulletproof. Someone, probably Paul, would be standing guard outside. His job was double sided. He would have to keep anyone out as much as keep Set in. Paul would come in to keep him company if he'd wanted, but he never did. Imogen always made him 'rest' for a full night after he'd turned. It had more to do with allowing the potion to fully heal him. Even though his limbs and skin were torn apart during his turning, whatever was in that drink helped him fuse back together, so it never looked like anything had happened. From the outside. His mind was another matter.

Set shuffled out of the sterile room, ignoring all the gauze and skin grafts he could see through the toxic waste bins. Imogen had kitted the rest of the caravan as a normal space. Another bedroom was just ahead of him and the small kitchenette area even had a couch and large screen TV. His mother had wanted to make sure he was as comfortable as possible during his 'recovery time'. He made it to the other bedroom but was breathless enough that he needed to sit on the bed. Just for a moment.

Blinking repeatedly until his eyes focused, Set found his head precariously hanging off the side of the bed, one arm trapped underneath his torso. He must have dozed off because when he woke, dark shadows coated every surface and the sound of the fairground had shifted from Ferris wheels and bumper cars to the live band they played in the dancing tent. His body shaking, he forced himself upright and selected sweatpants and a loose t-shirt to replace his hospital gown, his arm dead after spending so long trapped under his substantial weight.

After an eternity, he made it back to the living space, where he pulled snacks and water out of the mini-fridge. He still hadn't bothered turning on any lights and didn't see the point in doing so as he sat on the couch and ate, not tasting his food as his troubled thoughts consumed him. He thought back to what he'd said to his mother about not killing anyone. They both knew it was a possibility that he had.

It wasn't until Set had grown into puberty, and the episodes had got much worse and more frequent, that she'd refurbished this caravan for his 'needs'. That was after his father had tried to stop him single-handedly. Set had woken up bloodied and naked in a forest so far away from camp that Imogen had sent out a search party for him. She'd admitted she'd almost involved the gardaí. Her consideration of involving any outsiders was arguably the most disturbing thing of all. Gluttons could not be trusted.

His father had gone missing that day and never returned. Paul coughed outside, probably to let him know he was there. As Set continued to munch, his jaw still throbbing, he wondered if he should ask for his sister to come. She was the only one who really listened to him after an episode. Without judgement, without dismissing his fear and guilt. She would be on stage now if the band music outside was any sign.

The silence inside almost drowned out the jovial noise happening feet away.

Alone. He was so very alone. It was better this way.

CHAPTER 11

MAEBH

"Fuck me, it's too early for this." Maebh groaned as an obstinate amount of light yanked her from unconsciousness.

"That's a weird thing to say to your brother." Setanta's voice was irritatingly cheery as he leaned against the doorframe of her bedroom. "Get up, you drunken mare."

"Turn the light back off first." Maebh moved her swollen tongue against her upper teeth and knew without opening her mouth that her breath was terrible. Memories of last night assaulted her as she tried but failed to widen her eyes any more than slits. "On the scale, how pissed is she?"

"She's moved off the scale into a new, undiscovered scientific calculation." Setanta laughed as she cursed.

Moving further into the room; his aftershave was strong, like he'd just doused himself with it, his blond hair wet with their identical natural curls dampening his grey sweatshirt. No doubt he'd spent the hours she'd been snoring training with the other Fianna warriors. She groaned, annoyed she'd missed out, but knowing she'd needed to sleep off the night before.

"Oh, joy." With her forearm covering her eyes from the glaring light Setanta hadn't switched back off, Maebh replayed last night's events that ended with her mother storming off and her finishing the bottle of whiskey. Everything after that was a black hole. Blurry visions of re-entering the dancing tent tried to break through, but no. She didn't do anything stupid last night. Had she? "Coffee?"

The welcoming smell of Arabic caffeine filled her nose, and she peeked through one eye to see her favourite cup inches from her face.

"And you claim I'm a terrible brother."

"You're a god." Maebh carefully sat up and leaned against the bedframe before she took the cup. The shift in gravity finally righted itself as she drank and groaned, causing her brother to glare at her while muttering something that sounded like 'gross' under his breath.

The end of her bed dipped substantially as her twin sighed. "Why do you do this to yourself?"

"I didn't ask for a side of judgemental asshole with my morning coffee."

"It's six o'clock in the evening."

"Well. Fuck."

Setanta tapped her foot as if to say he wouldn't be an asshole about the fact she'd slept the entire day. The room smelled awful. Underneath Setanta's aftershave and besides her bad breath, there was an undertone of vinegar. It was only when Maebh had drunk half of her coffee that she realised her brother's jovial facade didn't hide the anxiety rolling from him. Groaning internally, she berated her alcohol soaked brain for forgetting that he had spent the last couple of days trapped inside their mother's awful caravan.

She leaned forward, peering at the bruise blue stains under his grey eyes. "You're okay now?"

"Just peachy." Setanta squeezed her calf but didn't elaborate and Maebh didn't push. He'd talk when he was ready. "She wants our presence in her tent before the show."

"Why?"

"She didn't say," Setanta said as Maebh detected a note of dread on his scent. They both shared the rare ability of sensing emotions, so didn't bother lying to one another about how they truly felt about anything. "Clearly, I don't think it'll be about anything good."

"Is it ever with our mother?" Maebh muttered, leaning over to her bedside table to retrieve her perfume, always within reach.

Spraying herself twice, and one more for luck, she downed her coffee but couldn't bring herself to get up. Smelling emotions didn't seem to bother Setanta, but no matter how much she sprayed her most overpowering perfume, surrounded by feelings she didn't want to know about was impossible to ignore.

With no inclination to follow her mother's summons, she stared at her brother, waiting for him to say what it was he'd really come in here for. Droplets of shower water dripped onto her bedspread as he leaned on his arm. Even in his baggy top, she could make out the muscles underneath. Stronger than any man she'd met, her brother was more vulnerable than anyone she knew.

"I heard what happened."

Her eyes narrowed. "Which version?"

Setanta's nose flared as he opened and closed his fist. "The one where you were assaulted. Why didn't you come to me after?"

Maebh lifted her cup to drink, only to realise she'd no coffee left. There wasn't enough caffeine in the world to prepare her for this conversation. All sensible and calm responses crossed her mind. She settled for the least reasonable.

"And interrupt your day at the spa?" Her laugh was humourless as she set her cup on the table, lifting her duvet up to her throat. "Did Mother pamper you with a pedicure while she had you sedated and strapped to a bed?"

"Don't be gross." Setanta shifted in the bed, his heavy frame taking up most of the space in her entire room, which wasn't a lot to begin with. He gripped her ankle above her crumpled duvet. "I can be there for you, if you'd only let me."

Maebh couldn't bring herself to say what she really thought. She was truthful about everything with her brother except this. He could barely be there for himself these days. He was one of the few people she cared about, the thought of hurting him with that much truth . . . she couldn't.

"You're not my knight. I can handle myself."

"I'm not talking about that shithead that groped you. I heard you handled him. You know who I'm talking about, Mae."

Maebh steeled her expression at his nickname for her. She wouldn't yield to this golden boy; their mother's joy. He would never understand how it felt to be the poor man's Setanta, loath of their mother. Even as a monster, he was still Imogen's favourite. Maebh chastised herself again. She knew she wasn't being fair. It had to be her throbbing headache.

"I know." Maebh dropped the duvet, finger combing her own mess of blonde curls. "Answer's still the same."

They sat in a fury-dense silence until she couldn't take his unspoken disappointment any longer. She gestured for him to let her pass and closed herself within their shared bathroom. Relieving herself and splashing ice cold water on her face, Maebh glanced at the mirror, noting her blue eyes were rimmed with red, but at least she'd taken her makeup off last night. Her cheek bore a mark thanks to her mother, but she'd looked worse. Women hated her for her looks, but she didn't care. Although, they didn't have an issue with Setanta knowing he was handsome. For him, it was charming, for her it was arrogant.

Donning her baggiest joggers, a jumper that she had stitched the slogan 'Guess my favourite f word' and a pair of oversized sunglasses, she hugged her ankle grazing puffer coat as she followed Setanta through the fairground. It was already dark, and the sunglasses were a ridiculous choice, but she kept them on. Her trainers did little to keep out the freezing autumn air as she hugged her body tighter. Her stomach was a hollow pit of uneasiness as last night's drinking binge gave her the feeling of dread. 'The Fear' is what her dad used to say. 'Leave me be, love, The Fear has its grip on me'.

Maebh used Setanta's broad frame as a shield against the wind. It was a rarity that she was ever thankful her brother loomed over her at almost seven feet. She was taller than most women but hated any advantage Setanta had over her. Especially in physicality. Missing training was a sin in her books and she mentally planned out what exercises she'd do after tonight's performance. She was too pent up for a gym workout, needing something more physical. Maybe she'd sweet talk Malachy into the ring for boxing. If her mother's second was too busy, she could easily antagonise any of her clan into wanting to punch her. She was due a round or two with her obnoxious aunt Lorna.

Her mind drifted to the tent Setanta performed in. It was all showmanship and strength, something she would love to be a part of. Dancing was fun, but the hair, makeup and short dresses were something she wasn't a fan of. Their physiques were vastly different, but Maebh knew she was just as strong as Setanta. Yet every night, Imogen forced her to flaunt her ass on stage.

Tall gas lanterns were scattered around the fairground, illuminating the multicoloured tents as they passed. Setanta pointed to a large puddle for her to avoid, and she marched through it, kicking rain water at him. Her feet were now sodden, but she couldn't hold back her smile at his glare. She watched his broad shoulders move as he stormed ahead. Laughing as she followed his string of expletives, she ignored the twinge in her chest. She loved him more than anyone, but it was hard to be his sister.

They made it to the matriarch's tent in near silence, with only greetings from their clansmen who were lumbering around, making sure they'd set everything up for the shows, starting in an hour's time. Imogen's tent was the only one made from navy silk with gold embroidered Celtic symbols covering its tall structure. It looked flimsy, but Maebh knew inside was dark as night with no sound breaking through other than the smell of incense and the clang of bells her mother liked to use for paying customers. Imogen often said that bells and whistles had nothing to do with her gift, but it kept the Gluttons happy. Maebh wasn't sure her mother's gift was anything more than being a know-it-all bitch.

They remained outside as the curtains were secured with a thick rope, signalling Imogen had company. Setanta stood apart from Maebh, his arms crossed and head dipped, clearly still mad at her. Both of their breaths puffed upwards in the chilly night. Whether it was his soaked grey sweats, or not coming to him last night, she wasn't sure. Probably both.

Maebh pushed the frames of her sunglasses higher on her nose and wrapped her oversized duvet coat securely around her body.

"If your image doesn't scream 'hangover' I don't know what would."

"Shut up," Maebh said, but without heat.

Relieved he was letting the argument drop, Maebh inched her glasses lower, hoping the red mark on her cheek wasn't visible in the dim light. She would take the glasses off once she was in front of Imogen. They'd played this game before and she wouldn't give her mother the satisfaction of trying to conceal her mark. Huffing, Maebh glanced at her watch. It was too damned cold for them to be standing outside this ridiculous tent.

One curtain swept aside, followed by a rustle of the rope, and a petite woman appeared. She barely acknowledged either of them as she clung to a tissue, muttering to herself before hurrying off. Setanta motioned for Maebh to enter first, but it indicated an act too gentleman-like, which infuriated Maebh's already soured mood. She planked her feet apart and gestured with a flourish for Setanta to go first. They silently argued about who would enter until a silken voice floated outwards.

"You're letting the cold in."

Setanta tutted and shook his head when Maebh remained where she was, a smirk playing on her lips, knowing that she had already won. He ignored her chuckle as he disappeared through the curtain, not holding it out for her to follow. Good. He was finally learning.

She removed her glasses, stowing them in her coat pocket as she entered the dark room. The smell of incense hit her hard and she wondered if her mother had burned more of the suffocating fumes, knowing the twins found it difficult to smell her emotions through it.

"Sit." Imogen sat behind her small circular table, the billowing sleeves of her cream blouse fluttering around her slender arms as she clasped her hands beneath her chin, watching her children enter with an unreadable expression. Over her blouse, Imogen wore an embroidered floral corset laced at the front, no doubt with billowing skirts to match.

When Setanta dutifully sat, and Maebh remained where she was, Imogen sighed dramatically. "I don't need my gift to see you wouldn't follow even that simple request, dear daughter." She shuffled her tarot cards and placed them neatly to the side of her table. "How's your hangover coming along?"

"Just fine, thanks for asking," Maebh said in a sweet voice. Examining her nails, she added. "You summoned us?"

"The Cath."

"Ah." Maebh pretended those two words meant very little to her when her animated heartbeat told a different story.

It was finally happening.

Setanta, who wore every emotion, straightened from slouching son to rigid warrior. "It's our year."

"No, darling." Imogen leaned back, every bit the regal queen of her midnight tent. "It's *your* year."

Maebh didn't register her meaning, but Setanta seemed to as he began speaking before she finished. "You can't—"

"Don't forget who you're speaking to, Setanta. I can. The High King is finally selecting a new set of warriors from each clan to join him. No matter what you've read about the trials, trust me, you can never be too prepared. And she," Imogen muttered while pointing a dismissive manicured finger in Maebh's direction. "Is not worthy."

Numb. Maebh felt numb. She couldn't move her lips to speak and her mind grew more foggy with every conversation piece floating around her and *about* her. Setanta was wrong. This wasn't their year, this was *her* year. She would finally prove to all of her clan that she was faster, stronger, and better than him. She had other reasons for taking part in the Cath, though. A secret reason so important she didn't dare think of it in the presence of anyone, let alone a wannabe Seer. Whether she believed her mother truly had the gift was something she wouldn't risk.

Her mother wanted to cut Maebh down before she had the chance?

"No." Maebh was just as surprised by her quiet voice filling the dark space as her family.

Imogen leaned forward, a wicked smile on her darkened lips. "Who am I?"

83

"Matriarch of McQuillan Fianna clan," Maebh muttered.

"And. Who. Are. You?" She said it like a rhetorical question, but Maebh answered anyway.

"The badass bitch who is going to win the Cath."

Setanta's grey eyes pinned her with a look that begged for her to keep her mouth shut, but they both knew that wouldn't happen. A soft chuckle came from their mother, signalling the beginning of something far more dangerous than a slap across her face.

"Do you remember what happened last night? After our . . . discussion." This time she asked it like a question, but Maebh couldn't answer. "You interfered with a Fair One."

Setanta angled to face her, clear horror shining through his eyes. "What happened?"

He had directed it towards Maebh, but it was Imogen who answered. "One minute she's crying about a little groping, the next she's luring the same man away from a dearg due. Honestly, Maebh, do you know the danger you have put us in? The dearg due is not a creature to make your enemy."

Maebh stared at her mother, her mind racing. Her memory was hazy, but the recognition of her mother's words drew a sharp breath from her. She remembered now. How she'd returned to the tent and flirted with the men, drew them away from the harmful hands of the fanged creature who'd clearly planned on feasting on their necks.

"What happened with the bloodsucker?" Maebh asked, ignoring Setanta's curse at her confirmation of what had happened.

Imogen sighed. "In a gesture of goodwill, she is welcome to attend our fair and take whomever she chooses."

"You can't be serious?" Setanta stood and as his chair fell back as it scuffed Maebh's shins. She didn't feel it.

"For how long?" Maebh took one step back, dislodging the chair from her feet.

Imogen's face was grave as she answered. "For as long as necessary."

This was her fault. The dearg due was a fearsome creature. She would feed on humans, anyway. Being complicit about the Fair Ones harming unsuspecting humans was a part of being Fianna Maebh struggled with, but now they had invited a blood drinker into their home to feast at their table. Why had she stopped that fae last night? And for the man who'd groped her.

Staggering out of her mother's tent, she somehow made it back to her room. The journey was as hazy as last night's stupidity had been until Imogen had hit her with the truth. There was nothing heroic in what she'd done. Not when the dearg due had likely found someone else to feed on. Someone who'd probably kept their hands to themselves. A decent man, on his way home to his family. Or a child who'd enjoyed the festival.

She'd torture herself, conjuring up images of the act, but she sat on the edge of her bed, retrieving her journal from underneath her pillow, she'd choose another activity that brought both solace and its own torment. In her hands was the real reason she so desperately needed to take part in the Cath, and to make the journey to Tír na nÓg.

CHAPTER 12

MAEBH

T he worn leather notebook, the length of her forearm, rested on Maebh's lap. She traced the familiar tan cover, its warmth and smell filling her with a clarity like nothing else could. The pages were filled with cramped handwriting, so much so that she'd begun tacking on loose paper along with all the old newspaper clippings she'd saved over the years.

Maebh pressed her palm against the cover that was held together with elastic binding and sheer will. This notebook didn't dedicate its pages to just one missing person—even though one was the only number Maebh cared about. She'd dedicated these pages to all five souls who had vanished seven years ago.

"I'm sorry, Dad. I was so close."

Maebh didn't realise she was crying until a tear splashed on the back of her hand. The first page held just one word. The nickname given to the group of missing Fianna.

Caillte.

Lost.

What the journalists hadn't realised, or perhaps didn't care to mention, was that the missing Fianna didn't belong to the same clan. They each belonged to five of the most prominent clans in Ireland.

She sifted through pages with the greatest care until her dad's face stared up at her in the dull black and white newspapers used. He was, in her opinion, the most handsome of the caillte, and because of that, the papers had used his image the most. The Cath would help her solve his case, giving her access to people and places she hadn't before.

"I'll talk to her again, Mae. It's not the end." Setanta's voice was as solemn as a prayer by the doorway.

She didn't raise her head, and he took this as an invitation to sit beside her. Once again, her room shrunk at his overbearing size.

Squeezing her shin once with his large hand, just as scabbed and calloused as her own from their years of training to become warriors worthy of winning the Cath, he nodded at the aged image of their father. "He was quite the man."

"You say 'was'. Past tense. Why?"

"You know why."

"I really don't."

"Mae . . ."

Maebh shirked out of her coat, the room unbearably hot. "He's alive."

Setanta's silence fuelled her anger. Perhaps she directed all her rage at him when it should be with the mother who barely raised her, but at that moment, she didn't care. "I'm surprised you can move around so freely, with you still being attached to our mother's umbilical cord."

"I'm trying to help you. There's no need to be such a—"

"What? Go on. Say it."

Setanta lumbered to his feet in such a force that their caravan swayed. "Bitch! There, I said it. Are you happy?"

Maebh laughed. She laughed so hard that tears spilled through her clenched eyes until she sobbed. Setanta stooped over her, placing his hands on either side of her slumped shoulders.

"Mae, tell me how I can help you."

They stayed that way until all emotion seeped out of her.

"There's nothing you can do." *Especially if you believe our dad is dead*. She closed her notebook. "Get out."

"What are you going to do?"

"Cause trouble, dear brother. What else?" Before Setanta could reply, Maebh held up her hand, gesturing for him to run along. "You're going to be late."

He swore when he looked at his watch. In one swift motion, he tore his jumper from his upper body, reminding Maebh she hadn't worked out today. After disappearing into his room, he reappeared in the kitchen she'd slinked into, not bothering to get ready for her own performance. Maebh rolled her eyes at his 'costume'. Bare chest to show off his muscles, leather pants that were far too tight to be decent, and boots. This was it. Their mother was a sick fuck. She noted that his tanned skin was blemish free. The only sign that anything had been amiss was the bluish shadows under his bleary grey eyes.

"Break a leg." Her words hit an empty doorway as the main door slammed shut and a gust of cold air assaulted her.

She opened the mini fridge with immediate disinterest in filling her hollow stomach with food. Orange juice and prosecco clinked side by side on the door shelf. She smiled. Hadn't she promised her brother trouble?

"Ladies, gents and all that's in between, welcome to the McQuillan clan festival. We hope you've enjoyed our many attractions . . ." Malachy's words floated towards Maebh as she swayed on stage, hidden behind the other dancers. They were already positioned in front of the crowd, but the tent was pitch black as they were being introduced.

Why did she have to fuck everything up?

She must have asked out loud because one of the Corrigan twins snorted a nasty little laugh. Maebh could just make out her look of disgust. It would have felt more judgemental if she wasn't dressed up as a crow. Black feathers jutted out at all angles in a crown and black and white makeup covered her face as she sneered at Maebh. "You're pissed."

Before Maebh could think of a comeback—she was in fact quite pissed—the overhead lights swallowed her vision, the crowd gasping in appreciation.

"The girls have a special dance to perform in their costumes depicting the three faces of Morrigán: crow, maiden and war goddess." With a flourish of Malachy's hands, the band played and their dance began.

Muscle memory rather than sobriety kicked in as Maebh moved on stage. She was the War Goddess, dressed in red, black and white. Her costume was comprised of sheer panels and uneven hemlines, her legs covered in leather tights with heeled shoes that shone in the strobe lights as she moved.

Setanta's large silhouette appeared in the back of the crowd and her steps quickened with an anger she couldn't place but knew there was only one way to release it.

In front of this crowd.

Even though it was not part of this routine, she signalled for the band to stop. Murmurs from the dancers surrounded her as she tried to steady her breath before addressing the audience "Everyone, I'd like to invite my brother on stage. You may have seen him in the Warrior Tent, with his many swords and even more muscles . . ." She smiled as a spotlight hit Setanta's frame. The backstage crew must have thought this was part of the act and were going along with it. Setanta's expression was stone-faced as the crowd murmured their appreciation. Maebh continued. "What do you say, bro? Care to give these folks a show they won't forget?"

The crowd began chanting and stomping their feet in encouragement, and Maebh could see the exact moment Setanta knew he had no choice. His eyes never left hers as he made his way on stage, and the scent of annoyance mixed with fear prickled her nose as he stood by her side.

"What are you playing at, Mae?" Setanta whispered, but she had no intention of revealing her prosecco infused scheme.

It was glorious in the way half-baked plans were.

"Shall we let our new friends decide our performance?" Maebh directed this to the crowd rather than her brother and tried to move her tongue in a way that made her words less slurred. "The loudest cheer decides. Who wants us to have a dance-off?"

A loud cheer greeted them, but Maebh had no intentions of dancing. In fact, she wasn't dancing on this stage ever again.

"Or, who would like to see us have a good old-fashioned bare knuckle fight?" Maebh knew that under normal circumstances, this crowd would not normally go for this type of performance, so she filled her words with the suggestion that this was exactly what they wanted to see. They filled the room with a thunderous noise that she almost couldn't hear Setanta's warning.

"Maebh, stop it right now." He grabbed her arm. "Don't do this."

Maebh shrugged him off and took a fighter's stance. "Let's begin."

Before she could find out whether he was going to lift his arms and fight her, Maebh punched him so hard his head knocked backwards and the crowd gasped. She could feel the surprise and almost heard their thoughts, even though that trait wasn't part of her gift.

How could this blonde dancing girl get even one punch in against the hulking warrior before her?

Easy. She spun out with her foot and contacted Setanta's stomach. She shared the same womb of hell.

Setanta bent over, wisps of hair coming out of the bun he wore while performing. She charged him off the stage and into the now silent audience. Luckily, the crowd had dispersed in time and a large empty floor broke their fall. She let out a roar as Setanta stood upright, but did not make a move towards her. He raised his hands, palms up, and spoke, but she lashed out. She noticed his split lip and warning bells rang in her ear, begging her to stop, but she ignored them.

She was just as strong as him. If the bastard would just fight her, she could show them. She punched him again and still Setanta did not strike back. Fianna began circling them, sending the audience out of the tent. A few made to join the fray and Maebh smiled widely, beckoning them forward.

Setanta's voice rang out. "Nobody intervenes."

She tackled him to the ground with a roar.

"I'm just as golden, just as worthy." Her words tore out of her as she sat on top of him, beating at his arms that now covered his face.

Fuelling her rage, he still did not fight back. A sting to the neck caught her off guard and then she fell forward into a sheet of black.

Maebh didn't know how much time passed but when she came to, she was lying beside Setanta in an empty tent, a red cloth doing little to stop the blood pumping from his broken nose. She winced, but it had little to do with her throbbing headache from whatever sedative they'd given her. Usually on hand to subdue her brother, but this time, she'd been the one to turn into a beast. When Maebh glanced up, she met her mother's assessing gaze.

"Not. Worthy." Imogen's soft tone was filled with more than disappointment.

Maebh couldn't scent her emotion with this much blood surrounding her—both Setanta's and the blood pumping hard in her ears. Before anyone could say another damning word, Malachy walked into the tent. The look on his face was frozen in shock, but not from the scene before him.

"There's been a murder. Cara Breen is dead."

CHAPTER 13

AISLING

A sh watched her mother float in a river of fire.

She had been late to her own mother's funeral. So much so that she couldn't ask anyone where Conor was. How the clan got Cara released from the morgue so quickly, Ash didn't know. A messenger had called to her door that morning to tell her where the funeral was taking place and that Mary and Dom weren't allowed to come. Even though her self-proclaimed foster parents had argued about it, Ash insisted she would go alone.

She'd stood by the River Boyne while a druid, standing with an archer on a small fishing boat, performed the ancient Fianna rite in Gaelic. Her mother had been shrouded in linen; Breen crest flags whipping and snapping in the wind, standing like sentinels along the rows of clans who'd come to pay their respects to the fallen matriarch. Ash couldn't hide her shock at the vast number standing for miles along the river in either direction. Her skin pricked with mixed emotions brewing from the knowledge that the majority probably felt she shouldn't be there.

The matriarch's final resting place was lit in flames by the archer. An offering to the great Manannán mac Lir, ruler of the sea, to allow her passage to the afterlife. The sky had remained dry so far, but there was a threat of rain, as there always was in Ireland. Ash cast her eyes skyward at the clouds that seemed to grow heavier as she watched. What would happen to her mother's pyre if it rained?

Staring numbly at the raft that had been cast to the middle of the river, weighted down so it wouldn't drift downstream. It would remain until there was nothing left, and then someone would reel it back in, her mother's ashes lost to the river. Her gaze wandered to her people. She knew most of the Breen clan that stood around her, almost as if they were flanking her. Though she'd been late, she'd been guided to the front of the river's edge. There were some unfamiliar faces, but they all may as well have been strangers to her.

The druid droned on, but she couldn't hear his words over the rushing river and now the roaring flames that turned her mother to ash. Her face stung in the freezing air as unshed tears blurred her vision. Even though she'd dressed warmly in her black padded coat, a woollen hat and gloves, and jeans tucked into her heaviest boots, she could not stop shivering. Everyone remained stationary until the floating pyre was engulfed in flames and the druid and archer came to dry land.

As if on cue, everyone moved, soft chatter accompanying the rushing water beside them. Ash remained steadfast, staring at her burning mother until, one by one, her clansmen approached her. *Her.* What was she supposed to say? She hadn't spoken to her mother in years. She felt like an intruder. It didn't seem to matter if she didn't respond as hands clasped hers, but words meant to provide sympathy barely made it through her barrier of forced indifference.

Faces blurred into each other as Fianna from other clans approached. She noticed the McQuillan twins, their fierce beauty like a beacon, setting them apart. Even at her mother's funeral, she was too intimidated to speak to either Setanta or Maebh McQuillan. He offered his sympathy, his attractive face solemn, her hand dwarfed by his. Ash noticed cuts and bruises on his nose and jaw, the hazards of being a warrior, she supposed. Maebh stood before her, uttering her own words of comfort, but when Ash thanked her and looked to their next clan member, the tall beauty remained standing in front of her. Ash glanced up at the blonde again, and Maebh looked ready to say more, but seemed to shake herself, offering a small smile before stepping away.

"Aisling, you'll come back to camp?"

Ash recognised the voice before lifting her gaze to meet one of her elders. Not her elder. One of the Breen elders, Mrs O'Malley. The woman hadn't changed in the seven years since Ash last saw her. Grey hair, wide set shoulders; she was a large imposing figure, a woman who looked like she'd lived hard years, but had come through them with determination and a few tales to tell.

"Alright." The words left her mouth before she realised what she'd agreed to. Years of obeying the older woman had rendered her unable to say otherwise. She needed to see her brother anyway, and this would be the quickest way to find out why he wasn't among the Fianna at the riverbank.

Her boots squelched in the grass and mud as she walked towards the rows of caravans in the short distance. She wondered how long they'd been camped here, only a ten-minute drive from her home. If she'd gone to her classes, she would have driven by them. As it was, she hadn't stepped near the cobblestones of Trinity college and the past couple of days were a blur of her bedroom and conversations forced from her by Mary.

Someone had built a campfire at what seemed to be the centre of the encampment. She noticed there were none of the larger vans that stored the equipment for the Breen fairground. Maybe they'd camped somewhere else? Or were her suspicions right, and they'd stopped performing? Ash didn't look to see who else stood beside the firepit, flames crackling when someone added more logs, and she stretched her gloved hands towards the flame.

She didn't care about any of it. Why had she agreed to come? A shiver ran through her as the front part of her warmed, chilly winds still pounding into her back. Her brother. That's why. She needed to see him. To make sure he was okay.

Mrs O'Malley carried a large tray of cups filled with tea around the gathering crowd. A cup was thrust into Ash's hand and even though she wouldn't have taken one through awkwardness, she was grateful for its warmth.

"It was a beautiful ceremony, don't you think?"

"Aye, the druids sure know how to send a spirit off."

Murmured conversations drifted by her as Ash stared into the fire. It was only when a gentle tap on her shoulder made her realise that someone was speaking to her.

"Aisling, I'm sorry we are meeting under these circumstances." Mrs O'Malley's lips tightened as the surrounding crowd quietened. "May Cara's soul continue on."

"And her love remain," the nearby group murmured.

Ash blinked at the Fianna blessing, realising she'd momentarily forgotten it after her years apart. She made a movement mixed between a shrug and a grimace and tried to figure out the best way to leave the literal centre of attention. She found what felt like the entire Breen clan staring at her. What were they expecting? Her gaze drifted back to the fire. She didn't care. Taking a drink of her tea, hiding her grimace at its bitterness, she opened her mouth to ask where her brother was.

Mrs O'Malley stepped in front of Ash, blocking its warmth. "We now need to move on with our clan."

Ash didn't like how that sounded and her gaze met the old woman's. "What are you saying?"

"As Cara's daughter, you are next in line to take on her role as matriarch," Mrs O'Malley said; she was silhouetted against the fire and darkening sky, making it hard to see her expression.

She could have sworn she sensed the woman's unhappiness. That made the two of them.

"You can't be serious."

"That I am. Brehon law is clear on the matter." Mrs O'Malley sniffed, tightening her shawl around her wide shoulders. "There's the matter of the Cath and we need a matriarch. . ."

"The what?"

"The Cath! Oh come now, girly, has it been that long since you swanned off?"

"It wasn't like that," Ash grit out.

But recollection appeared on Ash's face, so Mrs O'Malley continued with a little more geniality. "It is an honour to serve our High King, and it's the only time our clan has a chance of living beyond."

Ash knew that 'beyond' meant the otherworld, Tír na nÓg, a place her parents had told her much about. Her mother especially talked about it during her bedtime stories. She'd settled herself to the idea that there wasn't any chance she'd ever travel to the land of the Fair Ones, and she wasn't about to change her views. She remembered those early morning training sessions, something she'd carried on after she left, though the reason she'd continued had nothing to do with joining the elite warriors in the other realm.

Mrs O'Malley stood closer, her pale wrinkled face unreadable as she said, "We want to win, and to do that, we need a matriarch worthy of leading us. I think we can both agree that isn't you."

"You said so yourself, Brehon law is clear." Ash didn't know why she wasn't agreeing with the woman, but the way she was being so easily cast aside caused a reckless anger to swell. She didn't want to be their matriarch, but she sure as the realms wouldn't let this woman make her feel like shit at her mother's funeral. Ash scanned the crowd, annoyance warring with worry in her stomach. "Where's Conor?"

"He's . . . away. He'll be back shortly. Aisling, you need to—"

"I need to do nothing. I want to see my brother."

A man in his twenties stood beside Mrs O'Malley. He was one of the new clan members, and Ash didn't know his name. His dark features were hidden by a peak cap and high-collared coat. "He's not here."

"Where is he?"

Mrs O'Malley gripped his arm as if in warning. "He'll be back—"

Peak Cap shook his head and moved closer to Ash. She noticed his deep hazel eyes were striking against his brown skin and sharp cheekbones. "No, Mrs O'Malley. She deserves to know. You expect her to give up her birthright at the side of her mother's funeral pyre? Give her the respect of truth."

Mutterings of foul-mouthed brats filled the space as Ash regarded her only potential ally. She wondered when and why he joined the clan, but as she glanced around at those gathered, she realised there were quite a few faces she didn't recognise. The ones she did, left her shifting on her feet. It seemed Mrs O'Malley spoke for everyone.

It was highly unusual for clans to take in members from different families. Not that everyone within a clan was related, but there was always one head family and most of the remaining clansmen comprised of cousins and marital joinings. Mrs O'Malley was Ash's distant aunt or cousin, or something; she couldn't remember. Not that they were ever close, and by how Mrs O'Malley looked at Ash now, she would never consider her family, let alone, her leader.

She met Peak Cap's gaze. Maybe he'd married into the clan. Frowning, she realised once again, she didn't care. But her confusion must have been apparent, as the brown-eyed stranger explained.

"My mother is one of the caillte, so our clan divided among a few others. There was no female line willing to take on as matriarch."

Ash racked her mind for the names of the other missing persons besides her father. "Your mother is Nessa Cassidy. You're . . ."

"Tiernan. And your father is Lorcan Breen. Hopefully, they're together somewhere."

"Where's Conor?" Ash realised she sounded rude, but she'd just been to her mother's funeral; she was as welcome in this clan as a chocolate teapot, and her brother was missing. Being polite was not high on her list of priorities.

"He said he couldn't go to her funeral," Tiernan replied so slowly she thought he was stalling. "He came back shortly after . . ."

Ash waited, but he didn't finish. She noticed the entire camp was quiet, the only sound the fierce breeze and fire crackling beside them. The sun had made its descent; the only light source now was the pit and a few surrounding caravans with their lights on. Everyone was listening. Even the children who had been running amok until now had stopped.

"You said I deserved the respect of truth."

Something warred in Tiernan's face. "Come on. Let's go to my caravan."

CHAPTER 14

AISLING

A sh had a feeling it wasn't the cold but the many prying eyes and ears around them that had them walking towards one of the smaller caravans far from the blazing fire. Mrs O'Malley had half-heartedly tried to stop her as she passed, but she'd ignored the woman.

She debated whether this was wise. To go to a stranger's caravan alone wasn't exactly the safest choice, but she would rather risk being attacked by a potential psychopath than standing in front of that many eyes for another second. Stalling in her steps, she chastised herself. That was a terrible thought. Ash shrugged it off, quickening her pace to catch up to Tiernan's long-legged steps. The most honest thoughts were usually the ones that shouldn't be shared.

Tiernan opened the caravan door and gestured for Ash to step inside. One glance behind decided it for her. Everyone was still looking their way. She supposed that if he was a murderer, there were witnesses right outside. Then again, she had seen her mother's body. Ash gripped the mug of half drank tea she was still holding. What if one of them had been involved? What if this Tiernan character had? Before she could talk herself out of it, Ash took the two steps inside.

A light came on and Tiernan moved around her and over to the kitchenette, closing his laptop and gesturing for her to sit at the fold-down table. Setting the mug down and discarding her outerwear, Ash took one of four seats, taking in the small room that brought back memories of a time she'd lived in her mother's caravan.

Cara's was bigger, but Ash and Conor had shared a room. She had begged her mother for her own caravan. Something like this, only tidier, Ash thought as she cast her gaze over the floor covered in devices and computer parts. But Cara had refused even though there were other seventeen-year-olds living on their own. Ash sighed as she looked outside from the small shuttered window to the clansmen still convened at the fire pit. It wasn't as if you were ever alone in a Fianna encampment.

Tiernan retrieved a bottle of whiskey and two glasses, sitting across from her at the small table.

"What happened?" Ash asked as Tiernan poured her a drink.

"I honestly don't know, Aisling."

"Ash," she corrected, wrapping her stiff fingers around the glass.

When he turned to look at her, he smiled, his face transforming into something almost ethereal. "I like that, it suits you."

Ash returned the smile, but it was forced. Why had that sounded like he knew her enough to make that statement? She tucked a strand of dark hair behind her ear and studied the man across from her as he poured his own drink. He was beautiful, regal looking, as he sat twisted in his seat so his long legs jutted towards the kitchenette. His black hair was coarse and curly, shaved at the sides, and there was something calming about the way he moved, his long fingers hypnotic as they wrapped around his glass.

"I found her," Ash blurted.

Tiernan's smile faded, and he turned his gaze back to his glass. He lifted it, but didn't drink. "I heard."

"I need to see my brother. I need to know he's okay."

"I'm not sure that he is." Tiernan set the glass down, leaning forward, his brown eyes simmering with a concern that made her throat tighten. "I promised you the truth. But that's not easy."

"Just tell me."

"They were missing for two weeks. He and Cara had gone off on one of her usual excursions. He returned, but your mother didn't."

She twisted, ready to stand, but Tiernan was quicker. Moving around the table, he kneeled before her as she sank back into her seat, not sure where she had intended to go, anyway. "Ash, I joined this clan right after . . . you left. I've spent the last seven years with your brother and mother. They're like family. If something had happened to him, I wouldn't be sitting here with you, not drinking whiskey."

"Where is he now?"

"He left early this morning, but assured me he'd be back. He's eighteen, free to make his own choices." Tiernan moved back to his seat, sitting with a heavy sigh. "Conor won't speak about what happened, but I believe he will talk to you."

"Where did they go? You said they went on her 'usual excursions'. What does that mean?"

Tiernan's thick eyebrows bunched together, but she knew his frown was more to do with his thoughts than her question. "We've travelled all over Ireland and the continent. At first I thought it was about finding the caillte, and I was hungry to help your mother so that I could find my own. But in recent times, I've had my doubts."

"Why?" Ash lifted her glass, sipping the amber liquid, grimacing as it burned its way down her throat.

"Cara kept coming back to Meath. Close by, but never near enough for you to find out." Tiernan looked at her in apology before continuing. "Then she would disappear for a couple of days while we waited. It drove Conor crazy. He was so close to you, but terrified of disobeying her orders to stay away. I noticed a change in Conor recently."

"How?"

"He was moody. Withdrawn. It's no secret he's angry with your mother for leaving before you could return. He learned your address from me. That's how he could write to you."

"How did you know where I lived?" An unease gripped Ash's throat, burning its way down worse than the whiskey.

Tiernan looked sheepishly at her before taking another sip, and gesturing for her to stay in her seat. "I have to show you something, Ash."

He disappeared, presumably to his bedroom, and returned moments later with a brown leather journal. Passing the counter where he'd placed his laptop, he grabbed that too and sat across from her once again.

"Your mother took me in when I was at my worst," Tiernan said, his face illuminated as his laptop woke up. "I didn't want to, but she begged me to keep an eye on you."

He glanced up at her, his brown eyes dripping with remorse. When he was met by her rage-filled green, it seemed to make him hesitant to go on. She knew her mother had always been a persuasive woman, and persistent.

Ash sighed, taking another sip even though she detested the taste. "What did you do for her?"

"I'm a hacker."

Ash stared at Tiernan, waiting for him to go on. Instead, he turned his laptop to face her. She blinked several times, staring at the screen and then looking up at him. He had the decency to look embarrassed.

"Those are my accounts."

"Yes," Tiernan answered, twisting to look over the laptop.

"They're logged in."

"Yes."

"They are logged in as me, Tiernan."

"I'm sorry, Ash. I didn't want to, but Cara wanted a way to ensure you were safe."

Ash slammed the laptop shut, the absence of its glaring light blinding her for a second. She shoved her glass at him, standing. "You have some nerve."

She reached the door, but paused when Tiernan asked her to stop.

"There's more."

She twisted to face him with a glare, realising she'd forgotten her coat. Retreating to her seat, she ignored him, wrenching it on along with her hat and gloves. The fire in her temper made the extra clothing unbearably warm, and she rushed towards the door, anticipating that even the cold night would do little to cool her down.

"Take this." Tiernan offered her the brown leather journal he'd dropped onto the table before revealing what a creeper he was.

"What is it?" Ash eyed the book as if it were a púca baring its fangs.

Tiernan stood, but kept his distance, reaching across the space to give her the book. Still, she didn't take it.

"It's your mother's journal," Tiernan said, and Ash reached across without thinking, taking it from him. As she turned, he added, "It's not the type of diary you might think, Ash. She had you followed. I don't know by whom. These are her surveillance records and notes on what she'd been really up to."

Ash didn't turn to face Tiernan, but didn't leave either as she stared down at the brown, aged cover. He took it as a sign to continue, his voice interrupting her thoughts. "She'd been looking for something. A lost treasure. It's full of notes about finding what she's initialled, 'TFHK'. I don't know what it means, but Teamhair seems to be an important location."

Teamhair holds the answer.

Remembering the letter stained in blood, Ash's heart raced at Tiernan's words. She'd been wrong to think he was soothing or trustworthy. Normally a good judge in character, Ash scolded herself for thinking she could open up to a stranger. He had lured her to this caravan under the guise of being a friend of her brother's, but she'd leave with the knowledge he was nothing more than her stalker, sanctioned by her own mother.

Ash opened the door, a gust of wind stealing her breath. She didn't turn to Tiernan, her words as harsh as the autumn air. "Stay away from me."

CHAPTER 15

AISLING

"I'm sorry my assignment is late, Professor. I've had a family bereavement." Ash fought the tightness in her throat as she stood on the cobblestones of Trinity college, the mid-morning hustle of students and tourists traipsing past.

The clouds had finally relieved themselves of rain soon after she stormed away from Tiernan and the Breen camp the previous night, and it hadn't stopped raining since. She stood, shivering, her hood doing little to keep the rain from her face. Gripping her heavy crossbody bag strap, she looked to her black boots, raindrops bouncing from the tops.

Professor Mathews sighed, his impatience as apparent as his preference for brown clothing. Adjusting his umbrella, which he didn't offer to her for shared shelter, he said, "Yes, I received your email. And I'm sorry for your loss. Truly, I am. But the deadline has been and gone, Aisling. You have until the end of the week or I'll have to fail you."

Ash swallowed her retort, wanting to ask whether he'd be as hard on the other students, but decided against it. She nodded, blinking through the downpour. "I understand."

"What a shit show," a woman's voice sounded behind them and Ash turned towards her at the same time as the professor.

Maebh McQuillan stood before them, her blonde curly hair as wild as her statement. She had on oversized sunglasses, but Ash could still make out the glint of amusement in her eyes. Unlike Ash's all black attire, Maebh was dressed to be anything but subtle. Skin tight faux leather jeggings, red boots and a jumper printed with the words, "If you're reading this, stop looking at my tits." Her long navy coat was open, hood down, as if she welcomed the elements. She looked gloriously unapproachable as always, and Ash couldn't think of why she was standing in front of them now.

"Excuse me?" Professor Mathews asked, straightening his beige blazer as he looked at Maebh with clear disbelief.

He was Ash's least favourite lecturer, his clear prejudice against the Fianna community apparent with every glance her way, but she would never dream of confronting him. It wasn't worth the marks he would deduct, and she was barely going to pass his class with a late assignment. Apparently, 'murdered mother' was an unacceptable excuse.

"You're not sorry for her loss." Maebh lowered her glasses, her blue eyes trailing down the man's hideous corduroy pants right down to his brown boat shoes.

"Beg your pardon?" Adjusting his cross over satchel, he looked ready to continue with some authoritative bullshit.

Ash opened her mouth to interrupt, but Maebh beat her to it.

"I enjoy a good begging, but I'm not very willing to pardon." Maebh paused, lifting a finger to her full lips. "I suppose you could try. Go on, give it your best shot. But it's Aisling who you should apologise to."

Ash tried to hide her smile, a thrill running through her that Maebh McQuillan was standing up for her. As the professor glared at her, her smile quickly turned into a grimace. She was definitely failing his class. She watched him depart without another word to either of them and almost forgot Maebh's presence, but her perfume made it impossible. It was overpowering, a hint of lavender but also a stronger woody scent, something Ash couldn't place.

"Aisling Breen, we need to talk." Maebh signalled for her to follow as she walked through the crowds that seemed to part for her as she sauntered away.

She'd never seen Maebh without Setanta, and couldn't help looking around in the hope he was close by. Why, she didn't know. It's not like they'd ever held a proper conversation before, but he was nice to look at.

"Why are you here?" Ash asked, weaving through the passersby with less ease than her new companion; the rain slicked cobblestones slowing her down.

"I'm here to check in on my new best friend."

Ash sighed and looked towards where the lecturer had departed, her mind not fully registering what the blonde beauty beside her had said. "I'm not in the market for best friends right now."

"What about someone who can help you find your mother's killer?"

Her attention snapped back to Maebh, the flush on her face a stark contrast to the chill in the air. "Excuse me?"

"Look, we all know that people without the Sight are clueless. And to add to that joy, they irrationally hate us." Maebh gestured between the two of them. "Fianna. They don't understand our culture and get nervous when we don't let them in. Sure, they get a hell of a show out of us, but they never see the real us. And for good reason, obviously."

"What's your point?" Ash asked, her gaze constantly moving around them to the onlookers who stared as they passed.

Nobody paid them much attention, and her shoulders sagged in relief. She wasn't sure if news had spread that she was the daughter of the murdered Newgrange woman. It had been on every news channel and radio station since it had happened, and Ash feared it wouldn't take long for her identity to be released. She was already the daughter of Lorcan Breen, one of the mysterious 'caillte', and the media would no doubt trudge that up once her parents' cases were linked, no matter how coincidental it was.

"The detectives on your mother's case won't find anything. Trust me, I know how useless they are." Maebh readjusted her glasses and looked at the students milling around them. "What are you even doing here? You're the head of the Breen clan."

"Keep your voice down."

"Are you embarrassed by your heritage?"

"Yes." The word slipped through Ash's mouth before she realised, and she straightened when Maebh sneered, quickening her pace as she continued, "I'm embarrassed to associate myself with any community that thinks it's okay to stand by and watch as . . ." Ash's voice quivered, but she ignored it, lowering it in fear of being overheard. "As Fair Ones wreak havoc on innocent people. On babies.

"You can swan around in your 'look at how Fianna I am' shirt all you want, but I've put my time in amongst these 'clueless' people and I'm not about to let you ruin it for me."

She wanted to mention that she also found it hard to be proud of being part of a family where her mother, instead of reaching out to her, thought it was okay to have her stalked. She'd spent most of the night reading through Cara's journal and could only assume there were more of them. The date on the first entry had been a year ago. If Cara had kept surveillance on Ash for seven years like Tiernan had admitted to, then this was just the most recent. It seemed her mother had her followed everywhere—from college, to her sporting events, even to working at Newgrange. Not to mention Tiernan rifling through her online accounts.

"Actually, Aisling, my shirt refers to my ample chest."

"I'm leaving. Stop calling me Aisling." Ash adjusted her hood to conceal more of her face; the rain had stopped, but she was tired of the looks she was getting.

"I'm following." Maebh said, her long strides easily keeping up with her own. "Until you hear me out, bestie. If I can't call you by your name, what can I call you?"

"My mother just died. I don't need this."

"Couldn't agree more." Maebh's outstretched arms smacked a student as he walked by. She ignored his glare. "You don't need this. You don't need to be here. Fuck 'em."

She stopped walking, causing another collision with more passersby. They were near the large gate at Front Square that led out to sprawling Dublin city, and it was only then that Ash realised she was headed in the opposite way to her next class.

"Fuck 'em? I've spent the last three years studying here. I'm almost finished getting my degree and you think I'm just going to throw it all away because some old woman in a clan has the nerve to tell me it's my duty to take my dead mother's place?"

"Okay, Nameless. I thought you said you didn't want a scene?" Maebh smirked as she looked at everyone who'd stopped to gawk at them. "You're quite shrill when you raise your voice."

"My name is Ash."

"Finally. We're getting somewhere in our relationship." Maebh stopped smiling as she placed a hand on Ash's arm. "I'm truly sorry for your loss. Cara didn't deserve that."

Shrugging from her grasp, she didn't move, instead fighting back the brewing emotion that wanted to explode out of her as she looked anywhere but at Maebh. She didn't deserve to mourn, not after walking away from her family, and not with the way she couldn't forgive her mother for keeping tabs on her without reaching out. Mrs O'Malley was right. She had no right to prolong the inevitable. She would relinquish her right as matriarch as soon as she knew Conor was okay.

"How can you help me?"

When Ash finally looked at Maebh, her wide smile had transformed her already exquisite face into something angelic. "Let's find somewhere warm, preferably with coffee."

After a half-hearted protest that she should go to her next lecture, she agreed and led Maebh to a cafe close to Trinity. It was nothing like Newgrange's, with modern furnishings and copper light fixtures that hung so low from the ceiling they both had to duck in places as they headed to the long queue.

"What are you doing?" Ash asked as she noticed Maebh moving past the people already waiting at the front counter.

"I'm not waiting in this line; it'll take too long," Maebh replied, winking at her before turning back to the harried looking barista. He opened his mouth to presumably state they couldn't skip, and as Ash looked between him and the annoyed expressions from the next patrons, she could feel heat creep up the back of her neck that had little to do with the packed room.

"You don't mind if we go next, right?" Maebh let out a breathy laugh and Ash noted the space filled with a sweet smell. She could just about make it out over the blonde's strong perfume, but it tugged at her stomach, making her feel . . . confused. Her eyes snapped to Maebh, who looked at her with arched brows as she murmured, "Interesting."

To her astonishment, they received their order next, with no charge. Maebh led them to one of the remaining seats by the front window. Maebh took a sip of her coffee while Ash slouched into her chair, discarding her bag and coat while trying to figure out what had just happened.

"Out with it," Maebh said, shirking out of her own coat before sticking her fork into the generous serving of apple tart that the barista all but climbed across the counter to offer her.

"How did you do that?" Ash whispered, glancing around the cafe to ensure nobody was listening. Everyone had seemed to snap out of whatever had happened, but the barista continued to stare at Maebh, his expression dazed as he clumsily completed orders.

"I have a gift that allows me to manipulate emotions." Maebh shrugged, tossing her blonde hair across her shoulder, as if it was a normal occurrence. She set her fork down. "Technically, I'm not supposed to use it, but a girl needs her caffeine."

Ash stared, dumbfounded, at the woman sitting across from her, but something was bothering her. She knew magic was something humans couldn't comprehend, but when you witnessed Fair Ones roaming freely amongst them, your ability to grasp impossibilities became easier. Ash sat up straight, an uneasy flutter settling in her stomach. "Is it through smell?"

Maebh smiled at Ash, tilting her head as she contemplated her. "Yes. I sensed something strange about you when I used it. I've only ever noticed it before with two others. You could sense what I was doing, right? And you currently don't have the hots for me."

Ash spluttered, her latte dripping down her chin. She reached for the napkin Maebh offered. "No, I don't. You're clearly attractive but—"

"Relax. I'm not fishing for compliments." Maebh gestured to the barista. "I made the mental suggestion that everyone near that counter wants to have sex with me. When people want sex, they tend to give you what *you* want."

"That's kind of despicable," Ash said, but Maebh only waved her off. "What strange thing did you notice about me?"

"That you don't want to have sex with me because, obviously, that's weird." Maebh laughed when Ash rolled her eyes. "My brother has the same gift, but we're twins and I can't have anything without him stealing at least half of all the good things. There's also a guy I know who is the only other person immune to my . . . charms."

Ash contemplated that for a moment as they drank their coffees and watched the day continue in a blur of rushing bodies and honking cars outside. The clouds were as grey as wood ash from a fire. Dublin was cement grey and brick brown; full of the smells of pollution, litter and impatience, Ash realised with a frown. She'd always been good at reading people, but she could have sworn she'd known how that detective felt as he questioned her. And then, when she'd reunited with Mary and Dom afterwards, she'd sensed their feelings.

Ash leaned closer. Tucking her dark locks behind her ears, she glanced around once more before asking, "How does it work?"

Maebh turned her attention towards Ash, her blonde hair glinting in the temporary appearance of the sun. Her tanned skin gave the impression she spent a lot of time outdoors, and Ash glanced down at her own pale arm that seemed to deflect any sunlight.

"I'm able to make people feel certain emotions temporarily, but I also feel their true emotions constantly." Maebh wrinkled her nose. "Through smell. It's interesting to know that not many people share what they really feel."

Ash's frown deepened. "How long have you had this gift?"

Maebh leaned against her high-back chair, glancing out the window to the bustling street outside, and Ash copied her. It had started to rain again, so people were rushing by as the heavens continued their assault on anyone unfortunate enough to be walking.

"Fianna have Sight, but Mother told me that some also have gifts that lie dormant until they need to call upon them. It's rare and my mother ordered me to never speak about it."

"You obviously don't listen, do you?"

Maebh laughed. "Clearly not. Why are you so interested?"

Ash straightened, playing with her damp hair again before lifting her cup. She studied the woman before her. She had no reason to trust her, but she'd just openly told Ash about her own secret. "I may have the same gift. But I'm not sure."

Maebh's face lit up as she set her cup down. "Tell me more."

Ash recalled her experience with the horrible detective, and also with her foster parents. As she spoke, she realised there had been a few occasions where she'd sensed emotions, but had always put it down to being good at reading people. "Is it your, I don't know, aura I can smell? It's woodsy and floral."

Maebh chuckled as she shook her head. Reaching into her bag, she retrieved an expensive looking bottle of perfume. "It's the strongest scent I could find. Myrrh and tonka bean. Here, take it. I always carry a spare. Trust me, you're going to need it if your gift grows. From what you've described, it's similar to mine."

Ash protested but Maebh insisted, showing her she did in fact have another bottle. Thanking her, Ash started, realising for the last hour she hadn't thought about her mother's murder, or her brother's wellbeing. A pain tore at her chest, the guilt of the unlikely reprieve catching her breath.

"Don't do that." Maebh leaned back, frowning.

"What?"

"Feel guilty. Whatever it's about, you have no control over it. Stop it, you also smell bad when you do it." Maebh signalled to the barista for more coffee, who diligently ignored the next customer and gave Maebh a thumbs up.

Ash couldn't help the smile that formed. "Despicable."

Maebh laughed. "Shall we talk about the reason we're here?"

Pressing on her chest as if it would somehow dull the ache, Ash nodded.

"I have a proposition for you. I want to help you solve your mother's case." Maebh paused as the barista approached, clearing their table and setting down fresh coffees. He stalled, as if hoping she would do more than provide the thanks she offered, but he gave up with a sigh and returned to the counter. Maebh's eyes were trained on Ash, excitement clear as she spoke. "We team up. When you take on your matriarchal role, you make me your second in command."

"First," Ash said, taking a drink before scrutinising the woman across from her. "Why do you want to join the Breen clan? Second, what makes you think I'm accepting the role? And last, why would I agree to this even if I was?"

"Why in all the realms would you not be matriarch? It's your birthright."

"They don't want me." Ash lifted a finger with each sentence. "I'm in my last year of college. There are several reasons, actually."

"What does your brother think?"

Ash frowned, looking out the window as she answered. "I don't know."

Where was Conor?

"Ash," Maebh began, her tone serious, which seemed like a rarity at this brief encounter. "You forget I can smell how you feel. It's slightly different with you, I admit. Maybe because you share a similar gift, I don't know. But I know you care way more than you're admitting."

They sat in silence and Ash let the noises of the busy cafe wash over her as she contemplated. Glancing at the Fianna woman beside her, she felt . . . comfortable. Maebh was intimidating from afar, but up close, she was actually a soothing presence. Ash felt more herself than she ever could be with any of her college friends, even more so than with Mary and Dom. She had forgotten what it felt like to be with someone who knew her deepest secret. Who experienced it too.

"Do you know anything about Teamhair?" Ash asked when her second cup of coffee was half empty.

"Teamhair?" Maebh's face scrunched, but she shrugged. "As in the Hill of Tara?"

"Yes." Ash said, looking at the bag where she would normally hold her letters. She'd left them at home, hidden. They technically no longer belonged to her. Evidence from a crime scene she had no business tampering with. Shaking her head, she turned to Maebh, a fluttering in her chest as she steeled her resolve to pursue an answer to the question left to her by her mother. Fianna often used the original names for places and she was confident the letter meant the ancient hill.

"Teamhair holds the answer." Ash waited for a sign of recognition from Maebh, but when she received none, she continued, "My mother's last words to me. What would the Hill of Tara hold?"

She waited as Maebh's eyes drifted towards the window, peering out but glazed, as if she didn't really see the scurrying figures go by. She turned, shaking her head, but then her face brightened, a triumphant glee in her eyes as she smacked the table. "My seanchaí will know."

"Your storyteller?" Ash's brows furrowed, unconvinced. She remembered the seanchaí tent at the Breen clan, where a robed Fianna would tell stories of lore and magic. They'd had a rota, different clansmen taking turns performing. She didn't know how a glorified storyteller could help.

"Diarmuid is not just a performer like some of the other clans have, Ash. My seanchaí has a gift like ours. He can recall stories from the past with the help of druid magic and wiccan blood. If there are tales about Teamhair holding answers, he will know them."

Ash opened her mouth to argue, but her phone rang. It took a few seconds for her to realise it was hers as the ringtone was unfamiliar, but the vibrations by her feet were the only sign. Frowning, Ash stared at the screen, Tiernan's face peering up at her. She was about to hit ignore, unsure how he'd programmed his phone number into hers, but then his picture blinked and Ash realised he'd somehow video called her and forced her to answer.

"Ash, I'm sorry to call you like this."

"How did you . . . never mind. I'm hanging up."

Maebh stood, peering across the table to see her phone. Ash heard her curse softly when she saw who it was.

"Don't hang up. It's about Conor. He's back."

"I'm on my way," Ash said, her internal temperature rising as her throat tightened.

Tiernan hung up and she jumped to her feet, banging into the table as she shoved her arms into her coat and hoisted her bag from the floor. In a fluster, she turned to leave before realising she'd said nothing to Maebh.

"Go. Be with your brother. Here's my number in case you change your mind about my offer." Maebh handed Ash a napkin with her digits scrawled across it.

Ash nodded, but didn't commit to anything, her mind wrapped around finally reuniting with Conor. She only hoped he wanted the same thing.

CHAPTER 16

AISLING

A sh's reunion with her brother didn't go exactly according to plan.

"I can't believe how much you've grown, Con." She hated herself for the senseless words spewing out of her.

What did it matter how much he'd grown when their mother had just been murdered? He sat hunched on his bed, barely registering where she stood at the narrow doorway of his one bedroom caravan. Where had he been during her funeral? Tiernan had met her at the side of the road where she'd parked to walk back to their camp. She'd ignored his attempts at apologising for his earlier confession. Even if she wanted to understand why he'd invaded her privacy for years, she was consumed with anticipation of reuniting with her younger brother. The last time she'd laid eyes on him, he'd been a child. Now, he was a young man, and her first words to him were nonsense.

Tiernan had said that Conor had showed up just before he'd called her, but hadn't said a word so far. When the elders had tried to talk to him, he'd ignored them, staggering straight to his caravan where he'd stayed since. In the short distance between the road and his small home, Tiernan had admitted that Conor refused to say what had happened before his solo return after Cara's death.

A woollen blanket lay uselessly limp across him, and he didn't seem to have the strength to hold it as silence stretched on. His black hair was a mass of unwashed curls and as she studied him, she took in all the changes to his appearance in the years they'd been apart. Although she'd desperately wanted one of his letters to contain a photo, there had been none. The clans didn't use social media, so she had found no photos of any of her family online. All except a blurred black and white of her father who'd gone missing. She cast a weary glance at Tiernan, who stood in the main living space behind her. The hacker was clearly more up to date with the outside world.

He raised his dark brows as he caught her glare, but she wordlessly turned back to her brother. Time made little difference to people like Mrs O'Malley's appearance, who was already in her later years, but to someone as young as Conor, it was as if she was looking at somebody else. Not quite a stranger, but enough time had passed to transform his face and lengthen his frame. She realised with an inhale that he looked strikingly like their father. There was no trace of the baby fat that once was, and the man before her had stubble, a more structured jaw, and haunted brown eyes.

He stared at his hands as if they were about to reveal a secret, and he didn't want to miss it. His dark clothes were muddied, but it wasn't proof he'd been sleeping rough. He needed to tell her, but she swallowed down the question. Where had he been? For years, Conor had been the only connection to her past life. He'd communicated the day to day of his Fianna life, and she'd cherished every word. Now, he sat mute before her, caught in a pit of sorrow.

All she wanted to do was to gather that blanket and wrap it tightly around him. But that would involve sitting on his twin bed. Even though she was his sister, it felt far too intimate.

Were they strangers now? It had never felt that way until this moment.

His bedroom was barely big enough for two of them, but Ash was grateful Tiernan loitered behind her, despite how much she hated how he'd invaded her privacy at her mother's request.

"Con, I'm going to make us all a cuppa. Why don't you chat with Ash, buddy? I know it's not the way you wanted it, but your sister is finally here with you."

She gave Tiernan a tight-lipped smile before he turned to take the ten steps into the kitchenette. He motioned for her to sit down beside Conor, and her gaze returned to his slumped figure. She wondered why it was so hard to do it. He was her younger brother. He was barely an adult at eighteen, but it still counted. She had certainly thought so when she had turned that age. She moved into the room directly across from him, her arms crossed over her erratic heartbeat.

"Con?"

"She's dead." His voice came out hoarse, like it hadn't been used in a long time.

Something snapped within her ribcage at the sound and she rushed to his side, jostling the bed as she sat. "I'm sorry."

He leaned into her, and even though he was now taller than she was, she cradled an arm around him. A sob tore from his throat so loudly that it sounded more animal than man, and she gripped him, fighting the lump in her throat, until he lowered himself to rest his head on her lap. The tinkering of cups and kettle had quietened as she shushed and petted his hair, reminding her of when they had shared a room, and he'd had a nightmare.

Continuing to stroke his head, she leaned against the wall and took in the room that looked similar to the one they'd shared in Cara's caravan. She could never house all of her belongings in such a tiny space now. Ash glanced at the boy—no man—on her lap. He seemed so delicate. Breakable. Would he be able to overcome this loss? She blinked back tears she knew weren't about their mother, but about the broken brother she was failing miserably to comfort. His heartbreak tore her own apart.

Every time he sucked in shuddering breaths, her throat constricted, until it was impossible to swallow without wincing. She would do anything to take away his pain. She had a million questions for him, but couldn't ask a single one. The air smelled charged, like how it did before a heavy thunderstorm, and Ash realised she could smell Conor's despair. Thinking of her conversation with Maebh earlier, she wondered whether she *could* take away his pain.

She let out a soft breath, willing a sense of calmness outwards. She wasn't sure if she'd made any difference, but when she took a tentative sniff, the air had shifted. Hints of lavender filled the space and Conor's sobs grew less and less until they were only sniffling and uneven breaths. They sat that way until his breathing steadied and he began to softly snore.

Tiernan returned with only two cups. Handing her one as he hunkered on the floor across from the bed, she bit the inside of her cheek when he sniffed the air and his attention snapped to her. They studied each other for a moment, but he said nothing and she didn't offer an explanation. They both drank their tea and listened to Conor's breathing.

"That's the first he's spoken since he came back."

"Where was he?"

"I think he was in Tír na nÓg." Tiernan set his cup down and adjusted the blanket over Conor before returning to lean against the wall. "It'd explain why they weren't here sooner."

She stared down at her brother in surprise. He'd been to the otherworld?

"Why would he be there?"

121

"Because Cara was searching for something. I think that's where she was going on her quests." He let out a heavy sigh as he rested his head against the wall. "It's the only explanation I have. We travelled everywhere, Ash. In this realm, I mean. France, Italy, Africa. We even went as far as China and Russia a few years ago. All for what?"

She hoped he didn't expect her to answer because she was speechless. As she sipped her tea, begrudgingly realising he'd made it just the way she liked, she thought about the otherworld. Even though she knew of its existence, she never considered it a tangible place before. It was like the sun or moon; it was there but never somewhere she would visit. Why was her mother visiting the other realm?

Time shifted differently, so much so it was rare for Fianna to travel to it. One reason they didn't let outsiders know too much about their community and whereabouts, either. Only the High King and his Fianna warriors were permitted unrestricted access to Tír na nÓg, so what Cara had been doing was prohibited. And forcing Conor with her?

They drank their tea in contemplative companionship, but Ash couldn't help but steal glances at the man sitting across from her. She couldn't trust him, not after what he'd admitted to doing for her mother. How much had he read of her private messages? Every conversation, search engine entry, even her journal where she tracked her dealing with Fair Ones. Her skin heated at his audacity and she glared at him, gripping her cup tightly.

She knew it was her mother's orders, but he was the one who'd done it. As if sensing where her thoughts had gone, Tiernan sighed and clasped his long, brown fingers together in front of his raised knees. His look was imploring as he said, "Will you let me explain?"

"What is there to explain? You know everything about me, and yet I know nothing about you."

His smile was small. "I'll tell you anything you want to know."

"Where do you get the nerve to think it's okay to snoop into my life?" Ash winced as she realised her raised tone elicited a movement from Conor. She held his head with care, shuffling from the bed. Once she'd stood and was confident Conor was asleep, she turned to Tiernan, signalling they move out of his bedroom.

Leaning against the cluttered counter in the tiny kitchenette, she took in the scattered sketch books and random drawings that covered every counter. Tiernan stood at the wall beside the dining table, his arms clasped behind him. He was much taller than she was, the black curls on the top of his head almost reaching the ceiling. It was only when he spoke that she looked at him.

"I never felt okay with what your mother asked of me. Please know that I didn't delve too deeply, only skimmed to make sure you were okay."

Ash crossed her arms, taking a deep breath and holding it in. Exhaling in a loud breath, she narrowed her eyes at him, realising she would never understand, but an idea had come to her.

"Can you hack into anywhere?"

"Yes." Tiernan freed one hand trapped behind him, scratching the back of his long neck as he frowned at her. "Why?"

"Can you hack into the detective who is investigating my mother's murder?" Ash stepped forward, closing the gap so she stood directly in front of him when he was about to protest. "You owe me."

"So, let me get this right," he began, moving around her to sit at one of four seats around the dining table. He stretched his long jean-clad legs out, warily watching Ash as she sat across

123

from him. "You want me to hack into An Garda Siochana, find out what the detective knows, and you'll forgive me?"

"Who said anything about forgiving you?" When his expression turned wary and he shook his head, she waved her hand. "Fine. I'll think about it if you do it."

"Why don't you call the detective? He's obligated to keep you up to date, right?"

"Not if I'm a suspect." She sighed, giving him a rundown of her uncomfortable interrogation, and he shook his head, cursing.

"Typical Glutton."

Ash laughed, despite their conversation. "It's been a long time since I heard anyone use that term about outsiders."

Her face heated, realising she'd insinuated she was part of the clan. Gluttons was a term clansmen often used about humans without Faerie Sight. They called Fianna a lot worse, and Ash was all too familiar with the hostility that was felt by both sides.

"You know you are still one of us?" Tiernan said, again somehow knowing where her mind had gone.

"I need you to see if they've been able to read a piece of evidence," Ash said in a rush, wanting desperately to change the subject and also to get out what she was about to reveal before she lost her nerve. "A letter."

His face was unreadable as she admitted to the torn letter. She watched him closely when she quoted the only words she could make out.

"Teamhair holds the answer," he repeated softly, his features furrowed in contemplation.

A knock on the door caused both to jump and Ash cast a wary glance toward her brother's room. Luckily, his snoring continued as the door was opened and Ash heard a softly spoken feminine voice. "I need to speak with Aisling."

Tiernan murmured, "It's not a good time, Niamh."

"It's okay," Ash said as she stood by his side and looked down at her red-haired cousin. "We can talk out here."

She grabbed her coat and took the two steps down to stand level with Niamh, whose freckled face was smiling. She looked the same as she had seven years ago, when Ash would have considered her a best friend. Similar in height, the women were both athletic, whereas Ash was more lithe and Niamh had broader shoulders. She had always been competitive during their workouts, and Ash had yet to meet anyone who had stronger upper body strength. Maebh popped into her head then, followed quickly by Setanta. She was confident the twins could each out-perform her cousin in the Cath. A wave of nostalgia at her old life crashed into her, and something else. Something she hadn't expected. Her stomach fluttered with longing for just a moment before she shook herself.

"How are you?" Niamh asked, her long red hair plaited down to her lower back. She wore a green fur-lined coat, dark pants and boots to combat the cold. The sun had already descended, the darkness taking its place causing a greater chill to creep around Ash, making her wish she'd stayed inside.

"I'm fine," she said lamely, looking beyond Niamh to the woman standing behind her.

Her black hair was thick and long, flowing in the surrounding breeze, and her skin was a rich brown. Deep set eyes studied Ash, her plump lips pressed together without acknowledging her.

"This is my cousin, Emer," Tiernan said in a cool tone, standing beside Ash with crossed arms. He'd donned his heavy coat and peak cap, his collar pulled up but not reaching his chin.

"And my wife," Niamh added, her smile widening as she gazed at Emer, taking her hand.

"Congratulations," Ash said, her own smile forced.

She was happy for her old friend, but there was something in the air that she sensed, an unease between her and the pair. She wouldn't blame Niamh for resenting how Ash had left. They'd been friends, and Niamh had known how unhappy she'd been, but it didn't mean she had understood. Niamh was Fianna in every sense. She could never grasp Ash's frustration when Cara would make her shadow her, and how her overprotective nature smothered her.

'Being matriarch means sacrificing any social life,' Ash would complain, to which Niamh would laugh and tell her to stop crying and get back to work.

"I'm sorry for your loss," Niamh said, breaking through her trip down memory lane. "May Cara's soul continue on."

"And her love remain," Ash murmured, sniffing as she shivered in the cold.

"My aunt tells me she spoke to you about our plans for the Cath," Niamh began, her look apologetic. "I'm sorry for whatever she said. She isn't the most tactful woman."

"Contrary old goat, more like," Emer said, a smile finally forming on her lips as she tugged on Niamh's hand.

"You'd better hope she doesn't hear you say that." Niamh giggled, smacking her wife's arm before turning back to Ash. "When you're ready, can we talk about it? I don't want to rush you, but we must plan to leave soon, and a new matriarch needs to be appointed."

"Niamh is next in line once you renounce your claim," Emer said, her expression stony. She ignored Niamh's muttered admonishment as she continued to stare at Ash. "You can continue on with your life and so can the clan."

"Emer," Tiernan warned, stepping in front of Ash. She gripped his arm, pulling him back. Despite the coldness in the air, her shivering stopped. Straightening her back, she took a step closer, having to angle her head to meet Emer's gaze.

"Has the detective been here to question any of you yet?" she asked. When both women looked at each other and then returned blank stares at her, she added, "About my mother's murder."

"What are you insinuating?" Emer asked.

"She doesn't mean it like that," Niamh said, shaking her head, but there was a clear look of uncertainty when she met her gaze again.

Ash swallowed, her head throbbing. She meant nothing, of course, but she was sick of being looked at like an unwelcome nuisance. "I'm leaving," she said, turning to Tiernan. "Let me know when he wakes up?"

Tiernan looked like he wanted to say something else, but only nodded.

"I'll talk to you tomorrow, Niamh, okay?" Ash said before taking a few steps in the direction of the road and the solace of her car. "I'm just not able for it today."

Niamh reached for her hand and squeezed gently as she passed. Ash could hear rapid whispers between them as she retreated, and she picked up her pace before anyone else confronted her. If they did, who knew what would come out of her mouth.

Taking one glance behind, she caught Emer's gaze, before turning away again. She was unwelcome here, so why couldn't she let them have what they wanted? Her resolve was clear as she opened her car door. As soon as she spoke to her brother, she would renounce her claim as matriarch.

She'd move on, and so would the clan. Hopefully, without one more clansman. She was taking her brother with her.

CHAPTER 17

AISLING

S itting around the dining table in the cosy cottage, Ash let Mary's continuous conversation flow around her, adding a one-worded response or grunt when she felt it was needed. Dom sat near the fire hearth in his favourite worn chair. It was probably older than the stones that held their home upright, but he refused to replace it with a new one.

As she ate the dinner Mary had placed in front of her, not tasting one bite, she thought about everything that had happened since she'd found her mother's body. She didn't know how she was supposed to feel about any of it. Would Conor want to speak with her when he woke up? It had been hours since she'd left, and Tiernan hadn't called.

Once she could have a decent conversation with her brother to ensure he was okay, and to offer for him to move in here with her, she'd tell the Breen clan to appoint whomever they wanted in her mother's place. Mary and Dom had already agreed to letting her brother stay. They could start a new life together, one without warrior training and impossible burdens on their young shoulders.

Ash barely registered the sound of the door knocker until she heard Mary's voice turn high pitched—something she did when an unexpected guest arrived. When Conor's lanky frame appeared, Ash dropped her cutlery with a loud bang.

"Conor!" She jumped from her seat, reaching out to clasp his arms.

"Hey, sis," Conor said, enveloping her in a tight hug. "Sorry to intrude like this."

"Nonsense." Mary gestured for him to take a seat at the table. "I'll get you a plate."

Ash sat beside her brother, drinking him in as he smiled politely at Mary and shook Dom's hand, who'd stood as soon as he'd entered. He'd showered, his black hair still thickly curled around his angular pale face. Purple and blue stains were painted under his eyes, and she noted how bloodshot they were. He turned to look at her, those russet eyes taking her in, too.

"Come on, Mary," Dom said once she'd placed a hefty plate of chicken, potatoes and steamed vegetables in front of Conor. "Let's leave these two to catch up."

"How are you really?" Ash asked once they were finally alone. She reached for his hand, and squeezed, her earlier awkwardness gone over the need to make sure her brother was okay.

Conor squeezed her hand once before dropping it, resting both elbows on the table. "I'm not okay. You?"

"I'm . . ." Ash paused, unsure of how to respond. "I don't know. Once I know you're going to be okay, I think I'll be fine."

Her brother looked everywhere but her, taking in the low, wooden beamed ceiling to the mismatched furniture that had made its way from the cafe over the years. She scanned it as if it was the first time she had set foot in there. An antique fire range took up a large portion of one wall, where Mary often cooked stew. Dom's hideous chair where you could clearly see his indent into the fabric. To many people, it was a small room. To Conor and other Fianna, it was more space than their entire caravan.

"I'm not okay," Conor repeated, but then his eyes trained on her with more focus than before. "I've missed you."

She felt sick with guilt and regret, the chicken dinner that she'd managed swirling in her stomach as she nodded. "I'm sorry I left you."

He leaned forward, his eyes searching hers. "Why did you?"

"I don't know," she began, but shook her head. She did know, but embarrassment at her selfishness stopped her from disappointing her brother further. "It was just so intense with . . . her. Mam never let me out of her sight for five minutes. It got worse as I grew older. She wasn't like that with you."

The fire crackled in the hearth, and she watched it, avoiding the look she feared she'd see on his face.

"I remember," he murmured, reaching over and taking her hand in his. His fingers were long, stained with charcoal at the tips. "I understand. Mam did too; I think that's why she let you leave."

Her attention snapped to his face as she sucked in a breath. "Did she tell you that?"

He nodded, a sad smile playing on his lips as he released her hand and ran it through the errant curls covering one eye. "Tell me, how has life been here for you? I told you all about what I've been doing in my letters. My tattoo apprenticeship, warrior training, the trouble our cousins always seem to get me into. What have you been up to?"

Ash smiled as her heart warmed, relishing in the moment of reuniting with her brother, and the much needed subject change. It was how neither expected, but things rarely went as planned. She told him about her archaeology studies and how she hoped to travel after she finished her degree. He told her about his art, his friendship with Tiernan. She swallowed down the unwarranted jealousy at hearing him speak as if he was talking about a brother.

She hadn't been there for his teenage years, and Ash should be glad somebody had looked out for him. Casting her gaze toward the closed door, as if she could see down the long hallway and into her room, she thought about the bundle of letters that lay in a drawer. Responses to every letter he'd written. She felt silly for writing them now. He wouldn't want them.

As if sensing her mood change, Conor took her hand once more. "Tiernan is a good guy. I know what he did for Mam was wrong. But you said it yourself; she was always overprotective. It didn't stop after you left."

She only nodded, forcing a placid smile onto her face. "I'm glad he's been there for you."

Conor's smile was wide as he said, "You two would get along if you gave him a chance."

They both picked at the food on their plates as comfortable silence finally fell around them. As if they'd picked up where they'd left off, and their sibling relationship was as steadfast as before. There were topics they both avoided, but it seemed her brother was ready to broach the one she still wasn't.

"The Cath is an important Fianna rite, and it sucks that it's happening so soon after . . ." Conor's jaw ticked, but after a moment he continued, "We need—"

"You can move in here with me." Ash knew before she'd finished that it had been the wrong thing to say, but she hadn't wanted him to continue that sentence. She didn't know if he wanted her to give up her birthright, or come back, and she was afraid of which one would hurt more.

Conor stood, his chair scraping against the tiled floor.

"Move in, here?" He stretched his arms outside, circling the table. "This isn't for me. I love my clan. I love you, too." Conor stopped in front of her again, his voice breaking as he stared down at her slumped figure. "I need you to come back."

"Conor," Ash began, but she didn't know what to say.

She was wrong to leave him. She'd had a duty to her family, and she'd let them down. Cara had been overbearing, and they'd fought constantly until Ash left. Her mother had scrutinised her every move, and wouldn't let her have as much freedom as the other teenagers, because she was to be matriarch. It had always felt like it was a punishment, and she couldn't understand her mother's decisions, so she'd run away instead of standing up to her.

He turned to face her, a sad smile on his pale face. "There's nothing stopping you from coming back now. We need you. I need you to be our matriarch."

"Why? Nobody else wants me there."

"That's not true. Mrs O'Malley wants her great niece to take the place, and she'd have you believe that's what everyone wants. Niamh wouldn't make a good leader. Only her wife and Mrs O'Malley think she would."

Ash studied her brother as he stood by the hearth, the flames highlighting his sharp features. She swallowed, her throat tight. Reaching for her glass of water, she said, "You didn't answer my question. Why do you need me to be matriarch?"

"To finish what our mother started," Conor said. He returned to the table, sitting across from her. "All the clans are going to Tír na nÓg in a few days, and we need to be ready. She took me there. That's where we . . . got separated."

Conor reached for his glass, lifting it with a shaking hand. Ash waited for him to speak, fearing if she said anything, he'd clam up and not share what he needed to.

"Mam was looking for the caillte. For our father," Conor eventually said, his eyes glazed. Shaking his head, he glanced at her before standing to pace once more. "She wouldn't share much about her mission, but she admitted that the High King was involved."

"What?" Ash gasped at the mention of the Fianna High King, someone who lived in the background of her acceptance of the reality of their worlds. He was human, a Fianna, but lived in the other realm, and was as elusive to her as the Fair Ones.

"They knew each other," Conor added. "King Aedan was friendly with our parents and had tasked our mother with finding the lost clansmen, the caillte."

Conor continued to pace as she studied him; her lips pursed as her heartbeat thrummed in rapid bursts. Tiernan had convinced her that perhaps Cara had been lying about looking for her father and the others who'd disappeared, including Tiernan's mother. But why should she believe someone who'd been hacking into her life undetected and uninvited for years before she even knew him? Her brother was so sure that this was what Cara had been doing.

Her mother's journal came to mind. In between having Ash's every move tracked, there had been notes scrawled in the narrow margins about possible locations. The initials 'TFHK' popped up continuously, and she wished she knew what it meant.

"I'm going to Tír na nÓg with or without you, Ash," Conor said, fully facing her once more, the change in his tone sending a coldness through the room. "There is more to what you know about the Cath. About our missing father and the others. I've trained, like all warriors do, and I can take on what comes during the trials. But I will find our father. It was Mam's dying wish."

If Niamh took her place, would she protect Conor? Would she keep track of what he was up to, if it didn't involve the High King's trials? Ash opened her mouth to insist he needed to drop their mother's quest, but he put his hand up and stopped her.

"Either I go on my own and risk my life or we go together and do it the way our mother wanted. With you as matriarch. She trained you most of your life to take over, and this is your one chance to make her proud."

There was a strange glint in his brown eyes, something that forced Ash to lean forward. "Are you feeling okay, Con?"

She tried to sense his emotions, but gave up when nothing happened. It was as if a void had filled the room and she was sure she'd done something wrong with her untested gift.

"Where were you when Mam was killed?"

His face immediately crumpled, but he blinked back tears. His voice was hoarse as he spoke. "She'd left me at the Hill of Tara. There are tunnels there that lead between the realms. There was something wrong. I knew I shouldn't have left, but she'd insisted."

"I found her in Newgrange," Ash said after a long pause. Their eyes met in the shared loss of their mother.

"I should have never left her in that barbaric realm." Conor coughed, clearing his throat as he made his way to the door.

Ash jumped up from her seat. "Where are you going?"

"Back home." Conor gave her a small smile as he bent and kissed her cheek. "Hopefully, I'll see you there."

Ash watched from the hallway as he said goodbye to her foster parents who'd materialised from the sitting room as soon as he stepped into the hallway. She stood at the open front door and watched him fold into a small car and drive away.

She replayed their conversation over and over until she couldn't see his taillights any longer and Mary called for her to shut the door as she was letting all the cold in.

They'd been in the other realm when Conor and Cara had parted ways. Ash grabbed her coat, calling out that she was going for a walk before stealing the set of keys to the Newgrange security gates. The stiff wind clawed at her, pushing her back as she headed in the dark night towards the shrouded monument in the distance. On a whim, Ash dug out her phone.

Ash: If you still want to join the Breen clan, you're welcome.

Maebh: ARE YOU TAKING YOUR CLAN BY THE BALLS AND SHOWING THEM HOW IT'S DONE?

Ash: Something like that. I'll be there soon. Haven't told them yet.

Maebh: DED. See you there.

Smirking, she stashed her phone in her pocket, sending a silent prayer to the sky that she'd made the right choice. Ash would need all the help she could get if she was going to take on the impossible task of the role she'd thought was dead to her.

Staring at the ancient stones before her, she hugged her torso, embracing the shivers that came from both the weather and the inconceivable revelation that had awakened something in her. She knew where her mother had really been murdered, and if she was right, the detective had no chance of discovering Cara's killer.

CHAPTER 18

MAEBH

M aebh hadn't expected a parade, exactly, but this welcome was ridiculous. It was borderline hostile.

"Go back to your own clan."

Maebh mentally scratched off the borderline part. "Where's your matriarch?"

The old woman huffed as others murmured around her. "You were at her funeral, girl. Does your mother know you're here?"

"Ash is your matriarch." Maebh raised her brows at the gasps and objections from the surrounding group.

"It's true," a deep husky voice said from behind, and Maebh pivoted towards her saviour with one of her winning smiles. It turned into a scowl when she saw Tiernan standing a few feet behind her. His frown matched his clansmen. "Come with me."

He turned and walked away, ignoring the many voices demanding he explain. Maebh hesitated only long enough to smell sulphurous anger seeping from the growing group in front of her.

"Where are you taking me?" she asked, catching up to his long steps.

"To your new home, of course." Tiernan's tone was anything but welcoming as he gestured to one of the smallest caravans Maebh had ever seen. Sure, she'd shared hers with her brother, but it had been much bigger than this match box.

"You can't be serious? I'm Ash's second."

His smile was asinine. "That remains to be confirmed."

Maebh tossed her wild hair behind her, only for the blonde locks to sweep forward from the wind, shielding the tall, unhappy man in front of her. "What did she tell you?"

"Nothing." Tiernan scowled, his brown eyes boring into hers as he stepped closer. "Let's get one thing clear. I just lied to the clan elders in order to protect Ash, not you."

"Still holding a grudge over our . . . misunderstanding, I see," Maebh muttered, waving her hand to dismiss whatever he was about to say.

Tiernan opened his mouth, but closed it just as quickly, his jaw clenching. Tossing a key at her, he said, "We drove this around for storage."

As she opened the door, she had to press her nose and mouth into the crook of her elbow. Her perfume soaked coat did very little to overpower the stench. It would be hard to smell any emotions coming from this tin can. "What did it store?"

"Horseware." Tiernan's wide lips curved into a smile as Maebh gagged. "Welcome to the Breen clan. If you need anything, don't come to me."

"Your cousin got all the people skills you lack, I see."

"Still mind molesting folk?"

Maebh glared at Tiernan. "That is *not* what I do."

Before he could retaliate, their attention was drawn towards the main road where a gardai car had parked. A plain clothes officer got out and walked towards the encampment. Without speaking, Maebh and Tiernan made their way to where that old woman who'd harassed Maebh was now speaking to him. As they approached, she heard they were asking about Ash's brother.

"He still hasn't returned?"

"No."

"Do you know where he is?"

"No."

"And he hasn't come back since the thirty-first of October?"

"No."

"Does he have a contact phone?"

"No."

"Does he—"

"I think we all see a pattern forming here." Maebh stood in between the detective and the old woman. "It's safe to assume all answers lead to a one word response."

The male detective looked Maebh up and down and she returned the favour. "Who are you?"

"Maebh McQuillan," she said with forced enthusiasm, stretching her hand out in which he reluctantly shook. "Nice to meet you."

"Can I look around?"

"Absolutely not," she said with the same pasted smile on her face.

"Is Aisling Breen here?"

"Why do you ask?"

"Because I want to know."

"Have you any suspects?" Maebh asked, inspecting her nails and relishing in the detective's clear annoyance.

"Everyone is a suspect."

Maebh laughed. "I'm sure you're doing a stand up job, detective. As always."

"McQuillan," the detective drawled, scratching his bearded chin. "Don't you belong to another clan? Your mother's, in fact. Oh, yes, I know more about you people than you realise."

"She's not my keeper," Maebh retorted through gritted teeth, ignoring the clear delight of the surrounding clansmen at the detective's words.

"That's not true, is it?" the detective replied with a chuckle before glaring at her. "Where's Conor?"

"Haven't seen him."

"Where's Aisling?"

"No idea."

"I will get a search warrant for this camp. You know that, right?"

"Go ahead." Maebh turned to leave, noticing the others were standing mute right behind her.

She arched a brow at Tiernan. *Not the second, indeed*. He shook his head, seeming to know what her look meant, and muttered under his breath.

"I'm still working the caillte case."

Maebh stiffened, noticing Tiernan wore a similar expression. When she turned back towards the detective, she was impassive, her voice showing how bored she was. "That case was closed."

"Officially, yes. But I'm still working on it. You people . . . intrigue me."

"And I'm sure you're going to solve the case any day now." Maebh chuckled, mimicking his earlier tone and hating how his words felt like a threat. "Like you are for this one."

The detective offered a small rectangular piece of paper. After an uncomfortable amount of time, Maebh accepted it.

"If you need to speak about either case, call me."

Maebh crumpled the card in half and stuffed it into her coat pocket, smiling at the detective. "I will do that."

She stood apart from the others, watching until the gardai car pulled off. Tiernan's voice took her by surprise. "Come on, we need to talk."

Maebh smiled at the old woman, who glared back as she followed him to a caravan close to her new home. It was bigger than hers, but not much cleaner.

"Explain why you're here."

Maebh looked around, noting the scattered computer parts, crudely drawn maps, and what looked like miniature satellite dishes lying around the floor of the small kitchenette. She felt a pang when she imagined Setanta walking into her empty room of their shared caravan. He had always kept it immaculate, nagging her for being untidy. If he had left her to clean on her own, she imagined it would have looked more like Tiernan's, but instead of broken down devices, it would be clothes, makeup, and weapons. Now Setanta would have the entire home to himself. At least it would be clean. His broken nose and the marks she'd left behind were just proof he was better without her. She'd acted like a savage, causing her brother to spill blood. Although it wasn't on Samhain, it was still assault. Before her matriarch could bestow a fitting punishment, she'd left, deciding exile was a fitting sanction.

He thought he was the monster but really it was her.

She looked back at Tiernan, who was standing, arms crossed, by the counter, contemplating whether she could trust him or not. He was no fan of hers, and when she'd jokingly referenced their last encounter, he'd clearly not forgiven her for attempting to use her gift on him. She'd been desperate back then, and still was. Finding her father meant he'd find his mother, but he was too stubborn to see that. She often wondered how much he knew about her previous relationship with his cousin Emer. Sighing, she met his eyes and relayed her conversation with Ash, but left out the part where she'd asked her seanchai for more information on the Hill of Tara. She would share what she'd learned from the storyteller with her new matriarch first.

"I'm glad she's decided to re-join us, even if it means you're here," Tiernan said, and before Maebh could retort, he added, "I wonder what changed her mind?"

A knock sounded and then the door opened, letting in a cold breeze and a young man with unruly black hair and pale, freckled skin. His brown eyes met Maebh's before greeting Tiernan. "Is she here?"

Tiernan stepped forward, placing his long hands on the newcomer's shoulders. "Conor, I thought you were still sleeping. Come, sit, I'll make tea."

"Nice of you to offer." Maebh sat on one chair at the fold-down table, smiling sweetly at Tiernan's glare before adding, "Milk, two sugars."

"You're Maebh McQuillan," Conor said, taking the seat across from her. She opened her mouth to answer, but he turned his attention to Tiernan, who was filling the kettle. "Is she back yet?"

"No," Tiernan responded, facing them as the sound of the kettle filled the small room. He cast a wary glance at Maebh before adding, "She might be returning."

"She is." She leaned forward, trying to catch Conor's darting gaze, his leg bouncing up and down. "I'm sorry for your loss."

His eyes snapped to hers, a pain so raw filling the space that Maebh sucked in a breath. He broke eye contact first before muttering, "Thanks."

Conor shirked out of his dark coat, rolling up his jumper sleeves, and Maebh noticed his colourful tattoos. Leaning close, she saw pixies, selkies and other Fair Ones depicted across his skin. Some were drawn whimsical, others, lifelike.

"Those are beautiful." She gestured to his arms.

Conor cast a glance downwards before shrugging. "Thanks. I've just finished my apprenticeship as a clan tattoo artist."

Maebh was impressed. He looked so young. She had pegged him for possibly only sixteen. "Have you seen these guys up close or are they just imaginings?"

"Some were up close. Others from the scrolls."

Maebh knew he meant the teachings the elders made them learn. She frowned at his cagey tone. "So you've been to Tír na nÓg?"

"A few times."

Tiernan placed a teapot in the centre of the small table, along with cups, a milk jug, sugar and biscuits. She noted he was quite hospitable despite his unfriendliness. Maebh wondered how Conor had gone to the other realm, undetected, more than once. It was forbidden.

"I visited Ash at her cottage," Conor said, running his fingers through his black hair. "I thought she would have come back by now."

"Why didn't you tell me you were leaving?" Tiernan asked, taking the seat beside him.

"I'm eighteen, Tier, I don't need permission," Conor snapped before slumping in his seat. "I just needed to see my sister."

Maebh remained quiet, and Tiernan stared at the young man, a frown creasing his thick brows. She could see how deeply he cared for him.

"Do you remember anything from that night?"

Conor set his cup down with a clatter, and Tiernan glared at her. She shrugged and took a sip of tea. Conor tried to comb his fingers through his mane of unruly black hair, but it ended up tangled and his fingers stuck. "I want my sister."

"She'll be back soon."

"I thought she'd be here by now. It's not safe!"

"What do you mean it's not safe?" Maebh asked, but he didn't answer.

Conor pressed his palms against his eyes, his tone weary. "I can't do this right now."

Tiernan's frown deepened as he watched the other man rise from his seat and pace the small space. Wafts of sour lemon radiated as he tugged at his hair with one hand while hugging the other close around his middle. She looked at Tiernan in question, and for a moment, he pretended he didn't know what she was asking. As Conor grew more agitated, he nodded once, his wide set lips firmly pressed together. Maebh let out a calming breath and immediately the room filled with the soothing scent of lavender. Conor stopped pacing and looked at Maebh.

"Ash can do this too." His expression changed him from a young man to old and Maebh couldn't help feeling pity for what he must have gone through. Before she could apologise, he murmured, "I'm going to lie down."

He went to what Maebh assumed was Tiernan's bedroom and closed the door. Maebh and Tiernan sat quietly, drinking their tea, until they could hear the slow, gentle snoring of Conor. Tiernan yawned deeply, too.

"I forgot how everyone around you feels the effects."

"You don't feel it as much as others," Maebh reminded him, setting her cup down and smirking. "You didn't mind my mind-molesting there."

"It wasn't for your own gain."

"Who am I, Peter Parker?" Maebh laughed. "I promise to use my power only for good, Alfred."

"You're mixing up superheroes."

"And you're just as big a hypocrite as ever."

"What's that supposed to mean?"

"You hack into private files but judge me for using my gift to do basically the same thing."

"It's not the same. I didn't seduce you."

"Oh please. Anything you felt for me was on you, kitten."

A knock on the door was followed by a loud, bubbly voice. "Mae, is that you?"

Maebh felt a pang of guilt at the use of her nickname, but she knew it wasn't her brother on the other side of the door.

Why hadn't she said goodbye to Setanta? Knowing the reason was selfish, she pushed it to the back of her mind as she ignored Tiernan's scowl and opened the door for his cousin.

"Hey, Em." Maebh couldn't help returning the smile Emer gave her. "Guess who's joined the misfits clan."

"Oh, don't let Mrs O'Malley hear you say that." The women embraced in one of those awkward one armed hugs and Tiernan gestured for them to all go outside as Conor's snores grew louder.

Emer pointed to the caravan as they walked away. "How is he?"

"Not talking much," Tiernan replied. "He's pressing to see his sister. Can't blame him after losing Cara. They need each other right now."

"Wherever she went off to." Emer eyed Maebh as she rubbed her hands together in the brisk wind. "Do we have you to thank for convincing her to come back here? We had other plans in mind for a matriarch."

"Don't start that now." Tiernan sighed, rubbing the bridge of his nose that had started to turn a rosy pink. "The decision has been made."

"She hasn't deigned to arrive and announce her plans herself. Great start as matriarch."

As the cousins bickered, Maebh stood silently by and watched. Her ex-girlfriend had always been a force of nature, but it seemed she had a good match in Tiernan.

She'd made peace with what had happened between them. They had been young, a first love for both, but when Emer had accused Maebh of only using her, it hurt. She hadn't meant for it to look like that. When she'd discovered Tiernan was a hacker, she'd badgered Emer to introduce them. And when he'd been less than receptive to her suggestion they work together in solving the caillte case, she'd been frustrated enough to try to force his decision.

That hadn't gone down well.

With a painful swallow, Maebh's attention drifted to the encampment. Children were running around, carefree in the way only they could be. Everyone else she could see seemed worn out. This clan had stopped performing, and she wondered how they made their income. Never having to perform in that stupid dance tent was another reason she knew she'd made the right choice. Setanta wouldn't have understood. Shaking off guilt, she turned to the cousins who seemed to have started a staring competition.

"I want to speak to the elders."

"Mae, you've only just arrived." Emer broke eye contact first, and Maebh noticed Tiernan's smirk. "Are you planning to start trouble already?"

"That's exactly what she is going to do." Tiernan gestured towards the largest caravan beside a crackling fire pit. "There's a private meeting now and we're both going. You're welcome to join us."

Maebh walked towards the caravan and heard Emer berate Tiernan about his lack of invitation, never mind the newcomer's. His response was quiet, but she made out just enough to know he thought this was the quickest way to get rid of her. She smirked. He didn't know everything, it seemed. Ash needed Maebh. She was confident Ash also didn't trust any of the Breen elders after making it known how unwelcome her return would be.

Smoothing down her coat, she opened the caravan door without knocking and entered the large common area. The soft-spoken conversations from the already convened halted. Maebh smiled at everyone, throwing out "hello's" and "how do you do's" as she sauntered into one of the few remaining seats.

"Oh, lovely." Maebh reached to the centre of the long table where a spread of scones and tea and coffee pots were laid out. As she helped herself in the now silent room, she realised the interior reminded her of a hotel conference room. She'd only seen her mother's elder room a few times, as she wasn't allowed to go to meetings, and it looked decidedly drab in comparison.

Tiernan and Emer took the last remaining seats. Helping himself to a scone, Tiernan said, "Aisling Breen's first role as matriarch was to accept Maebh McQuillan into our clan."

The old woman from earlier glared at her. "That does not mean she's permitted to attend this meeting."

Maebh took a large bite from her scone. Through mouthfuls she said, "This is delicious. Did you make them?"

When the old woman didn't respond, Maebh took a swig of her tea and continued. "Ash made me her second, so I believe that means I'm here in her stead. That's how this works, right?"

Murmurings of surprise sounded, and she smiled.

It was Tiernan who responded, "That remains to be confirmed. But let's get on with this meeting, anyway."

"Where is Aisling?"

"Mrs O'Malley, the only thing I can tell you is what she told me," Tiernan lied. "She'll be back soon and she left me in charge until then."

Maebh scoffed, spraying scone on the table, much to the distaste of the elders beside her.

"Let's not waste this time with a pissing contest." Maebh waited until all eyes were on her. "What are your preparations for the Cath?"

"You do not decide what this meeting is about, girlie."

"What's this meeting about?"

After a beat, Mrs O'Malley addressed the room, "The Cath is in—"

"Aha!"

"Two days' time and we need to confirm our selection. We can't send as many warriors as previously planned. We need to keep some strong clansmen here to protect the rest of us. If there is someone targeting us, we can't leave anyone vulnerable."

"Agreed," an older man said from near the centre of the table.

Maebh let them converse back and forth, pretending not to be too interested. When she thought they'd finished, she piped up. "Anyone you want can go, but I'll be joining the Cath."

One elder protested. "You're not—"

"It's not up for debate." Maebh set her cup down with enough force that its contents spilled onto the table. Everyone in the room stilled as her quiet wrath filled the space. "I am going and so is Ash."

"The matriarch does not take part." Mrs O'Malley gathered her tweed coat tightly around her. "This is folly."

"You can't speak for Ash," Tiernan said, his attention solely on the older woman and Maebh found herself struck by his fierce beauty. She was used to his scowls being directed at her and found watching him from the sideline a treat. "If she wants to go, that's her choice. As it's mine."

His eyes were steel, as he dared anyone to disagree. He had been one name bandied around for entering, but the elders had tried to dissuade him. Something to do with not being as athletic as the other clansmen. Maebh had rolled her eyes, knowing that brawn was not the only trait needed to win in a Cath trial. He looked fit enough, but she supposed the elders considered warriors like her brother the only viable contenders.

"I know you think I'm not physically as strong, but I'm smarter than everyone and you need wit as well as strength in the Cath."

A red-haired woman sitting beside Emer quietened the growing argument. "I vouch for him. As one of the few Cath warriors you all agree on, I get more of a say on who joins me than the rest of you."

Maebh was impressed and by the look on Tiernan's face, he seemed to be, too.

The woman took Emer's hand as she added, "That obviously includes my wife going as a warrior, too."

So this was the wife. She'd heard Emer had married and Maebh smiled as she realised she wasn't jealous. She hadn't been with another woman since, only having had a few superficial encounters with men. After Emer, she'd realised relationships weren't her thing.

Emer squeezed her wife's hand before turning to where her cousin and Maebh sat. "These two, and Niamh, are my choices. You choose the remaining warriors."

As the group grew more agitated and arguments ensued, Maebh stood. "You forgot to add Ash to that list. But other than that, we're done."

She made her way towards the door when Mrs O'Malley addressed her. "We have one more thing to discuss, and now you're here, it concerns you."

"Oh?"

"We need to perform again and, seeing as you've come from one of the more favoured clans, you will be in charge of entertainment."

"I will not."

"Excuse me, girlie, but you will—"

"I will not and you can talk until you're one foot in the grave, but it will do you no good." Maebh slammed the door behind her.

Fury boiled her blood as she stormed towards her matchbox caravan. She was in the right mood to attack the mess inside. How dare they assume she would dance for them? The elders in the McQuillan clan knew their place. They were advisors to her mother, but didn't have as much sway as they seemed to have here. The audacity to question Ash's right to rule as matriarch would not have been tolerated in her former clan. She didn't want to think about what she'd given up by coming here.

Brehon law still recognised her as matriarch after her mother, but she'd placed herself in the same situation Ash had by leaving. They couldn't outright deny her birthright, but they could put a case to the High King that she was unfit. It hadn't been done in her lifetime, but the history scrolls they were taught as children referred to it happening. It was a long drawn-out process, one that was as tedious as a Glutton court case, but it seemed like something the Breen clan elders were arrogant enough to do. Although she'd promised to help Ash solve her mother's case, she was nobody's puppet and wouldn't play the game these elders expected.

CHAPTER 19

SETANTA

"You knew this wouldn't last forever." Setanta tried to keep his voice calm, but he could hear the exasperation in it.

Orla deserved better than his current state of mind, but he was too exhausted to give her anything more. He'd come home to an empty caravan and most of Maebh's belongings were gone. She must have left in a hurry because on the floor near her bed lay her notebook, full of her investigation into the caillte. There was no way she'd have left her journal behind intentionally.

Setanta had spent the night reading through it, feeling a double dose of guilt from prying and from not telling her she may be on a hopeless quest. There was a high possibility he'd killed their father years ago. So there he was, ending things with Orla, and although she'd continuously told him how casual they were, it had felt a lot like a breakup when she'd tried to talk him out of it. All he could offer were weak excuses from an even weaker man.

She stared at him a moment longer before watching the fairground fill with outsiders for the start of the evening shows to begin. They both had work, but she had cornered him after days of his avoidance. She worked in the ale tent and was wearing the medieval style wench costume his mother made all the bartenders wear. She looked good in it, and Orla knew it. Set glanced at her low-cut top and short skirt, knowing it was clearly a ploy from her mother for the bartenders to get more tips. The men's uniforms weren't much better.

His cheeks reddened as she caught his appraisal, but instead of being mad, she smirked and leaned closer, her breasts rubbing against his front with every breath she took. He should step back. He needed to step back, but her fragrance sent a jolt of fire downwards. Setanta rubbed the back of his neck where his muscles had tightened, his shoulder length hair tied in various plaits, and his shaved undercut growing out too much. When was the last time he'd shaved it? Usually, he was on top of his appearance, ensuring his 'Viking look' was up to his mother's standard. She insisted on perfection, on the outside at least.

"What happened the other night? You literally pushed me to run." Orla trailed her fingers up his bare arm all the way to the nape of his neck. His hand automatically moved to her waist. "I thought a Fair One had got into camp again. And then the sounds..."

Setanta looked down at her warily as she trailed off with a shudder. Shane had told him she had approached him later that night to find out what had happened. Luckily, she'd done what he'd said and ran to her caravan, alerting her sister that something was wrong. And when he hadn't shown up the next day, she had come searching for him. She didn't seem happy with Shane's answers, but when Imogen told her not to worry about it, she hadn't pressed further. Nobody pushed against the matriarch.

Fighting with himself internally, he removed his hand from her side and took hers away from his neck. After releasing her, he stepped further away, crossing his arms against his chest. Even though it was one of the coldest nights this month, he was unfazed by his bare torso.

"Shane told you. We had a pack of púca try to attack a few patrons. Luckily, they thought it was a pack of rabid dogs."

"It sure didn't sound like that to me," Orla said, her calm demeanour vanishing as her words turned clipped and she stepped closer. "You're hiding something from me."

"Orla," Set began, but she cut him off.

"Don't bother." Flicking her dark hair behind her shoulder, Set felt a pang as the action reminded him of Maebh. "As you said, this wasn't going to last forever."

Without waiting for a response, Orla marched towards the ale tent, her shoulders tense. Setanta rubbed his face, his three-day stubble scratching his calloused palms. He was a coward. It was Imogen's order to keep his secret from his clan, but he willingly hid behind it. He didn't want more people to look at him the way Shane and the others did. He knew Orla wasn't the one for him, but would he ever be able to get close enough to anyone to reveal that part of him? Maebh was the only one who had never judged him about what he became. If he'd have protected her from their mother, would she have stayed?

Not everything is about you, Golden Boy. He could hear her retort and smiled despite the pain in his chest. He stood stationary, watching his warm breath hit fairground lights overhead, the carnival music playing through speakers. The scent of popcorn and fast food filled the air. When was the last time he ate? His stomach growled for attention, but he ignored it. He knew as soon as he bothered to even try to eat, his appetite would disappear and he'd have to run to the toilet with an upset stomach. It was the joy of the comedown. His limbs still ached from whatever it was his body did when he changed.

Cracking his neck, he forced himself to move towards his tent. He should do some stretches before the show. Three steps was all it took. Blood. He could smell it, see it pulsing in the necks of passersby. It was the first sign he was about to turn.

Not again. Not so soon.

A mix between a growl and a cry escaped his lips as he turned and hurdled through the woods that ran along their temporary fairground. He wouldn't make it back to the caravan of horrors. It was parked too far away. Letting instinct take over, he pushed further into the woods, hoping he could move away from the crowds and get lost for the hours it would take for this episode to last. Their fairground was on the outskirts of Meath, Imogen deciding it was best to station close to where the funeral had been so they wouldn't miss out on performing. His greatest fear merged as he felt his teeth loosen, ready to fall out and be replaced with fangs. *What if he never turned back?*

No. That was unacceptable. An unearthly groan filled the air, and it took a moment for Set to realise it was his own. Whipping his head at an inhuman angle, he could still see the lights from the fairground blur in and out of focus. He was still too close.

Anywhere but here.

Set wished it with his ever changing fibre. He did not want to be around people; he wanted to be in a world where he couldn't harm anyone.

Falling over a growing tree root, he landed on a patch of damp ground. His heart beat erratically in his chest and he clawed at it, willing it to slow down. He could barely hear the voice over the rushing in his ears.

"Calm yourself, boy." He wanted to tell the unseen voice to get away—get far away from him—but the feminine voice grew nearer. "Hold this."

Setanta convulsed on the ground as a warm clothed bundle was pressed on top of his body. Instinct to move his bulging arms kicked in as he heard a soft whimper and then a weak cry.

A baby.

The woman had placed a baby on top of his chest? Could she not see what was happening to him? His arms were threatening to break within his sockets and fuse again after twisting. He clung to the baby, terrified he would crush or drop her as easily as a grape. He fought both his mind and body as the monster tore him apart from inside. The baby closed her eyes as if his jerking movements were rocking her to sleep.

Fear took hold as his vision blurred further. He knew that one of his eyes was about to move inward while the other grew and the final shift from man to monster would happen. All while he was holding a baby. He blinked furiously until both eyes set on the fragile body in his arms. He could see through his reddened vision that the baby was a newborn, he would guess not even a month in this world. And he could kill her tonight.

No.

He tried to sit up but couldn't. With blurred vision, he found a cloaked person standing feet away. His monster-self knew that this was his most vulnerable. The time between shifting. The baby whimpered as a gust of wind blew past them and Set cradled her close as he covered her bare shoulders with the blanket. She had downy hair and cream skin. It was minutes later before he realised his arms were still his own and his body had stopped stretching. His breathing returned to normal and his vision cleared.

"Feeling better?"

Set's attention snapped to the pale woman standing a foot away from him. Her voice had a distinct lilt to it, but he couldn't place where she was from. She wore a dark cloak, wisps of silver white hair falling from her hood, framing her exquisite face. He could make out colourful tattoos that decorated her long neck. *A druid*.

As he stood, careful not to jostle the baby who had fallen asleep, he whispered, "How could you put a baby's life in such danger?"

"It stopped you from ríastrad, did it not?"

Set's mind whirled as things clicked into place, the term 'ríastrad' rushing to him with an impossible realisation it made perfect sense. *Warp spasm*. His mother could never explain what happened to him during his turning. This druid was claiming he had the same affliction as the great warrior, Cú Chulainn?

"You are gifted with ríastrad but you do not know how to use it. Interesting."

Setanta rocked the baby in his arms. "Take your baby back."

"What baby?"

Setanta stopped rocking as he looked at his now empty arms. "How—"

"How did you get here, boy?"

"I . . . don't know." Set frowned, and it was only then he realised he couldn't hear carnival music and the fairground lights were no longer visible. Before he could process anything else, the strange woman's smile widened and her next words sent a shiver down his spine.

"Sifting is a great gift, indeed." She studied him for the longest time, but he remained speechless. Finally, she clasped her hands and took a step closer. "Your destiny greets you under this moon. Stay close until you cross paths."

Setanta tried to call out, tried to move, but he couldn't as the druid approached him. She caressed his face in an almost motherly embrace before disappearing from his line of sight. He couldn't turn his head, but heard her retreating footsteps. When she was truly gone, he stumbled forward, taking unsteady breaths as he scanned the area. The trees were unfamiliar and even the air smelled different. Citrus and pine and springtime bloom covered the foliage. Nothing like the throes of frozen autumn in Ireland.

He had wanted to be anywhere without people and had got his wish. He was in Tír na nÓg.

CHAPTER 20

AISLING

Newgrange had been closed ever since Ash found her mother's body. Because it was a national treasure, it couldn't be cleaned in the same manner as any other crime scene. A team of specialists was debating the best way to preserve the stone without damaging it. If it had been a stranger's crime scene, she would have had a string of suggestions, using her archaeological studies as an educational crutch. Something Dom often teased her about. She wouldn't have many opportunities to put her degree to good use, according to him.

There was a small part of her that was working through the best solutions, even as she walked the quiet dark passageway to her destination, but it would have felt perverse to share them with anyone, knowing it was traces of her mother being erased from the ancient stone. Even still, she couldn't deny there was a fascination to it, a puzzle to solve where the modern world met with the old.

Standing in the antechamber, she willed her breathing to slow, forcing a semblance of calm she didn't feel. She tried not to look down at the now empty basin where traces of dried blood remained. Casting her phone light around, she inspected the walls and had to agree with the detective's crude remarks. The injuries inflicted on Cara had been horrific, and as she willed her erratic heart to stop pounding in her ribcage like a trapped bird, she tried in vain not to picture her broken mother by her feet once more.

Swallowing down bile, she continued surveying, pretending it was someone else's crime scene, the lack of blood just another puzzle to solve. If she knew anything about how these things went, it would be a long time before the specialists agreed on how to safely remove the damage caused by the few bloodstains that were there.

She looked back through the narrow passageway. From this angle, all she could see was the dark, cloudless sky, bringing her back to the memory of the red colour of the clouds that day. Thankful for no more blood omens, Ash continued her assessment, but this time it was in search of any sign that linked the realms. For all the tours she'd given, the one thing she absolutely kept from non-Fianna was that Newgrange was a bridge, not a tomb.

She needed to access the other side, but her mother hadn't included that part during her bedtime stories. Tracing her hands along the uneven stone wall, and spending over an hour in every other space than the room with the basin came to nothing. Thirty minutes into her second hour, she knew there was no avoiding it. With a sigh, she took a step into the darkened basin chamber. She tried to avoid the dried blood, afraid that she may leave evidence. Nobody except law enforcement and the specialist team were permitted there. Mary and Dom were the caretakers, and even they were still denied access.

A rush of fear barrelled into her. If she was caught there by anyone, especially that detective, how would she explain herself? As she searched the walls, her mind wandered to the letters. She'd re-read the ones she could, confirming they were the ones that had been in her bag. Why would her mother be clutching the newly arrived one in her last moments?

Hunkering down, she trained her light on the granite basin. She had looked at it so many times both during her studies in college and her own time working there. It was small, just over a metre in diameter. Her mother had been laid over it, both limbs and head sprawled at awkward angles. Taking a steadying breath, she looked into the now stained stone.

Ash stooped over, holding her hair back with one hand as she aimed the light at the two small indents within the stone. They'd always been there, but even in all her studies she'd never learned their use. She frowned as she noticed bloodied fingerprints, as if someone had pressed on them. The only person who could have done that with blood was Cara, or her killer. Her pulse quickened. That was good. The detective had fingerprints to work with. If they didn't match Cara's, this murder may be solvable knowing nothing about the existence of the Fair Ones.

Ash hesitated. Those indents could identify the way through to the otherworld, but if she pressed her fingers to them, she would tamper with even more evidence, replacing these fingerprints with her own. What if the detective hadn't noted them? He'd be pretty useless at his job; Ash had seen them almost immediately. She had to know if she was on the right track, though. She pressed her fingers to the stone.

Nothing happened.

Frustrated, she pressed harder, but the stone did not yield. A soft, otherworldly meow echoed behind her, and Ash jumped. The ginger and brown púca, tinged with green, ambled in, brushing its body against her before hopping into the shallow basin. Before she could blink, it lashed out with a claw, scraping her arm. She yelped and placed her hand against the now bleeding cut. The creature pressed a bloodied paw against the indent and looked at her with feline eyes. It lashed out again, not scraping her this time, but again pressed its paw against the indent.

Pressing her fingers against her bloodied arm, she placed them on the two indents and heard the púca purr before it licked her blood from its claws, clear impish delight in its eyes. A strange humming sound echoed around the chambers, followed by a faint bluish glow and rumble of stone.

Swallowing her cry, Ash forced herself to remain as she was, her fingers pressed against the stone, until the blue light turned blinding and a cold wet substance filled the basin. Yanking her hand back, the light dimmed and she had time to see the dark stains on her fingers.

The chamber was filled with blood. Aiming her light in every direction, she stumbled away from the basin, her bloodied hand held away from her body, unsure what to do with it. The púca scampered away, but she barely registered its movement.

The walls were splattered in a pattern of violence and Ash's nostrils flared as the smell overcame her. She was going to be sick. Racing down the passageway, she hoped nobody would hear her storm through the creaking gate. If Mary or Dom caught her, she didn't want to think about trying to explain. Panic set in. She was going to vomit *right then,* but as she reached the place where a gate should be, there was nothing. She blindly went through the opening and gulped up too much fresh air and vomited.

"It's better out than in, my girl."

Ash's vision blurred with tears from retching, but she gratefully accepted the cloth her unknown companion placed in front of her face. Righting herself, she wiped her mouth. The once white cloth was streaked with blood. She scrunched it tightly as she stood upright. The tarmac road leading to the cottage was gone. The warmth in the air and sweet scent of spring did little to ease her nausea.

She was in Tír na n Óg.

Her breathing quickened as her eyes adjusted. In place of the cottage lay a woodland, fireflies flashing in and out of visibility, or were they pixies? Turning to Newgrange, the structure was the same, except any modern furnishings like the steel ladder were gone.

"Come."

Ash spun toward the hooded woman, her voice breaking through her spiralling mind.

She followed her new companion until they stood facing one another by a grassland near the woods. The moon shone brightly overhead, with billions of stars burning the sky. Ash shirked out of her coat as the young woman let down her hood, tendrils of snow-white hair whipping around her alabaster face at every whisper of wind that blew between them.

Her attire was like nothing she'd seen on a living person, other than costumes at medieval fairs. A grey shapeless dress peeked underneath her dark cloak, but she could see the swell of her full chest and thick curves. From the rare glimpses of exposed skin she could see the woman was heavily tattooed in multiple colours. Her ink reminded Ash of the page borders in the Book of Kells and her silver white hair matched her complexion to the point where it was hard to tell where her skin stopped and the silken tresses began.

The woman clasped her hands in front of her with a docile smile. "You may keep the cloth."

"Thanks," Ash said as she stuffed it into her pocket. Should she explain why she was covered in someone else's blood? Looking around, she tried to grasp where she stood. This should be the beginning of the cottage. She peered beyond the trees, but couldn't make anything out through the shadows and branches. "I'm in Tír na nÓg."

"You are."

"Who are you?" She didn't mean to sound rude, but she took a tentative step back from the woman, who seemed unconcerned by Ash's blood splattered clothing. Her mother had been murdered in Newgrange in this world, the scene she'd just left clearly showed that.

Was this a Fair One that stood in front of her? She had been told countless stories. The Tuatha Dé Danann looked more human than any other fae. Her mother always said "the more they look like us, the more barbaric they are".

The woman smiled. "I am Ethne, druid to High King Aedan. Who are you?"

Ash let out a breath of relief but then realised she was in Tír na nÓg without permission, and a stranger was asking to give up her name. Shit. What would the High King think if this druid told him about her prohibited arrival? She had been away from Fianna life a long time, but remembered the basic rule of never revealing your real name. There was power in that, and only a fool gave it willingly. "Ash."

"The dead matriarch's daughter," Ethne stated, but not without kindness. "I'm sorry for your loss."

"Is the High King looking into her murder?" A thought struck Ash as she stumbled over a raised branch. "Is that why you're here?"

"He is, but that is not why I am here. I have been waiting to meet you."

"Why? I mean, how did you know I'd be here?"

"I foresaw your arrival." Ethne looked at the stars and then back at her. "Walk with me?"

As they headed into the woods, not without trepidation on Ash's part, she thought back to what she knew about druids. They were neither Fianna nor Fair Ones. More likened to what people might think wiccans were. They did not have power of their own, but could use nature as a catalyst to spark it. Druids were highly respected as wise and powerful, revered in an almost saint-like manner. She regarded the woman beside her, ensuring to keep enough distance in case she needed to run. Not all druids were considered 'good' but this was the Fianna High King's advisor; she must not only be wise but extremely powerful.

"How did you foresee me?"

"The stars talk," was her only response, as her silver eyes gleamed.

She couldn't make out Ethne's accent, but it seemed from a different time, never mind place.

They walked on and Ash took in the alien views. They were in a forest and everything could be named the same as at home: trees, shrubbery, foliage, dirt paths. But that was where the similarities ended. She couldn't place what was different until she saw a tree move; its trunk sucking inwards and exhaling like a breath.

It *was* breathing; alive like everything else here. Ash didn't know if it was because she was on high alert, in shock or her blood pressure was too high or low, but she struggled for breath. She couldn't hear anything. The forest was a deathly silence. The only noise was the rustle of Ethne's cloak and Ash's own clumsy footsteps beside her elegant strides.

Seemingly oblivious to Ash's distress, or perhaps letting her have the dignity of a discrete meltdown, Ethne spoke. "You are now matriarch and the king wishes to extend to you a welcome through me. He hopes you are prepared for his Cath."

She breathed in and out, in and out, trying to right herself before she spoke. Being called matriarch was alien to her, and she cursed inwardly. Maebh would have arrived and announced it at camp by now. She couldn't deal with that when a strange druid was staring at her, waiting for a response. "What is the deal with this Cath business? Why does everyone care so much?"

Ethne stopped walking, causing Ash to have to retreat a few steps. "It is a great honour that your High King bestows. You will find no one as gracious as he."

Ash fumbled for words while trying to figure out the change in Ethne's tone.

"I'm sorry. I don't mean to sound disrespectful. I've been out of the whole Fianna loop for a long time."

Ethne regarded Ash as she tried, but failed, not to fidget. The druid seemed to decide something and smiled. "I will guide you."

Ash felt like she was being pulled down a path that she had no business going. In less than a week, she had found her mother's mutilated body, been questioned as a suspect, reunited with her brother and was now a leader to a clan who did not want her back. Ash looked at the female before her. She needed all the help she could get.

"Thanks. Thank you. I don't know what to expect with any of this."

"Your elders are deciding who to send as we speak." Ethne regarded the stars as if they were speaking. "They have selected a strong band for you to lead into battle."

"Hold on. I have to take part in a battle?"

"You are matriarch." It was the first time Ethne sounded exasperated.

That made two of them.

"But . . ."

Ethne reached into a fold in her pocket and took out a sand-like substance. As she raised it in front of her face, she only had time to wonder why the woman kept loose grains in her pocket when the druid blew the substance into her face.

Coughing, Ash blinked away the stinging sand, only to realise Ethne no longer stood in front of her. Noise erupted around her as she took in the blood bath before her. Stumbling forward, she watched in horrified silence as an army of men and women unleashed hell on one another. Their faces were covered in mud and blood, contorted in rage, some in pain, as steel clashed and arrows whirred.

CHAPTER 21

AISLING

A sh ducked as a warrior barrelled towards her, his axe raised high, ready to strike. She fell to the ground and looked up in time to see his weapon rushing down, crying out as the blade sank into her. Through her. She blinked as she stared at the blade sticking out from her stomach, but no pain came. Her attacker didn't bother to dislodge his weapon as he picked up another that had fallen by the muddy ground beside them. Without looking at her, he moved on to his next target.

"Get up." Ethne's voice came from nowhere.

She took a tentative breath, but still no pain. With gritted teeth, she grabbed the axe hilt, but her hands went through it.

"The scene will not affect you." The druid's voice floated around her, carried in the wind.

Ash crawled back until the axe was no longer embedded in her. She realised then that it was sticking out of the leg of another fallen warrior. How had she not felt the blade or the man below her?

"This is the first Cath."

"Where are you?"

"I cannot be inside your head. This is for you."

Ash wondered how it was possible *she* was inside her head but didn't want to dwell on it. More warriors rushed through her

165

before she could jump out of the way, and she looked down to see her body was only partially corporeal.

"I think I've seen enough," Ash called out to the sky.

"When you see enough, you will return."

Ash regretted her acceptance of this druid's help. Giving herself a moment to adjust to her new reality, she moved around the battlefield, avoiding red puddles and fallen bodies, but nobody noticed her. It was hard to make out where she was. A high stone wall surrounded them, and she squinted towards a familiar structure, but her gaze snagged on the foreboding castle in the distance. A hulking figure seemed to be at the epicentre of the fight at the bottom of the sloped hill she stood on, so Ash moved towards him, now convinced she would not get attacked by anyone.

He was the tallest man she'd ever seen. His unruly red hair was almost as long as hers, with sections braided. Unlike the others, he didn't wear protective armour. He looked barbaric, like a Viking out of one of her textbooks. Ash marvelled at his speed and strength as he fought ten men at a time. When a bell gonged from the direction of the castle, everyone stopped fighting, and the giant warrior in front of her cried out in victory. All, including the injured, cheered.

"What the . . ." Ash watched as the Viking held his hand out to the woman he had just sunk a blade into. Her side seeped with gushing blood, but she smiled through gritted teeth as she allowed him to hurl her upright. "You nearly nicked me."

She laughed and tried to raise her fist, but stumbled. A robed, monk-like man appeared at her side, holding a large cloth to her wound. As he assisted her towards the castle, Ash saw that more monk-like healers appeared on the battleground, attending to the injured who couldn't stand. The Viking's booming laughter caught her attention once more and she watched him retreat toward the castle, both injured and victorious, hollering and cheering behind him.

She felt a pull from deep inside and she was standing in front of the druid again.

Ethne smirked as Ash took an unsteady breath and began walking.

"You just witnessed Fionn Mac Cumhaill create the first Cath."

"Fionn Mac . . . *that* was the first Fianna High King?"

"You see why he was nicknamed the giant, yes?"

Ash caught up with her companion. "Are Caths still as bloodied?"

"Unfortunately, no. They no longer allow battle at the end. A pity, it was my favourite part."

With a frustrated swipe at stray strands sticking to her face, she was about to argue that Ethne had just said she was going to lead her clansmen into a battle, but pressed her lips tightly together. She had a feeling that this woman spoke in riddles and wasn't sure if it was on purpose or not. She suspected the former.

Ash continued to sneak glances at her companion as she followed her. It was hard to put an age on Ethne. She was beautiful in a savage way, and looked no older than Ash, but she'd just declared to have been present at the Cath over a century ago. She lived in Tír na nÓg, the land of eternal youth, but asking the druid if she had been at that first battle, felt rude. If Mary got tetchy over her joking about her age, she didn't like to think about a woman who might be thousands of years Mary's senior, even if her skin was as flawless as a social media filter.

They continued in silence, and Ash could hear water up ahead, but she turned behind, worry pooling in her stomach. What reaction would she get from her clan? She'd let Maebh break the news she was returning and shame coated her. It was cowardly. Would Tiernan back her up? Or had she alienated him by not telling him her intentions before she'd even returned?

"I need to get back."

"Not yet. First, you meet an ally."

Before Ash could ask anything else, Ethne's cloak rippled at the edges. Her body darkened until she melted into the night. She stood, stunned, waiting for her eyes to adjust to the lack of a figure before her. Was that it? Was the druid gone? She stood there blinking, listening to the oddly ordinary sounds of the otherworldly forest around her: crickets underfoot, owls calling out from unseen branches, a howl that sounded worryingly like a wolf, and much closer than Ash would have liked. Had those sounds been there this whole time? She hadn't noticed the teeming nocturnal activities until the druid had left her alone.

Shaking herself, she debated turning around, not wanting to meet any other strange characters here, regardless of Ethne's suggestion of meeting an ally. Time moved differently in this place and she didn't want to waste hers by getting lost in a strange wood at night. A blue-white light flickered right before her, but any time Ash tried to look directly at it, it would lose shape and vanish. It seemed to be suspended in mid-air, and whatever it was, it was watching her.

She reached outward with one hand, trying to locate the source, but wherever it came from, it was beyond the cluster of trees. Shielding her eyes as the light pulsed, the trees before her became ink black silhouettes. As silent as it arrived, the light drifted away towards the sound of rushing water. Feet moving before her mind could keep up, she pushed through trees, quickening her steps as the light floated on. It was only after she had weaved through her fifth or sixth interlocking tree trunk and stumbled over a raised web of roots that she remembered she was headed in the opposite direction from where she'd come. Newgrange was nowhere in sight.

Ash waited for that dreaded sensation of worry to creep over her, but it didn't. Instead, her shoulders relaxed, her spine popping as if she'd spent the last hour in her weekly pilates class. A tranquil lullaby floated through the jasmine drenched air and the source of light circled a wide oak until she was close enough to touch it. No longer blinking out of focus, it twinkled like a dozen stars suspended above the leaves strewn ground. It shifted into many shapes and patterns, ending up taking on the form of a glistening hand, beckoning Ash closer.

"Will O' The Wisp," Ash's voice came out croaked, breaking the mesmerising silence the small being emanated.

Licking her lips, she realised she was parched. The sprite transformed again, now a shapeless, fluid like light—perhaps this was the sprite's true form? It pulsated again and then disappeared through the oak. *Harmless beings*, she remembered her mother's bedtime stories about the sprites who led travellers through the woods at night. Ethne had said she needed to meet an ally. Perhaps this Will O' was taking her to them? Her tongue became sandpaper with every step she took, but her senses were consumed by the now even louder music that was beckoning her on.

The water penetrated her clouded senses as she walked around the trunk. She surged towards a night-glistened river as a thirst and need to drink was all she could think about. She barely registered that the star speckled sprite had disappeared, not unlike Ethne moments ago. At the sudden absence of light, her eyes took a long time to adjust. Her sudden thirst drove her to blindly scoop mouthfuls of water into her mouth, and it was only after three or four scoops that she could see her own reflection. Rippling from contact, she frowned at the feverish look on her face. *What was in this water?* Dispensing the water in her hand, she surveyed her distorted reflection again.

And found several clouded black eyes peering upwards from beneath the surface.

Ash was frozen in place, her hand suspended just above the surface as the eyes blinked in unison and began swimming around like dolphin sized tadpoles. One broke the surface, displaying a piggish nosed face, a red cap fashioned with turquoise feathers adorned its green scaled head. Before she could register how odd it was for a water creature to be wearing a hat, slender shoulders emerged, then two claw tipped stubby fin-like arms. A tail flicked upwards out of the dark water, moving back and forth, disturbingly like a dog, but this creature looked anything but docile or playful.

Merrow.

Ash made to move back, but the creature bared two rows of needle-sharp teeth and grabbed her arm. She cried out as warm blood oozed over her dimpled flesh. It was much stronger than its size would suggest. She almost broke loose and would have if the other merrow had remained submerged. Four more talons clawed at her skin and, before she could gasp a decent lungful of air, she was underwater and being dragged to the deep riverbed.

CHAPTER 22

SETANTA

B linking through the disappearance of the Will O' The Wisp, Set stumbled through a cusp of trees to find a rushing river to his right. Why had he listened to the druid? Following the tiny ball of light had only led him closer to Tuatha Dé territory. His attention snagged on a lone figure by the river in the distance, and he retreated behind the first tree, cursing under his breath. Studying her for only a few minutes he breathed out a sigh of relief, she was human. He couldn't see her fully from this distance, but the moonlight bounced from the water, accentuating her curves and framing her as if she was a painting.

"Shit," Set said, when she leaned over the river, scooping mouthfuls of water from her hand.

His teeth clenched as he fought against the pull to drink, knowing it would be enchanted. What was a human doing here, drinking from fae water? Although they still stood within the relative safety of Fianna land—the Kingdom of Mede—the waters that ran throughout were fae. Stepping away from his hiding spot, he faltered as a merrow emerged from the river. Cursing again, he raced forward, his pace quickening as she cried out. No matter how fast he was, it was no use. He was too far away before she was snatched by the repulsive monster.

The river swallowed her whole.

Scanning the rushing water where she had once stood, he tried to see beneath, but only stars floated on top. The half-formed moon made it impossible to see how deep it went. As he leaned over, his reflection stared back and there was no sign of her or the green scaled merrow. If he hadn't seen her being dragged under, he wouldn't have known she'd ever been there.

Set kicked his shoes off but left his pants on, thanking the gods for his mother's idea of a costume. Making his last breath a good one, he plunged in and almost gasped from the icy dark that embraced him. They were now in Tuatha Dé Danann territory. He'd only realised when the druid had left, how far he was from safety, and with every step he was sure to encounter a Fair One. Brehon law was clear, and he would have no protection so far from the boundaries of Tara Court. Set felt the deadly allure of the water, tempting him to drink his fill. To drink so much, he would drown himself. It slithered around him like watery snakes hissing in his ear.

This water was poison, and he could only hope he could get to the woman in time. Humans would die in an instant, Fianna were slightly luckier. If he didn't find her within the next few moments, they'd both die in this watery graveyard.

It took a couple of blinks before his eyes adjusted while he swam blindly to the bottom. Training for the Cath most of his life meant he was a strong swimmer, and the last time he'd tested himself, he could hold his breath for almost seven minutes. The woman would hopefully have one to two minutes, but they were coming up to that second minute fast. Only a few pairs of hands had gripped her and, from the look of their green and hideous appearance, a school of males had taken her. Unlike their beautiful female counterparts, these sea hounds were bloodthirsty and vicious. They liked to play with their food. He needed to find her before playtime began.

As Set swam deeper, the heaviness of the water and soundless depth spiked his adrenaline. With each descending breaststroke, coldness tore at his bare skin, as if he was swimming through fire, not icy water. He needed to calm down, or he'd use up too much oxygen. Shadows circled him and he prayed they were normal fish. Using all his strength, he plunged deeper. How many merrow would he have to kill?

Almost blind in the heavy darkness, Set's hands hit the river bed, grazing sharp rock, plants and something that felt like bone. He only hoped it wasn't human. Twisting in different directions, he swam in a tight radius. Time was running out. His own lungs burned. *Was it already too late?* Movement and dark shadows caught his attention and he was upon them in seconds. Two merrow had the woman's arms pinned to the riverbed while the other was tearing her top open. He had just gripped the waistline of her pants when Set snapped his neck.

In the seconds after, the woman clawed at one merrow's eyes, its grip loosening on her as another charged towards Set. He saw her rip off the blinded merrow's hat while he swivelled out of the other merrow's attack. Ensuring she placed it on her head, he swam to the dead merrow he'd just killed, who was already floating towards the surface. His lungs screamed at him as he tore the hat from the dead creature and placed it on his head.

The change was instantaneous. The painful forming of multiple slits replaced the need to breathe, circling his neck right up to behind his ears. His nose and mouth no longer screamed to be allowed access to air as his newly formed gills gulped water, easing the painful spinning in his head.

As the blinded merrow's gargled protests pierced his ears, he realised he could hear echoing sounds, cursing as the creature pursued the woman. He pivoted just in time to see the other creature charge toward him. He back-stroked as the sea hound swiped a claw towards him, but he wasn't fast enough. Talons shredded his chest, and his roar was a gargle of bubbles. It wasn't deep enough to cause fatal damage, but blood obscured his vision as he grabbed the merrow's neck and squeezed. The beast stabbed his forearm with its claws, but he held on despite the pain, keeping it as far away from the rest of him as he could.

He risked a glance upward; the blinded merrow or the woman no longer visible. The merrow's attempts at dislodging him had weakened, and he kicked hard from the silty riverbed.

Breaking the surface, he gasped, but the burning air was alien to him. It took a panic-filled moment to realise why he couldn't breathe. Ripping off the merrow hat, he ignored the stinging sensation on his neck, treading water until he spotted the woman. She was crouched on all fours, wearing only her bra and shredded leggings, coughing out river water through painful sounding breaths. The blind merrow lay by her feet, drowning in air. Her own discarded hat lay on the ground beside her. Without its enchantment, the creature would have died instantly after breaking the surface.

The merrow in his clenched hand grasped his forearm weakly as he swam. If Set let it go, he may survive. Hoisting himself up, he crawled on to the bank, dragging the creature with him. The woman watched, wide-eyed, as he let go of the merrow's neck. Its breathing was weak, but it looked up at him with hateful eyes, a smirk playing on its too big lips. Set stood. Grabbing its tail, he hoisted it over his shoulder and, in one swift motion, slammed its head against a river rock. The impact reverberated up his arms, the sickening sound of splitting bone twisted his own gut before he released the now dead merrow back into the water.

Pivoting towards the still coughing woman, he noticed her skin was a greenish white, and her hands seemed to shrink as he watched. He looked at his own hands and then his feet, noticing for the first time that they were elongated, with a thin layer of weblike skin in between each digit. She cried out, snapping him out of his fascination. Coin sized welts formed across her skin, angry looking and multiplying as they both watched with equal expressions of horror.

His own body burned, and he blinked away as much of the water as he could, hoping by wearing that merrow hat, it helped cleanse him of most of the water's poison. Would they be that lucky? Fianna scrolls only taught them so much about the Tuatha Dé Danann, and he was impressed this woman had remembered about the magical breathing qualities a merrow hat gave. He had forgotten in his own panic.

Kneeling beside her, he helped her sit upright. She didn't shy away, just looked up at him in a confused daze.

"We need to wash this water off you as soon as possible."

"Newgrange. I live in the cottage beside—"

Set caught her as she began retching up what looked like an oily substance tinged with blood. Just as quickly as she started, she slumped over, her breathing sharp and painful sounding raps with every inhale.

"Shit."

Laying her down only long enough to ensure she was still breathing, he ran to retrieve his shoes. His wet feet slipped into the open laced boots. Tucking both hats into the back of his pants, he raced back to the unconscious woman and noticed her familiar face for the first time. Considerably heavier than a merrow, Set hoisted Aisling Breen over his shoulder and ran. Slowing his pace only when the forest got in his way, he ignored the knife-like stitch in his side and they made it to Newgrange in minutes. He fought against an urge to massage his ribs as more welts formed up her back. Set cursed as one looked large enough to burst. He wasn't sure what would happen if it did.

Aisling's breaths were mere wheezes by the time he finally made it to the mouth of the passageway. Manoeuvring her so that he now held her at her armpits, he walked backwards through the passage while dragging her through. He grimaced at how limp she was, making sure her head didn't hit the floor as he squeezed through the most narrow part. Set took in the sight of blood only long enough to ensure there wasn't anyone else here. Cradling her in one arm, he dipped his cold fingers into one of his open wounds where the merrow's claws had sliced his chest. Pressing his fingers in the basin, he held her tight as the humming and rumble of the portal sounded around them.

The only tell-tale sign the portal had worked was the lack of blood on the stone walls, something he didn't have time to dwell on with the injured woman. Set dragged her through the passage once more and cold autumn air hit him as he lifted her into his arms. He barrelled towards a stone cottage in the distance, his gaze darting to Aisling's pale face. He had offered his condolences at her mother's funeral, but had never spoken to her before. Hoisting her closer to his chest as her skin turned ice cold, his heavy legs pumped harder.

CHAPTER 23

TIERNAN

Tiernan stomped between the staggered caravans, weaving through children who were playing 'tip the can'. One of them called to him to join, but his head was pounding from the hour long torture session that was an elder meeting.

"Not now, pal." He smiled at the young boy as he continued towards his caravan, stuffing his cold hands into his pockets.

It hadn't exactly been a typical meeting. Not when Maebh McQuillan had showed up halfway through, demanding to know why costumes had been delivered to her door. The elders seemed determined to perform again and not even Maebh's mood meltdowns would sway the cunning clansmen. What was Ash thinking? *Where* was Ash? Almost a week had passed with no sign of her.

"Tier!"

He contemplated ignoring his cousin, but sighed and slowed his pace. She would only follow him.

Emer jogged up to him, her breath hitting the autumn air in puffs. "Don't mind those old farts. *I* know we need you at this Cath, despite your unwarranted loyalty to Ash."

Tiernan's jaw tightened, but he nodded. She'd already cornered him about Ash returning as matriarch and there was no point in arguing with his cousin. She believed her wife would make a better leader. He liked Niamh, but there was something about Ash that he just knew made her a better fit.

"They don't need to list my faults with such enthusiasm."

He didn't mind his physique. Not every man wanted to look like Setanta McQuillan, all muscles and easy smiles. Okay, maybe he did sometimes. But normally he was content to be the tech guy, lean and tall. He ran, he trained in combat like all potential Fianna warriors, but nothing he did gave him that 'muscle man' look. But to hear his elders argue, *actually argue*, about how he wasn't strong or fast enough to be an asset in the Cath stung. He thought their decision had been final the day of Maebh's debut into the elder meeting. He should have known better.

"You're fast. Okay, you're not the fastest, and my wife can beat you in a fistfight with one arm tied behind her back but—"

"That only happened once and—"

"But we need your calculating mind. Your brain makes up more than enough for your spaghetti arms. Plus, you'll be the tallest team member. You can, I don't know, move branches out of our way in the forest . . . as long as they aren't too heavy."

"As much as I'm enjoying your motivational speech, cuz, I'm going." Tiernan gave her a look that gave no allusions to the fact he didn't want to be followed.

Reaching his caravan, he grabbed his oversized duffle bag and headed back out in the night, away from the Breen caravans. His phone pinged, and he breathed out a sigh of relief after wrestling it from his deep pocket.

"Finally."

When he had first admitted Cara had tasked him with monitoring her, he hadn't mentioned the tracker he'd planted on her phone. She was his matriarch, even if she hadn't told him directly. He'd already lost two, and he wasn't about to lose another. Her last known location had been Newgrange, but then it seemed to glitch. That glitch could only mean one thing: Tír na nÓg.

The alert he just received—that she was back in this realm—left him with lighter steps as he weaved through the conifer trees, scanning the area to find the perfect place for his experiment. If this worked, he'd no longer have to worry about his matriarch disappearing into the black hole of the otherworld.

He spotted what he was looking for and trekked inland to an ancient oak tree. Its girth was so thick it looked like multiple tree trunks had formed it. He estimated it would take around six people to surround it, their arms outstretched and barely touching. From its height, it had to be thousands of years old. Perfect. Let this show the elders just how much of an asset he was.

Placing his bag on the ground, he set about his work, pulling out a mini satellite dish, several arm-length solar panels, an ancient druid scroll he'd stolen from Cara's office, and an iron cast cauldron that fit snugly in his palm. Taking out bundles of crushed herbs and flowers, he glanced occasionally at the scroll even though he'd read the instructions to the spell he was attempting so many times he knew it by heart.

Jogging to the river's edge, he scooped a handful of water into the cauldron and winced as the concoction stung his eyes. The druid who'd written the instructions mentioned the foul smell, and Tiernan wondered again why Cara had needed a cloaking spell in the first place. He was stirring the potion in the eternity eight symbol for his seventh time when a twig cracked behind him.

"Either you're about to have some sort of eco-friendly seance or I've had more whiskey than I thought." Maebh's voice was too close.

He groaned internally for losing himself in his work. Twisting his head, faint fumes of toffee and butterscotch tickled his nose, along with her favoured perfume that made his eyes water at its overpowering scent. He had to admit it was a welcome reprieve from the fumes coming from the cauldron.

"Did you follow me?"

"Yes." Maebh hunkered beside him, a bottle of whiskey in one hand. "So. What'cha doing?"

"You don't want to know."

"Try me."

Tiernan sighed. "I'm manipulating the two realms to believe they are talking to each other, therefore creating a pool of space where they merge."

"Cool. Why?"

He had expected her to come up with some snarky comment, so it took him a moment to answer.

"By doing this, I can have cell service while I'm in Tír na nÓg."

Maebh chuckled, playing with the cap from her bottle. "I've heard of people being addicted to their phones, but this is a whole other level."

"It's not just about my phone," Tiernan began, but stopped to use his tracking scanner. He squinted at Maebh. "What phone do you have?"

"This one." She pulled out a brick like device straight from the nineties. "Still works a treat."

It took several attempts to formulate his thoughts. He felt more disturbed by her than the first time she'd tried to alter his mood to get access to his caillte files.

"Why?"

"Why would I want a new one? This does what I need. I call people and ignore them just as quickly. No social media gnomes judging me."

"Trolls."

"Same difference." Maebh drank straight from the bottle. Wiping the rim, she offered it to Tiernan, but he shook his head. "Also . . ."

"What?" Tiernan noted the hesitancy in that one word and he couldn't help how it piqued his interest.

She gripped her brick phone tightly as she stared down at it. "It was my father's."

He stared at her in silence, knowing the weight of what she didn't say. He felt the loss of his mother swell up in that moment, the wave of frustration that constantly crashed against his chest whenever he tried to solve the mystery of where she'd disappeared to.

"I get it." He offered a small smile in which she returned.

"You're really smart, so I have a question."

"Hmm." Tiernan returned to his work, uncurling cables.

"Why haven't you found them?"

He stopped, lifting his head to look at the blonde pain in his ass. "Why haven't you?"

"Hey buddy, I never claimed to be smart."

"Neither did I!"

Maebh gestured towards his equipment and then at him. "I can answer the question. Want to know what I think?"

Before he could respond, she continued. "It's because you need both tech wizardry like what you have and my mind . . . what'd you call it?"

Tiernan turned back to his equipment with a sigh. "Mind molesting."

"Right. That. Think about what we could achieve together."

"You're beginning to sound like an evil villain in some fantasy book, trying to groom me to the dark side."

"Steady on. I'd buy you a drink first." Maebh wiggled her eyebrows as she shook her whiskey.

"We need to protect Ash. That's what we need to achieve."

Maebh stopped twisting her bottle lid. Her eyebrows scrunched as she scrutinised him. "Do you think she's in danger?"

"Cara went missing for a week in the other realm. And Ash has done the same thing." Tiernan sighed. "Yes, I think she's in danger, because I think whatever Cara was doing was about Ash."

"What makes you say that?"

"What happened between Ash and her mother seven years ago?" Tiernan paused, trying to find the right words. "Cara was a good mother, and I could tell she felt guilty about never reaching out to her daughter. You know Ash left the day before my mother and your father—and Ash's—disappeared? That's not a coincidence. Cara always said she was trying to protect her by keeping her away."

Maebh moved to lean against the oak tree, her tone more serious than he'd ever heard. "What if it's all connected, Tiernan? Cara's death, Ash, the caillte?"

Something twisted in his gut at the sound of his name on Maebh's lips. He didn't need her mood detector to know she was sad, and he realised then that she was as desperate as he was to find their parents. They only had different approaches. He'd never admit it, but he knew he had no right to be mad at her for trying to use her gift on him to get answers. Was he any better considering he'd spied on Ash for the last seven years? Not liking the answer, he pushed his now empty bag aside and leaned against the tree beside Maebh. Tiernan took the bottle from where it lay pressed between her raised knees. It was still three quarters full. Taking a small sip, he sighed. "If we were to join forces, what do you propose?"

"Compare notes on our parents' disappearances, get matching tattoos, solve a murder case, win the Cath." Maebh's blue eyes sparkled with mischief as she winked. "That's a good start, right?"

"Right. Second one is easy. Let's go to Conor right now."

Maebh laughed, and he turned to face her, caught up in the bewitching allure of her tone, a rasp that hinted she had a mesmerising singing voice.

"What? You think I won't get matching tattoos?" He smirked at her wide eyes and pushed her further. "Maybe you're scared. Don't worry, it only stings a little, kitten."

"You think *I* won't? Get your scéance done and let's go."

His head threw back in a laugh, but then remembered who he was talking to. With a smirk at her apparent desire to goad him further, he jumped up and hoisted the satellite on his shoulder. It was compact, but still heavy and he grunted as he climbed up the grooved trunk until he couldn't see Maebh's still seated form. Taking out his phone, he scanned the distance he'd climbed while straddling a thick branch and marked the exact spot where he secured the dish, using cable ties he'd stuffed into his coat pocket. After a few close calls where he almost fell from his perch, he surveyed his work. He scaled back to the ground, satisfied it wouldn't fall, his arms and legs tensed from the climb.

"What next?" Maebh had stuffed her bent knees into her long coat. It looked more like a quilted blanket.

"I need to erect the solar panels somewhere safe where they won't get trampled on or stolen."

Maebh's head reclined, her oval face cast in moonlight as her blonde tresses swayed in the breeze coming off the river. "The only way is up."

"It's too far. I got as high as I could with the dish."

Maebh unzipped her coat, letting it fall to the ground.

Tiernan stared at Maebh's outfit, a smirk on his lips. "Why are you wearing one of those dance costumes? I thought you were going to rip Mrs O'Malley's throat out over them."

Maebh looked down, as if it surprised her she was wearing it. Green and black sequins glinted in the moonlight, her black tights opaque but still showing how toned she was. "I don't hate dancing. I just hate being forced to dance. Here, hold my whiskey."

Grabbing the solar panels, she was about to climb when Tiernan stopped her. Should he insist he should do it? That seemed like what the elders would expect, but he knew his limits and he also accepted hers were far greater than his. Maebh was a McQuillan, and that costume revealed enough to show she wasn't just fit from dancing. She clearly took her warrior training seriously, too. She was much more capable of climbing than he was. "You need these to tie the panels."

Maebh smirked. "I've no more hands."

Opening her mouth, she wiggled her eyebrows again. He wouldn't let her win this. He bent the long cords inwards before snapping them, causing her to jump. It was his turn to smirk.

Stepping so close she had to tilt her head to look at him, he placed them between her lips. "Bite down."

With a soft chuckle, she bit the cable ties between her teeth. Holding the small panels over one shoulder, she lifted herself to the first branch of the tree with one hand, and Tiernan let out a whistle of appreciation at her superior strength. From her height, he could just make out her wink before she scaled the rest of the tree in a blur of blonde and embroidered green. A cool breeze rustled the night drenched trees. Tiernan had just poured the contents of his cauldron around the diameter of the trunk when he heard Maebh's descent.

"All done." She clapped her hands. "Now, let's get tattoos."

"Lead the way, tiny dancer."

"Never call me that again."

They made their way back through the caravans, with Tiernan's bag a substantially lighter weight on his shoulder.

"Will he be okay? Conor. Will he be able to do it?"

"You're serious about getting tattoos?" Tiernan stopped when she stared back at him in challenge.

"Are you scared?"

Shaking his head, he unzipped his coat, lifting the hem of his top enough to show it wouldn't be his first. His cheeks darkened as Maebh's eyes widened and she hunkered lower to his abdomen.

"How many tattoos do you have?" She reached a hand as if to touch his skin, but he pulled his top down and started walking again. He heard her soft chuckling as she followed.

"My clan brother is a tattoo artist and needed to practise, so . . ." he trailed off with a shrug and pointed to Conor's caravan where the light was still on. "Tattooing is his first love. If anything might bring him back to himself, it'll be two eejits knocking on his door to get matching tattoos."

"I get to choose!"

Tiernan couldn't help but laugh at her enthusiasm. Her determination to make everything a joke was infectious. If only this was the only version of Maebh. But the obnoxious, pushy pig-headed side seemed ever present underneath the surface. It wasn't true, though, he realised, as he stole glances at her as they walked. He didn't just want one version. Maebh had just shown a more vulnerable side underneath that oak tree, and it was the first time he felt he had seen a side few did.

When they reached Conor's caravan, many of the others were dark behind shuttered windows. Most of the clan would get an early night. The Cath began tomorrow, and even though only a small group were going, everyone would wake early to send them off and wish them luck. He hoped Ash would make it back in time. If she didn't arrive soon, he'd call, but he wasn't sure if she'd ever forgive him for hacking into her personal life.

He'd promised he'd make it up to her by finding out about her mother's case, and he'd planned to do that tonight.

He rapped his cold knuckles against the doorway and they stood in silence until it opened and Conor's pale face peeked through.

Tiernan silently assessed his brother. He seemed tired, but more alert than he had been since he returned to camp. "Hope you're not too busy, Conor. But we need your help in marking our skin permanently."

"You want tattoos?" Conor's voice was quiet. He pointed towards the whiskey bottle in between Maebh's hands. "I don't tattoo drunk people."

"I don't get tattoos sober, so I guess we're at an impasse." Maebh shivered. "We're not drunk. But we are freezing our nads off, so will you let us in?"

Conor shrugged before leading them to his room. It had been transformed into a tattoo parlour when he finished his apprenticeship. Most of his work was on his fellow clansmen, and Tiernan when Conor had a new technique he wanted to try, but other clans had started to come to him to get inked. Tiernan looked at the photographs he'd displayed on the walls, showcasing his best work, and a lump formed in his throat. Such talent for a young person. Tiernan prayed he'd see Conor's usually bubbly personality again. This shadow of his clan brother was heartbreaking.

"Who is going first?" Conor asked as he disinfected his hands, tools and workspace.

Tiernan gestured at Maebh, but she smiled, shaking her head. "Gentlemen first."

He raised his eyebrows before unzipping his coat. Lifting his jumper and then shirt, he felt Maebh's gaze on his bare chest as he sat with his chest leaning against the chair back. She moved to stand in front of him and he couldn't help but smile at her look of appreciation.

"You're like a work of art."

Scratching the back of his neck, he coughed, avoiding her attention, and glanced at his colourful arms where two half sleeves depicting various designs were inked. Rich reds, blues and greens spotted the mostly black ink to compliment his dark skin tone. He knew she meant it as a compliment to Conor. "When you have a talented tattoo artist living beside you, of course you're going to have ink."

One look at Conor and he could see a shy smile and blush creeping on his cheeks and Tiernan saw a glimmer of his brother before it disappeared once more and Conor turned away with a frown.

"Where am I inking this time?"

Tiernan gestured at the right side between his back and torso, hoping whatever Maebh decided would not be too hideous.

"So what will it be?" Tiernan asked, hugging the back of the chair as his legs sprawled outwards on either side.

Maebh tapped her chin with one pink tipped finger. Her eyes lit up. "I know!"

"Care to share with the entire room?" Tiernan grumbled as she leaned to whisper into Conor's ear.

Conor frowned in concentration, but then nodded as she grabbed a blank sketch pad and wrote something on it, showing it only to him.

"Traitor," Tiernan muttered, and Conor wordlessly drew on his skin.

It felt like he was writing something, and Tiernan regretted calling Maebh a tiny dancer. She came to stand in front of him once more; her curved waist at his eye level and he tilted his head up as the sting of Conor's needle penetrated his skin.

Her smile was all teeth. "No peeking."

He almost told her to stand right there so he wouldn't want to look anywhere else, but he kept his lips pressed together. What had got into him tonight? A few hours with Maebh McQuillan and he was like every other swooning lapdog at her bidding. "This better not be a kitten."

"You'll find out soon enough."

"Whatever it is, you're getting the same."

"A deal's a deal, kitten."

"All done."

"That was quick." Tiernan hopped up, gesturing for Maebh to take his place while Conor wrapped his side. Before he could even look at what Conor branded on his side, his attention was drawn to Maebh's hands as they unzipped the side of her dress. Without a word, she eased her arms out of the top part of her costume, leaning against the chair with her now bare back facing Conor to work on.

"Aren't you going to see what it says?"

Tiernan's face flushed as he examined his side. Angling his head, he squinted at the black calligraphy styled script through the clear wrapping that scrawled up his skin. "Níl sé ach ina thús."

"It's only just begun." Maebh winced as Conor began.

She reached towards him. Did she want him to hold her hand? Tiernan took a step closer, unsure what to do, but she traced her finger along the border of his tattoo. It was tender, but he didn't dare to move. "So whenever you get really pissed off with me, you need to remind yourself that we're starting fresh. No mind molesting, but a partnership."

"I would have preferred that as our tattoo."

Conor was finished soon after, and as he put salve on and wrapped Maebh's tattoo, Tiernan stepped into the other room. It felt weird standing there as she dressed. She didn't seem to mind. Even though he had taken off more than she had, he'd only felt naked when she'd displayed her own pale skin.

Conor's caravan was in its usual messy state. Sketch pads and loose paper everywhere. He noted a sink full of dirty dishes and began cleaning them when a particular sketch caught his eye. It was a hand. Conor was always sketching different body parts, practising shadowing and positioning. He'd spend an entire month drawing the same sketch of a pair of eyes until he deemed them acceptable and moved on to the next challenge. So the hand wasn't out of place, but it looked oddly familiar. It wasn't simply a hand; it was one gripping paper. A letter. Although it was only a pencil sketch, Tiernan was sure that the shading was blood.

CHAPTER 24

SETANTA

E veryone knew the story of Aisling Breen, but Set hadn't
had time to assess the fact that he held the new matriarch in
his arms when a short, plump woman opened the cottage door
before he was close enough to knock. He sent up a silent prayer
that he wasn't about to reveal the existence of The Fair Ones as
the woman's shocked expression turned to fear when she looked
at Aisling.

"Dom!"

A tall, grey-haired man appeared at the doorway, his
expression stern as he wordlessly reached for Aisling.

Set backed away only long enough to explain, "We need to get
her in the shower. She has poison on her skin."

"Come in. Dom, take him to the bathroom. I'll get towels."

Set followed him down the narrow hall, having to shuffle
sideways to avoid bumping Aisling's head, but they finally made
it into a large bathroom. A clawfoot cast iron bath sat under a
window and Set kicked off his shoes and climbed in with the
unconscious woman between his legs.

"We both need to wash it off," Set explained as he saw Dom
about to protest. "She also needs to drink fresh water with salt."

Dom shouted to the woman, calling her Mary, for his salt
water request.

As Set arranged Aisling's back to lean against his chest, Dom turned both taps on. Set grimaced as both hot and cold water hit his feet, but Aisling didn't react. He motioned for the handheld shower head and Dom switched the water to pump through it. Set angled the nozzle directly over Aisling's head and a soft hiss filled the air as a rainbow streaked oily substance slid off the still unconscious woman in his arms. He didn't have time to feel awkward as Dom stood directly over him, hands gripping the tub as he scrutinised Set's every movement.

Set didn't blame him. He'd just shown up, holding a half-naked and unconscious woman, covered in deadly looking welts. Not to mention he was also shirtless, wearing only leather pants and black boots. Mary rushed in, holding a tower of towels in one hand, which she dropped unceremoniously to the floor, and a glass of water in the other.

"Why aren't you helping him, Dom?" she scolded before turning her attention towards Set. "Here, dear. May I."

It wasn't asked like a question, so he handed the nozzle to her outstretched hand and Dom took the glass of water. He wasn't sure what to do with his now empty hands, so he let them hover awkwardly over Aisling's arms while the woman continued to wash her down. He ground his teeth every time the water touched him, so he knew it was working. It was a mix of relief and agony with every contact it made to his skin and he noted he, too, leaked that oily substance.

After what felt like hours—and a tonne of now lukewarm water—Aisling stirred. Set dutifully looked away when Mary inspected under her bra and leggings. He didn't dare look at Dom, whose constant glare burned more than the poison.

Aisling's welts had become less pronounced and her skin seemed to cool down to a calm creamy colour between the sores. As she murmured, Set held her forward so Mary could tend to the welts on her back.

"Heavens above," Mary muttered as she let the water pelt down.

"We need her to drink," Set said as he leaned her across his chest again, tilting her head back.

Mary continued to water her down as Dom pressed the glass to her lips. He had to hold her chin to coax her mouth open, but Aisling gulped it down, her eyes fluttering.

When half the salt water contents were gone, Aisling heaved forward, vomiting again. There was no longer any blood.

"That should hopefully do it," Set murmured.

"Water," Aisling croaked before opening one bloodshot eye to a slit. "No salt."

Dom left without another breath and returned with two glasses as Mary hosed Set's shoulders. His jaw clenched as she worked on him, the now cold water pouring over his eyes and face as she moved. He hadn't realised his own skin had formed welts. Dom thrust a glass in Set's hand as he held a fresh drink to Aisling's lips and she shakily gripped the glass. When she drank her fill and handed it back to Dom, she seemed to realise Set's presence. She sat bolt upright, a blush appearing on her neck and cheeks as she squeezed water out of her ink black hair, never turning to look at him. He sat upright too, but kept as much distance as he could between them as he drank his glass of water and Mary hosed his back. She gestured for him to loosen his pants.

"That isn't necessary."

He was afraid she would insist, but Mary eventually turned the taps off. Ash gripped the tub, hoisting herself up, but slipped. Set held her waist as she made another attempt. The welts no longer looked ready to burst. Mary engulfed her in a large towel, and Set noted the way Aisling stole glances his way as Mary fussed over her.

"I can dry myself," she snapped as Mary tried to rub her down.

Set stepped out of the bath, his low slung trousers dripping large puddles on the floor. He towered over them, but it was something he was used to. He fought the smile on his lips as Aisling's gaze roamed his body. Dom threw a towel at him with more force than necessary and he almost dropped his glass.

Mary stood in the doorway. "We'll leave you two to dry off. Will you join us in the kitchen for tea."

Again, it wasn't a question. Dom seemed reluctant to leave, but eventually allowed Mary to direct him out of the room. Set and Ash stood facing one another in silence. Every time he tried to meet her gaze, her attention drifted anywhere but him, and he realised she didn't know who he was.

"I'm Set McQuillan." He reached his hand out and she accepted.

He winced on contact from a welt that was on his palm. Her hand was tiny in his, and Set noticed a Celtic knot tattoo on her inner forearm as they shook.

"I know. I mean, I'm Ash Breen."

Underneath her welts, Ash's complexion reminded him of a fairy-tale princess . . . with chickenpox. Her green eyes were rimmed with red, but underneath her injuries, he found himself mesmerised by her beauty. He took a step back, drying himself. After his breakup with Orla, he'd decided he would not put another woman in danger. He was a monster in the skin of a man. His muscular body and good looks were all part of the arsenal of the deadly creature within and he may not have the strength to control it, but he wouldn't allow it to harm anyone but himself.

Hints of a blush had faded as Ash hugged the towel tightly around her sleek body. His jaw ticked at what he might have witnessed if he'd been only mere seconds later. There wasn't one shred of guilt at killing either merrow, and he was happy that she had killed one on her own. He fought the images of possibilities that could have happened as he draped the towel across his shoulders before setting his now empty glass down on the floor beside the tub.

Her black hair dripped water on the floor, tousled long strands sticking to her face. Set couldn't help but think she looked too young to be a matriarch. She was around his age and hadn't lived in a clan for years. How could she possibly lead one? And why was she in that river?

"What happened?" She scrunched her narrow nose, and he noted a piercing that twinkled in the overhead light. "After you killed that merrow, I mean."

"You passed out. That water is in Tuatha Dé territory. I'd always heard it would kill us if we went in." Set frowned, keeping his voice low so the couple wouldn't hear. "I honestly wasn't sure if washing the water off would work."

Emerald eyes scrutinised him as she pieced everything together. "You carried me the entire way here?"

"Tea's almost ready!" Dom's voice bellowed down the hall through the still open bathroom door. Ash stepped further away as they heard his footsteps approach. He stood at the doorway with a bundle in his hands before dumping them on the edge of the bath. "Here's some of my clothes. They may not fit, but at least they're dry."

Set thanked him, in which he received a grunt in response. Before Dom left, he gave Ash a pointed look. She followed behind him, but turned at the door. "I'll see you in the kitchen. Down the hall to the right."

He didn't have time to reply before she closed the door. *Shit*. He had wanted to get their story straight before answering questions. Could he trust she would know what to say? He stared at the closed door for a moment before realising he had little choice.

Peeling off his wet clothing, he dried himself and started putting on his borrowed clothes. Dom was right, they certainly didn't fit. No matter how many times he tugged on the T-shirt, it sat above his midriff. The jeans Dom had loaned were even worse. He couldn't fit them over his thighs, no matter how hard he pulled. Fearing he'd rip the seams, he gave up and contemplated wearing his soaked leathers, but didn't think Mary would appreciate his traipsing through her house in wet clothing.

Wrapping the towel around his hips, he bundled his belongings in one pile and draped Dom's jeans over his shoulder. He had to stoop as he moved through the doorways, and even though he was used to small spaces in his own caravan, these walls were full of framed photos and delicate ornaments on side tables that he didn't want to break. When he reached the kitchen, he noted Ash still wasn't there. He stood in the doorway as Dom and Mary whispered to one another at the table.

"Here, love. Let me take them. I'll dry your shoes and pants before you leave. I see Dom's jeans weren't up to the job."

Set thanked her and felt the need to apologise to Dom—for his jeans not fitting or for bringing Ash home in the state she'd been in, he wasn't sure. Neither was his fault, but Dom's wordless assessment made him feel like they possibly were. He sat where Mary suggested, close to the lit fire range where she placed his shoes on the hearth and lay his pants across a clotheshorse nearby. The merrow hats fell to the floor, and Mary frowned as she picked them up. Sighing, she placed them beside his pants without further comment.

Wood crackled and spat as Dom poured him a cup of tea. He thanked him and took a long drink of the hot liquid. When his stomach rumbled, reminding him he hadn't eaten properly in days, Mary put a bowl of steaming stew in front of him, insisting he tuck in. The rich smell of gravy and meat filled his nostrils, and he didn't need to be told twice as he devoured the entire contents in minutes. Cold fingers pressed on the back of his neck and Set tensed as Mary stood behind him.

"This is my homemade calamine lotion."

Set didn't argue as she administered the cream. In between mouthfuls, he gave a brief introduction to who he was, and they told him of their relationship with Ash. He was halfway through a second helping of stew when Ash reappeared in the doorway, dressed in a pair of black leggings, a baggy cream jumper and her midnight black hair pulled up in a messy bun.

"Finally. Aisling, sit down and tell us what happened." Mary nodded to Dom, who poured Ash a cup of tea, placing it in the seat farthest away from Set. "We were beyond worried since we haven't heard from you."

"I've only been gone . . ." Ash began but stopped, a deep burrow appearing between her dark eyebrows.

Time moves differently, Set wanted to say, but he turned towards the older couple. "What date is it?"

"Eleventh of November," Dom answered before returning his fierce gaze to Ash. "One full week since you walked out that door."

Ash opened her mouth but closed it again, her frown still prominent on her tightened pink lips. Mary put cream on Ash's neck, but she grabbed the tub and lathered it carelessly on herself. As she opened her mouth once more, Set tried to hide his shock as she revealed everything, but his jaw tightened with every revelation. How she'd been to Tír na nÓg in search of her mother's actual murder scene—that explained the amount of blood he had seen in Newgrange.

Stealing glances his way, she described meeting a druid named Ethne, and Set realised Ash could somehow be linked to the destiny the druid had told him about. What did this all mean? Had he been destined to save her? If so, the white-haired druid knew. He tried not to spiral as he heard Mary talk about the Fair Ones as if it were an everyday subject. Had Ash told them everything before? If anyone found out, she and this couple would be in grave trouble. As if sensing his thoughts, Ash turned to him.

"Mary and Dom knew about the existence of the Tuatha Dé Danann before I came to live with them."

She didn't elaborate and, by the sad expression on Mary's face, Set didn't feel it was his place to pry. Dom reached across and squeezed her hand; her grip turned her knuckles white.

"Are you considering moving back to live with them, Aisling?" Dom asked after a considerable pause.

"No, of course she isn't," Mary replied as Ash opened her mouth. "She's in her final year of university."

"Actually . . ." Ash began, but Mary heaved off her chair, muttering about needing the patience of a saint.

Mary began wiping down countertops as Ash tried to speak again, but before she could, the woman whirled around, cloth waving in the air through her clenched fist.

"You're going to throw away your degree for what? Those people don't want you back. You said so yourself."

"I'm not doing it for them. Conor—"

"Can come here; he can live with us."

"It's not that simple. I'm lucky to have you. But he has no family and needs me. He won't leave our clan. I *want* to go back and take part in the Cath."

Set almost spat out his tea as the two women began arguing over the sacred rite that Fianna only dreamed about fighting in. His eyes danced between them as he let out a low breath. Mary seemed to know so much about it, to the point where she could ridicule it with a scornful mirth that made him shrink in his seat. He noted Dom lower his chin, his eyes fixed on the fire as the two women argued. Set caught his gaze, and Dom shook his head. He mimicked the man and remained quiet.

The argument went on for what felt like an eternity, and by the end, Set wasn't sure who had won. He wasn't even sure it was over, but raised voices were replaced by scowling silence and it was only then that Dom spoke.

"Aisling is an adult, Mary. It's her decision."

Set decided that Dom was a brave man when Mary turned on him. She plonked back on her seat, still clutching her washcloth, and began arguing the same points that had been bandied about moments ago. Dom raised his hand and, miraculously, Mary stopped.

"Aisling knows this is her home, and she can come back when she's ready."

The fire had died down and Dom went over to tend to it as Ash rose from her seat.

"I'm going to pack." She made to walk from the room, but Dom stopped her.

"I'm not finished. You have our blessing—"

"No she—"

"You have our blessing, but only if he agrees to watch over you."

It took a moment for Set to realise Dom meant him. Ash bristled, about to speak, probably in protest. Dom raised his hand, and again, silence ensued.

"We're in different clans. That's not really how a Cath works," Set began, but Dom gave him that silent assessment and he felt as if he'd shrunk in size. "Of course. I'll look out for her."

Dom returned to his seat and lifted his mug. "That's settled, then."

CHAPTER 25

AISLING

It was difficult to resist looking at Set's towelled crotch as Ash drove towards his clan's encampment. With every bump—and there were many on this stretch of country road, Ash's gaze watered from staring straight ahead. She knew it was right there, jiggling around, prominent through the sea foam, one hundred percent cotton towels Mary favoured. Ash would never look at those towels in the same way again.

"So, that's where my sister went off to?" Set's voice was quiet. She hummed in response, surprised he hadn't known.

He seemed unfazed by the fact he was sitting in the passenger seat of her Ford Fiesta in what looked like a crop top and bath towel. He'd stuffed his ridiculously large feet into still damp boots, but the rest of his clothing was unwearable in the frigid November air. Some might say those leather pants were unwearable prior to his night-time swim.

November eleventh. Seven days had passed. The unread emails on her phone were like an angry pimple, daring her to poke and prod, not to mention the alerts from her social accounts. Without reading, she knew there were classes she was failing, but it didn't seem to matter anymore. Three intense years of study at a prestigious university, and she was failing before the first term of her final year. It was a worry for another day. Tonight—or yesterday, or whenever that was—she had killed a merrow and vomited in front of the most gorgeous man she'd ever seen in person. The latter bothered her more, which should worry her, but again, it didn't.

Set rested his head on his fist, looking out his window, so Ash took that as an opportunity to sneakily gawk without crashing her car. He had sandy blond hair secured with random plaits, curling at his shoulders. His jaw was firm, coated in a thick, short beard that was slightly darker than his hair, but equally matched his brows. Shadows cast his features, adding to the troubled look he wore. She could still make out his wide set lips and the hollows of his perfectly formed cheekbones. He glanced at her, and her neck spasmed at how quickly she faced forward. It was almost sinful how thick his lashes were. She could still see them from the corner of her eye.

Her hands gripped the steering wheel. This was not what she should focus on. Only a week had gone by since her mother's murder. Or had it? The days were a blur. That's what she should think about. But she wasn't. She cringed as she remembered how it felt laying against his broad chest in the bathtub while Mary and Dom watched. Freeing her mind of that painfully awkward memory, she tried to remember what they were talking about.

Maebh. The type of girl who made you realise you were slouching just by looking at her. The resemblance between the pair was undeniable. Perfection encased in human forms. The Fair Ones were known for their beauty, but that was expected from them. Another deadly tool used to lure their prey. Although Ash hadn't seen the noble-blooded species, the Tuatha Dé Danann, in person, she imagined the McQuillan twins were the closest thing in human form to rival the fae's infamous beauty.

"She seriously didn't tell you she was leaving?" Ash glanced sideways but quickly turned straight ahead as her Fiesta jostled over a pothole.

The road was pitch black, sporadically lit up by a scattering of street lamps. Ash had thought little more about Maebh's offer and her insistence on transferring to the Breen clan. *Her clan*. She gripped the steering wheel with slick palms. The prospect of returning to face Mrs O'Malley and the others after she'd sent Maebh to declare her intention of taking her mother's place now seemed impulsive.

Archaic in ways, clan members were cult-like in their loyalty to the matriarch. One female leader passed down within the head family clan. And now it was her turn. She had accepted that her birthright was non-existent. The clan elders could petition to the High King to overrule her claim, but she didn't think she'd have to worry about any of this yet. Now, it was upon her far too soon.

"We weren't exactly on speaking terms." Set sighed, his deep voice penetrating her drifting attention. Rubbing a hand roughly against his jaw, he added, "Our mother is . . . difficult. It doesn't help that Maebh acts first, thinks second, and refuses to apologise. Ever."

"She seems determined to be part of the Cath." Ash's thoughts turned to Ethne's vision and her stomach twisted.

Set only nodded in agreement, so Ash's attention fixated on the winding road. It had narrowed to where she would have to drive into the ditch if any car bigger than her Fiesta were to approach. Sure enough, a tractor appeared around the corner and she groaned. As she slowed to a crawling pace, her thoughts went back to the Cath. What had she agreed to?

She would need any help the druid could give if she were to lead herself, never mind her clan, into the unknown trials. Fionn Mac Cumhaill, first High King of Ireland, had looked every bit the warrior she was not, but thankfully they wouldn't battle like the first Cath. Sliding her glance sideways once more, she looked at the tight torso of the man beside her. He was certainly Cath-ready.

Set laughed, his defined muscles rippling as he did, but it still didn't sound like he was truly amused. "I didn't want to believe it when I found her empty room, but my first thought was she's determined to piss our mother off."

"There has to be more to it than that."

She stopped the car, the tractor now upon them and its driver, who looked no older than fourteen, making no effort to give her any space. When she glanced at Set, he was staring at her. Her breath caught as he lifted his hand to her face and stroked her hair. *What was he doing?* She remained still, not sure if she should tell him to stop.

Holding something dark and thin between his thumb and forefinger, he said, "River grass."

"Thanks," she murmured, willing her stupid heart to slow down. The tractor barrelled past, and she sped on. "Do you know much about what a modern Cath is like?"

She was reasonably fit. Finding athleticism had always come easy to her. Maybe she'd be fit enough for this? It was a big fucking maybe. She'd been a part of nearly every sports club Trinity University offered. Judo, karate, rowing, Gaelic football. Not to mention being a member of the rifle club. A part of her knew it was because she'd always hoped to rejoin her family, even if Mary wouldn't listen to her reasoning at the cottage. Her mother's death hadn't been part of that dream.

Fianna were raised to be warrior-ready if, when they were in their adulthood, the current set of warriors were to 'move on' in Tír na nÓg. It didn't happen often, as warriors couldn't age in the Land of Youth. Fianna were mortal like every other human, so giving that up was something very few did willingly. As far as

Ash could remember, it was the High King who decided when this happened.

"I don't know how she knew, but my mother has had the McQuillan clansmen training heavily since we were young. More than what Brehon law requires. She always said a Cath would happen for me. For both Maebh and I. It's supposed to be . . . intense. The last one was around one hundred years ago, and it followed the series of trials written in the scrolls."

"Fuck."

Set laughed, this time it rumbled deep within his chest. "Yes. Couldn't have put it better myself."

She remembered the type of training Fianna had all children undertake from an early age, and the McQuillan matriarch had insisted on more than the requirement? Her head pounded at the thought of it. Brehon law was never something she had questioned when she was younger. Being raised under the various ancient laws that all Fianna clans followed was just another part of her life back then.

It had felt odd to wake up that first morning after Mary and Dom had found her wandering the road that led to their cafe. No sunrise call to boot up and play battle with blunt swords. No pre-breakfast wrestle match with her clan peers. Mary had told her she didn't have to take on any sports, that she could live her life however she chose, but when she told them she wanted to continue her training, Dom had driven her everywhere. To all of her training sessions, matches, and competitions. They were both supportive, but he knew all of her teammates' names, even the names of her competitors. He was there for everything, even after she had eventually bought a car to drive herself. A lump lodged in her throat. When would she see them again?

It had taken over an hour to pack: with Mary's constant interruptions at attempting to change her mind and her own indecision on what she should take. Dom had come to the rescue, loaning her one of his camping rucksacks. With his and Set's input, she'd squeezed in everything she would need. She hoped. There wasn't exactly a manual on what to bring to the otherworld.

The scrolls Set had mentioned were vaguely familiar. During their lessons, they would have to learn Fianna history, including the different species of Fair Ones and how the Tuatha Dé Dannan overruled Tír na nÓg. The Cath trials had been widely publicised in a popular collection of published stories in the early twentieth century. Everyone believed it to be fiction, of course, and that was the only reason the author had lived to tell her next tale. If the Tuatha Dé had decided otherwise . . . Ash didn't want to think about that.

While no one had been looking, she'd stowed away the purse full of her letters. When she was alone again, she would read them, even though she'd read them so many times before. The one she needed was torn in half and covered in blood. Hopefully, Tiernan could solve that problem for her. Conor wasn't ready to talk, but she hoped she could ask him about that letter soon. There had to be something different about it. If it meant enough for her mother to clench it in her dying hands, then she had to use every resource possible in discovering why.

Maybe Cara had written the name of her killer and Ash had it all along? Internally kicking herself, she realised, not for the first time, how utterly foolish she had been for taking evidence from her mother's murder scene. Shivering, she turned the dial to blast more hot air through the heaters.

"About what Dom said. You don't need to worry about looking out for me. We're from different clans. He doesn't understand that, but I do."

"What do you mean?" Set twisted to face her, his broad shoulders sandwiched between his seat and dashboard. Her eyes watered and she blinked, not before noting the fine coating of dark hair under his navel, leading underneath that damned towel.

Ash's eyes snapped to the road, and she laughed, internally cringing at how false it sounded. "You're off the hook. No babysitting necessary."

"I gave Dom my word."

"Yeah, but—"

"You think I'm going to go against him? No way."

Ash smirked, glancing once at Set's serious expression before facing forward. "Are you afraid of my foster dad?"

"Of course I am." Set's head tilted. "What's so funny?"

"I find it hard to believe you could be afraid of anything."

"Size isn't everything."

Ash resisted the overwhelming urge to look at his towel again. *I beg to differ.* "You jumped into a poison infested river to rescue someone you didn't know."

"When you put it like that, I do sound impressive." Set flashed a grin and she smiled, realising it was the first time she had in a long time without it feeling forced. He gripped her forearm gently before pointing ahead. "We're here."

The fairground had been halfway dismantled as they pulled into one of the parking spaces.

Before Set moved to get out of the car, he reached for something at his feet. "Here, this belongs to you." He handed her the deep red merrow hat. She played with the turquoise feathers peaking out of the rim. "The cohuleen druith."

She'd forgotten the hat's proper name. Studying it closely, she murmured, "Thank you."

"Make sure you pack that. You never know when you'll need to breathe underwater."

"The breathing part was handy, but those webbed hands and feet." Ash made a yacking sound and Set chuckled.

"I'd take webbed feet over blue lips any day."

Just as he was about to step out of the car, another parked beside them. Ash glanced at the driver. "Shit."

"Who is that?"

"A detective working my mother's case."

Set resumed his seat, closing the door. The detective opened his and Ash could see he was alone. Recognising her, he gestured for Set to roll down his window.

The detective nodded to Ash as a way of greeting. "I'm canvassing other clans to see if they know anything."

"I'm sure that's going well for you," Set replied, flashing a dimpled smirk.

"Setanta McQuillan, I believe. Your sister has the same charm."

"And you are?" Set leaned back, looking completely at ease, and Ash knew that nobody could pull off the appearance of not giving a shit dressed only in a bath towel quite like him.

"Detective Garda Raymond O'Leary." He leaned against the car door, making a point of staring at Set's towel and then Ash with raised brows before continuing, "Ms Breen, I visited your clan, but there was still no sign of Conor. Have you seen him?"

"No, I haven't." Ash shivered against the cold air seeping through the open window, but she refused to fidget under his gaze. Her blood thrummed hot inside her as she remembered how horrible he had been only hours after discovering her mother's body. She was glad the clan had hidden Conor from this man.

"I wanted to discuss something with you. About your mother." He looked at Set with a frown. "It might be best to do so in private."

"He can stay." Ash didn't know why she said it. It wasn't like they knew each other well. She didn't want to be alone with the detective and seeing as they'd fought merrow together, and he was wearing one of her towels, she felt safe with Set.

"We didn't get to speak as much as I'd wanted the day I initially interviewed you."

"You mean the day my mother was murdered, and you treated me like shit on your shoe?"

The air thickened and Ash's nose crinkled as the smell of rotten eggs filled the space. Set was still leaning back, one arm casually on the doorframe, but he reached towards her with his other, and without taking his eyes from the now seething detective, he placed a hand on her arm and squeezed gently.

In his next breath, the car filled with a calming hint of lavender, and she was reminded that Maebh had said he shared her gift of manipulating emotion. She let it seep into her too, even if it didn't take on quite the same effect.

Set said, "What do you want to say to Ash, Detective O'Leary?"

The detective blinked, his shoulders drooping before shaking his head as if to clear it. "The coroner's report has come back. It's officially a murder case."

"Clearly she couldn't have done that to herself, so bravo to the coroner who solved that." Ash didn't need Set's warning squeeze on her arm to tell her she was being rude, but she patted his hand before moving it away.

When their gaze met, she could see he wanted to say something, but the detective ignored her jibe and spoke, still impassive from Set's manipulation. His next words were anything but calming. "There were puncture wounds just below your mother's collarbone. The coroner's report suggests they came from an antlered creature. Other notes suggest that it would have to have been more than one assailant.

"Why?" Ash's question came out in a whisper as she tried to process what he was telling her.

"Reports were inconclusive how she received the fatal abrasion down her ventral cavity."

"What does that mean?" Set asked, and she was thankful that she didn't have to.

"Ms Breen, are you sure I should continue here?" the detective asked and for once Ash could hear kindness in his tone.

"I want to know."

Without realising, Set's hand was covering hers and she stared down at it as the detective's words ambushed her once more.

"The abrasion marks on her skin coincide with injuries occurring through flesh being torn apart without the aid of a sharp object." After a brief pause, he added, "The probability of Cara Breen being torn open by bare hands is impossible, so the report is inconclusive."

Torn open by bare hands.

Silence filled the small space while Ash let that sink in. Without her control, her senses opened up, and she looked at Set, whose hand remained encased over hers. His scent reminded her of when she'd come face to face with an ancient fae attempting to steal a newborn. Nothing scared her more than failing to stop a changeling attempt. Was he scared of whatever creature could do that? The detective may think it was impossible, but Ash and Set knew better. There were monsters in this world capable of far worse.

"Was there anything else at the scene?" Detective O'Leary's voice penetrated her thoughts and she jumped.

Set removed his hand and Ash felt the absence of warmth disconcerting. She crossed her arms as she looked at the detective, but then back through the windscreen. "What do you mean?"

"Did you notice anything else out of place?"

The letter. She should hand them over and beg for forgiveness. Maybe she could use her mood gift to get away with it? She'd have to figure it out first. She looked at Set, who was frowning at his hands. Would he or Maebh help if she asked? That was putting a lot of trust in people she'd only met.

"No."

A tall, shapely figure appeared behind the detective. "Setanta, it's time you join your clan."

Ash had met the McQuillan matriarch at her mother's funeral. She had been dressed much like she was now, a silken dark layered skirt with a long vintage tweed coat. Her blonde hair was styled in an elegant knot, and even in the darkness, Ash could see her makeup was perfect. The detective began to speak, but one look from Imogen McQuillan made him hesitate. "Your presence is not required, detective."

The detective stepped away from the car and murmured with the matriarch, but Ash could tell he would make no progress in attempting to speak to any of the McQuillan clan.

Set turned to Ash, one hand on the door lock. "Are you okay?"

Ash let out a breath. "Not really, you?"

"Set." Imogen tapped the window before turning and walking away after nodding once at Ash.

Gritting his teeth, he sighed but opened the door. Once outside, he turned to her with a look as solemn as if he was standing by her mother's funeral pyre. "I'll see you soon, Ash."

CHAPTER 26

AISLING

Ash pulled up to the Breen encampment at midnight. Looking across the blackened sky to the treeline she could barely see, she imagined pulling away and driving another ten minutes to the safety of her cottage. One word stopped her: Conor.

She leaned against the headrest, wondering where she should go. She was the matriarch, not that she'd earned it, and she didn't have anywhere to call home. There was no way she was stepping foot inside her mother's caravan. Morbid curiosity didn't outweigh her need to shield herself from the inevitable pain it would cause.

Would she find more evidence of her mother's surveillance? Cara had wanted to know her every movement, but didn't want her close? Why would she do that? Who had she chosen to carry it out? Tiernan had admitted to the tech side of the warped spy detail, but insisted he hadn't been involved in physically following her. Ash didn't know what to do with those answers if she searched for them. Not yet. Conor's caravan was the obvious choice.

She didn't pass a soul as she made her way to the centre of the encampment. Embers of a dying campfire were a mix of grey and orange, a shadowed figure sitting on one of the low benches. It took a moment for Ash to realise it was Tiernan.

"Are you okay?" His voice was quiet, as if he had been deep in contemplation.

He wore his grey coat buttoned up, his peak cap tucked low over his face. She'd always associated those caps with old men and farmers, but it suited him. The weak flames of the fire illuminated Tiernan's dark skin; his nose and cheeks were rosy and she wondered how long he'd been sitting there.

With a sigh, she sat beside him. "I was in Tír na nÓg."

"I know."

"How . . ." Ash began, but Tiernan took out his phone, waving it in answer. Her eyes narrowed. "That's creepy."

He shrugged, and Ash realised she didn't care. She stared into the embers, processing the fact that Tiernan, with a few taps on his phone, could hack and track her phone. He was the type of person she needed by her side, working alongside her if she was going to be anything other than Cara's prodigal daughter.

His voice penetrated her spiralling thoughts. "Why did you go?"

Her sigh went deep into her bones. She had trusted him with her confession of stealing evidence, and he hadn't reported her to the gardaí. She had to trust her gut and continue to do so. It wasn't like she had a lot of options. She told Tiernan about her encounter with the druid, her lucky escape with the merrow and meeting Set, who was the potential ally Ethne had told her about. She left out the embarrassing parts of being half naked and vomiting, not once, but twice, in the warrior's presence.

Tiernan remained quiet throughout her tale, his frown deepening at everything she said until she finished with what the detective reported.

"Do you know what it means to be matriarch? Have you thought past the fact you want to find your mother's murderer and protect Conor?"

Ash didn't answer because she hadn't.

Tiernan moved to straddle the log facing her. "It means you have a clan—a family—who depend on you to lead them. But you need us as much as we need you, Ash."

They sat in silence, watching the now only grey ashes in the pit. How could the clan need her? Why? She was too young for all of this responsibility. But she'd said yes to all of it, even against what the elders wanted.

Ash sighed. "I'm sorry."

"Look, I understand that this is all new and scary and difficult for you." Tiernan squeezed her arm. "All I ask is that next time you have an important announcement to make, do it yourself and not by sending a McQuillan."

"I shouldn't have done that." Ash cringed, her stomach dropping at how childish that had been. "How did Mrs O'Malley take it?"

"As well as to be expected."

She slouched in her seat, feeling every bit the incompetent fool she believed she was.

"Did you make Maebh your second in command?"

Ash's attention snapped to Tiernan's face, noting the edge in his tone. "No. I haven't decided who to choose. I'm sure Mrs O'Malley is happy to continue until then."

He only nodded, but she noticed his shoulders relax.

"There's more. I want to talk to you about Conor."

She sat upright, a painful lump forming in her already tight chest. "How is he?"

"He seems okay, but I saw a few drawings. Ash. He was there. He saw your mother's body."

Tiernan described Conor's sketch of a hand gripping a letter, and Ash could only agree with him as even more questions piled on top of a tower she'd constructed in her mind, dangerously close to collapsing. Visions of her mother's torn body forced their way in, circling her mind along with what the detective had just revealed. Conor had been the last known person to see Cara alive. Had he been there when she'd been attacked? "I'm going to his caravan now. Hopefully, he'll talk to me."

"The Cath is tomorrow."

"I'm aware." Ash lifted her backpack. "I'm already packed."

"The elders held a meeting. You should know, they'd rather I wasn't one of your warriors."

"They also wish I wasn't matriarch," Ash said but when she saw he was about to disagree, added, "Why?"

"I'm not strong enough."

Thinking back to what she saw from Ethne's vision of the warriors surrounding the first High King, and looking at Tiernan, she could see why they would assume he wasn't capable. He didn't have the bulking physique like Set, but she didn't care. Her own body was athletic, not muscular. She wanted people she could trust, and although she still had questions about Tiernan, she believed he was one of few people in this world that she could depend on.

"You're strong enough to be my warrior. I trust you, and that means more than muscle."

She couldn't tell if she'd said the right thing, but Tiernan moved on to the logistics of what she should expect tomorrow. As he listed timeframes and weaponry they were taking, Ash realised she was playing a role that felt wholly out of her capabilities. Who did she think she was? Just because she had been born into leadership, did not make her worthy, or competent. She felt neither of those qualities as he continued, seemingly oblivious to her increasing discomfort. She silently prayed that Set had meant to keep his promise. Would Ethne seek her out to help, too?

"Do you know anything about the High King's druid?"

Tiernan shrugged. "Not much. Only that she was the former king's advisor before Aedan took the throne a decade ago. He's the youngest High King in recorded history. The last one had ruled for over a century."

"I forget how absurd Fianna history is." Ash laughed as Tiernan frowned. "Magical lands that keep you young? Oh, but only if you stay there forever."

Tiernan smirked as he scratched his chin. "I've known no different, but I suppose it sounds out there."

"So Ethne is . . . old?"

"Rumour has it Fianna have spotted her in our realm, but she never ages. Druids are a mix of Fianna and wiccan, so she *should* age. I don't know of anyone personally who has seen her, so it's probably a load of rubbish." Tiernan stood. "Ash, there's more I haven't said."

"What?"

"Mrs O'Malley and the others weren't sure if you'd return in time. And because Niamh couldn't take your role as matriarch after you claimed it, they were going to forfeit the Breen clan's right to enter the Cath."

Ash closed her eyes, weariness seeping into her core. "What made them change their minds?"

She opened her eyes when she heard him chuckle. "Maebh. She told them that if they so much as contemplated forfeiting, they wouldn't have time to hear a banshee's warning before she slaughtered everyone dear to them."

"That's . . . extreme."

"You should have seen their faces." He grinned. "She's a nightmare, but you picked a fierce ally."

Ash smiled at the admiration in Tiernan's voice, and wondered if he had fallen under the spell Maebh seemed to cast with her gift, too. She had text her earlier to say she was back and to make sure everything was in order for the Cath. She didn't realise Maebh would need to threaten the elders in order to do it.

"Can I ask you something?" Tiernan began, a small smile on his lips. "It's about your Fair One journal."

She raised her brows. "It might be too soon to bring up your stalking tendencies with me."

He had the decency to look embarrassed and he nodded, standing. As he turned, she sighed. "Go on, then. What do you want to ask? I'm not promising that I'll answer."

"Why did you interfere? With Fair Ones."

She scrutinised his face, and instead of finding contempt, his open expression was genuine . . . and curious. Tucking loose strands from her face, she looked toward the direction of her unseen cottage.

"My . . . Mary and Dom took me in when I had nowhere else to go. Before I arrived, they had lost their newborn to one of those ancient fae."

"A changeling," he murmured, sitting once again beside her.

She nodded. "I know we aren't allowed to meddle in their acts, but I decided I couldn't live with myself if I didn't. What good are Fianna if we don't protect the innocent? They can't fight against something they don't know exists. How is that fair?"

Tiernan didn't respond for a long time and they both sat with the silence pressing in on their own thoughts.

"You're really something special, you know that?"

A warmth spread across her chest as she bumped his shoulder. "Still doesn't excuse you for being a creepy stalker."

She soon said goodnight and rapped on her brother's caravan door. The interior was lit like a Christmas tree when Conor's hunched frame filled the doorway. When they were both inside and sitting at the dining table, Ash looked at him, really looked, and felt a sadness radiating off him in waves. She didn't think she would need her gift to notice it. Reaching across the table, she took one of his hands in hers and squeezed.

215

"I'm sorry I didn't return sooner."

"Where'd you go?"

"Tír na nÓg. To the Newgrange in that realm."

Conor's hand clenched under hers, but he said nothing. The nervous energy that had radiated off him at her cottage was gone and in its place was a tiredness that could only come from loss.

"That's where she was murdered, Con."

"I can't remember what happened."

"You were there?"

Conor shuddered. "Yes. I don't know. Fragments of seeing her dead have come back, but I can't remember how it happened."

"It's ok—"

"But it's not okay, is it? She's dead. What if I could have stopped it? What if I was there?" Conor's voice rose, his eyes darting to her but scrunching shut.

"It's not your fault, Con."

"You don't know that."

"I do."

They sat in silence, and Ash removed her hand from his when he fidgeted. Taking in his artwork hanging around any available space, Ash felt a pang in her chest. She wished she knew him better, in order to know what to say. She knew he was an artist and had taken on a tattoo apprenticeship a few years ago, because his letters were filled with his doodles and descriptions of what he had inked onto fellow clansmen's skin.

"Your letters always gave me hope."

Conor's gaze met hers again.

"Every time I got one, I felt closer to you and the possibility that I could come home to you felt real. Your drawings were my favourite part, but also how you would write out all the old bedtime stories Mam used to tell us when we were young."

Conor sniffed, his brown eyes darting back to his pale clasped hands, charcoal stains visible on his fingertips. "They weren't from me."

"What do you mean?"

"The sketches were mine. And so were most of the letters." Conor's grip tightened. "But the stories were from Mam."

Ash's breath hitched as she looked at her brother and then at her rucksack at her feet. Some of those letters had been from her? She mentally categorised all the past letters and what old fairy tales they'd held. They were mostly about Tír na nÓg, and about the quests the original Fianna used to go on.

"Why?"

It was Conor's turn to reach across the small space between them. Gripping her hand, his voice was pained. "I wanted to tell you everything, Ash. Or at least the small amount I knew."

"Do you know why she did it? Why she left that day without me?" Ash remembered the last time she saw Conor, a boyish fullness to his face. She looked at the almost gaunt face he wore now. A lot had changed since then.

"At the time, no. But later . . ." Conor leaned back, lowering his hands under the tabletop. "She wouldn't talk about you much, but I wore her down, eventually. She told me she had always known you needed protection. I don't know who from, but she made it sound like . . . like it was from everyone. She said 'if they found out about Ash, we would all perish'. Whenever I pushed her for more, she'd shut down and refuse to speak."

Ash's eyes darted back and forth, trying to make sense of what that meant. She came up blank. The bloodied, torn letter infiltrated her thoughts and her breath hitched.

"What did your last letter say? The one you only sent in the past two weeks."

Conor's eyebrows scrunched high on this forehead. "The last letter I posted was over two months ago."

The humming of Conor's refrigerator was the only sound as Ash processed this revelation. If the letter hadn't been from her brother, it had to have been from Cara, who had been involved in writing them all along. The pumping of her heart matched the pounding in her head. Why would her mother post something only to steal it back before she could read it?

"That night, she told me I had to come with her to meet someone. We got as far as the Hill of Tara and then . . . I can't remember anything else until I woke up by the River Boyne."

"In this realm or the other?"

"This one."

"That doesn't make any sense, Con. She was murdered in Newgrange: Tír na nÓg. Why was she at the Hill of Tara?"

"I wish I could remember." Conor's voice cracked, his hands gripping his floppy black curls.

"Hey, it's okay. You're doing amazing." The words felt flat even to her. "Come on, we'd better get some sleep."

Conor nodded, gesturing to his room. "You take my bed. I won't get much sleep, anyway.

"I'm not taking your bed, Con," Ash's voice was forceful and she continued when it was clear he was about to argue. "I'm quite happy with the floor."

Conor's mouth twitched. "I laid out a sleeping bag in case you came back. It's not very matriarch-like."

"It's perfect. Like old times." Ash smiled, remembering when she would bunk with him, when he was too scared to sleep on his own.

They made their way into his small room and he explained how this space was also used as his tattoo station, pointing out the different tools attached to the imposing chair that took up nearly as much space as his single bed. As he placed an extra pillow by the sleeping bag, she noticed two garment bags hanging on the built-in press handle. "What's this?"

"Our Cath uniforms. Tiernan had yours delivered here earlier."

Ash unzipped one bag, tracing the Breen family coat of arms stitched onto the leather jacket. A knight's helmet resting on top of the heraldry, green and red plumage, encompassed a red hand at its centre. Two u-shaped crescent moons on either side of a star floated above the hand. It had been seven years since she saw it. Not bothering to uncover the rest of the uniform, she noticed another bag on the floor. Glints of silver greeted her when she unzipped it. Unsheathing the top sword from its scabbard, she studied the intricate designs of the blade all the way up to the hilt. The pommel was made up of a copper trinity knot, balancing the blade. It had been recently cleaned and sharpened. She knew who it belonged to even before her brother spoke.

"It was Mam's." Conor stood close behind her. "Now, it's yours."

She nodded once before re-sheathing it, the weight of that statement far heavier than the steel in her hands. She knew how to use it, but never thought she'd need to for a Cath. After cleaning up and changing in his small bathroom, Ash settled on the floor by Conor, knowing fully that she would have no rest tonight.

CHAPTER 27

TIERNAN

The early morning hike did little to clear Tiernan's head. After his talk with Ash, he'd spent far too long searching through the detective's private files. He'd already done it, but hadn't told her last night. She had enough on her mind with the impending Cath. After she admitted to stealing the torn letter, he'd immediately hacked into the investigation files, finding they hadn't been able to clean the letter enough to decipher anything on it. Ash had sent him a photograph of her half and he'd scanned it into a private Chinese company software system. The full letter should be readable soon.

He'd spent the early hours re-reading anything, making sure he'd missed nothing. Detective Raymond O'Leary was meticulous, continuing to work the caillte case and Cara's murder case. Even though *he* had more files on his mother's missing persons case, he could appreciate the detective seemed competent in his handling of both. If only he could solve them.

Tiernan couldn't bring himself to look at Cara's body at first, having avoided the photos on his first visit. He'd read all documents, both official and on his private drives, as well as the coroner's report. It was clear from the detective's documents, Ash remained high on his list of suspects. It was only when there was nothing left to read, he forced himself to open the first digital photograph.

It wasn't an image of his matriarch he had wanted imprinted on his brain, but if it helped Ash and Conor find their mother's killer, he needed all the facts. His heart had plummeted to his stomach when the first image opened. After only a few clicks, he had to exit the carousel.

Through searching the thumbnail images, he only opened ones that were zoomed on particular wounds. From quick research, he had to agree with the coroner's report. The two puncture wounds around Cara's collarbone looked like they were from antlers.

As for the abrasion that ran down Cara's torso, that was something he would have to trust the coroner knew about. Searching for 'torn flesh from bare hands' led to some even more disturbing images, so that's when he switched off. The headache he got from staring at his screen, along with disturbing data running through on repeat, was an unwelcome companion as he trudged through a wet field towards the Hill of Tara alongside his clansmen.

Most of the clan, and all the elders, had woken early to see the warriors depart. Ash had been hauled into one vehicle with half the elders, including Mrs O'Malley. Tiernan was furious when he was forced to take a car with the others. The little confidence she'd seemed to have last night had vanished as he watched her pale, pinched expression wordlessly exit the car and begin trudging towards their destination. It would have been too risky to drive directly there, even in this early hour, and they couldn't abandon any vehicles for however long their time in Tír na nÓg would be.

He couldn't get much out of Ash, but apparently, they had made it clear that her disappearance confirmed she was not fit to rule as matriarch. Nothing short of winning first place in the Cath would change their decision to petition for a new matriarch—or disband the Breen clan. Tiernan knew

Brehon law as well as any of the elders. It was difficult, but not impossible.

If they won, that would mean Ash may choose to remain in Tír na nÓg, and therefore a secondary matriarch was a requirement for this realm. He looked to where Niamh walked with his cousin. She was kind, much nicer than Emer, but he didn't see the qualities needed in a leader. Mrs O'Malley clearly disagreed. Nobody would take that place other than her great niece. He was placing his trust in Ash and even though she couldn't see it yet, he knew she was their true leader. If only they had more warriors to have a fair chance of getting through the trials.

The more likely event would be for their clan to lose and if the elders split up . . . His jaw tightened. He would not let that happen. Moving to a new clan once was hard enough. These people were his family now.

Glancing at Ash, walking alongside her brother, their dark hair a perfect match to one another, his resolve was as steadfast as his heartbeat. He would help her win. The group was quiet; the only sounds coming from their bags and weapons jostling, along with footsteps from their black boots in the short grass. Birds chirped overheard, already hunting for their breakfast.

They each wore almost identical clothing, fit for the unknown terrain of what they'd face on the other side. There were many scrolls about Tír na nÓg and the High King's court, and tales told from seanchai. Fianna storytellers could only talk about that past, they knew very little about what this modern trial would be.

Tiernan looked to his chest, where a fist size emblem of the Breen coat of arms rested on their leather jackets, and he wondered how Maebh felt about it. His chest tightened when he imagined wearing his mother's family crest, but that clan was gone. He would find her, and his world would be righted once more.

Looking skyward, he noted it was a cloudless morning, muted by dusk but brightening; with every step brought the promise of sunlight.

Tiernan's attention shifted ahead, where the rolling hills had emerged. "Hopefully, the gate isn't too rusted to use."

"Why would it be?" It was the first Ash had spoken since admitting what the elders had said. As he looked at his new matriarch, he realised how the uniform suited her. She looked like she belonged, if only she'd believed it.

Hoping to distract her, Tiernan continued, "It's rarely used. The Cath is the only reason the High King has granted us access."

An old padlocked gate kept tourists out of the underground passage, but fear of breaking Brehon law kept Fianna out. It wasn't the offence that deterred them, but the punishment if caught. The archaic laws were every bit as barbaric as 'an eye for an eye'. If caught breaking a code, the breaking of bones and a stay at the High King's infamous dungeons was an unwelcome reality. He had heard that anyone who went down there did not come out the same person, if they came out at all.

Cara had always been brave, but she was never foolish. Or so he had thought. Spotting the hill in the distance, he wondered why she had come here leading up to her death. He turned towards Ash and opened his mouth to speak, but when he saw Conor's pinched face, he thought better of voicing his questions. His complexion was paler than normal as his eyes scanned the area like a nervous tick. He would speak to her later when he told her about his research last night.

Cara and Conor had been missing for days before her body was found. Time was fluid in Tír na nÓg so it was hard to know when they'd come here, and Conor couldn't seem to answer even that simple question. Had she intended to use the portal? She must have been desperate to do something as drastic as using the High King's personal access to his court. Although, there had been rumours about her history with him—

"What are you thinking about?" Ash asked beside him, her pace quickening to match his longer strides.

Glancing again at Conor, he shook his head, mouthing, "Later".

She sighed, her shoulders dropping, shifting her rucksack. "Just say it. You don't think I'm capable of this either."

"What?" Tiernan stopped, frowning down at her as she crossed her arms. "Don't let the elders get to you. Remember, they think I'm not strong enough to be here. Look at these shoulders; I've managed to carry my own bags for this entire trip . . . so far."

Ash let out a reluctant laugh as the others, including Conor, walked ahead.

"Why do you have more bags than anyone else, anyway?" Ash gestured to her rucksack that towered above her head.

"Ah yes, you don't know about my experiment yet. Let's just say I can't bear to be without cell service for more than a few minutes. I'm going to fix that problem."

Maebh chuckled up ahead but kept moving. They hadn't spoken much this morning, and Tiernan felt strangely unnerved by that. After waking from the little sleep he had got, the first thing he'd thought about was how she had looked straddling the tattoo chair. It probably had something to do with the fact he'd woken lying on his newly inked side and the pain a reminder of what they'd done. It had nothing to do with how beautiful her sun-kissed skin was, or how there never seemed to be enough air when she was around.

He took a step towards his matriarch, placing a hand on her shoulder. "You're more than able for this. And you have us."

She looked towards the clansmen, lowering her voice. "I barely know any of you. Not even my cousins. They haven't even spoken to me yet."

They both watched their small group continuing towards the grassed mound in the distance. Ciarán and Tomás Breen remained a few feet behind everyone else, the brothers deep in conversation. Both had the same black unruly hair, an attribute that all Breens seemed to share.

"We all still have your back," Tiernan said, signalling for them to follow.

Ash gave a noncommittal grunt in response, but walked alongside him.

"I was thinking about your mother, and the reasons she had come here before . . . she was attacked."

Ash seemed to tense for a moment but nodded as she kept up with him, both careful of where they stepped as sheep grazed only feet away. "Any ideas?"

"Not really. Her focus had waned in the weeks leading to her—"

"Murder. It's okay, you can say that. I'm not going to fall apart."

Tiernan's throat tightened as he kept the fact that he might be the one to fall apart to himself. Swallowing it down, he said, "She rarely spoke at meetings and whenever she did, it had been in riddles. Her body was found in Newgrange, so why had she planned to meet somebody on this hill? What if she'd been meeting someone from the High King's court?"

"Why would you think that?"

"It would make sense to meet here if it was someone who needed to sneak under the king's nose."

Or was he way off base? Tiernan looked at the grass just in time to avoid stepping in sheep droppings.

"We'll talk more later," Ash said as her focus turned to her brother, who had distanced himself from the group ahead. She didn't wait for his response as she hurried towards him.

Adjusting the weight of his bags, he jogged to join the others, his attention still on their conversation. The High King's court lay on the other side of the veil.

At the thought of court, Tiernan's jaw ticked. The High King's rígfennids would undoubtedly be present today, instead of ruling over their province on behalf of their king. It had been a long time since he'd seen his dad. Being Rígfennid of Leinster would put a strain on any father's time. But Tiernan knew it had more to do with his mother's disappearance. Bradan Cassidy hadn't been the same after his wife disappeared. Tiernan wondered if his father believed what the papers had reported, the ridiculous rumours she had run off with her lover, Gearoid McQuillan. What did Maebh think of the rumours between his mother and her father?

"It's a grand day for it," Maebh's voice carried in the wind as she led their party.

Emer called from just ahead of him. "For what, Mae?"

Maebh twirled, her rucksack spinning with her as she raised her arms. "To kick some ass."

The surrounding group cheered. All except Ash. Conor's sombre demeanour still hadn't morphed back into the cheerful man he was so used to. By the time Tiernan realised he hadn't joined in either, it was too late. Not that he was feeling Maebh's enthusiasm at that moment. He glanced at the others. His cousin was a few feet ahead, with Niamh, who was fussing over one of Emer's bag straps, her ginger hair shining in the low hanging sun that had just appeared.

There had been at least half a dozen more who Cara had selected to join the Cath trials, but after her death, the elders had insisted they needed them to stay behind and guard the remaining clan. Tiernan felt sorry for the ones left behind. He had nearly been one of them, but not for reasons as grand as protection. Disappointment burrowed deep in his bones at the possibility. It would only be a shadow to how they must have felt watching the group depart. Not that he wanted to undergo the gruesome trials, but it was an honour that everyone should be allowed to take. The only person who should be able to decide their fate was them—not a group of wrinkled fools who couldn't switch on a phone between them.

"We're here." Maebh ran towards the mound as the others quickened their pace.

In the early morning, no tourists roamed around the undulating, frost-crusted grassland. A renovated church lay in the distance, surrounded by a stone wall and large oak trees, tendrils of fog still present. The group chattered excitedly as they crossed the field that transformed into sloping hills that would be any rally biker's wet dream. Maebh raced to a hill in the distance where a metre-high cylindrical stone and tombstone lay. Tiernan jogged the incline, his heavy packs jostling across his back.

"Lia Fáil," Maebh whispered, her breath sending a wisp of steam in the cold air.

Stone of Destiny. He stared at the ancient stone, full of unknown power, a gift from the Tuatha Dé Danann to the Fianna High King, Fionn Mac Cumhaill, after the Peace Treaty that was signed over a millennium ago. The scrolls he'd read during his studies had said little about it other than giving it two names, the other being the Speaking Stone. If Tiernan ever accessed the High King's library, he was sure he'd discover more about them. They said the stone had cried out when the rightful king was ordained. It did for Fionn, but not for their current king, Aedan O'Dwyer.

Tiernan wondered if it did more. The Fair Ones weren't known for their generosity. When they gifted you, it always came at a price. A humming current rumbled on the grassland, something strong enough to get through his heavy boots. He imagined it was like an electric circuit board, and the energy originating from the standing stone. Tiernan knew of magic in this world. How could he not with the gift of Faerie Sight?

He leaned towards the things he could control: technology and science. This, however, was raw. He felt its power, and almost swore he could see it ripple underneath, deep below the soil. The grass didn't just sway in the breeze; it pulsed. Like a slumbering presence, the stone waited to be woken, to be used for something *more*. He raised his hand to touch it—

"Does anyone else think it looks like a penis?" Maebh asked, arranging her hands as if measuring the stone.

"Sweet, suffering . . ." Niamh muttered as Emer burst into laughter, the next pair to have crested the hill.

Tiernan lowered his hand and smirked at Maebh, whose smile radiated more warmth than the weak autumn sun. "You're all thinking it."

"Anyone know how to use this portal?" Ash asked as she appeared, a bemused tone mixed with what Tiernan guessed was nerves.

They retreated to the remaining group, and then towards the hill they would use. A padlocked gate sat at its base, where the opening lay for the passageway. The lock looked old but standard. Tiernan reached into one of his deep-set pockets at the leg of his combat trousers. Taking out his thin canvas kit, he opened the fabric to display his tools as the others watched.

"So we can add breaking and entering to your long list of skills, kitten," Maebh murmured close to his ear as he stuck a pronged key into one side of the lock and twisted a similar prong to the other side. Her breath tickled his skin, but he didn't answer as he concentrated. Within minutes, the padlock dropped to the floor. Tiernan didn't hide his smile as he wrenched the creaking gate outward and gestured for Ash to enter. "Matriarchs first."

Her smile was tight as she grabbed Conor's arm to follow her. One by one, the others went through the small space. Through closed bars, it looked no larger than a caravan bathroom, but having just witnessed six other people disappear through the low entrance, Tiernan knew fae glamour was at play. Bending himself nearly in two, he walked through the opening before securing the lock back in place.

Four or five strides in, the smell of damp earth filled his senses. He could hear the shuffles and murmurs of his group, but the farther away from the only source of light, darkness consumed him. With his vision impaired, his other senses kicked in. Every sound was heightened to the point even hearing a light cough up ahead made him jump. The feeling of cold, stifled air and earth made him shiver. The strain on the back of his thighs was a signal they were descending.

"Anyone have a light?"

Somebody wordlessly turned on a flashlight, something he wished he'd thought to bring as he followed. It was like a pinprick of guidance in a depthless black. Tiernan fumbled inside his pocket, scolding himself for not remembering the constant in this life. The thing that never let him down. Technology.

Tiernan cast his phone torch from floor to ceiling and left to right as they moved deeper through the tunnel. There was a very real possibility he could fall into a bottomless crevice, and having the others moving ahead of him did little to ease that fear. They would fall first, but then he'd have to save them.

Saving wasn't one of his strong points.

CHAPTER 28

MAEBH

More lights shone as the others turned on their torches. There was a dampness to the air that Maebh could both taste and smell, along with the scents she associated with excitement wafting from the others.

She used a slimy, low hanging stalactite to right her slippery footing, the constant sporadic dripping of unseen water an ever present companion. Ducking low, in fear she'd smash her head, she paid attention to the footsteps of the others. Nobody spoke, all caught up in staying upright and moving forward.

Tiernan cursed behind her, and she turned in time to see him stumble into a deep puddle. Aiming his torch to the ground, he leapt up to the dry path on the other side.

"Mind your step, kitten," Maebh said, training her light on his face so he had to raise his hand to block her. It elicited a curse from his lips, causing her own to turn up.

Tiernan shook his foot, his trousers already clinging to his leg. "Thanks for the warning."

"You've got to keep your wits about you." Maebh chuckled as she walked backwards.

"Don't you think you should face forward?" Tiernan quickened his pace but scowled at her chuckle.

Soft murmurings floated back to them, but they were growing fainter. She opened her mouth to retort, but before she could, her foot met nothing and she stumbled backwards. Raising her arms, she tried to lean her body weight toward safety, her heavy rucksack weighing her down. Tiernan lurched forward, grabbing Maebh by one of her bag straps, pulling her toward him until she could feel solid ground underneath her feet once more.

Maebh's phone slipped from her hand in the process, and they both watched as it descended into the nothingness below, and with it one of the few remaining connections she had with her father. As her flashlight disappeared, she strained to hear any sign it had collided with the ground. The only sounds that met her were their rasping breaths and the damned dripping water.

Tiernan's torch was muted by his grip on Maebh and it was only then that he seemed to realise he was holding her. Releasing her, he took a few steps back, training his torch along the ground to see how big the hole was.

She turned towards the pit with a frown, her curled ponytail sticking to her neck. "I guess I should thank you."

"Maebh, your phone . . ." Tiernan gripped her arms. "We can try to find a way to get it."

She just shook her head, even as her heart spasmed and she fought back tears. "It's only a phone."

She heard the hollowness in her words and wondered if he did too. They both knew it wasn't just a phone. They stared at each other as the voices of the others came back to them. She fought the jolts of nerves taking over her limbs, and instead of concentrating on losing another piece of her father, she remembered how lucky she was. If she'd fallen, she'd have died.

"Are you guys okay?"

He angled his phone to find Emer and Niamh standing on the other side of what could only be described as a manhole. It was roughly circular, the pathway on either side large enough to walk around. Maebh continued to look at the pit, grateful she wouldn't find out if it was bottomless.

"You could have warned us about this," Tiernan's tone was filled with a fury she hadn't heard before.

Sure, she'd heard him severely aggravated, mostly by her, but this was different. His face was contorted in a scowl, his chest heaving as he gripped his phone tightly. When his gaze snapped to hers, she felt an odd thrill run through her. His gaze softened as he offered his hand and helped guide her around the pit cave.

Emer aimed her own torch at the hole, a look of puzzlement on her face. "No one else noticed it."

"I guess I'm the lucky girl," Maebh said, righting her straps and jutting her chin towards the others. "Come on, we have a High King to meet."

They trudged on through the ever narrowing tunnel, the moistened air pressing on her as she fought against the thought they were walking willingly into a grave. The sound of Tiernan behind her was a comfort and he held his torch high enough to aid her steps instead of his.

Just when the roof and ground met to where they had to crawl, she wondered when the nightmare would be over. All she wanted was to get to the High King's court.

"There's more light up ahead," Ash's voice drifted back.

Several people sighed in relief. After a couple of feet, she could see the darkness had broken. The ceiling finally rose and as she righted herself, she found the others huddled together in a small cavern. With Tiernan joining soon after, it was a tight fit.

"Which way?" Ash asked, directing her torch to several openings.

Maebh frowned as she cast her gaze over each of them, all as clueless as one another. Why didn't the damned scroll give them a map to Tír na nÓg? Each clan had received an invitation by the High King to come, but it seemed the trials began now, with finding how to get to his blasted Tara Court.

Tiernan dumped his bags on the already cluttered ground and reached for his toolkit again, scratching above the entranceway they'd just crawled through. "Let's each choose an entrance and walk a few paces in, but no more, and then meet back here. Keep a lookout for anything that might direct us to the High King's court."

"Good idea," Ash said, and Maebh couldn't help but notice her clipped tone.

Tiernan did too, because his attention snapped to her with a frown. He opened his mouth to say something else, but Ash disappeared through a tunnel, its opening almost identically low to the one they'd come through.

From her unseen positioning, she called out, "Pick a tunnel and walk in fifty paces and then come back here."

As the others disappeared, Maebh turned to Tiernan. "I'm sticking with you."

He raised his brows, but she gestured to her free hands. "No flashlight."

With a shrug, he motioned to one tunnel that was barely larger than a crevice. "We'll take this one."

"Can we even get through it?"

"There's something down there," Tiernan said, angling his head toward the narrow opening. "Can you hear that?"

She stood closer, straining for anything out of the ordinary, but other than cold blasts of air, she shook her head. "But, gentleman's choice."

Loosening the clasps of her own bag, she let it fall beside his, only then noticing a slumped figure where the rest of the discarded bags were.

"Con, do you want to check this one out with us?" Tiernan asked, his light angled just above the young man's head.

Conor hugged his arms to his chest tightly, his rucksack towering above his head. "I'll wait here."

Tiernan entered his passageway first, and when she followed, she was relieved to find it was tall enough that they didn't need to stoop. What it made up in height, it lacked in width.

Heading forward was a struggle, and Tiernan angled sideways, shuffling through the bubbled walls. She grit her teeth. "Remind me again, not to let you choose."

Cursing, she ignored his chuckle as her chest felt like it was going through a compressor, but she eventually pushed through to another antechamber. This time, there was only one tunnel entrance and she peered into it as Tiernan trained his light. Nothing but darkness greeted them and then a force of air so strong they both stumbled back.

"I don't think this is the way, kitten," Maebh shouted over the ever increasing wind.

He ignored her, his attention fixated on the wall in front of him, his light moving up and down it until it zeroed in on something. Even in the dark, this wall looked different to the others they'd passed. It was too smooth, and the stone was so sleek it looked like marble.

Turning her back to the tunnel, she caught her breath as she looked at the markings he'd found on the wall. Nothing like the crude x-shape he'd used to distinguish their entrance; these were swirls and lettering of an ancient tongue. Moving close enough their shoulders touched, she ran her hand along a symbol she recognised: the triskelion. Two swirling spirals topped with a third, all joining at its centre. It was a symbol that both Fianna and Fair Ones used to depict the act of life, death and rebirth.

"Do you hear that?" Tiernan asked, his voice almost lost in the rising wind.

She shook her head, wiping stray strands of hair from her face.

"Not the wind," he said, looking at the unknown tunnel. "There's a thrumming."

"We better get back," Maebh said, a shiver running through her. She tugged on his arm when he stepped closer to the other entranceway. "Tiernan."

He stood for another moment, his expression pinched as if he were trying to solve a puzzle, but he nodded once, signalling for her to lead the way. Sucking in a breath, she charged through the narrow opening, thankful for the thick coat she wore as a barrier.

Conor's panicked voice came from ahead, almost unheard over the wind. "They went in there ages ago."

Several torches trained on Maebh as she sidled through the tunnel opening. She shook her head to the many questioning eyes, dusting off her jacket as Tiernan appeared from the cave mouth. Emer's gaze flicked back and forth between her cousin and Maebh, and she swallowed.

"I think I found the tunnel leading to the court," Ash said, a small smile on her lips. "But, Tiernan, you both were in that tunnel for longer. Do you think yours has a better chance?"

Tiernan opened his mouth, but closed it with a frown, directing his torch behind him.

"No, it seems to go on forever, but I don't think it leads to where we want to go," Maebh answered, an unease she couldn't place covering her. She refused to look at her ex-girlfriend, focusing on her new matriarch instead. When she thought of going back through that tunnel, she sensed something in the air, a buzzing warning that seized her throat and made her heart beat faster.

Tiernan stepped forward, once again their shoulders touching. "Maebh's right. Lead the way, Matriarch."

Her smile widened as she nodded once, a look of determination on her face. "Let's go."

They followed Ash in the same order they had before, the Breen brothers directly behind Conor, Emer and Niamh after him, and then Maebh ahead of Tiernan.

"Did you feel that?" she asked, staying close to the tall warrior behind. "That tunnel was … off."

Tiernan's frown was almost indiscernible in the dim light. "There was something strange about it. I trust Ash found the right path."

After several minutes of quiet trudging through a much wider tunnel, but low ceiling, she saw why Ash had chosen it.

Depictions of Fianna warriors and coats of arms for prominent Fianna clans lined both walls. She traced her fingers along the McQuillan drawing, the standard knight's helmet and heraldry, and then a lone wolf on hind legs, its claws outstretched. She couldn't fight the pang in her chest, her thoughts immediately going to her twin.

"Anyone hear that?" Ash asked, directing her torch forward, her brow creased.

When everyone's footsteps halted, Maebh heard it, too. "Music."

The group collectively increased their pace, and soon there was an incline and more roof space, along with glorious flickering light. Once more convening in a small opening that barely fit all seven of them, but this time there were sconces holding flaming torches. The sound of a fiddle drifted towards them.

"Everyone ready?" Ash asked, her slight frame still leading the group.

"Ready as we'll ever be, Matriarch." That was Ciarán or Tomás, she wasn't sure. They'd barely spoken to her, but then again, none of the Breen clan had been welcoming so far.

It was hard to tell the brothers apart in broad daylight, never mind here. Both similar height, they were muscular and fierce, everything you'd expect from hardened warriors. She'd enjoy training with them and kicking their asses.

Ash's shadowed figure pressed against the stone wall between two torches, and it gave way. It was only when Maebh passed through the opening that she saw the handle embedded in the wall. They were now in a slightly bigger room, like some sort of antechamber, the new selection of stone doorways easier to distinguish in the flickering torches along the stretch of wall. Two guards stood to attention, directly facing them.

"Who are you?" a gruff voice greeted them. Dressed in all black, their long cloaks did little to shield the array of weapons each carried.

"Aisling Breen, and this is my clan." Ash's voice sounded strong, if not a little rushed. "We are here for the Cath."

One guard pressed the wall behind him and again, another door opened. Fresher air greeted them as they walked the stone arched pathway, along with the mouthwatering smell of savoury meat. She wasn't sure whose stomach growled, but she echoed the sentiment. Windowless, and almost as narrow as the passageway, she followed her new clan as a guard led them on.

"You're the last clan to arrive," the guard stated. "This way."

They walked in silence for another few minutes until finally a wooden door greeted them. More guards manned it, but this time, they were let through without question.

"Fina-fucking-ly," Maebh muttered as they walked through to what appeared to be a night-time festival.

CHAPTER 29

AISLING

S tars twinkled with a low hanging crescent moon, and Ash stood with her clan as they surveyed the festival. They'd emerged from a base of a hill, but the lantern lit dwellings were far below. The air was much warmer than the tunnels, and beads of sweat formed along her neck, joining her already drenched skin. The uniform fit perfectly, and Ash wondered if Tiernan had had a lucky guess, or he'd known from his hacking what size she wore. Deciding the answer would only piss her off, she left it unquestioned. Straightening her leather jacket, she smoothed out her dark combat trousers that were tucked into her laced boots. The black shirt she wore underneath stuck to her, and she already wanted to change.

Shifting her bag, its weight heavy with the weapons attached, she was hesitant to join the throngs of people. From this high vantage, she could see the entire village and impossibility of where she now stood. She'd entered this realm through Newgrange before, but to stand within the High King's court, where hundreds of Fianna gathered, stole her breath.

They stood near the Hill of Tara, but besides the familiar slopes she was used to, it was another world. A tall stone wall stretched for miles, encompassing them within a village lower down. It was as if they'd dug into the ground by the ancient hills, and they now stood on the only elevated ground for miles besides the mountainous walls. She craned her neck and could only just make out movement from the top of the wall where she assumed guards stood watch. If the High King needed a wall that tall for protection, Ash dreaded to think what creatures lay beyond. She knew of the merrow and realised just how lucky she had been that Set was on the outside of this wall at the exact time she'd needed him. The druid Ethne's words of finding an ally replayed in her mind.

"Let's go," Ash said, still unsure whether she'd made the right choice. She tugged on Conor's arm, ensuring he walked beside her as they descended. He was the only one who'd refused to carry any weapons and although Ash wondered why, he'd insisted on coming. It was one of the few things her brother was clear on. He needed to be in this realm. If he'd been content to stay in the human world, she knew deep down that she wouldn't be playing matriarch and the Breen clan would have been a larger group than what now followed behind her.

Thatched cottages and stone storefronts were the first buildings they passed and it was only when they reached the first dirt road that Ash realised how many narrow alleys and streets there were. She stopped when they stood on the outskirts of what looked like an old town market square, where throngs of people were enjoying food and drink while listening to music from an unseen band. In the distance, a castle she could have plucked out of a fairy tale loomed; nowhere near as high as the stone walls surrounding them, but impressive in the way grand buildings were.

Dancing had broken out around sporadic fire pits, the many instruments and merry footwork vibrating through the soles of her boots and up her bones.

"I didn't realise there would be so many people," Ash muttered as the group convened around her. "What do we do now?"

"Greet the High King and thank him for the honour of being here," Maebh advised, her ice-blue eyes darting everywhere. It was the first time she'd seen her look nervous. "He should be this way."

After checking their bags in at a designated area, but holding on to their weapons at the insistence of Tomás and Ciarán, Maebh led the group through the festival, a mix of clans dressed in warrior gear like them and frocks and attire from every known century. Fianna who had been granted the privilege of living in Tír na nÓg often kept their dress sense from the era when they were born. Walking through this crowd was like walking through a fancy dress party. Bell-bottoms and ruffled shirts, flapper and bustle styled dresses mixed with tweed suits and high-waisted trousers. Ash had to dodge a pair of shoulder pads that nearly poked her eye.

"There's the throne," Emer said, directing Ash by the arm, subtly pushing her close to a wooden platform at the centre of the market square. "Wait, do you know the proper protocol when addressing the High King?"

"Too late, he saw us," Niamh whispered, taking Emer's hand from what had turned into a vice grip on Ash's arm.

Tiernan cursed under his breath, but Ash didn't turn to look at him as the High King's table quietened and he waved his hand to stop the person beside him from continuing their conversation. His dark eyes found hers.

"So the new matriarch has finally arrived." The High King of Fianna lounged on his throne, a crown glinting from the brown hair that curled around his thick neck. He wore a dark cloak which fell over one broad shoulder, the other displaying a loose white shirt. Although there was a table and a raised platform between them, Ash could see chocolate-coloured eyes glinting over the raised goblet he held to his lips, curled in a smile that hinted he was a man that laughed at you more times than with.

All she could think was, *that's* the High King?

Somebody, probably Maebh, pinched her arm and even though she wore a leather jacket, it hurt. Shaking herself out of her stupor, she stepped closer to the platform. Bowing from the waist, she placed her right forearm across her body, thumping her chest three times in what she hoped to have correctly remembered as the greeting all Fianna made to the High King.

"It is an honour to be here, High King," Ash said, still lowered. She didn't dare lift her gaze, afraid that at any moment he would admonish her for not greeting him correctly, or the crowd would burst out laughing at how foolish she looked. She wasn't sure which one was worse. The air moved behind her and she could sense rather than see that her clan had also bowed.

"Rise, Breen clan," the High King said. His smile displayed a dimple as he added, "It is lovely to see you again, Aisling."

She blinked. *Again*? Was she allowed to ask if they'd met before? As if knowing what she thought, he continued.

"You were very young the last time we met. I knew your parents well. I was saddened by the news of what happened to Cara. May her soul continue on."

"And her love remain," Ash murmured.

A prickle of emotion danced on the rim of her lashes, but she blinked the tear away. She didn't know whether it was because she mourned her mother, or that she seemed to have got something right for once, even if it was only a simple greeting to the king. Other than continuing with her athleticism, she hadn't kept many other traditions. She had spent most of her life immersed in their culture, *her* culture; at least some things seemed to have stuck.

The surrounding merry goers came to life around them, and music trickled back to her ears. Or had they really stopped and gawked at her like she had thought? She stepped back, closer to her clan. Did he expect anything else? Should she bow again and move away?

"And is that your brother I see standing behind you? Conor, I never had the pleasure of meeting you. You look like a good mix of both your parents." The High King set his goblet down, his gaze darting behind Ash for a moment before snaring her once more. "Aisling . . . I could never make out who you looked like."

Ash nodded but couldn't help the frown that formed. Conor made no attempt at responding and she wanted desperately to check if he was okay, but she couldn't risk offending the High King by turning before he dismissed her. A grey clad figure appeared behind the High King and as Ash noted the mix of pale flesh and colourful tattoos, the white-blonde druid placed a hand on his broad shoulder and whispered in his ear.

Her clansmen remained as still as her as they watched their brief exchange. Then, King Aedan's smile widened and he gazed at Ash, winking before signalling to the druid. Ethne straightened and clapped her jewel clad hands once in a loud bang. The surrounding noises muted instantly, and it was only when he spoke, she realised the druid had performed some sort of trick to make all other sounds dim.

High King Aedan raised both hands in greeting. "I welcome you all to Tara Court, my fellow clansmen."

Ash looked at the crowds while placing her palm to her right ear, rubbing to clear the ringing in it. Even though fire pits were lit and there were hundreds of people around, it was as if someone had used a remote control, decreasing the volume so that only his voice rang through. She noticed most people were in similar discomfort and cast her gaze on Ethne, whose grey eyes met hers and a knowing smiled splayed on her pale lips. Ash shivered as she tuned back into what Aedan was saying.

"Many of you have never been here and I humbly hope it is all that you've heard it would be. Brehon law declares that when Fianna warriors retire, the High King must choose a new set of warriors through our Cath."

The crowd shuffled excitedly and Ash imagined there would have been cheers if everyone hadn't been placed on mute. She cleared her throat and noticed that no sound came out, just an increase in that humming white noise, the pressure on her ears growing. From beside her, Maebh's face lit up in a rare smile at the mention of the trials. Her own stomach dropped at the realisation she was really doing this. Glancing to her other side, she cast her eyes on the reason she was here. Conor looked paler, more withdrawn, as he stared up at the raised table.

The High King continued, "What you have read in the scrolls, and the rumours circulating about the trials are not what I have planned for you. To be deemed worthy, you must . . . impress me."

This time, Ash didn't need to hear anything to know the discontent and shock emanating from everyone around her. She frowned. What did he mean? Her gift kicked in and the smell of soured bread filled her nostrils as some in the crowd tried to speak, but only that white noise increased to a painful level. The High King beckoned for order, raising his hands for a silence he already had. "Fear not, you are all loyal warriors and I'm sure you will succeed."

He sat back in his throne, raising his goblet with a gleam in his brown eyes as Ethne addressed the crowd. She stood to his right, resting a hand on the back of his chair. "The High King has given you a worthy quest. One right here, in this court. The Kingdom of Mede is full of legends of lost treasure. Find one, and your High King will reward you. At sunrise, you will be granted access to the castle and all the lands within the court.

"You know the lore. It is time to put your knowledge to the test. Strength is not the only value of a Fianna warrior. You need wisdom, courage and luck."

Ethne clapped her hands once more, and the festival noises came back in that one motion. The thunderous sounds of many voices filled the air, and Ash fought to keep up with the change in energy. When she looked back to the raised table, the High King and druid were gone.

CHAPTER 30

AISLING

"That was confusing as fuck," Maebh muttered beside Ash.

She had to agree as she stared at the space where the High King and his druid had vanished. A man who looked vaguely familiar stood from his spot beside the vacant throne. His cloak wasn't as ornate as the king's, but his position of power was clear in his attire, along with his seat at the high table. Before turning, he nodded to Tiernan and then exited the platform.

"That's Bradan Cassidy," Tiernan murmured close to Ash's ear. "Rígfennid of Leinster. And my father."

"Your father rules over Leinster?" Ash looked back at his retreating figure, swallowed up by the moving crowd. She hadn't seen him long enough to draw any similarities, but the rígfennid was far burlier than his son with a look of a warrior who had seen battle. There hadn't been one between Fianna and the Fair Ones since long before their time, but being a human leader in this realm was wrought in danger. The Tuatha Dé Danann were not known for their empathy or patience when it came to any human breaking Brehon law. The ancient laws were known to only favour one race, and it wasn't hers.

"Yes, under High King Aedan's favour. Did I not mention that before?"

"You definitely didn't."

"Oh," Tiernan stated, his brown eyes trained on the stage.

There were others still seated on the long table, and only one whose face stood out to Ash. He was looking at her in between an exchange with his companion, both dressed in ornate robes similar to Tiernan's father. Her grandfather, Cara's father, was Rígfennid of Munster. Although matriarchs oversaw clans, rígfennids were answerable to only the High King. All were answerable to the Fair Ones, of course. She refused to meet his gaze. Turning before he attempted to address her, she linked arms with her brother.

"Are you okay, Con?"

Conor's face was still withdrawn, his delicate features cast in dancing shadows, and if possible, he looked even paler as his attention remained to where the High King and his druid had retreated. The dark circles under his eyes told a story of a fitful night before. That made two of them.

"It's just . . . a bit too much."

She gave her brother's arm a squeeze and he let her angle him away from the crowded centre of the party.

"Come on. Let's get something to drink," Maebh suggested, her gaze constantly moving.

Perhaps she was looking for the McQuillan clan. Ash did her own scan and couldn't fight her disappointment that she hadn't been able to spot Set. He was nowhere near, she noted, because he would have loomed above everyone else. They made their way to a row of stalls lined around the square. The rich smells of crackling meat on spit roasts, along with gravy and roasted vegetables, made Ash's mouth fill with watery appreciation. She hadn't eaten since Mary's stew the previous night and even though it was technically only noon; it was nighttime here. The time warp was mind-boggling. As they passed a stall serving sugary treats, her cousin, Ciarán, took her arm with a gentle pressure and gestured to the following stalls serving drinks.

"Everything is safe to eat and drink, except poitín, Matriarch. Don't even smell it or you won't be able to see until next week."

"Thanks, Ciarán. Please call me Ash."

He only nodded, which made her think he wouldn't. It was strange. She'd grown up with Ciarán and his brother, Tomás, who trailed behind them. They had been childhood friends and family. For her first seventeen years, she would have considered them her best friends. Her cousins had said nothing to her since her return, nor had they tried to reach out to her beforehand. They were a couple of years older and had behaved like overprotective brothers when they were younger. It had hurt that not one of her clan had ever tried to contact her, except Conor—and also her mother, according to his confession last night. Seeing them now didn't make that pain any less. So much had changed, and now she was their matriarch.

The stalls were teeming with patrons, all queuing in disarray. Ash joined one line at a food stall, the aromatic spices floating to her, along with what she now realised was wafting of surrounding emotions. She wasn't sure what each scent meant and made a mental note to ask Maebh if they experienced the same smells for feelings. Any time she caught an alien smell, it sparked a memory that had caused her to feel a certain way.

She was almost to the front of the line when a couple of warriors from another clan pushed in front of her, one of them swaying so much his jug of beer sloshed onto her boots. Before she could so much as lift her foot to shake off the unwanted beverage, a flash of black curls loomed forward and the drunken warrior was shoved away from her and out of the line.

"You owe my matriarch an apology." Tomás' voice was low and deep; teeming with simmering anger.

Sulphurous, Ash noted. She put her hand on his thick arm, about to tell him it was okay, and she could fight her own battles.

"Matriarch?" the warrior asked, looking her up and down in a way that made her teeth grit. "You're the newly orphaned Breen girl, right? Kicked out of her clan only to rule over them. Bet they're sorry now, love."

A warning growl sounded from Tomás, and her grip on his arm tightened. "Leave it, Tom. They're drunken idiots."

"You know what we heard about you, wee girl?" The other warrior said, joining his friend's swaying side. "That you killed your mammy out of revenge. Drank her blood on Samhain and made a deal with the devil himself. Rumour has it you wore his horns as you did it. There's dark wiccan blood in you, lass."

Ciarán was by his brother's side in an instant, both now flanking Ash and holding her back. With one hand on his scabbard, her newly arrived cousin went face to face with one of them, who chuckled. Ash stopped trying to push past to get to them as Ciarán began laughing, much louder and more obnoxious than either, until the surrounding crowd had all stopped and stared. Slapping his thigh, he withdrew his sword.

All traces of humour, that had never matched his scent, disappeared as he said, "Apologise, if you're fond of those tiny balls remaining attached between your legs, boys."

Ash wasn't sure what would have happened if the kingsguard hadn't walked by. Wearing steel armour and mesh helmets, their dark cloaks rippled behind them like trapped midnight. Armed with weapons, Ash was sure she wouldn't be able to pronounce the names of, their imposing figures stopped in their patrol. A penetrating gaze never wavered from the six-piece until the drunken clansmen muttered their apologies—not directed toward her, she noted—and moved away. The king's highguard remained stationed by the stalls until Ash and her clansmen filled their plates and hurried away.

Those were the warriors the winning clan would join?

After retrieving drinks, Ash followed her group to a long bench close to the lively céilí band. There were around twelve musicians, all sitting on a lone bench nearest the dance floor, which was really the cobblestones of the village square. They didn't need a raised platform to command attention. The musicians looked chaotic, hollering and yipping in between, raising a toast with the crowd before downing their drinks. All while never missing a beat from their instruments.

As Ash looked beyond the band and to the other tables, it was clear they were the smallest clan here. Others filled several rows of tables, their coat of arms displayed proudly on similar uniforms to her own. Did they all think the same as those two fools? The detective had made it clear she was a suspect, and her fellow Fianna seemed to agree. To think anyone would believe she'd kill her own mother . . . A shudder ran through her.

Between mouthfuls of delicious food, she tried not to think about how slim of a chance they had at winning the Cath, and at how thinly veiled the threat was from the Breen elders. One look around and she knew that their claim of needing to keep all their warriors with them instead of joining Ash was a way of ensuring she would fail.

And with that failure, her days as matriarch would end. She was about to ask if she should send word to the Breen clan and insist that more join them, but stopped. She wouldn't send Conor, Tiernan, or Maebh, and if she sent any of the others, could she trust they would return? Her cousins had defended her during that confrontation, but why would they barely look at her since she'd returned? If she sent either of them, would she be leaving their small group with one less warrior? Time was different here, so even if they intended to return in time, they may miss the entire Cath.

The elders had screwed her.

"Your address to the High King went well," Emer said in between eating a caramel glazed pear. Ash noted how clipped her voice was, but ignored it as the dark-skinned warrior studied her from across the table. Her brown eyes were unreadable, but her stench of animosity was undeniable. "How did you know what to do?"

"I was raised in the Breen clan." Ash shrugged. "I guess some things stuck."

"Well, thank fuck for that." Maebh patted Ash on the back as she took a deep drink from her mead horn. "I heard that sometimes it doesn't matter how well your clan does. It's really the High King's decision who he permits into his warrior clan."

Tiernan scoffed from the seat beside her. "Where did you hear that? The last Cath was a hundred years ago."

"Do you think he will let you in if he doesn't like you?" Maebh retorted. "Of course he has a say. This is the first time High King Aedan has changed his guard; he's doing it for a reason."

"Tradition dictates—"

"Who gives a fu—"

"Daughter, there you are." A delicate, tanned hand landed on Maebh's shoulder, causing her to flinch. "Perhaps we can have a word."

Maebh lifted her drink as she stood. "I'll be back in a while, Matriarch."

Imogen's smile tightened at her daughter's address, but she only inclined her head towards Ash before gliding through the crowd. Ash took a sip of her sweet wine as she watched Maebh follow her mother. Imogen was every bit how Ash imagined a matriarch should look. Beauty didn't matter, but her presence was commanding and her walk sure.

Set was probably where Maebh was now headed. Maybe she should go look for her in a few minutes? It was clear Maebh had a complicated relationship with Imogen. She could check in, and just bump into Set in the meantime. Visions of the god-like Viking sitting in her car caused her cheeks to flush, and she hoped it would look like it was from the celebrations surrounding them.

Ash ate until her pants protested, all the while listening to Emer and Niamh discussing potential strategies for tomorrow. Ciarán made a couple of contributions, but Tomás remained silent, his piercing blue eyes continuously scanning the surrounding area. Ash was just glad Conor had eaten a little.

Turning on the long bench to face outwards, she watched the now full dancing area. Tiernan turned too, but his attention didn't seem to land anywhere in particular. She reached over to tap his shoulder as he twisted the straps of his heavy looking bag in between his long legs. He'd been the only one to keep his belongings with him, insisting on his experiment needing attention as soon as possible.

"You're distracted."

He glanced her way before facing forward once more. "I haven't spoken to my dad in a long time. We don't exactly see eye to eye."

Ash wondered if she should ask him to elaborate. Ever since they'd met, they'd only spoken about her problems. Naturally, a murdered mother was a pretty big deal, but she didn't want to be that friend. Ash stilled, realising she wanted to be his friend, despite their beginnings.

"Do you want to talk about it?"

"Not really."

She guessed she was that friend, even if she didn't want to be.

"It's not that I don't trust you; it's just . . ." Tiernan gestured, as if trying to find the words. Glancing at Emer for a moment, he leaned forward, lowering his voice. "Dad believes my mother is dead. And . . . There were rumours circulated about her when she disappeared. About why she left."

Ash nodded. She'd seen the stories about Nessa Cassidy running off with her secret lover, Gearoid McQuillan. Maebh and Set's father. "And you don't believe them."

"Of course I don't." Tiernan glanced towards his cousin again, but Ash noted she was busy canoodling with her wife. It didn't stop him from lowering his voice once more. "It's all bullshit. I'm probably the only one who doesn't believe it, though. And the only one who knows she's still alive. They all are, Ash. Your father too."

It was in that moment that Ash realised that she didn't care her father was part of the missing group dubbed the caillte. A pang of guilt anchored her to her seat. Both of her parents were gone, and she probably didn't feel how she should about that. There were different stages of grief, but was numbness one of them?

Before she could think of an appropriate response, Tiernan stood. "I know we have a lot to discuss about tomorrow, but I have to go do something. If I'm not back before the end of the festivities, set up camp to the west of the stone castle wall. Will you be okay?"

Ash angled her head so she could look into his deep mahogany eyes. "Of course. See you later."

She couldn't help her frown as she watched him retreat through the crowd, his heavy bag looked like an extra burden on his already overloaded shoulders.

She was one of those burdens.

A familiar figure appeared before her, and Ash blinked. Had she walked, or just appeared? How did that work?

"The High King wishes to speak with you," Ethne declared. The druid shook her head as the others stood, her silver white hair straight and flowing underneath her raised cape. "In private."

It was Conor who Ash turned to in question. He nodded but didn't speak, his eyes trained on his half eaten supper.

"I won't be long. You heard where Tiernan said to camp?"

"We'll remain here or set up camp for your return, Matriarch," Ciarán said, his freckled hand resting on the hilt of a dagger strapped to his belt.

She would get used to his protective nature. And his weapons.

Ethne led her, not towards the castle as she'd expected, but through the gate of the high stone wall where a heavy door remained open only long enough for them to pass. She only noticed now that around the halfway mark, there seemed to be narrow openings on the wall where guards patrolled the torch lit battlement. As they passed a barren expanse of ground outside the High King's court, Ash realised it looked like the same battleground where she had witnessed the first High King, Fionn, create the Cath in Ethne's vision.

"Time has changed since the first king stood on these lands. Through here," the druid advised, her grey cloak trailing behind her like rippling water.

"Did you know I would be attacked by merrow?"

Ethne didn't slow her steady pace as she continued towards a forest that stretched for miles parallel to the walled fortress. Ash waited for a reply, but it got to where she believed one wouldn't come and they'd made their way deep into the woodland.

"You met him, did you not?"

"Who?"

"Your ally."

"Set is my ally?"

"Then all is well."

Ash couldn't fight the huff of annoyance. "I was nearly killed."

"No, child." Ethne finally turned, her eyes blazed like molten silver and it was the first time Ash had felt unsafe with the druid. "If you were meant to die, then so you would."

As they continued through the trees in silence, Ash wondered if the High King really had called her away. What if this was some trap laid by the druid? She should have insisted Ciarán or Tomás had come with her. If Maebh hadn't wandered off somewhere with her mother, would she have demanded to come, too? Would Tiernan have told her not to go? She was a foolish girl, barely a woman. Why had she got herself into this mess?

"You are more than what you believe."

Ash's heart hammered in her ears as she sucked in a breath. "Can you read my mind?"

"I can do many things." Ethne smiled, her face illuminated by the appearance of the moon in between the clusters of high trees they weaved through. Her skin was so pale it almost looked like she belonged up there, suspended with the stars.

"What do you mean I am more than what I believe?" Ash asked after a moment, too afraid to antagonise the strange female walking alongside her by insisting she answer one damned question plainly.

"Like all Fianna, you have the gift of Sight."

"Faerie Sight, yes, I know, but—"

"Take care who you call a faerie, child. Some only answer to Tuatha Dé Danann." Ethne's lilting accent pronounced every syllable with equal measure, the d's and n's harsh with the softness of her a's. Her piercing gaze never wavered from Ash as she continued walking in elegant strides. "Offend a Fair One, welcome strife."

Ash stiffened as she scanned the surrounding trees. Tiernan had warned her about her words carrying in the wind back in their realm, and now wondered how much easier it would be to be overheard here.

Ethne smirked, as if knowing what she thought. That was getting annoying.

"You have other gifts." Her smile grew wider.

"Reading emotions?" Ash quickened her pace to catch up to Ethne's long strides. "You know about that? Wait, of course you do. I don't really know how to use it, though."

"It doesn't matter. The well is still full of water, even if there is no bucket to retrieve it."

While Ash tried to figure out if the druid had referred to her as a well or a bucket, Ethne stopped walking. "I will leave you with this advice, Aisling. If the wrong kind found out about your origin, using faerie as a term would be the last worry you'd have."

"Wh—"

"Because you'd be dead." Ethne folded her long fingers together before concealing them in her robe. "Your destiny awaits. The High King is just beyond those trees."

Ash only nodded before scurrying forward. The woman was clearly toying with her. She didn't bother turning around to confirm the druid had disappeared before stepping forward, her head buzzing with riddles and non answers.

CHAPTER 31

MAEBH

M aebh spotted her brother's imposing figure even before Imogen signalled to where the McQuillan clan was located. Taking a steadying breath, her eyes darted to Setanta's before scanning the others. The first thing she noticed was his nose no longer looked broken and his skin was bruise-free. Not having to see her brother in pain—because of her actions—only made her throat restrict to the point she could hardly breathe without wincing.

That he was already healed meant one thing. She glared at the back of her mother's perfectly styled hair. Imogen practically force fed Setanta those healing potions. It couldn't be good to have that in his system so often. Who knew what prolonged use did to someone?

She'd abandoned him to the tyranny of the McQuillan matriarch in order to pursue her own selfish goals. The surrounding crowds only seemed to press into her further, but Maebh swallowed past the lump in her throat and squared her shoulders as she continued towards Setanta and the others. Finding the caillte wasn't selfish; there was more than just her family missing a loved one. It had been seven years, and she was the only one who still cared. She thought of Tiernan and realised that wasn't true. He'd agreed to help, and she'd hold him to it.

Maebh's breath turned into a ragged hitch as Setanta looked at her in the same way everyone else was. Weaving through passersby, she followed Imogen's languid steps. The clan all wore similar expressions, and the wafts of disgust and disappointment infiltrated her nostrils before she could turn away for one last fresh breath. Her back straightened as it always did when faced with the onslaught of how much of a failure she was to her clansmen.

"Evening all."

Silence.

Her *former* clansmen.

But it was her brother's matching scent to the others that triggered water to form at the rim of her lashes. Blinking, she forced it back. There was no weakness in tears, but she had made a vow years ago that her mother would never see her cry again.

"What do you think you're doing, Daughter?" Imogen's soft-spoken voice grated in her ears.

She always seemed louder than anything else in the world, even when it came out in a whisper. Maebh was sure that if her mother wanted, she could make herself heard over the lively band and partygoers surrounding them so that everyone, including the High King, would stop and listen. Maebh grabbed another drink from a passing servant's tray, discarding her now empty horn.

"I'm doing what brings me joy, Mother." She took a slug of the honey flavoured ale. Wiping her mouth with her sleeve, she levelled a deadpan stare at the McQuillan matriarch. "It's such a rare commodity, don't you think?"

Imogen's smile turned into a thin line as her elegant hands twitched. She knew the warning signs, but surely her mother wouldn't slap her in front of so many? Gripping her drink, she forced a smile to her own lips. *Let her try*.

As if sensing the shift in Meabh's resolve, Imogen frowned. Her eyes widened as she looked behind Maebh. She turned but couldn't see what had got her mother's attention. There were throngs of people milling about, enjoying the festivities of the Cath opening ceremony. Before she turned back, she noticed Ash retreating through the court gate, the grey-clad druid ambling beside her. She should find out where they were headed; Ash was more capable than she believed herself to be, but that didn't mean she should wander off with strange females in even stranger woods.

As Maebh turned, she noticed her mother had taken several steps back. Before she could so much as raise an eyebrow, her mother muttered, "Excuse me," before disappearing amongst the crowd. She was so busy puzzling over Imogen's strange departure that she only registered the lumbering shadow of her brother when she heard his voice.

"You left."

Looking up at her twin, knowing she'd hurt him, was like staring at the sun for too long. She couldn't do it. Her sleepless nights were filled with self-loathing and wondering if she was turning into her mother. Violent, spiteful, quick to pass judgement; all the signs were there. The other clansmen spoke quietly around them, giving her pointed glares and she couldn't blame them. Nor could she bring herself to care. No matter who was kin, they all knew what her mother was like. What Maebh had been forced to endure by those delicate looking hands. And even if they didn't fully know what Setanta's 'condition' was, they feigned ignorance over what that caravan was for. She had never told her brother that his secret was the worst kept lie of their clan.

She should say sorry. "Was my clean room the giveaway?"

Setanta's sigh coated her with sadness. She knew it was a mix of her own as well as his.

"I understand why—"

"You do? Good, that's settled, then."

"I'm not finished."

"Are you sure you can't just leave it there?" Maebh tried to smile, but it felt alien to her; she let out her own sigh as her shoulders hunched.

Setanta lowered himself to her level, waiting until she met his gaze. "You should have talked to me."

Squinting at her brother, she nodded. Taking a long sip of her drink, she grimaced. Honey turned to vinegar around the lump in her throat.

"I'm sorry, Set," she whispered.

His booming laugh was not the reaction she'd expected, and she stared at him as he threw his head back, his long blond locks plaited to show his newly shaved undersides. The others stopped their glaring judgement towards her enough to look at him as if they, too, thought he'd lost his mind.

Setanta punched Maebh's arm, and she winced, spilling most of her drink. "The snark queen has apologised?"

"Shut up." Maebh laughed, shaking her hand so the ale landed on his jacket. "And nobody says that."

"They should." He grabbed two horns from another passing tray and gestured to her to move away from the sour-faced clansmen. She winked at a Corrigan twin as they walked by, the returning sneer only lightening her mood further. Setting her now empty horn on a table as they passed, she gripped her fresh drink while they manoeuvred to a new spot. The crowd tilted slightly as she walked and she realised she needed to slow down on the ale consumption. She was used to drinking, but the alcohol in this world was much stronger.

When they could walk side by side, Maebh tapped Setanta's jaw. "What's with this fluff? Either grow a beard or don't."

"I was going to say the same to you, Mae." Setanta winked as she spat out her drink.

Wiping her chin, she muttered, "Rude."

Setanta led them to the outskirts of the party, passing the rows of food and beverage stalls. She could make out Conor's slender frame sitting beside the other Breen clan a few feet away. Neither Ash nor Tiernan were anywhere to be seen. Perhaps Tiernan had followed their matriarch, and Maebh hadn't seen him. Were they an item? She tried to picture the two of them together, realising they would make a beautiful couple. Ash had flawless porcelain skin and black hair, soft pink lips, and an athletic physique. Tiernan was nearly the same height as Setanta, but that's where the similarities ended. He was the stereotypical tall, dark and handsome, but had the bonus of an intellect she could only be impressed by. His clothing choices left him to appear on the slimmer side, but she'd seen his toned physique underneath. He was strong looking, like a panther.

Although she had thought him a stiff bore, he'd shown a more playful side recently. Smirking at the memory of them getting matching tattoos, not believing he would go through with it, she pictured him straddling the chair, his long fingers gripping its back. What else could he do with those fingers? As her thoughts went to the darker deeds a beautiful couple could do, she found herself engrossed in a secret moment of longing. It had been too long since she'd felt that way for anyone.

Emer had been the last, but their relationship hadn't been widely publicised. A blush crept up her cheeks as she realised she had just fantasised about her ex's cousin. They had been young, and Maebh had wanted to keep their relationship secret, so she doubted even Tiernan knew about it. She had known she was bisexual from a young age, but it wasn't the fear of judgement that had sparked her discretion. She kept anything important to her far away from her mother. Imogen would only use it against her or turn it into shit.

Leaning against the stone wall, she surveyed the crowd for the worst mother in history. "What do you make of Imogen's behaviour?"

Setanta took a long drink before answering. "I'm sorry I never stuck up for you, Mae." He gently gripped her arm when she opened her mouth to protest. "Don't make a joke right now. She has always been harder on you, and ever since Dad . . . I should have protected you from her."

"Don't take on that guilt, Setanta. You're her son. She has this power over us. Nobody else gets it. Nobody will ever understand what it's like to be her child." Maebh stepped closer to him, surveying his unblemished features. "Speaking of, how much of that healing potion did she make you drink?"

"What?" Setanta frowned at her. "Why?"

"Your face was fucked up the last time I saw you."

Setanta chuckled into his ale. "You didn't get me that good; don't flatter yourself."

"She must have slipped it into your drink or something. Sick bitch."

"There's no way I wouldn't have known. That smell . . ." Setanta shuddered as he raised his broad hand to his nose, wincing for a moment before frowning. "My nose is healed. Huh."

"You seriously didn't drink it? But how do you not have cuts and bruises on you? I'm glad you're feeling better, because I'm the worst, but I don't understand it."

"Neither do I. Maybe there're some aftereffects from the last time I turned?" Setanta whispered, looking around as the vinaigrette fragrance of his anxiety overtook her senses. "But, wait a minute."

He took her drink and ignored her protests as he brought both horns over to a nearby table. When he returned, he took her hands in his, examining them.

"It's weird that my brother is holding my hands."

"Shut up." Setanta raised her hands so they were only inches from her face. "You beat on me pretty hard, especially because I wouldn't fight back. Yes, you *should* look that guilty, but look. Your hands have healed."

Maebh shook out of his grip, squinting down at her knuckles. She hadn't realised that they were no longer swollen; her scabs, gone.

"Maybe it's the air in Tír na nÓg."

"Maybe," Setanta agreed, sounding unconvinced. After a brief pause, he added, "I brought something for you."

"Thank you!" Maebh squealed as he uncovered her caillte journal from his inner jacket pocket. "I can't believe I left it behind."

"I know how much it means to you; to find him. But, Mae, there's something I need to say—"

"You did nothing to him, Setanta. Don't start that again," Maebh said as she clutched her journal close to her chest.

"But what if I did? What if I've done something again . . . recently?"

"What are you saying?"

"What if I killed Cara Breen?"

Eyeing their surroundings, Maebh pulled her brother further away from eavesdroppers, down a deserted alleyway that smelled like cat piss, but it was better than the wafts of despair coming from her brother. Her head scrambled to catch up to what he had said.

"Why would you think that?"

"She was torn apart. By bare hands. Do you know anyone capable of doing that?"

Stopping only when they were far away from everyone, she turned towards her brother. "Setanta, you can't do that. It's not *you* when you turn—"

"Who is it, then? Going by your logic, it still could be my other self." Setanta hugged himself, as if trying to contain what was inside. "My other hands. I need to know. I need to stop it from happening again."

"What do you mean by that?"

"It's not safe. I'm not safe. I have to be stopped." Setanta paused only long enough to glare at her as she opened her mouth to protest. "If no one else will do it; I'll have to be strong enough to do it myself."

It was only then that Maebh looked at her brother. Really looked. She'd been so concerned about his missing injuries, she had noted nothing else. His usual cocky persona was always an act. When they both looked the way they did, it was hard to break out of the mould people shoved them into. His McQuillan clan uniform was impeccable, his hair recently groomed, but his stubbled jawline and the bruise-blue eye baggage told a different story. Although he was outwardly healed, she didn't need her gift to sense the despair and anguish radiating from him.

"We'll look into this together." Maebh hated the next words that came out of her mouth, but she knew it was what her twin needed to hear. "If it comes to it; I'll stop you."

The relief pouring from Setanta only made her heart burrow further within.

"Do you mean it?"

"Anything for you, Brother."

They stood with each other, facing towards the merry crowd feet away, the darkness of the deserted alley a brief reprieve before Setanta spoke again. "I almost turned, and I ended up here."

Maebh's attention snapped to him as he described what happened after he broke up with Orla. Her head spun when he came to the part about rescuing Ash from a merrow attack, and she knew it wasn't from the ale she'd consumed.

"Fuck."

"Yep," Setanta said before finishing his drink.

"This is good news." Maebh swatted her brother's arm when he raised his brows. "The part about you stopping yourself from turning. The rest sounds horrifying. But, Setanta, you can do it. You can control it. And apparently you can teleport."

"Sifting." Setanta shrugged as her brows rose. "That's what the druid said. But that's not the point. I can't conjure up a fake baby by myself. I can't control it."

They'd returned to the edge of the square. A grey dress caught Maebh's attention, and when she saw who the druid approached, she turned to her brother. "We'll figure this out. I promise. You need to get some rest before the quest tomorrow. Find me in the morning."

She waited until he promised he'd retire for the night before weaving through the crowds of partygoers once more. Maebh hid behind a group of women dressed in simple smocks dawning from a time long past. Peering through the bodies, she watched Imogen and the druid talk. She'd never seen her mother so . . . rattled. The druid had her back turned, so she could only see her mother's many facial expressions. She couldn't hear her words, but her mouth was firmly set, her hands twitching at her side. The crowd moved, leaving her exposed and it only took a moment for Imogen to spot her. When she shook her head, Maebh took that as an invitation to join.

She revelled in her mother's glare as she approached. The druid tilted her head; her hooded cloak flowing to the floor, a sheer silver dress revealing a curvy body and colourful tattoos that could be seen continuing underneath the scant material. *Fuck me on a fiddle.*

"Maebh, it is so nice to see you again."

Maebh met the druid's gaze, realising she'd been caught checking her out. She couldn't remember ever meeting her. With her white unruly hair and colourful tattoos, it's not a sight she would easily forget. Before she could ask when they'd met, Imogen reached forward, squeezing Maebh's hand.

"You should go back to your clan, Daughter."

"Come now, Imogen. I haven't seen your daughter since the day of her birth. Surely you will allow me a few moments to marvel at her beauty."

Maebh tugged her hand free from her mother's vice-like grip. "How do you know each other?"

"I delivered you and your brother. I was the first to hold you in my arms." The druid turned her piercing gaze towards the now mute matriarch. "I can't believe you didn't include me in your birth story, Imogen."

"Ethne," Imogen's voice was a quiet warning, but one the druid seemed to have little intention of heeding.

"You remind me so much of my own babies. Look a little like them, too. Not just in your looks; more to do with your aura."

Maebh looked at the two women. She could sense Imogen's growing discomfort but frowned at the nothingness radiating from Ethne. Was she blocking her somehow? "I'm not a baby anymore."

"I forget how much age matters to you. Twenty-odd years is but a blip." Ethne surveyed Maebh before adding. "You are made of more, Maebh. I know you. The real you."

Imogen opened her mouth, no doubt to contradict any nice thing said about her daughter, but when Ethne cut her gaze towards the matriarch, she began coughing. Maebh took a reluctant step forward as Imogen's complexion darkened and she clutched her throat.

"I will see you soon, Maebh," Ethne said sweetly, clearly unconcerned by Imogen's choking.

She turned and popped out of focus as Imogen drew in a sharp breath.

"What was that?"

"You need to listen to me." Imogen grabbed both of Maebh's arms, digging her nails in when she tried to move away. The phantom bruise on her cheek from their last encounter throbbed as though her mother had slapped her again. "Never speak to her again."

CHAPTER 32

TIERNAN

It was easy for Tiernan to forget he had a parent still present. That was the wrong word to describe Bradan Cassidy. Even before his mother had disappeared, along with the other caillte, his father had been absent. Tiernan had been only a boy when his father had accepted the coveted title of Rígfennid of Leinster by the then newly appointed High King, Aedan O'Dwyer. Bradan was a natural born leader and all the Leinster clans respected him. He and Nessa Cassidy had been a power couple within their community.

To everyone else, Nessa had been a fearsome matriarch to the Cassidy clan. She had the same calculating mind of Imogen McQuillan, but the caring nature of Cara Breen. To him, she was always Mam. A mother who tucked him in at night, who told him to be whomever he wanted, regardless of what others expected. He sometimes wondered if she could foresee the tenuous relationship he'd have with his father. As he walked among the ever-flowing crowd, he remembered the days when they were still a family. A time when Nessa led one of the strongest clans, and Tiernan would try to stay up late and eavesdrop when his parents hosted late night gatherings with 'Uncle Aedan' and their other close-knit friends.

Tiernan gripped his bag as passersby stumbled across his path. Most of his parents' friends were missing, like his mother.

Others were rulers, like the High King and his father. He clenched the strap tighter at his next thought. *Or dead, like Cara*.

Spotting Bradan's imposing figure in the distance, he stopped only long enough to watch him laughing with a large group of admirers. Court members, Tiernan gathered by their ornately robed attire. Readjusting the heavy load on his shoulder, he altered his course. His father had changed the day Nessa left; but he couldn't blame him for that. He had too. The difference was he hadn't shut him out. Somebody bumped into him, causing his bag to slip, but he caught it before it fell to the ground. All of his tools were inside for replicating his experiment. He didn't know whether it would work, but if it did . . . it would change everything.

The night was still young, but the party had shifted. Less food was being consumed and more alcohol was present in the hands of his fellow Fianna. Even the music had changed from the high tempo beats of multiple instruments to a lone bodhrán. The beating drum brought the sporadic fire pits to life, each thrum of wood on leather causing the flames to dance higher and higher. Edging around the sizeable crowd, he spotted dancers floating towards the centre of the dance floor. Once noticed, everyone stopped what they were doing and faced the floor, solely focused on the performance to come, in anticipation he could almost smell. These dancers wore costumes that were nothing like Maebh's. Long panels of sheer white fabric tangled around their legs, held together at their waists by gold belts. Loose tops under leather corsets covered their upper bodies and more gold plated jewellery adorned their necks, arms and ankles, gleaming against the firelight.

This was the part of being Fianna Tiernan struggled with most. The dancers were beautiful, and he enjoyed watching half-naked women writhe around one another, but this was only the beginning. Fianna would make offerings to the Fair Ones tonight; the beings who allowed them to set foot in this realm. Tuatha Dé Danann, fairies, fae—they had many names—Tiernan preferred to call them power-fuelled assholes.

The primal, gods-worshipping ritualistic side of his people was the part he didn't care for. Give him technology, something his mind could break down into strings of coding. Why did the Fair Ones deserve their reverence? Because they had power and supernatural gifts that made all other beings somehow inferior? Watching the dancers' lithe bodies move to the beating drums, he pictured Maebh amongst them. Her fuller figure *not* covered in that clothing would be a sin, and as his blood heated at the images he conjured, it was one he would be happy to commit.

"Enjoying the show, Son?"

Tiernan's jaw ticked before he forced a smile and turned to Bradan Cassidy. He'd twisted his hair in dreadlocks adorned by gold circlets, a style he'd had for as long as Tiernan could remember. "Hello, Dad. You're not being trailed by your minions tonight?"

"They're enjoying the festivities." The rígfennid stood beside him at the outskirts of the growing crowd. "It's hard work running a province. One I hope my son will aid me in soon."

Tiernan glanced up at his father, and then at the surrounding Fianna, who had put a respectful distance between them. He fought a sigh. "We've been through this. I have other things going on."

"Other things? Anything to do with that heavy load on your shoulder?"

Before Tiernan could stop him, Bradan opened the zip and peered inside his duffle bag. Seeing the satellite dish, cauldron, and cables, his eyes darted to his son's. "What are you playing with?"

"It's just an experiment."

269

"No doubt one to find her."

The way his father said '*her*', as if his mother meant nothing, made Tiernan's already strained patience snap. "Just because you've turned your back on Mam doesn't mean I ever will."

"You're like her. Loyal to a fault. She was the current High King's puppet." Bradan looked towards the dancers, the sharp angles of his face making him appear more fierce. "Times are changing and I want you by my side when everything plays out."

He surveyed his father, trying to hide the surprise at hearing him speak with contempt about the High King. Perhaps 'Uncle Aedan' was no longer a friend to his father. So much had changed since that time, Tiernan hadn't realised. "What do you mean?"

"What is Aisling Breen like?"

An overwhelming urge to protect her washed over Tiernan, and he gritted his teeth. "She's . . . learning."

Bradan grunted. "She has no loyalties yet. Good."

Strings of coding, technology, that was what he was good at. Cryptic conversations with his father were another matter. "You didn't answer my question."

"I will answer all of your questions if you join my side. Become my apprentice."

"Right." Tiernan lifted the bag onto his shoulder once more. This was a conversation he understood all too well. "This has been fun."

Leaving his spot, he moved behind his father, who remained at the edge of the dancefloor, his back straight and arms clasped behind him. His eyes were a burning laser at his back. Closer to the castle, he realised he was walking in the wrong direction and would have to loop around the other side of the dancers in order to avoid his father. Deciding it was worth the added journey, he moved through the dispersing crowds, only to appear in front of Maebh and her mother. They weren't speaking, just fuming at one another with matching stances of crossed arms. Seeing them facing each other, it was easy to see their similarities. But there was something more to Maebh, like the glow of a candle in a darkened room.

"Hey."

It took a moment for Maebh to tear her stormy eyes from her mother's gaze, but once she did, he could have sworn he saw relief there. He fought the thrill that brought him, but she no doubt had already sensed it.

"Oh, yes, we're doing that thing now." Maebh took the bag from Tiernan's shoulder, and he knew better than to protest with whatever had just transpired between the two women. Without looking at either of them, she ambled past Imogen. "Lovely chatting to you, Mam."

Tiernan flinched at the look on Imogen's face as her daughter marched towards the castle gates. He nodded in farewell, but the matriarch didn't acknowledge him as she continued to stare at her daughter's retreating figure.

Through the gates and into the surrounding forest, he followed Maebh until the symphony of night creatures muted the sound of the party they'd left behind.

"I can carry that now," he said, but Maebh only hoisted the bag higher.

"Do we need to find the exact tree used in the other realm?"

Tiernan was equally surprised and impressed by her observations, and her smirk confirmed his emotions were filtering through to her.

"Can you ever turn it off?"

"Nope."

Tiernan sighed, unsure whether to believe her. "I've just had the weirdest conversation with my dad."

"There must be something in the air because my mother isn't exactly making sense either."

After checking the coordinates he'd written earlier, he pointed toward where the ancient oak tree should be, excitement already brewing. His focus lay on the experiment, but his gaze drifted towards the blonde at his side more times than he cared for.

"Did you follow Ash when she left with the druid?"

Tiernan's head whipped towards Maebh's. "Ethne? When did they leave? Where is she now?"

"I'm not sure." Maebh frowned as her pace slowed. "I never thought to ask the druid where Ash was when I spotted her talking to my mother. She was too busy being cryptic and strange."

Tiernan looked behind him, debating whether they should turn around and look for their matriarch, but a quick squeeze of his arm forced him to face his companion. "She's probably sitting beside Conor right now. She seems reluctant to leave his side for too long."

Gripping the straps at Maebh's shoulders, he gave her a look when she was about to protest. Hoisting it on to his shoulder, he reluctantly continued towards the tree. "I don't blame her, do you? He's been through heaven knows what, and she hasn't been around the past seven years."

"Can you imagine? Living outside our Fianna bubble?"

"I'd probably live in a shitty one-bed anywhere with the fastest broadband; and never leave my room."

"Sounds fun. I could window shop while you worked and bring home sustenance for your tired, overworked brain." Maebh winked as she quickened her pace. "Over here. I think I've spotted our tree."

Tiernan couldn't help his grin at the image of them living together, but shook those thoughts from his mind as he jogged to catch up. She was right; it was their tree. Hunkering at the base, he set out his tools. Maebh stood back and he could feel her gaze on him as he got to work. Wordlessly handing her the satellite and cable ties, she scaled the trunk, securing the equipment. She was back on the ground in less than two minutes. "What's next, Boss?"

From his crouched position, he smiled up at her, handing over the solar panels. "Want me to go?"

"I got it." Maebh took the panels and bent low, opening her mouth.

He blinked before realising she wanted him to place the cables in her mouth again. Their eyes locked and something came over him as he took his time, letting his fingers trail her cheek and down her neck as he obliged. The playfulness in her stare only made his own eyes pool with heat, and he could have sworn that the smell of her perfume grew stronger. He hadn't noticed there were hints of jasmine in it before. He never acted this way; only with her. She bit down on the ties, staring at him for a moment, as if waiting, but when he didn't react, she silently turned and climbed the thick branches.

What was happening between them? Why didn't he do something? What had she wanted him to do?

"Done!" Maebh called from somewhere above.

The night was black, with billions of stars lighting the sky, but he couldn't see her from her perch. Taking out his phone, he got to work, searching for Wi-Fi networks to log into. He barely registered Maebh's climb down as he watched the circular loading icon rotate. Around and around. After an excruciating amount of time, the glorious green light appeared, linking him to the personal network he'd programmed to the tree in the human realm.

"I don't believe it."

"Did it work?" Maebh peered around his shoulder, her perfume surrounding him, and it took a great deal of restraint not to inhale deeply as she continued, "You didn't do the seance part, though. What was that for?"

"The druid's potion should ward off anyone outside of its circle. Because we were both inside it in our realm, we're the only ones who can find it; everyone else will have a powerful compulsion to avoid that tree." He smiled at Maebh's awed expression. "Effectively, as long as we're in the circle, we're invisible."

"No fucking way." Maebh snapped up the container he had laid out, opening the lid and pouring the potion he'd already prepared into the brass cauldron. He muttered the incantation needed to finish the spell before Maebh created a wider circle than the one he had before, enclosing them and the tree within. "So if anyone walks by, they can't see us?"

"Theoretically."

"It's a pity it smells so bad. But it doesn't hide how hot and bothered you are." Maebh laughed as his head snapped from his phone to her. "Theorising is a real turn on for you, I see."

"Why do you do that?" Tiernan asked, his face heating as he grit his teeth, the jasmine scent turning rancid around him.

"What?"

He stomped towards her so he was close enough she had to crane her neck to look at him; the flush of her laugh a whisper on his face in the cool night air. "Make jokes about everything."

Tiernan watched as something in Maebh bubbled to the surface. In one of those rare glimpses of her true feelings, she didn't hold it back as she stepped into him, forcing him back without touching. "Because if I don't laugh at other people's constantly interchanging moods barrelling into me, I'll combust. Do you know how hard it is to be subjected to the assault of emotions that everyone feels?"

He instantly regretted snapping as he realised he'd never stopped to consider how her gift affected her. "Maebh, I—"

"Sometimes I'm so numb I'm not sure I can feel for myself anymore. I know everyone's emotions, but I don't know how to deal with my own. So I laugh." She turned away from him, hugging her arms around her torso, her blonde hair swirling with the movement. When she turned back, her eyes were like a stormy ocean. "If this is a gift, why am I the one paying?"

They stood facing each other as something zinged between them. Their eyes locked for another painful moment, and Tiernan let out a long breath. A myriad of scents infused between them, and he took another step back, stuffing his hands in his pockets. What was happening to him? Between them? His own senses had awakened and he couldn't fight his guilt as he became painfully aware of his constant feelings around her, *about her*.

There was only the chirping of night insects until he looked at her and she whispered, "Even you, right now. You're all consuming. Your emotions are charging into me and I . . ."

"What? What are my feelings telling you?" He dared to return to where he'd shared breath with her, his eyes darting to her mouth as her tongue swept over her bottom lip.

She leaned back to meet his gaze, the fire in her eyes matching his. The night went still. It was the two of them and the moonlight. She stepped even closer, standing to her full height so their mouths were just a breath apart.

"Kiss me."

He didn't waste another second before his lips were on hers. Knowing it was the only chance they'd have a first kiss, he slowed his pace, taking his time exploring her. Tugging at her bottom lip with his teeth, she let out a breathy laugh and he took that as an invitation to deepen their kiss. As her lips parted, he swept his tongue inside, holding the nape of her neck to angle her face upwards. The noises she made . . . Gods. A growl escaped him. Never breaking contact, he pushed her against the wide trunk of the tree. She wrapped her long legs around him, so he no longer had to stoop.

He broke away to trail his lips along her jaw and down her neck, and smiled against her skin as she arched her back. Those perfectly swollen lips, eyes lit with desire . . . his heart pounded louder than any drummer at the festival. He rested his forehead against hers, hoping to catch his breath. She gave him a moment, the tip of her nose brushing his. Maebh's hands moved from his shoulders up to his hair, tugging as he'd begun pressing lazy kisses against her neck. Another tug and he chuckled before he met her waiting lips.

This time, he didn't hold back, kissing her soundly. Those breathy moans of hers moved the pounding in his chest lower. His hips started moving before he'd realised. She arched into him, tightening her grip around his waist as he continued to move.

"You're beautiful," he whispered close to her ear as they broke apart once more.

He leaned away, staring at her glazed eyes and shock ran through him. She felt the same attraction for him. The heady scent between smoked wood and floral jasmine filled the air . . . that wasn't Maebh's perfume. He gripped her sides, fighting against that thought. Nothing would ruin this moment, not even the dawning realisation that something had changed within him.

Maebh whispered for him to kiss her again, and he obliged. A twig snapped close by, followed by soft voices and for a moment they both stilled, their breaths coming out ragged. When nobody appeared, Tiernan looked at Maebh, who shrugged, reaching to kiss him once more, but he stopped her.

"Don't worry about it."

Tiernan chuckled at her petulant tone. Snaring her with a look, he made quick work of shirking out of his jacket before unzipping hers. A leather book fell to the ground, but his attention snagged on the thin material of her top.

"Tiernan." Maebh's voice was a whisper and a promise and a plea as she gripped the hem of his shirt.

He lifted the top over his head, shivering, his bare skin tingling. Not from the cold, never with her here, before him like this. Those beautiful flame-blue eyes roving over his toned torso, scorching his skin, his heart raced so that he nearly forgot they were out in the open. With slow movements, he tilted his head towards hers and delighted as she shivered from his warm breath dancing on her skin.

"Beautiful." Tiernan murmured again before grazing his hand up her side, savouring every shiver he forced from her body as he pulled her shirt off and unhooked her bra. "Fuck."

He would never get enough of her. She was a stunning creature, utter perfection.

His eyes snapped to hers as she reached up and tugged his hair, rougher this time, and claimed his mouth for her own. They stayed like that, both sets of hands now exploring as their mouths devoured each other, but he needed more. She did too, it seemed, as she brought his hand to the buttons of her dark jeans, arching into him again.

He unfastened and slipped his fingers inside, his heart leaping at the sharp intake of breath his touch wrought from her. She unleashed herself on him, her fingers digging into his back, her tongue sweeping in as they kissed. He met her every savage stroke and a dark laugh escaped him as she whimpered.

His entire focus narrowed in on her. Taking his time, his fingers teased and circled, and she panted. He stroked her, over and over.

His name on her lips as she shattered was a prayer answered. They both stilled, her legs shaking around his waist until she signalled for him to release her.

"Your turn."

He chuckled as she turned so his back was against the tree. Maebh traced her fingers along his shoulders, his now bare arms holding her waist as her eyes roamed his upper body. She was probably used to a bulkier physique. Maebh traced her fingers over their matching tattoo, but didn't stop until her hand slid over the grooves of his torso, her eyes finding his when he reached for her hand.

"You're perfect, Tiernan," Maebh murmured as her searing eyes pinned him.

She raised herself to her toes, gripping his neck to kiss him. The tug on his zip was the only warning he had before she took him into her hand, and he gasped as she explored. He gripped her to him, desperate for release, but she broke their kiss, stepping back and smiling. She opened her mouth to speak when footsteps came from behind her and the chatter of a couple floated towards them.

"Fuck." He was about to fix his pants, but Maebh stopped him, a wicked smile on her lips.

"We'll see if your potion worked," Maebh whispered as she pressed him back against the tree and knelt.

The sight of her on her knees before him took his breath away. He gripped the tree behind him, the rough bark digging into his bare skin. The unseen hikers were louder now and Maebh turned to look behind her, one hand holding him firmly in place. As if he was going anywhere. He could make out shadows of two people dressed similarly to them.

Fianna warriors. At least they weren't Fair Ones, and so far it appeared they hadn't seen them. Maebh spotted them, too. She pressed her index finger against her pink lips, signalling for him to be quiet. With one last devilish smile, she took him into her mouth.

"Maebh."

He didn't care if the two warriors found them and stood watching as this blonde goddess knelt before him. His hands wound themselves into her hair.

Nothing else mattered. The warriors seemed to walk parallel to them, getting nearer but then wandering away. Through hazy eyes, he noted they weren't anyone he knew. His attention snapped to Maebh, the most beautiful creature he'd ever laid eyes on.

Breathing heavily, he waited until the world stopped pulsing before he sagged against the trunk. With her eyes never leaving his, she licked her lips with a smile. Helping her to her feet, he kissed her again, before they both fixed their clothing. He couldn't hide his smile as they regarded each other. Never in his wildest dreams had he thought anything would happen between them. She winked and a laugh escaped him.

"Do you think they saw us?" Maebh whispered, and Tiernan could have sworn he heard hope in her tone.

"Would you have liked it if they had?"

She laughed, and that was the only response she gave. Stooping low, he picked up the discarded book. "Here."

"Thanks. I need to keep better care of this. I've only just got it back."

"Is it your diary?" Tiernan noted the return of the blush to her cheeks, and his eyes widened. "Sorry, I didn't mean to pry."

Maebh smacked him with the book. "It's not a diary. I'm not twelve. It's my journal."

His eyebrows shot up. "What's the difference?"

"It's my investigative journal." Maebh gripped the leather book to her chest. "For my research on the caillte."

He nodded in understanding, and the reason he'd come all the way out here returned. "We can share our intel if you'd like."

He reached for his bag, taking out his laptop before switching it on.

"So, all it took was an exchange of bodily fluids for you to finally agree."

"Maebh." He groaned, casting a wary gaze her way.

"I'm joking," she said as she hunkered beside him, her journal resting on her lap. "You need to lighten up, kitten."

The taste of sugar on his tongue caused his attention to snap from his laptop to Maebh, but before he could say anything, he noticed her frown as she stared at his screen which had loaded to show a childhood photo of him standing with his mother and cousin.

"Are you okay?"

She nodded, but said nothing.

"I thought for a minute, it might have been Emer."

"What?" she asked, her tone sharp as she stared at him.

"In the woods. Looking for us."

"Oh." Maebh leaned against the tree, raising her knees close to her chest.

The air turned acidic, something astringent filling his nostrils as if he'd bitten into a mouthful of tart cherries. He swallowed, fighting the urge to gag. Something had changed.

"Hey." Tiernan set his laptop aside and reached over to cup the back of her head. Drawing her in, he pressed a soft kiss to her lips.

The sour tang filled his nostrils.

Somebody had hacked into his mind and overridden his circuit board. He realised two things. One, he had somehow tapped into the ability to smell emotions, and two, Maebh regretted what had just transpired between them.

CHAPTER 33

AISLING

"**A**isling, you made it," the High King said, appearing from behind a wide oak. "Thank you for agreeing to join me."

As if she had a choice. She tilted her head to look at him. He was taller than she'd realised, his appearance as dazzling and intimidating as before. As she bowed, he motioned for her to straighten.

"You wished to speak to me, High King?" Ash remained a short distance away, nerves taking over, her feet refusing to move closer.

"Let's walk. And please, call me Aedan."

"Then please call me Ash."

His face lit up with a smile and he nodded, flourishing an arm out from under his black and emerald cloak. He waited until she stepped forward before walking alongside her. Her heart pounded against her rib cage as she walked beside the mysterious king. Had he known her mother? Why had he singled her out tonight to meet in fae infested woods? They were still in his kingdom, but that didn't stop creatures like the merrow roaming like the predators they were.

She stole glances as they headed further away from the castle and through the dense forest. He looked only thirty, but that meant little in a place where ageing wasn't an indicator.

Thinking back to when she was a teen, she remembered there had been a different king.

"Have you spoken with your grandfather?" The timbre of his voice echoed the night time songs of unseen creatures.

"No." Ash gritted her teeth as she thought of her mother's father. Sitting at the long table with the other leaders as she'd greeted the king, Rígfennid Fintan Breen's black unruly hair claimed him as a Breen, but his boyish face also claimed him as someone who hadn't bothered leaving this realm in decades, not even for his daughter's funeral.

"I know he wishes to speak to you."

She looked at the king, questions bubbling on her lips. Why did he care? They walked further and Ash's breath became ragged from the steep incline, the scabbard on her belt growing heavier with every step. She was used to sparring and leaving her weapons behind when finished. Carrying them around was another task she'd have to get used to in this realm. She tried to think of where they were walking within the human realm. They were headed southeast from the hill of Tara, and although there seemed to be nothing but forest in this realm, she imagined they'd have made it to civilization by now.

"Are we still in your territory, my king?" Ash jumped at the sound of twigs snapping, aware of what happened the first time she'd wandered through these woods.

"Aedan, remember? For this meeting, please speak as new friends," he said, his tone light. "In a matter of words, yes, we are in my territory."

She only nodded as she continued to scan the trees, acutely aware of every sound. The air was cooler now. Far away from the court and festivities, the true temperature of the realm brought a chill and Ash could see puffs of her warm breath hit the air. She zipped up her jacket, wishing she too had a heavy cloak like the king beside her.

"I meant what I said earlier. About your mother." Aedan's tone was soft as he continued. "You found her. How traumatic that must have been for you."

"It was," she breathed, the sigh escaping her lips as heavy as the weight dragging at her heart. She couldn't think of anything else to say and she would not divulge gory details, no matter who walked beside her.

"Your father and I were best friends." He clasped his hands behind his back, concealed by the flowing cloak that trailed behind him. "We grew up together. Did you know?"

"You were part of the Breen clan?" Ash hurried her steps, her speech rushed as she tried to keep up with him.

"No, your father originally came from my mother's clan, the O'Dwyer's. I was there the night your parents met."

Ash only nodded. She had known that Lorcan had been part of a different clan, but she'd never asked him about it. He was a silent man who growled or grunted more than ever spoke to her. His side of the family had paid little attention to her, and it had somehow felt like it was her fault.

"Where are you taking me?" Ash averted her gaze when the king glanced at her, his thick brows raised. She hadn't meant for it to sound like an accusation.

"You have been out of our community for so long." King Aedan assessed her, clearly ignoring her question. "How was it living with the Gluttons?"

"Mary and Dom aren't Gluttons." Ash's lips pressed into a thin line. She didn't want to offend a king, but she wouldn't allow him to judge them before knowing their kindness. She'd experienced the prejudice that plagued her community. But they were no better. "They are good people."

"Of course. Forgive me if I caused offence. My past dealings with anyone outside of our clansmen have left me with poor impressions, and what I'm about to show you might help you see why." Aedan looked genuine in his remorse, and she was wise enough to know she shouldn't reproach a king any more than she had. She nodded, and he spoke again, his tone kind. "I'm sure anyone to take a young woman in from the fianna community are good people. How did you find keeping the truth from them? About the Tuatha Dé?"

Should she have told him the truth? It wasn't their fault that a changeling had opened their eyes to the fact of their existence. They had broken no law. Opening her senses to Aedan was easier than ever before, and she thought he seemed only curious, nothing more. She was about to admit that they knew, but a fierce sense of protection overwhelmed her. She couldn't take that risk with the only parents she had left.

Looking straight ahead, she noticed the trees had thinned, the sounds of the forest becoming mute. "It was fine. There's an annoying púca who shows up at the cafe they own but other than that we have been sheltered from any . . . visitors."

If he realised her voice was rushed, he didn't show it.

"What do you want to show me?" Ash asked as the only sound she now could hear was their footsteps on the brittle fallen debris of the forest. He only smiled in response, nodding in the direction she should continue. With every step, the air became heavier, with a return to warmth in the air. A column of water and steam erupted from the ground nearby and Ash noted fist sized geysers dotted the landscape. The crescent moon gave little light, and the king's face became more shadowed.

"Tír na nÓg has been my constant home for twenty years."

Ash did the maths as she unzipped her coat, the air pressing in, her hair sticking to her neck and reminding her of the warmth of the cafe during lunch hour. "That's why you look the way you do."

He laughed, his perfect teeth glinting in the faint moonlight. It said it all; he knew how attractive he was. How could he not?

"If you win this Cath, you have the choice of joining me here to live out your days, therefore never ageing, or rejoining the rest of your clan." Aedan peered down at her, his dark features unreadable as his wavy brown hair fell to his brow and she noticed for the first time he wasn't wearing his crown. "What would you choose?"

His question caught her off guard. "I would stay wherever my brother chose."

He nodded as if he approved of her answer, and it took a moment for her to notice he hadn't answered her question.

She took a breath. "Where are—"

"Here." Aedan pointed towards a cluster of trees and Ash noticed the tips of his fingers were stained green and dirt was lodged under his fingernails. Not very kingly.

As they took a step past the cluster of trees, the vibrancy of the surrounding forest dulled. Tír na nÓg was full of colours and shimmering plants that had already somehow become the norm for her. Until they reached this part. Trees were bleached white and as thin as brittle bones, the ground a scorched earth. In a couple of steps, they had walked from utopia into a barren wasteland. Another geyser erupted close by, welcoming their arrival with a thunderous roar.

"What is this?" Ash asked as she touched one of the dead trees.

It was spongy; she feared if she pressed hard enough, it would dissolve.

"This is a cry for help."

Ash took a step away from the brittle bark, her eyes trained on the king. "What do you mean?"

"We live here at the approval of the Tuatha Dé Danann as part of the Peace Treaty." Aedan began, his brows furrowed as he placed his hand on the tree she'd just retreated from. "Although they find all humans distasteful, they see our fianna community is set apart, and not just because we have the Sight. We live in harmony with the earth and do not gorge and destroy the planet. The Gluttons cause this. Their world has seeped into ours."

Ash took another few reluctant steps into the barren land, taking in the scorched earth, the smell of decay in the stale air, and a sense of deep loss overwhelmed her. She wasn't sure if it was hers or the High King's.

"You're saying that the human realm has somehow polluted this place?" Ash swallowed, her throat dry. "How?"

"How indeed."

Ash looked above to where a feminine voice had come from, but she couldn't see anyone. On a thin branch stood a glorious crow, its blue-black feathers glinting in the moonlight.

The High King looked surprised but quickly composed his features into something that looked like wicked delight. "Badb."

Badb. It took several moments of looking between Aedan and the crow, who had fluttered to the closest branch and strutted its length, to realise who perched above her. She had never seen a bird move so . . . sensually. Her hand went to the hilt of her sword before she'd realised her actions. She'd hoped the creature didn't see, but the bird's beady eyes seemed to narrow in on the movement.

"Your death comes soon."

Before Ash could register a Fair One had revealed herself in her presence, or to ask who she directed those ominous words to, Badb flew for her face, its beak aimed for her eyes.

Chapter 34

Aisling

Ash saw the shift from feathers to skin as a blinding light swept through the dead forest. Instead of claws scratching her, silken black tresses caressed her cheeks.

"Macha," Aedan murmured, in a reverence fitting to a worshipper at the altar as he bowed before the beautiful fae.

She was naked. And leaning in much too close. Was she sniffing her? The fae purred, a deep, guttural sound emanating from her throat as she inched even closer. She *was* smelling her. The phrase fight or flight came into Ash's head, but all she could do was freeze as the female circled her, the sword within reach as useful to her as if she'd left it back at Tara Court.

Aedan wordlessly removed his cloak, his broad shoulders even more impressive under the loose fitting white shirt he wore, and placed it over the naked fae. Macha left the cloak unclasped and flowing, doing nothing to conceal her perfectly formed body within, as if oblivious to the need for clothing. Her skin was flawless as satin, a faint glow causing Ash's eyes to involuntarily squint every time her gaze returned to her. Black hair was cut in a blunt angle to her chin, and no matter how hard Ash tried not to, she noticed the carpet matched the curtains.

Growing up, she'd read everything there was to know about the Morrígan, but had never imagined meeting them. Sisters from the Tuatha Dé royal bloodline, three female forms, encompassed within their shared soul. Badb was the crow. Her fae form, Macha, stood before her now. Ash had never come across a creature more beautiful and terrifying, and hoped she would never meet their third and most blood lusting form.

"You were right about this one," Macha said, her head rotating between Ash and Aedan at a distinctly non-human angle.

Finding her voice, she looked between the fae and High King. "Right about what? What did you mean, 'your death comes soon'?"

"Everybody dies."

Another cryptic stranger. She clenched her jaw, arms crossing over her chest, her own black hair clinging to her skin. It was much too warm. As the air itself closed in around her, she shed her jacket, clenching it between her clammy hands.

Aedan's smile was broad as he continued to stare in awe-like reverence at the ancient creature before them. "Macha is unique, even for the Fair Ones."

The female's returning smile was wide enough to highlight her sharp canines. "We are Babd, and we are Macha. Nemain will soon return." Her voice came out in an echo, bouncing from one bleach boned tree to another. She angled her head again, studying Ash, and perfectly pointed ears protruded through her feather like tresses. "We wish to speak with you, Breen Matriarch."

A splinter of panic ran through Ash and she stopped fidgeting. Why did they want to speak with her?

"She does not know." Macha's echoing voice penetrated her spiralling thoughts, doing little to ease the tremor raking through her body.

"Not yet." Aedan turned his attention to Ash. "I've brought you here to see the devastation of the worlds. The Gluttons have forgotten the power of the gods. You want me to call them human, but look at what they have done. They truly deserve the title."

Macha finally stopped staring at Ash, only to stand on her other side, looking out at the scorched wasteland. "My kind chose to go underground, to allow humans to forget. But time is running out."

Ash continued to look at the tragic scene before her, finding it better than the terrifying faerie beside her. Her voice was shaky as she asked, "Time is running out for what?"

It was Aedan who answered, "For Ireland. For humanity. If humans knew of the existence of all of this, would anything change?"

"Yes. Well . . ." Ash hesitated, a frown forming as she tucked her hair behind her ear. Would anything change?

"Do you think they would give up their cars, factories, nuclear plants? Global warming, pollution—these things would remain. They need to be governed by stronger hands."

Ash thought of Mary and Dom, and found her shaky voice gained strength. "Humans have a right to govern themselves. Nobody is perfect. We can change."

"You talk as if you are one of them." Macha angled, but she refused to meet her scrutiny. "Interesting."

"Tradition dictates I must hold a Cath in order to declare any new warriors for my highguard. But it doesn't state that only winners join me. I need loyalty. I need warriors who trust my judgement and who will stand by my decisions.

"The Peace Treaty between Tuatha Dé and fianna was necessary because the High Kings before me tried to impose a power over gods."

Aedan held his arm toward Macha, who stepped past Ash and to his side, lifting her hand to clasp his. Still totally nude, save for the limply hanging cloak.

Averting her gaze, Ash traced the cracks in the barren ground, noting particles floated every time she shuffled her feet. "I don't understand."

"There is none more powerful than they." Aedan inclined his head at Macha before continuing, "Our first High King understood it. He worked with them, treated them with the respect they deserve. It was only after he went to slumber that the battle between our kinds began."

Ash's mind reeled as she processed what he was telling her. Ethne's vision of Fionn Mac Cumhaill played through her mind. He'd been a fierce warrior king. Although Aedan looked fit, he wouldn't match the sheer size and imposing stature of Fionn. She contemplated his words, her eyes darting over and back as she tried to keep up. "So the tale of the first High King is true? He didn't die, but went to sleep somewhere in this land, and he will wake up—"

"When Ireland calls out to him in her most dire moment. Yes, it is true. We've sacrificed more than you know in order to find him. Ireland is crying. Look around."

"What are you saying? That if I declare my loyalty to whatever you're planning, my clan will win the Cath?"

"What I'm saying is, if you stand by your High King, I will help you find out who killed your mother."

A gasp left Ash's lips, but before she could correlate her jumbled thoughts into words, the High King pressed on, "My clansmen are my kin. I will do everything in my power to search for who tore our family apart. Ash, all I expect in return is loyalty."

What she wanted to say was her family had been torn long before Cara's murder, but what left her mouth instead was, "Thank you."

Footsteps sounded behind them, and in a flash, Macha turned into Badb once more. As the crow took flight, Ash could see a blond looming figure step out of the last remaining living trees.

"High King, my apologies." Set bowed low before Aedan gripped his shoulder in a fatherly manner, insisting he rise. Set's eyes met Ash's with a questioning look. "I didn't mean to disturb you."

It took a moment for Ash to realise Aedan's cloak was pooled at the ground beside her, and how this must look. She was out here, alone, with the High King and he'd discarded clothing. Shit.

"Setanta, gods, you are the height of Cú Chulainn by now." Aedan punched Set's arm good-naturedly, and Ash noted that she'd initially thought the king tall, but Set towered over him. "You have disturbed nothing. What are you doing this far away from the fun?"

Ash clumsily gathered the High King's cloak as Set answered, "I needed to clear my head."

As Ash handed the cloak to Aedan, and finally found the courage to look at Set, she noticed dark circles underlining his eyes. She took an inhale of breath but coughed it out, the stench of something sour and decaying crept up her nostrils, worse than the surrounding dying forest. The smell triggered a memory of the argument she'd had with her mother. After she had stormed off in a sulk and returned an hour later, the encampment had been abandoned and she was on her own.

"What happened here?" Set gestured to the bone white trees and earth at their feet. The moonlight highlighted the deep crevices scratching the ground as far as they could see.

"This is what I came here to show Ash. As matriarch, she can help me fight against this disease creeping any further into this land.

"It's awful," Set murmured, kicking up dust with his feet. "We have to protect this land."

Aedan's smile was small as he nodded. "Your father felt strongly about it, too. Did he ever tell you he was my right-hand man?"

Set's eyes widened at the mention of his missing father. "No."

"Yours too, Ash." Aedan turned and stood before them, his cloak draped across one shoulder. His smile was sad. "We will see them again in this life."

Neither answered as he stepped away from them. "Duty of the High King calls. Set, may I ask you to escort Ash back to the Tara court? You've only been here a short while, Matriarch, and you could do worse than such a fine escort, yes?"

Ash's cheeks blazed as she cast her gaze to Set's before looking at her boots.

"Yes, my king. I'll walk back with Ash," Set answered, but continued to look towards the barren lands.

She watched the High King retreat before turning her attention on Set.

"Nothing happened."

It took a moment for Set to look at her, but it was clear his mind was elsewhere. "What?"

Ash looked anywhere but him. "It looked suspicious. The High King de-robed. With me. Alone." She wished she could shut her mouth, but the words kept tumbling out. "It wasn't like that. Not that you'd care, of course, but he's old. Obviously, he's a hot looking old guy. But still, I couldn't go there. Not that the High King would be interested in me."

Set stared down at Ash until she wanted to be swallowed up by the barren ground. A smirk on his lips, his eyes shone. "De-robed? Hot looking old guy?"

She slapped his arm and turned away. "Shut up."

"Who says de-robed?"

"Someone around High Kings who wears robes."

"Fair point." Set laughed and then gestured for them to walk towards the court. "So, you had a midnight stroll with the hot, but old, High King, huh?"

"Just add it to the list of weird things that have happened tonight." Ash squinted, looking up at the sky. "Or today? This time zone is confusing."

"Care to share any of the others on your list?"

"I wouldn't know where to begin." Ash laughed. "How are you? You seem . . ."

Set stopped. "I seem what?"

"Like you have the worlds on your shoulders."

Set's sigh was so deep she could hear his breath hitch. "I wouldn't know where to begin either."

"How about a burden for a burden? We don't offer any advice, we don't even acknowledge what the other person says, and it never leaves this place." Ash gestured to the deadened trees surrounding them. They were only feet away from entering the vibrant woodland.

"So you're suggesting we unburden ourselves in the barren?"

"Catchy. It means it has to help."

Ash fidgeted in her spot, unsure why she suggested this in the first place. She had too much going on in her head, but she also felt like he needed to unload whatever he had pent up. With the few tentative sniffs she'd allowed herself, she could tell he was still wrapped up in some terrible despair. She wished she'd thought to douse Maebh's perfume earlier.

"Okay," Set said as he lowered himself to the ground, patting the space beside him. He shirked out of his jacket, displaying a green t-shirt underneath, so tight she could make out every plane of muscle. Heat crept to her cheeks as she carefully spread out her own coat in a way to force herself to stop staring before he caught her.

When Ash planted herself down on it, she immediately felt silly. Tucking loose strands of hair behind her ears, she cast a wary glance at him. "Who goes first?"

"This was your idea."

It took several attempts to speak as she processed her thoughts, and true to their agreement, Set waited silently until she spoke. "I have no idea how to be matriarch."

Silence greeted her as Set only nodded without looking at her. Tucking his legs up, he hugged them as he stared into the wasteland.

"I'm the reason my father is missing."

Ash continued to stare ahead, forcing herself to stick to her own rules, but she couldn't help her frown. Why would he think that? He had only been a teenager, like her, when their parents went missing.

"I'm not as upset as I should be that my mother was murdered."

The moment it left her lips, she regretted it. What must he think of her? They sat side by side, listening to the faint wind whistle through the brittle branches and Ash stretched out her legs, half-heartedly wiping off the powder white sand that covered her clothing.

"One minute I'm me," Set began, his forearms tensing with every word. "And then the next I feel this rage take over my body. I can't control it. I'm afraid of myself. Of what I might do."

"I stole evidence from my mother's murder scene."

Shit. She'd gone too far. She clasped her hands over her mouth. He turned to look at her, his grey eyes questioning, but he didn't ask. She found herself explaining anyway.

"It was a letter. One that had been delivered to me at the cafe, and then soon stolen. When I found her, it had been in her hand. I needed to know what was on it. But it ripped in half."

Ash didn't realise her voice had broken, or that tears had fallen, until Set placed his arm across her shoulders, drawing her close to his body. With a shuddering breath, she realised whatever burden he'd unloaded had replaced his scent with peppermint and a freshly chopped wood. She inhaled deeply, her breathing coming out in embarrassing gulps.

"Hey, it's okay."

"But it's not. Who does that? Who steals evidence from their mother's body?"

"You were in shock." Set rubbed her arm in a soothing gesture, eliciting shivers. "Did you read it?"

"I couldn't. It was covered in blood." Ash took a deep breath, wiping away her tears. She sat upright, and he moved his arm away after a gentle squeeze. "Tiernan is working on it."

"You need to find out what it says. There's clearly a reason she had it."

Nodding, Ash strangely felt more at ease than she had in a long time. Even before finding her mother. It wasn't like she was sitting beside a stranger. She was being comforted by a friend.

"Is there anything else you want to get off your chest?" Ash bumped her shoulder against his side. "I'm pretty sure nothing could be worse than that."

Set stiffened beside her, his jaw tensing as he turned his head again to stare straight ahead, and she immediately regretted opening her stupid mouth.

He lay on the dirt ground, shielding his eyes with one arm. "There are things I've done. Things I'm ashamed of. And things I'm afraid that I'm guilty of."

Ash lay beside him, the uneven earth rough against the thin material on her back as she let him unload whatever he needed, in however way he needed to. She was getting used to cryptic conversations.

"Maebh has always had to look out for me. She's had to go through so much shit. Our mother is not a loving woman.

She's nicer to me, but it's only because she thinks I'm some . . . experiment she can play with.

"It's good Mae left. She'll be able to live her life without the burden of Mam or me. But, and I'd never tell her this, I don't know how to live in our clan without her. I've always been alone, but now I'm completely lost in the darkness with nobody to care enough to pull me from it."

When Set finished and his shoulders shook, she took his free hand and clasped it in hers, his calloused palms more coarse than hers, a sign of the training he did. She didn't know how long they lay like that, but he became quiet, his other arm still covering his face. Ash breathed in deeply and let out a long sigh. Looking at the sky, she forgot they were laying on deadened land. The stars shone so brightly she almost lifted her hand to see if she could touch them. Billions of blazing lights connecting the heavens to them.

"When you're at your darkest moment, look to the sky."

Set rubbed his eyes against his large bicep, finally uncovering his face to squint at her. When she met his gaze, she was thrown again by how beautiful he was. The larger-than-life man, his vulnerabilities and uncertainties laid bare for only her and the stars.

"What will I see?" His voice was a whisper as his gaze captivated her.

She almost forgot her answer, but turned her attention back to the night.

"Hope."

CHAPTER 35

SETANTA

Had he killed Cara?

The thought was a constant buzzing in the background of every move he made through the awakening dawn. From the moment the detective had described Cara's wounds, he'd known it was a possibility. Laying still in his bed roll, staring through the opening of his shelter, Set watched the sky lighten to a muted grey, the stone castle the backdrop to the Cath warrior campsite.

Each clan had set up at different stages throughout the night. The only guidelines they'd been given were to stay close to the wall near the farmlands. The taverns and homes of the Fianna who lived there couldn't house the sheer numbers of clans who'd gathered for the Cath. They had given the warriors makeshift tents and told them to forage and barter for any food they'd need from then on.

Set supposed it was better than being left to deal with the savages of this realm. The Kingdom of Mede belonged to Aedan O'Dwyer by name only, it seemed. Outside, the high stone walls of Tara Court was said to be as savage as the rest of the realm under the Fair Ones' rule, giving just this sliver of land to Fianna.

Rumours had circulated that the wild faeries roamed, and the highguard had little power over them. Like the human realm, the Fair Ones gave little thought to upholding the Peace Treaty, and knew there wasn't much Fianna could do about it. The High King remained within these high walls, hoping that Tara Court kept him safe.

Set stretched in his bed before giving up on sleep that would not come. Dressing, he looked out to his clansmen who slept on. The smarter warriors had retired early, while others continued the celebrations long after the last sacrifice. He was glad to have missed those, having wandered into the woods at the druid's suggestion. She'd cornered him on his way to rejoining his clan, and instead of answering his questions about how he sifted between realms, she hinted some more riddles about meeting his destiny. Instead of referencing the moon like before, she'd said the stars would guide him. That's when he'd stumbled upon the High King and Ash. It seemed the druid was right about them being destined to meet, and they would continue to do so until he found out whether he was a murderer.

With every few feet he took away from his clan, the rest of the warriors stirred. Fire pits rekindled and soft murmuring drifted around him as everyone prepared for what today would bring. He smiled at a few warriors who sat huddled by a small flame, all looking worse for wear.

Malachy had rounded up all the McQuillan clan early, insisting the festival was the beginning of the Cath, and a test to see who was taking it seriously. Their second had dismissed the arguments that they only had to successfully complete a mysterious quest, an easy task for the mighty McQuillans. Set had already set up camp when Malachy arrived, their reluctant clansmen trailing behind. Some had grumbled about missing the fun but eventually quietened to snores upon their second's threats. He had seen the late stragglers of others and bed roll hopping of different warriors through the dark hours.

The band had played on; the sound of their instruments floating beyond the market square, and to where he lay in the farmland that had the castle as a backdrop, a looming, pointed shadow in the night. He glanced at it now in the morning light, the many turrets and towers not reaching as high as the wall enclosing them. Tara Court stretched for miles, and there was probably enough space if the visiting warriors were not here, but from every angle the stone wall blocked the view of what lay beyond.

The sky had remained clear last night, a blessing as he slept under the stars, leaving his tent open. He looked to the now lightening sky, blazing in pinks and reds as the sun made her way to bring a new day.

"What will I see?"

"Hope."

He hadn't told Ash how much last night meant to him when they'd eventually dusted off the white dirt from the barren land and headed back to Tara Court. She had been there to listen, no judgement, something he had needed for longer than he'd realised. He found himself with lighter steps as he weaved through the different groupings in search of his sister. And Ash . . . he smiled. He looked forward to seeing her again, despite the secrets lurking between them. She was a friend he hadn't expected, but abundantly grateful for.

Last night was the first in a long time he'd released his pent up emotion. He was usually too afraid to cry like that. It wasn't only rage that sparked the monster inside him to stir. Like when the druid had tricked his mind into thinking he held a baby, Ash had cast her own spell on him. One that made him feel like he was safe while she was there. He felt connected to her in a way he didn't think would be possible for him.

Orla and the women before her were just a physical release, and although he felt like a shit for admitting this, they were only a distraction. He'd reluctantly lumbered Maebh with his fear and guilt over the years, but afterwards he never felt relief like he had with Ash. Maybe it was because they were strangers? Or because he'd vowed to himself, he wouldn't get romantically involved with another, so she was safe from him. Maybe it was what the druid had said.

"Your destiny greets you under the stars. Stay close."

Even though he wanted to, and the druid had an unknown interest in getting them to connect, he couldn't fully admit his demons to Ash. The way she looked at him . . . as if he was a good person, someone worthy of admiration. It was easy lying to her when she wanted so badly to believe him. To believe *in* him.

The field was teeming with people. Although some bedrolls still held snoring bodies, other warriors were sparring with swords, or huddled by fire pits, murmuring intently. He was sure everyone had the same thing on their minds. The reason they were here. The High King's quest. What would today bring?

The draw to be with his family had diminished since his twin had left. There had been no sign of Imogen, to his relief. What Maebh had said about his injuries healing had planted a seed of doubt in him. What if she had been drugging him with more druid potion than he realised? He shook his head. There was no way he wouldn't know. That drink was something you couldn't hide. The smell alone would give it away. Maybe he should ask Ethne about it. She seemed willing to help him, and she'd know more about the side effects of those potions. Last night, he'd wanted to ask her if she knew how he'd somehow transported himself to Tír na nÓg at their first encounter, but the druid had shushed him, insisting he follow the woodland and his destiny.

Set weaved along the fenced animals, watching the farm workers heave buckets of feed around as they tended to their early morning duties. What would it be like to live here? A simpler life in some ways, no technology and few modern comforts, but there was an appeal to what this world offered.

Ash had told him what the High King had said about the Cath. It didn't matter where your clan ranked. Then what was the purpose of it? What was he planning? The highguard had remained unchanged for a century.

The Hill of Tara was the only other elevated land within the walls, one of a few places that remained unchanged in both realms. Crafted slopes surrounded the mound that held the Stone of Destiny, silent like any other rock, for hundreds of years. The magical stone only cried out when it recognised the right to rule by the High King. It had been silent for King Aedan, as it had been for the previous kings before him.

Spotting Maebh's blonde plaits as she sat on a log at the Breen camp, his breath hitched. What would it be like to leave the McQuillan clan and find your own? Set noticed that their tents were much smaller than any other clans. Why had they brought so few warriors? The Breens were just as big as the McQuillans, and although Imogen had insisted on intensive training far more than the Brehon law dictated, all clans were expected to be Cath ready in case the High King called upon them. He knew the Breens had far more warriors than they'd brought.

Set realised he needed to be more present, and ask questions. He was always so wrapped inside the torment of his mind, and he'd had enough. If he wanted to find out if he had been the one to kill Cara, he'd need to help Ash and his sister with whatever investigation they had. He didn't need to ask to know Maebh was actively investigating Cara's death. She hadn't given up on finding their father and the other caillte, even years after her search went cold and no fresh evidence being brought to light.

When he'd criss-crossed past other campfires and was just feet away, Maebh looked up. Her expression was pinched until she saw him, and then a forced smile appeared. He frowned. He hated when she pretended she was okay because she felt like he wasn't strong enough to know the truth. She was just as messed up as he was, but for different reasons. A faint scent reached him, but he had never been good at deciphering emotions. He thought it reminded him of something tart and sour.

"Good morning, Bro," Maebh murmured as she stoked the fire. "Did you know they expect us to find our own breakfast? After that enormous feast last night, you would think they could just give us left overs."

Set sat cross-legged beside her, the ground still damp from the early morning dew. "Our clan stole some of the food before they left the festival last night."

Our clan. As if she wasn't part of it. She would lead the McQuillans one day, when Imogen retired, or died. For Maebh's sake, the latter would be better, so their mother couldn't call into question every decision his sister made. She had to come back to the McQuillans. Set locked eyes with his sister, his grey to her blue, and for a moment he felt like she knew where his thoughts had gone. She broke contact first, and Set rubbed his jaw. His few days' stubble had already turned into a dirty blond beard.

Maebh would rule them fairly, even though she pretended she didn't care. In the rare moments she'd shared her true feelings with him, she'd talked about the changes she'd make. Set would be by her side, her second, supporting her leadership.

"Of course they did. Smart fuckers." Maebh placed a padded glove on before lifting a heavy tin teapot over the flames. "At least they provide water from their wells. If I had to go through today without at least one cup of tea, I'd end up slaughtering everyone."

"Where's the rest of your clan?" Set asked, trying and failing to hide the way he choked on the last part. There were a couple of rucksacks and bed rolls neatly stacked beside them, but there were only a couple of bodies still covered up and presumably asleep a few feet away.

Luckily, Maebh seemed too absorbed in her task to notice his stumble. "The Breen brothers went to find sustenance, Ash and Conor went for a walk together, Tiernan went to check on his tree, and"—Maebh gestured to the couple with her chin—"Emer and her wife, Niamh, are still asleep."

Set's eyes met Maebh's before her attention went back to the kettle in her gloved hand and he knew there was something she wasn't telling him. He had known about her relationship with Emer, and how it didn't end well. She had only told him fragments, and like always, he would wait until she was ready to talk. "Tiernan has a tree?"

"More like a satellite dish," a male voice said from behind him.

Set twisted in his spot and peered up at Tiernan. He was holding a small rucksack across his shoulder. It had been years since he'd spoken to Tiernan; they had little in common. The hacker didn't enjoy talking combat skills or weaponry, and neither had the same taste in books. Set had always felt a little wary around him, like Tiernan was secretly judging Set on some score that he'd never be able to reach. Set was judged on his appearance alone and his actions were ridiculed based on his name.

"Hey, bud. Good to see you." Set stood and clasped hands with Tiernan, whose gaze kept flitting to Maebh, and Set instantly felt sorry for him. Not many people could resist the attraction towards his sister, but she tried to put them off with the many thorns in her personality. All weapons to protect herself. "We were just talking about breakfast."

Tiernan went over to a trunk where they seemed to be keeping supplies and took out a pot. Reaching into his bag, he retrieved a container and dumped the contents in. "Can I please have some of that water you're heating, Maebh?" Tiernan asked, looking at her intently as he did.

"Sure, no problem."

Set watched in wariness at this polite exchange; it was completely out of character for his sister. Maebh didn't look at Tiernan once and went back to heating her own pot when he'd said he had enough.

"Mae, you're not usually so much a morning person. What's changed?"

Maebh cut him with a glare as she brought the pot to the ground unceremoniously and went over to the trunk. Tiernan gave him a tight smile as he stirred the contents of his pot with a long-handled spoon. The smell of oats and something sweet drifted through the air and Set leaned across to see inside. "You brought porridge? King of breakfasts, good choice."

"It's the only thing I'm good at cooking," Tiernan replied with a shrug.

Emer and Niamh stirred from their rucksacks. When Emer spotted Set, she gave him a tentative smile, one he replied with tight lips. Maebh believed she was the cause of their breakup, but he'd been there through some of their arguments. Emer was high maintenance, with a fiery temper and low tolerance level. Just like his twin. If anything, it was a case where they were too similar. When Maebh had approached Tiernan about comparing notes on their missing parents and had made the mistake of letting her emotions take over, it was as if Emer had seen her chance to break up without being the one to blame for it.

He'd been the only one from their clan to know about their relationship. It was hard hiding anything from your twin and

Maebh and he had given up long ago. It was why, when he discovered her empty room, it had hurt so much.

Niamh greeted them cheerily, Emer in a more quiet way, before the couple left to 'freshen up'. Set smirked. That was a nice way to put a morning piss in the woods. When Maebh had poured tea into cups for the three of them and Tiernan had given each of them a bowl of his porridge with blackberries, Ash and Conor joined them. The black-haired matriarch sat beside Set, taking her own cup and bowl, and nudged his side before tucking into her breakfast. He noted her hair was tightened into a plait that Maebh often favoured during combat training, and a reminder of what they could face today played in his mind. He nudged her in return and smiled before catching Maebh's questioning look. And then he remembered. He may have killed Ash's mother.

"Is your experiment working, Tiernan?" Conor asked, his voice as quiet as his presence. He could see similarities between the siblings, their dark hair and pale features distinctive to the Breens.

"It is." Tiernan looked at Set and then Ash, who nodded.

"You can talk in front of Set. I trust him."

Set's chest tightened at the unwarranted loyalty, but he returned her smile before concentrating on his breakfast.

"Maebh and I were able to connect this realm with the human one," Tiernan began, setting his empty bowl at his feet. Maebh stoked the fire at the centre, and Set noticed she looked at everyone but Tiernan, who constantly looked to her. He sighed when she refused to meet his eye and continued, "I don't know if you're familiar with druid potions?"

Set sat up straighter, cracking his neck. "Painfully so." When silence met him, he explained, "Imogen McQuillan is a dab hand at replicating a healing potion and I've needed it from time to time."

He met Maebh's stare and she looked ready to kill their mother. She hated a lot of things about the matriarch, but her ministrations on Set after a turning were probably the highest on the list. Even higher than her physical assaults, something he hated both his mother for doing, and him for being unable to stop her. Maebh was right. She had some sort of power over them that nobody else could understand.

"I'm not as good as your mother, I'm sure, but I created a potion that makes whatever it encircles invisible to only the people within, and to protect it from being tampered with. It's like a pocket in each realm that can talk to one another. The ancient oak I used exists in both realms, so technically, they are the exact same place."

Everyone sat in silence and Set thought he might not be the only one who didn't understand any of that.

"So what Tiernan is trying to say is, he's got great Wi-Fi, but only at our tree," Maebh added; a rare sight of a flush on her cheeks as she finally met Tiernan's gaze.

"Right," Tiernan said, a smile on his lips.

Set looked between the two, and when Emer and Niamh joined the circle, it clicked. Maebh became quiet and reserved once more, now refusing to meet, not only Tiernan's gaze, but his cousin's, too. Something had happened between his sister and the hacker, and Maebh felt guilty because of her past relationship with Emer. Set sighed as he smiled to himself. The trouble that his sister got herself into sometimes was comical.

A large hand clasped Set's shoulder and he looked behind to find Malachy standing there. "We need to get moving, Set."

The McQuillan clan second stared ahead as he got to his feet, and Set knew he was ignoring Maebh. When he cast his eyes to her, though, she smiled as if she had just heard the best news. Another protective reflex, Malachy's dismissal would kill her.

He was one of the few clansmen who stood up to their mother and tried to protect Maebh from her abuse.

"I'll see you later, Bro. Thanks for stopping by," Maebh said cheerily.

Ash stood and gripped his arm. "Good luck today."

"You too." Set patted her arm in return and before turning towards the second, he added. "And I meant what I said. I'm not going against Dom, so you can count on me out there."

He heard Ash's light laughter, and it caused a smile to play on his own lips. When he looked at Malachy, though, it disappeared. "What's wrong?"

"Imogen hasn't been seen since last night."

"She probably talked her way into staying in a room at the castle," Set said, knowing that's exactly something his mother would do.

"I'm going to go look for her, so I need you to get our clan in order for the quest if I'm not back in time. Rumour has it the druid woman has something in store for us."

"How do you know that?"

"I got chatting to one of the highguards last night."

Set laughed. "Translate that to you seduced a guard and he spilled secrets during pillow talk?"

Malachy grinned. "There was no pillow."

They reached the McQuillan clan, who were all dressed and prepared for the trial, and Malachy gave a quick briefing to everyone, explaining Set was in charge, before departing towards the castle. Orla stood at the front of the group, her pouting mouth twisting into a grin when Set walked by.

"Have you come to your senses yet?" she murmured as she grabbed his arm, right where Ash had moments before. He didn't get the same sense of contentment from it, but was mindful of not hurting Orla's feelings.

"We've been through this, Orla." He patted her hand before stepping away. "I thought I made myself clear."

He signalled for the clan to meet by their large fire pit, running his hand through his unruly hair. His mind had already moved on to the day ahead.

"Where did you go?" Orla's voice brought him up short, and he didn't turn around as she pushed further. "After you ended our . . . fun, I followed you. You had one of your anxiety attacks and ran, and when I tried to catch up, it was like you disappeared."

Set stared at her, thinking about what could have happened if he hadn't somehow teleported to Tír na nÓg. If Ethne hadn't been there to calm him from turning into a monster, would Orla be standing before him now?

Narrowing his eyes, he bit out. "You shouldn't have followed me."

Before she could answer, a horn sounded and all warriors began walking towards the town square. Set grabbed his weapons from his tent and led the McQuillan clan into the throngs of warriors. There was no chatter, only determined footsteps.

This was it. The quest to qualify for the Cath. His stomach clenched with every step until he stood facing the same raised platform where the High King's table had been the night before. Ethne now stood with highguards, her grey cloak flowing around her and her white hair like silken curtains falling over her chest. From this distance, he could only make out her pale skin and flashes of colour from her many tattoos. Although, when she spoke, it was like she was right in front of them.

"The High King wants you to seek what has been lost. A treasure more valuable than gold," Ethne began, the lilt of her voice like a soft caress. "Until it is found, no one shall join the highguard."

Murmurs ran through the crowds as feet shuffled and protests began. They were already on borrowed time, and it was a gamble they'd all been willing to take, hoping to secure a place in the highguard. If they stayed in Tír na nÓg for more than a few days, nobody knew how much time would pass in the human realm. The druid raised her hands, and Set wasn't sure if everyone was afraid she'd perform the same silencing trick as the night before, but the commotion died down.

"Take heed in what I say, as it will not be repeated. Coming from a time when both realms united, a great warrior king now slumbers in this land. Lore tells us to call upon him when Ireland needs him. She will not rest until he awakens."

Set's heart hammered with every word she spoke, the impossible quest dawning on him. He searched the crowds until his gaze met the green eyes he searched for. The High King's conversation last night could not be mistaken as coincidence to the tale being told on stage. Set nodded subtly at Ash, knowing she'd come to the same conclusion. Her brows furrowed before she turned back towards the druid, and Set knew she'd also realised how long this could take. He didn't know how long he stood staring at Ash, deep in contemplation, but he soon realised that Ethne was no longer standing on stage. A flicker of alarm ran through him when hot breath caressed his ear, and he flinched.

Ethne stood by his side, a knowing smile playing on her lips. "You must find the first High King, Fionn Mac Cumhaill."

CHAPTER 36

AISLING

"You're sure the creepy tunnels under the Hill of Tara are where you want to search for a dead guy?" Maebh asked from her seat across the rickety wooden table of the tavern they'd been in for the past hour.

Ash didn't answer, instead watching Tomás at the lone bar across the room, placing an order for their table. She sighed. Not that they had the luxury of time. Ciarán and Conor remained quiet also, their features highlighting their similarities. Seeing Conor now a man, they could be mistaken for brothers.

When she didn't respond, Maebh huffed a strand of hair from her face. She'd braided it tightly into warrior plaits, but the front strands came loose with her dramatic movement. Ash wondered if she'd get to see her in action as a member of the highguard, but with every passing moment of indecision, the chance to pass this quest was becoming an impossible task.

"Are you going to question my decisions like the other two?" Ash eventually asked through gritted teeth. Instead of running to random destinations like many other clans, she'd insisted they needed time to strategise. Something her mother had taught her. Now, as time ticked on, and they were nowhere closer to actually searching, she feared she'd made the wrong choice. With tense shoulders, she pointed toward the narrow door. "I sent Emer and Niamh to find supplies just to get a break from being judged with every breath I take."

"Fair enough." Maebh smiled as she raised both hands in surrender, only for Ash to give her a weary smirk in response.

She raised her clay mug, taking a long drink from the nettle tea they all nursed until her cousin came back with food. The tavern was dimly lit and already full of Fianna, both visiting clans like them and the settlers of Tara Court. Some still wore fashions from eras gone by, but most kept to simple tunics and pants.

Ash peered at the long bar to her left where a couple of trolls had perched on bar stools, Tomás keeping a wide berth from the pools of excretion on the dirt floor by their enormous feet. They were half her height but twice her gait, so the feat of sitting on the seat was an accomplishment in itself.

It had taken until now for her to stop holding the hilt of her sword. They were only there for the same reason anyone else was. Being around fae in the human realm differed from the more civilised kind here. These beings were clearly a different species to humans, but they didn't mean to cause harm. This was their world, and Ash and the others were the odd ones.

A table of Fianna warriors closest to their table raised from their seats, exiting the tavern in sure steps, and she watched with envy. They were off to do what her clan should be: searching.

With a weariness she only got when she felt sure she'd fail at something, she leaned her head back and stared at the ceiling. Why had King Aedan summoned her to that barren land? Why had he hinted at the quest before announcing it to the other clans? More importantly, *did* she believe the legend could be true?

The story of Fionn Mac Cumhaill was as legendary as it was far fetched, despite the insistence of its truth from their current king. Knowing the existence of fae and this magical realm was one thing, but she wasn't foolish enough to immediately believe a tale about a king who'd died long before the Peace Treaty between the fae and Fianna.

"I understand why you sent those two away," Maebh began, clearly gauging Ash's already tense expression. "But their arguments are also valid. The other clans are venturing beyond the wall. To the lands the High King seems to have forgotten are part of his kingdom."

"Keep your voice down," Ciarán said, his eyes trained on the neighbouring table which had just been occupied by highguard.

Clearly on a break, and seemingly unimpressed by the business of what was probably their local bar. Their armour was cut from black metal, weapons visible on their belts. Ash assessed the guards, but they paid no attention back. Ash and the other warriors had taken up a lot of space since their arrival. In truth, nobody had known what to expect for the Cath, but spending so much time in Tara Court hadn't been something she'd considered.

The door opened, letting light into the dimmed room, and Ash squinted until it was closed and Tiernan approached. Tomás came back to the table carrying a platter of food and the two men sat. Her stomach growled at the smell of warm bread and cheese, along with an array of berries that seemed to absorb the flames from their lone brass candelabra on the table. As she leaned closer, they changed colour, turning from purple to a red that looked like lava. She plucked one up, mesmerised by the dripping juices of varying colours and noting how it sizzled in her hand.

"What're these?"

Grabbing one between his own fingers, Tomás squinted at the fruit. "The barman said they were a local delicacy. I couldn't pronounce it. Sounded like 'choas sirain'."

She waited until he bit into one and gave a thumbs up, and she popped the fruit into her mouth. Her eyes streamed as she reached for the pitcher of water he'd brought.

"Oh." Tomás grinned. "He also said that they taste different depending on the time of year. Right now, they're like fiery chillies."

"Thanks for the warning," Ash grumbled as her cousin reached for another and she downed her drink.

Conor, who hadn't even looked at the food, rose from his seat and wandered off without a glance at anyone. She was about to follow, but Maebh reached across the table, grabbing her hand.

"He needs some air. Let him go."

"What do you think, Tiernan?" Ash asked in hushed tones as Conor exited the tavern. "He's not acting like himself, right?"

"He just needs time, I'm sure of it." Tiernan looked at the now closed door, his expression troubled. Eyeing the others before he met her gaze once more, he added, "I spoke to my father. He is completely against this quest. Called it a charade and intends to speak to the High King about what we've all come here for."

"Everyone else is treating it seriously," Ciarán said from the end of the table, in between mouthfuls of bread. "What do the legends say about Fionn Mac Cumhaill's resting place? I didn't pay much attention during lessons."

Ash smirked, remembering just how little attention her cousin had paid. "If I remember correctly, you got us into a lot of trouble with Mrs O'Malley."

"Is it my fault she has so many doilies in her caravan?" Ciarán's smile was wide enough to display his dimples. His brown eyes shone as he shrugged. "I didn't know they were that flammable."

"Oh, my mother would have hated you in our clan," Maebh laughed. "You sound like someone I need to introduce her to."

Ciarán winked at Maebh before saluting his cup to hers, and Ash couldn't help noticing Tiernan's frown.

After a few minutes, where the only sound was their munching, he said, "Fionn Mac Cumhaill was a fighter first. He formed the band of warriors known as the Fianna—"

"Whoop!" Maebh chuckled as he ignored her.

"And travelled around Ireland when the veil between our worlds wasn't as strong. During the Battle of Gabhra, they say Fionn died—"

"Or that he went to slumber," Tomás interjected. "Surrounded by his clansmen until his hunting horn sounds three times, and then he'll wake."

Ash gripped her mug, the story unfolding before her as she tried to piece it together. "But his horn was never found, and there's also the debate that there is no horn; that what will wake him is the three Fianna war cries."

"King Aedan doesn't want us to wake Fionn up." Maebh said. "Just find him."

"In between Ciarán setting Mrs O'Malley's caravan on fire," Ash said with a smile to which her cousin chuckled, "I remember her saying that Fionn slumbered in a cave. The Hill of Tara is riddled with them."

"But Ash, don't you think Aedan has looked in those caves?" Ciarán's use of her nickname caused her heart to skip. "They're right here in his kingdom."

"The cave we explored was off." Tiernan said, his gaze on Maebh.

She met his attention for a second before lowering her eyes to the bread roll in front of her, tearing it into chunks. Shrugging, she nodded. "It felt . . . unwelcoming."

"Did it feel like a repellent?" Ash sat up, excitement brewing right down to her fingertips. "Like your druid potion at the tree, Tier?"

His eyes widened as he nodded. "It could be similar. To ward off anyone."

Ash sat in contemplation, biting her inner cheek as Tiernan described the narrow passage almost not wide enough to walk through. All of her years of learning under her mother, playing scavenger hunts, mock battle strategies, puzzles and board games came to her now. She'd always wondered what good those games and hypothetical scenarios would be, but now she wished she'd paid closer attention. The door opened and Ash pivoted, hoping to see the black hair of her brother returning. She slumped in her seat for a moment, only to sit straight when Emer and Niamh returned, a burlap sack clunking at their feet.

"We have the torches and rope like you asked, Matriarch," Niamh announced. She nudged her wife, who turned to Ash with a tight-lipped smile.

"My better half wants me to apologise for my behaviour towards you, Aisling," Emer began, her dark brown eyes scrutinising her. When Ash raised a brow, she continued. "I still believe Niamh would make a better matriarch"—she grabbed Niamh's hand and gave a gentle squeeze before she could interrupt—"but she wants to give you a chance. I don't know you, but I knew your mother, so I will grant you this quest to prove your worth."

The table grew silent as Ash contemplated the women standing across from her. She'd had enough of this for one day. With slow determination, she stood, placing her palms flat on the uneven table. When she was sure she had her clan's full attention, she leaned in so they could hear her.

"I'm not here to be your enemy, but I am a person. I will prove myself, but you will all take note of how you speak to me." Ash's gaze pierced into each of them, lingering on Emer. "Like it or not, we are a team, or we fail. There are no other options. If you want the Breens to win a chance of being in the highguard, you will follow my lead. You have a choice right now. You stop arguing with me, or you can go home."

Her cousins sat up straighter, smirks on their faces. Maebh leaned back in her seat, saluting her before taking a long drink. Tiernan was frowning at his cousin, who looked ready to say something, but stopped when he muttered her name. Emer met her gaze, and they stared at one another for an eternity, but Ash did not yield. When Niamh patted her wife's hand, the other woman nodded, signalling for her to continue.

Hiding the surge of elation from that little win, Ash returned to her seat.

"I need to prove myself to you, and I plan to. But first, let's get out of here. We have a quest to win."

CHAPTER 37

AISLING

Tara Court was a bustling village in full swing of midday activities as they left the tavern, and Ash squinted in order for her eyes to adjust from the dimly lit room.

"Keep an eye out for Conor."

With the sprawling castle far in the distance, overshadowed by the great wall surrounding the king's court, they stayed within its boundaries as they headed toward the hills in the far distance. The wall must have taken ages to build, encasing the entire human village, though it shrank in size compared to the lands belonging to the fae. As Ash scanned the sky, low-lying clouds shielded her from glimpsing the top where the highguard patrolled.

Taking point, she weaved around the market that had taken over from the festival stalls from the night before. Stalls selling pottery, jewellery, healing tonics and fresh food now replaced where the cooked foods and delicacies had been during the party. The scent of spices and uncooked meat filled her nostrils, as did the assault of emotions that were becoming stronger every day. She turned to Maebh, noticing that she lifted her wrist to her nose often, perhaps trying to counteract the unpleasant smells. When she caught Ash's appraisal, she pinched her nose and made a gagging action as a particularly sour odour passed them, following an angry looking local.

"Does it get easier?" Ash asked, falling into step with her.

Maebh reached into her inner pocket and sprayed perfume on both of them. "Nope."

Her clan followed close behind, and Ash steered them closer to the hill in the distance, all the while looking for the dark, curly hair of her brother. As they wove through the crowd, Tiernan murmured to Emer and Niamh, filling them in on their discussion. Noting a quiet narrow alleyway in between two dwellings, Ash motioned for her clan to huddle close.

"Before we go any further, I want to prove I trust you all." Ash took a deep breath before gesturing to Tiernan. "I've asked Tier to help me solve my mother's murder case." When she saw Maebh's reaction, she added, "And also Maebh. That's why she's joined us."

Taking a leap of faith, she told the others about her discovery of her mother's surveillance, how she'd stolen the half torn letter, all the while ensuring her voice was low enough for any passersby not to overhear.

"Do the initials 'TFHK', mean anything to you?" Tiernan asked the group after they'd all reacted with either curses or silence.

"No," Maebh began, her nose scrunched in concentration. "But I spoke with Diarmuid and he had some interesting stories to tell me."

"Who?" Ciarán asked, turning from his surveillance of the busy street. He'd been quiet the entire time Ash had filled them in on her discovery, only casting unreadable glances at his brother occasionally, who wore an equally stony expression.

"Diarmuid is my . . . is the McQuillan clan seanchai. I talked to him about Teamhair before I joined you. He also spoke about the High King."

"Is it safe to tell us on the way?" Ash asked, her attention ahead and her body tensed with inaction. Time was not on their side, and she knew it would only be luck that gave them an advantage. She was sure underground was their answer, but knew others would be sure to think the same.

Maebh nodded, and they wordlessly fell into step, the small clan weaving through the crowd.

"What did he say?" Ash tried to keep her voice calm after a few minutes, knowing that if her seanchai had revealed anything important, Maebh would have told her already.

"The High King has sent loyal clansmen over the years in search of a lost treasure. They have even ventured beyond the Kingdom of Mede." She kept her voice low, and they all leaned in as they continued toward the hill. "He's searched the Tuatha Dé Danann territory. After years, he's concluded that the treasure is in his kingdom. And now we know this treasure is Fionn Mac Cumahill."

Ash looked around warily, realising if Maebh found reason to be cautious, then they should tread carefully. "Why does your storyteller know this? These aren't lore."

Maebh gave a smile. "Diarmuid is gifted with knowing all of our old tales, but he's also the biggest gossip I know. His favourite saying is 'there's no smoke without fire'. He wouldn't have told me this if he truly didn't believe there was something to it."

They were in the heart of the market now, and it was too hard to keep their voices hushed as they were forced to span out. In this quiet reprieve, Ash let everything sink in. She had to trust her instincts, and her gut was telling her she was right.

"Did your storyteller mention the tunnels under the Hill of Tara?" Ash asked when the group stood on the outskirts of the town square. She cast her gaze fruitlessly again for Conor.

Maebh nodded. "He said that they branched off, which we saw in that antechamber. He warned me to be careful because

319

if we took the wrong path, we could end up in dangerous lands, or lost like many other things down there."

"Exactly! That's why the tunnels make sense." Ash bit her bottom lip, the wheels of her mind spinning as she placed pieces together. "We know there are multiple tunnels because we've seen them entering Tara Court. He'd said the tunnels could take us to dangerous lands. I hadn't considered we might actually be hunting one of those lands. The right place to go hunting if we want to win." She raised an eyebrow, staring at her clan. "We want to win, don't we?"

"Of course." Emer said with a sigh.

Just then, Conor appeared through the crowd, his face pale as he approached.

"Are you okay, Con? Do you need to go rest?"

She took in the sheen of sweat across his face. He shook his head, shirking out of her grasp. "I'm fine."

Giving him a chance to change his mind, she swallowed before pointing toward the base of the hill. "Let's go."

A group of Fianna warriors were just exiting the tunnel mouth, and Set's unmistakably imposing figure came into view from the shadowed door. When he straightened, his smile widened when he spotted Ash.

"How's the search going?" he said in greeting. Standing in front of his McQuillan clansmen, he looked every bit a Viking warrior out of a storybook.

Her own smile was wide as she ignored the fluttering in her stomach. "We're only getting started."

"If you're planning on the tunnels, we've tried nearly all of them with no luck. We're taking a break to regroup."

"Aren't you going to introduce me to the little orphan matriarch, Set?" A brown-haired warrior stepped away from the rest of their clan, a sneer on her lips as she looked at Ash.

"Orla," Set said through gritted teeth. "That's out of order."

"Oh, so you're Orla," Maebh said, standing beside Ash. "She has a twin, but I can never tell them apart. One "—she flourished her hand towards the woman—"has a face like a slapped arse, but the other one is nice."

"Maebh," Set groaned, his hand coming up to rub his temple.

"You bitch," Orla seethed as she gripped her sword hilt and stepped in front of Maebh. "We're all glad you left. Your mother told me so last night. How now she can concentrate on training a worthy matriarch to take her place."

Maebh's eyes twinkled with amusement. "You're grabbing that sword handle with too much pressure. A light grip will wield higher control there, Orla. I guess some people can never be taught." She tsked. "Unfortunate really. But please, impress us with your empty threats. I love a good show."

"Stop it, both of you," Ash began, sensing her cousins move closer as she tried to step in front of Maebh. She turned to see Tomás gripping her arm, pulling her to his side; his glare solely on the fuming woman now unsheathing her weapon.

"Orla." Set placed his hand on her arm, stopping her from taking her blade fully from its holder. "Enough."

"Don't touch me." She shirked out of his grasp, her voice raising. His hands raised, as if he was trying to coax a wild animal.

Ash's breath caught in her throat as Orla raised her hand, ready to strike Set with a backhanded slap, but a whirl of smoke appeared and a pale hand gripped Orla's wrist. The rest of Ethne came into focus and she stood between a shocked looking Set and the angry female before her.

"Turning on your clan?" the druid asked, her tone deathly quiet. Her moonlit, pale face seemed to glow from something other than the sun above.

The world went quiet as everyone waited. Ash's own breaths were shallow as Orla stammered nonsense, trying to get out of the druid's grip. Ethne brought her closer, turning her hand and raising it to her lips. "Your hand was full of violence towards another. Therefore, it shall be the same for you." With those words, she kissed the woman's hand; a blinding light radiating at contact and Orla screamed.

In one blink, the light was gone, as was the druid. Ash waited for her eyes to adjust before she glanced at Orla's raised hand and stared at the puckered mouth scorched on it, a brand left behind. She let out an ear-piercing shriek as her hand twitched before clawing at her own face.

"What the fuck?" Maebh said from beside her, and they all watched, mesmerised, as Orla fought with her hand, that was attempting to gouge her right eye.

A few stunned seconds of silence followed before Set grabbed Orla's arm, and this time, she didn't fight him off as he held it away from her body. It continued to writhe like a snake, intent on causing harm. Ash watched in horror as Set winced. Orla's nails were digging into his flesh, clawing to be released.

She stood closer, ready to help, when Set's demeanour changed. His face turned red, sweat beading on his brow as he shook so violently the edges of his body blurred.

"Setanta," Maebh said, pushing Ash out of the way and gripping her brother's arm. He wordlessly shoved her before spinning Orla into his clansmen. His panicked gaze met Ash's and she opened her mouth to ask what was wrong before his body rippled like tarmac in the sun and then he was gone.

Vanished.

CHAPTER 38

AISLING

"Where did he go?" Ash turned to Maebh, but she only stared at the spot where her brother had been.

The other McQuillans hadn't seemed to notice the disappearance of their clansman as they gathered around a screaming Orla, and with sickening realisation, Ash watched her pull a fistful of hair from her scalp.

"This is some level of fucked up," Maebh whispered.

They all stood in shock, waiting for something else to happen, but Set didn't reappear. She turned once more to his twin, ready to plan out what to do in order to search for him, when Maebh shook herself. "Setanta is fine. I imagine the druid used her magic on him or something. They're probably knocking boots."

A sickening twist in her stomach formed and she winced. Maebh's gaze darted to hers and she offered a sympathetic smile. "Maybe they aren't, but he's fine either way. Let's get on with our quest."

"We need to go." Conor's voice was close to Ash's ear, and she blinked in surprise at the earnest expression on his face.

Before she could ask if he was okay, he turned toward the guards stationed at the tunnel doorway, who wordlessly opened it. As he disappeared, she took one last look at Maebh's former clan, and then the empty place where Set had been, before shaking herself and following behind her brother. If Maebh was so insistent he was okay, she had to believe it.

The tunnels were dark and uninviting. After everyone gathered at the first antechamber and the guards closed them in, they lit their oil soaked lanterns and Ash led them toward their destination. Her heart thrummed in her ears as she gripped her torch so tightly it hurt. She was sure she was leading her clan in the right direction, but what would she do if they actually found the first High King? What would Aedan do?

Scuttling sounds rushing past their feet did little to help the tension, but they made it to the antechamber that branched into different tunnels, one leading to the human realm. Ash traced the grooves of the markings Tiernan had made, contemplating what would happen if she just took that tunnel, dragging Conor along with her. He wasn't doing well here. No matter how much he'd begged for them to come, she wondered why he desperately wanted it. Ever since they arrived, he'd withdrawn into a shell and looked ready to crack.

Turning away from the path to home—and no doubt safety—Ash handed out a bundle of long rope to Tomás. "You, Ciarán, Emer and Niamh anchor yourselves together."

"I don't like this," Ciarán said, standing closer to Ash. "We should all remain together. Or at least take me or Tom into your team."

Ash stared at her cousin, wondering why he smelled of panic, and with a jolt she realised the smell hadn't been a mystery this time. Although it was an unpleasant odour, she could discern the emotion behind it quicker. "We'll all remain together, but it's too dangerous to tie everyone with one rope."

"We are capable of looking after our matriarch, too," Maebh said through a clenched smile.

Ciarán looked ready to argue, but Ash turned towards everyone. "In the unlikely event we're separated, go back to the entranceway." When both of her cousins opened their mouths to argue, she added, "It won't come to that, but stay safe."

Ash tied the rope around her waist, handing one length to Conor but he shook his head. She was about to argue when Maebh grabbed it and began tying it around her before handing it to Tiernan. Her brother wordlessly took the remaining length of rope dangling from her hands and tied it around his waist so that he was the leader.

"Can anyone else hear that?" Tiernan turned from the narrow tunnel. His face was cast in shadows, but Ash could see his frown.

She leaned closer, but shook her head. All she could hear was a whistling wind and cold blasts of air greeting her from the darkness.

"There's some sort of electric circuit coming from here," Tiernan said, gesturing towards the opening. "I felt it last time, but it's stronger now."

Ash listened again. It was faint, but she could feel it when she leaned into the mouth of the tunnel.

"We should go now," Conor's voice was barely a whisper, his pinched expression not matching his statement. It looked like it was the last thing he wanted to do, but he pushed past Ash and strode into the cave.

"Conor, slow down!" Ash's voice bounced around as she raced after him, feeling the tug of rope as her brother picked up speed.

The torch in her hand was more hazard than aid, and with every step she feared she'd burn herself within the ever shrinking cave walls. She had to shuffle sideways, all the while trying to call after Conor, who was barely visible in front. The tug of the rope was incessant, his pace quick, but he had no torch, and she didn't know how he could move blindly forward, as if he didn't fear what lay beyond.

She couldn't move to angle her head back to where the others followed without scraping against the uneven walls and she was about to call to Conor again, panic setting in, when his face loomed from the darkness in front.

Ash glared at her brother. "Why did you take off so quickly? There's something wrong, isn't there?"

He took the torch from her hand and she pushed through the last narrow part, coming to stand in a slightly wider section. When he didn't answer she stepped closer, but he turned his back on her, casting the torch light along the wall. Sighing, she peered over his shoulder as the others joined them.

"I forgot how much of a tight fucking squeeze this is," Maebh grumbled.

"I saw these patterns before," Tiernan said, aiming his own torch at the wall in front of Conor. The space was only large enough for them to huddle, and the other group was still wedged and unseen in the tunnel, her cousins' cursing reaching her. Ash leaned in, noticing how smooth it was compared to the others. Markings etched on the stone flickering in the firelight.

Conor moved his own torch until he came to an indent similar to the stone basin in Newgrange, and the bloody fingerprint she'd seen in the portal came to mind.

"Hold this," Conor said, his voice strangely calm as he handed Ash back the light.

She took it, trying to hold it away from the others in fear she'd burn someone. A small dagger glinted in his hand before he sliced across his palm.

"What are you doing?" Ash tried to grab his hand with her free one but he jerked away, slamming his palm against the indents.

Nothing happened.

Maebh took the torch as Ash grabbed Conor's wrist, inspecting the shallow cut on his palm.

"Let me bandage this," she began, but Conor grabbed her hand in one swift motion, slicing that too. "Conor!"

He lifted her hand to the wall, and she didn't stop him, shock freezing her limbs. *He had cut her.* White light beamed from the carvings in the wall, illuminating the fainter ancient language hidden below the symbols.

Instead of a portal, they stared at an endless pit of obsidian, the air rising in powerful gusts as it swept past them. A cavernous pit had replaced the wall and in the dim light it was hard to tell how deep it went.

The edge was just wide enough for all four to stand, and Ash found her stomach drop as her heart beat faster.

"Don't try to come in here yet!" she called to the others as she saw Ciarán appear in the narrow entranceway. His face mirrored her own, and she licked her lips, the fear of plummeting clawing at her erratic heart. Tiernan raised his torch, waving it back and forth to try to see something other than the black hole before them.

"Con, how did you know about this?" Ash asked, holding her cut palm to her chest. It stung, but it wasn't deep enough to cause concern.

"Eth . . . Ethne, the druid." Conor took the torch from Maebh, who looked ready to argue, but there was something oddly confident about Conor and Ash couldn't do anything but watch. He had the same determined energy as the evening he'd visited her at the cottage, insisting she had to return and take her birthright as matriarch.

He cast the torch into the pit and they all watched as it fell and fell, somehow never dying out, but also only disappearing once the distance was too great to see it anymore. Ash took a step back from the edge, her heart a heightened beat, drumming her fear of falling to her death. Conor moved behind her, the rope anchoring them together taut in his hand.

"She also told me this next part must happen." Conor's tone was impassive, as if he was bored.

The sound of the rope tearing from his cut was followed by a forceful shove, and Ash only had enough time to register her brother's pale face peering over the edge as she fell.

CHAPTER 39

MAEBH

M aebh fell long enough to remember every poor decision she'd ever made. Long enough to know she wasn't ready to die. Reaching out, she grabbed both Ash's and Tiernan's hands so that they were all joined, facing a death none of them were ready for, but would greet them anyway.

Gravity swallowed them as fear eventually stole her voice and tears blinded her vision as they continued their fatal plummet. She cursed Conor's damned name to the worst realm in the Underworld. This was really happening. It was too dark to see anything other than the blurred outlines of her companions but then Setanta's panicked face broke through the darkness enveloping her, and her blood chilled. What would happen to him without her? Why had she abandoned him to join this fucked up clan?

A faint light grew with each second of their freefall. Every muscle tensed as she gripped their hands tightly, but when she thought the painful impact of hard ground would greet her, the air became dense, their pace slowing as if they were falling through congealed matter. A wet mist clung to her flesh until she came to a stop, floating as if she were deep underwater . . . but not quite. It was no longer air and gravity, but a cold substance that was not solid, or liquid, or even gas or plasma. Heavens above, what *was* this?

She gasped, fighting for oxygen, as they drifted in the unseen element that stopped their deaths, but seemed deadly enough to suffocate. She wasn't sure who let go first, but both of her hands were freed as she clutched her throat, swirling just above a blue hued ground. Maebh's attention snapped to Ash as her arms and legs moved in synchronised strokes as if she were diving toward the bottom of a swimming pool. It worked, and the matriarch inched closer to the ground, the rope binding them tugging on Maebh's waist. Tiernan had almost reached Ash, and the two of them burst through the invisible substance, landing in a mass of limbs on the ground, gasping.

The rope had broken, leaving Maebh suspended.

She fought. Swinging her hands wildly as she frantically tried to follow. The burning in her lungs turned to ice, fear gripping her. She needed air. Now. Her ears rang as her vision blurred. They were right there, staring up at her, but so far out of reach as horror painted their faces. Maebh fought against the current forming within the substance. She would *not* give up. When her fingers finally passed through the barrier, the invisible film resisted for only a moment, but also a lifetime as she feared she'd never take a breath again.

Bursting through the membrane, air filled her lungs in painful, glorious gasps as she landed on the ground beside the others.

"Conor pushed me." Ash sat up, untangling from Tiernan. She angled her head upward as she hugged her legs. Her voice shook. "He pushed."

Maebh followed her gaze but couldn't see the substance or the tunnel ledge they'd fallen from. Wiping at her clothes, she realised she was deathly cold, but dry. "Why would he do that?"

"He said Ethne told him to," Tiernan said, his chest rising and falling rapidly, still lying on his back as he, too, looked into the darkness above. "Maybe he knew we would land safely."

Maebh watched Ash's face as she puzzled over her brother's actions and a leaden weight of worry fell on her as she thought about her twin. Where did Setanta go? He was about to turn, but disappeared, just like he'd said happened before. Her brother could sift between realms, so had he returned to the human world? Her stomach dropped as she bit the inside of her cheek. She hoped he was okay. What would happen to him if he'd remained here and the highguard found him after he turned? The druid had helped before, but would she this time? Or would it be too late? The highguard could think he was a Fair One attacking Tara Court, the only safe place for Fianna in this realm. The Peace Treaty ensured it was the one haven for humans, so they could attack Setanta, which would only leave a trail of blood on her brother's hands.

Tiernan pointed in front of him. "There's something down there."

The darkness was ever present, but somehow muted this far down. Glistening blue stones embedded in the walls and ground lit their path. As Maebh stood on shaking limbs, she took in the tunnel they'd landed in. The walls were wide enough that they could stand side by side, but they were at a dead end, with only one way to go.

Ash untangled the rope from her waist. "Let's go."

Tiernan did the same, walking ahead, and Maebh couldn't help but admire as he took the lead, his fitted jacket highlighting the width of his shoulders before tailoring to a lean torso. He was nowhere close to being the typical warrior build, but she knew how strong those arms were. A blush crept to her cheeks as she visualised how he'd held her against that tree.

The wind picked up from the faint, glowing light ahead and she chastised herself for getting distracted. Now was not the time to crave Tiernan's touch again, or cringe at how she'd reacted afterward.

Maebh's hand went to her belt, where she grazed the hilt of her dagger as comfort. There was a strange sound above the wind, and as she listened through their ragged breaths and unsure footsteps, she thought it sounded like a quarry or building site. Tiernan reached the bend in the tunnel just before them and Maebh tensed, ready to jump in front if anything attacked.

He didn't turn to see if they'd approached, his gaze staring at whatever lay ahead with furrowed brows. Ash reached his side and Maebh's throat bobbed as she allowed herself ten more seconds to relive their time together and at how awkwardly she'd behaved after. It was her fault; the pounding in her heart a mix of what had happened and what she'd made sure wouldn't again. She didn't know how to feel about it, not when Emer was her ex, so she did the only thing she could and pretended it didn't happen.

When she stood beside Ash, she frowned at what she saw. A large cavern lay ahead, lit by more gemstones. White stone statues filled the space in clustered formations, a clear path down the centre toward the end of the cave where a strange table stood. It was made of the same rock as the statues, and it was hard to tell from a distance, but it looked as if it was engraved with symbols or art of some kind.

She took a step forward but froze as the wind died and the sound of rocks banging against one another increased.

"What is that?" Ash asked, clear panic lacing her words as she stood beside Maebh.

Neither moved closer to the statues or whatever lay at the end of the cave, and Maebh decided she wanted to turn around and run as far away as she could. A foreign sense of dread melted over her, causing her mouth to dry, her hands to tremble. *Turn around*, her mind screamed. Shrouded in warning bells of danger, she could feel each forced breath, each blink as she searched the cavern for something to justify the fear that had taken over her mind and body.

Gritting her teeth, she swallowed, but found her mouth was dry, her heart racing painfully against her ribcage. She stepped back to the cave entrance, and her shoulders relaxed, her breathing more steady.

"It's like the druid ward I placed around the tree," Tiernan said after he attempted a few more steps but ended up beside her, a sheen of sweat on his forehead. Ash tried but had the same result; all three ending up at the mouth of the cave.

"It's powerful," Ash said, gritting her teeth as she pushed stray hands of ink black hair from her flushed face. "Whatever is being guarded is important."

"Let's try to reach the end, where that table is," Maebh suggested half heartedly, the idea of entering the room as repulsive as joining the bloodthirsty dearg due on one of her hunts.

"I don't think that's a table," Tiernan murmured, his eyes taking on a glint. "It's a sarcophagus."

"You're right, Tier." Ash gasped. She turned to both of them with a grin, triumph illuminating her delicate features. "This is it. Fionn Mac Cumhaill's resting place!"

"Let's hold hands," Tiernan suggested, offering his to each of them.

Ash took it immediately but Maebh hesitated, only for a second, remembering where his hands had been on her body and how much she'd wanted to go further. Before he could pick up on it, she grabbed his hand and stepped into the cavern again.

The push to run in the other direction beat against her as rapidly as the noise of crashing stone filled the space. What was that? Where was it coming from? There was no time to figure it out as they pushed forward, one painfully slow step at a time.

When one of them pulled against the repellent spell, fighting to turn back, the other two took charge. Taking it in turns to fight through the invisible ward, Maebh kept her gaze forward, trained on the stone coffin. It didn't seem to affect Tiernan as much as her or Ash, so he ended up dragging both of them. Halfway through the rows of statues, the tension lifted and her steps felt lighter.

"I feel much better. Do you both?" Ash asked, letting go of Tiernan's hand and shaking out her limbs.

"Yes," he said, looking at Maebh before dropping his gaze to their entwined fingers. He released her, moving toward one of the stone statues guarding the path.

The absence of his warmth caused her hand to flex, but she turned to the end of the cavern, ready to confirm they'd found the High King's treasure and find a way out. She needed to get away from her ex's cousin before she did something stupid like tell him how she felt.

"They look lifelike," Tiernan murmured. "Look at this one. He's dressed in warrior gear."

As Ash stood with Tiernan inspecting the statues, Maebh marched to the far wall. The sarcophagus reached her waist and was ornately carved in white quartz, flecked with blue gemstones, that gave off the same faint glow as the rest of the cave.

"It's beautiful," Ash said from beside her and Maebh realised she hadn't heard her approach above the constant sound of crashing rocks. She had got so used to the sound that she wasn't sure if she could hear a rhythm to it.

She reached forward, her fingers tracing over one symbol on the stone as she looked down at the face carved into the lid. The figure had arms crossed above their chest, dressed in armour from head to toe.

"What do we do now?" Tiernan asked, walking to the other side of the coffin facing Maebh.

Ash opened her mouth to answer, but Tiernan cursed, staggering back as he stared behind them. A keening sound filled the cave, and Ash gripped Maebh's arm as they both turned to see a banshee by the only exit.

Gripping her dagger, she realised there was no point. The ghostly pale creature cried out while reaching towards them but didn't come closer, her wails rising as blood dripped from her eyes and ears. Maebh winced as she clutched her own ears to muffle the sound. The same panic filled her as if she was standing before the ward to this place. As quickly as the banshee appeared, she was gone, the ringing of her cry lingering in the air. Ash raced towards the mouth, saying nothing, her pace a frantic race.

"Ash!" Maebh stormed forward, sensing Tiernan close behind her. "Wait!"

Halfway down the statue line, Maebh felt the need to leave, and she didn't fight it, letting it push her pace as she tried to reach her matriarch. She reached Ash as they came to the dead-end they'd fallen into.

"This can't happen again!" Ash cried as she scanned the walls.

Realisation dawned on Maebh as Ash moved to the other walls, her shaking hand pressing on the rough surface, looking for a way out.

"The banshee visited you before you found Cara?" Maebh asked as Tiernan inspected the wall.

Ash didn't meet her gaze but nodded, her face paler.

"I've found an indent," Tiernan murmured. Before either of them could reach him, he took out his switchblade and sliced his hand, slamming it against the wall. As bright light seeped through the cracks in the walls, he gripped Ash's hand and uttered the words they all thought. The person they all feared the cry was for. "Let's go find Conor."

The ground shifted, and it instantly threw them upward into the invisible membrane that took their breaths. Maebh was just as ill prepared as the first time, fighting against the unknown substance until panic subsided and she remembered to swim, but this time upward. As soon as she broke through, her ascension began.

Falling upwards was just as terrifying as down, and Maebh barely registered the others as they soared to the tunnel edge, landing ungracefully on the cold ground.

"Come on." Ash was the first to jump to her feet, picking up a discarded torch, mercifully still lit, and racing back through the narrow enclosure.

"The others," Maebh panted, a stitch burning her side. "They'll have followed him. He'll be fine."

Nobody responded as they pressed on. Tiernan was close on Maebh's heels as they reached the antechamber, their collective breaths a mix of disjointed gasps and panic. Through the roaring in her ears, Maebh listened, hoping for a sign to where they should go next.

"Should we split up?" Tiernan asked as he surveyed the dark openings they hadn't investigated.

A soft wail sounded from one tunnel and they wordlessly raced toward it. Sweat beaded Maebh's brow as her stomach dropped. Whoever made those sounds may be already lost by the time they reached them. The cave walls closed in on her as she followed Ash's frantic steps.

The matriarch stopped abruptly, causing Maebh to stumble into her, Tiernan catching her arms as she staggered. Maebh peered over Ash's shoulder at the cause of her halt. Drops of blood led to a slumped figure shrouded in the darkness of the cave. Ash stepped closer, training her torch nearer.

It wasn't Conor.

Faint gurgles reached Maebh before she pushed past Ash. Coming to stand close enough that she could see her face, her mind fighting to decipher the impossibility of what she saw.

"Mam?" Her feet carried her to the form of her mother, broken and torn on the cold ground.

She would think she was dead from the gaping wound at her centre, but the woman was moving her lips, no sound coming out.

Maebh fell to her knees, unsure whether to touch her. Her own stomach threatened to empty as her eye caught the dying woman's innards hanging out of the deep gash. Gasps sounded behind her, but she couldn't look. As always, her mother captured the entire area, and nobody spoke as her glazed eyes focused on her daughter. Her lips formed words, but Maebh couldn't hear.

Leaning in, she gripped her mother's limp hand. "I can't understand you. Who did this to you?"

Imogen's eyes rolled so only white could be seen until she refocused on Maebh. "Of my blood, but more."

"What? Mam, who did this?"

"Where's my boy?"

Maebh's throat thickened as she tried to swallow. "He's on his way."

"Of my blood."

Maebh finally glanced behind her to see the sombre faces of Ash and Tiernan. She pleaded with them through her eyes, knowing they were as useless as her.

"But more."

Maebh's head snapped back to her mother as she took a fit of coughing, blood splattering over her already ruined clothing. Imogen's hand grasped her daughter's weakly before going limp, and when Maebh looked at her mother's eyes again, they stared blankly back. The ghost of her last statement whispered through Maebh's head.

Of my blood, but more.

CHAPTER 40

AISLING

"We have to find help," Ash said as she stood behind Maebh's hunched figure. "We need to move her."

She couldn't look at Imogen McQuillan for too long; the similarities to her own mother's mutilated body were too much to bear.

When Maebh didn't move, Tiernan hunkered beside her. "She's gone, Maebh. I'm so sorry."

Ash crouched on the other side of the shaken woman, gently placing her hand on her shoulder. "We need to find Set."

That seemed to break her spell and she released her mother's limp hand, bloodied from her violent end. Maebh's own hands were stained, and she absentmindedly wiped them on her dark pants. Ash wanted to console her, but she knew words were not enough. She gripped Maebh's arm, squeezing, and trying to convey through her gaze that above everything, she knew how she felt. Her friend nodded, blinking rapidly before taking the torch and angling it further down the dark tunnel.

"Shouldn't we head back to Tara Court?" Tiernan murmured, carefully stepping over Imogen. "Find the others?"

"What if the killer is still here?" Maebh turned towards them, her beautifully defined features flickering in the torchlight. "Let's end this."

Ash's pulse quickened as she thought about coming face to face with Imogen's killer. With her wounds matching closely to her mother's, she'd already decided it was hugely improbable there were two murderers capable of inflicting such pain. Taking a steadying breath, she nodded in agreement.

The tunnel was as dark as it was quiet, weaving around bends deep underground. They walked in silence, and Ash wondered where they were within the Kingdom of Mede, her gaze drifting upward where the uneven cave ceiling was within reaching distance. Who was above ground, oblivious to the death and pain underneath them?

No matter how hard she tried to avoid remembering her mother in a nearly identical state, Cara's mutilated body forced its way in. If Ash had got to her mother before she died, what would she have said to her? Would she, too, look for her son rather than her? Swallowing the jagged rock embedded in her throat, she pushed those useless thoughts away.

Ash scanned the tunnel at every sound, every laboured breath from the others. The ground was hard under their feet and the walls rough but wide. There was no warmth down here; nothing but the offering of endless darkness.

A muffling sound drew her attention, and she noticed the others' heads snapping towards it too. She nodded for them to approach, her hand reaching for her sword. Unsheathing it, her companions followed suit, Maebh angling her dagger high as she held the light. Ash raised her mother's sword; it would be fitting to face her murderer with it.

Years of training kicked in, but there was a niggling worry at the back of her mind. Would she be able to use the blade to cause death? She knew the answer. No, she would rather bring her mother's killer to the High King to face a trial. Brehon law was clear, and they would be brought to a justice leading to death, but at least her conscience would be left untarnished.

The sound of steel dragging off rock reached them to the place just outside their torch's beam, and Ash hesitated only for a moment. Licking her lips, she willed her heart to beat steadily as they inched closer.

She let out a long breath as Set came into view, sitting cross-legged, a long blade resting on his lap. He didn't acknowledge them, raising a hand to rub against his beard, a habit she'd noticed he did when deep in thought. Ash stumbled to a halt, someone crashing into her back. Even in the dim light, she could see his bloodstained hands.

"Is she dead?" Set's voice was hoarse. The pain emanating from him took her breath away.

Maebh pushed past her and lowered herself to the ground, discarding the dagger. Squeezing his knee, she peered into her brother's face. "What happened?"

When Set didn't answer, Ash moved closer, taking in his haunted expression, similar to how he'd looked at her before he disappeared. Had he been here ever since? Had he seen the murderer? Her heart hammered painfully, the need to be sick, causing her to spin away from him. She pushed past Tiernan and made it only two feet before vomiting. When her retches became nothing but useless sounds, she righted herself.

Tiernan handed her a cloth, his gaze never leaving the twins, and his grip still tight on his blade. Maebh seemed to notice the same time Ash did.

"Stop that. He didn't do this."

"Mae—" Tiernan began, but she cut him with a snarl.

"I'm telling you. My brother didn't kill Imogen."

"Mae." Set seemed to come out of his trance. He went to grip the hand that still clutched his knee, but when he looked at his bloody hand he let it fall, open palmed beside him on the ground. "I think I did."

Nobody moved. Ash gaped at Set, thinking back to their starry night confessions. He had told her he was a monster. That he had an uncontrollable rage inside him. Had he been trying to confess then?

"Did you kill my mother?" Ash was surprised by how calm she sounded.

Set's gaze snapped to hers. His lips pressed in a hard line before swallowing once and nodding. "I think so."

The world tilted as she fought for clarity. Without realising what she was doing, she lifted her sword and stepped towards Set.

"Aisling. Stop." Maebh jumped to her feet, dagger back in her hand as quick as a blink. "He doesn't know for sure."

"Look at him," Ash seethed. She glared at her. "Look at how bloody his hands are. He told me he was a monster. I should have listened."

Maebh brought her dagger up in a sweeping motion, sparking off the low cave wall, when Ash tried to walk past, and even though hers was the longer blade, she didn't push past the blonde warrior.

"He has these episodes. He transforms into . . . someone else. It's not his fault."

Ash's back straightened as she glared at the woman she had thought was a friend. "You knew?"

Maebh didn't need to answer, as her chin raised in affirmation. "He's my brother."

"I'm your matriarch," Ash found herself saying, realising how stupid it sounded.

She was playing the role, and nobody found her convincing, least of all her.

"Mae. Step aside." Set's voice had become stronger, and as Ash turned, she noticed him kneeling on the ground, the discarded torch feet away, the light illuminating his features from below, casting him in the eerie light fitting for a killer.

"Easy." Tiernan stepped forward as Set unfastened his belt that contained another blade. Nobody moved and Ash barely dared to breathe as he let it drop to the rocky earth.

"I must be stopped."

Maebh shook her head as she turned away from Ash and lowered herself to the ground in front of her brother. Not seeming to notice the others or not caring, Maebh gripped his arm. "No. Setanta."

"At least this way, it doesn't have to be you," he whispered. "I hated to have to ask that of you. I'm glad I don't have to anymore."

"No."

"Maebh, you need to move aside." Tiernan didn't approach her, but he lowered his weapon, offering his hand.

She ignored him.

Set cupped his sister's cheek with his bloodied hand and lowered his forehead to meet hers. "You were always the best of us."

Set raised his gaze to Tiernan, and a silent conversation seemed to flow between them. With a firm nod to the dark-haired warrior, Set released Maebh as Tiernan sheathed his dagger and tugged the blonde's arms. When she pushed him off, Ash helped pull her away.

Maebh resisted the entire time, but when they were a safe distance away, Tiernan gripped her shoulders, murmuring softly in her ear. Ash refused to meet Maebh's furious stare as she turned back to Set, still kneeling. Her sword was heavy in her hand as she stepped in front of him once more; her mind racing, her eyes blurring with unshed tears. It took Set's softened voice to pull her back to him. She looked down at her shaking arm and into the eyes of the most beautiful, and now deadliest, man she'd ever met.

"You can do this, Ash."

She frowned at him, and then she realised what he meant.

"I can't." She lowered her sword, but he shook his head.

"You have to. As matriarch, you're permitted to bestow justice where you see fit. If any of the others kill me, Brehon law states they will stand trial."

"We'll take you back to the High King. You can stand trial for what you've done."

Set shuffled on his knees, slightly closer to her, but stopped when she stumbled away from him. He brought a hand up to his face, scrubbing as if he could wash away the guilt but only succeeding in spreading more blood.

"Why did you do it?" Ash asked softly.

Silence met her as she saw the war within Set battle. "I'm a monster."

Ash's blade shook so hard she had to hold it with both hands. "How did it feel, killing my mother? Your mother?"

"I . . . I don't know, Ash."

"Stop using my name."

He lowered his gaze and nodded, shoulder sagging. "I can't be trusted to stand trial. Maebh was right; I have episodes where I blackout, but I can turn at any moment. My monster will be freed, and I don't think he'll allow us to be captured."

"You can't control yourself?"

"Ash." Set stopped when he realised he'd used her name again and looked at her in apology before continuing, "I'm not talking about a figurative monster. I transform into a creature."

Silence filled the space as she processed what he'd said. Set sighed so deeply she could feel it.

"You can riastrad?" Tiernan's voice was closer now, and Ash turned in time to see both him and Maebh just behind her.

Maebh's weapon was still drawn, her eyes trained on Ash, who frowned, releasing her tight grip on her sword. Lowering it, she looked at Maebh with arched brows, wondering if it was safe to turn her back on her. Tiernan gripped Maebh's arm, and she eventually lowered her blade before shirking away from his grasp.

"Cú Chulainn's infliction," Maebh murmured, as if she, too, were surprised by the term being used in relation to her brother.

They all looked down at Set, and when he nodded in confirmation, she let out a curse.

"Ethne told me the first time I met her. Riastrad, also known as warp spasm," Set began, his voice monotone as he sat back on his calves, his large arms resting on his thighs. "The ability to transform into a monster."

Ash sucked in an unsteady breath as she remembered the legends. The others seemed to have caught up, too. Maebh staggered back, her face marred by tears and dirt. The legends of Cú Chulainn told of a fearsome warrior, taller and stronger than any man, with the power to transform into a hulking beast during battle. During his transformation, he wouldn't know friend or enemy, and would kill anyone who stood before him.

Her stomach lurched as she pictured his monster form slashing her mother's body. He was right. She gripped the handle of her sword tighter. He needed to be stopped. Set's gaze snapped to hers as if sensing where her thoughts had gone and he straightened, nodding at her in encouragement. How would Dom and Mary feel if they knew what she was about to do? How would Conor look at her?

"Where's my brother?" Ash let out a gasp as she closed the gap between her and Set. Lowering her weapon, she gripped the collar of his jacket with her free hand, bringing her face inches from his. "Was he here? Did you hurt him too?"

Set's brows furrowed, and then he looked up at her with wide eyes. "I remember seeing him."

"What?" Maebh's voice was high pitched as she pulled Ash away by the back of her collar. Her strength took Ash by surprise as she let out a yelp, her hand reaching backwards to break free. Maebh discarded Ash by Tiernan's feet, who immediately stooped to help her stand.

"Maebh," he warned, but she ignored him and Ash patted his hand, rubbing her neck and thankful for the dim lighting to hide the blush on her cheeks. She'd been cast aside by the woman like a rag doll.

Maebh stormed towards her brother. "You never remember anything when you turn."

"I don't usually, but I think I only half turned. Ethne appeared again. She helped me fight against turning."

"That druid has taken a keen interest in you," Maebh said. "She had us flung off a cliff earlier so I wouldn't jump to trust her." Turning to where Ash and Tiernan stood, she glared at them. "No more pointing weapons at my brother. Understood?"

"He admitted to killing our mothers," Ash spit out through gritted teeth. Stepping up to Maebh, she glared at the seething woman before Set stood, casting an arm between them as a barrier. She scowled at him. "Whose blood is on your hands?"

"It's a fair question," Tiernan said, taking Ash's arm and pulling her close to his side.

The twins stood side by side as she remained with Tiernan, who raised his hands in supplication. "Maebh, nobody wants to hurt Setanta. We just want answers. We need to find Conor."

"I remember. I saw . . ." Set's eyes widened as he looked first to Maebh and then Ash. His words came out in a whisper. "I didn't kill her."

Ash couldn't fight the frustration crawling out of her throat. "But—"

"Ash, I'm so sorry." Set stepped forward, closing the gap between both sides, Maebh flanking him and raising her blade slightly in warning.

Tiernan stood in front of Ash, ignoring Maebh's low voiced threat. "What do you mean?"

"I need to bring you to Conor." Set looked at Ash, his face full of pity that caused a boulder to drop in her stomach.

"Is he alive?"

Set nodded before sweeping his arm forward, asking for permission to take the lead. Having no idea what else to do, Ash conceded, following as Tiernan and Maebh fell into line.

A myriad of emotions barrelled into her as she followed closely behind the blond brute leading them further down the black tunnel. Tiernan lifted the torch and the hissing of the dimming flames was a warning that they needed to find more light, or resurface from the tunnels.

Ash watched Set's looming figure retreat further. What could he mean by confessing to murdering both matriarchs to then claiming he hadn't? A moment ago, she'd contemplated killing him. It was only for a second, but it had been real. Her limbs felt foreign, like they belonged to someone else as she warred with her turmoil. Why were they willingly following him? Where was the rest of her clan? They'd seen Conor push her over the cliff. Surely they'd have kept him safe.

"Where are you taking us?" Tiernan asked, breaking through her spiral. He hadn't moved farther than two feet from Ash since Maebh flanked Set's back.

The tunnel didn't continue in one endless path, but branched off into several forks and she tried to remember the way back, conscious of Maebh's earlier warning from her seanchai. It was easy to get lost, and she now saw how possible it would be to end up in Tuatha Dé Danann territory. Did the Fair Ones know of these underground paths? Surely they would, as ancient and cunning as they were.

Ash looked to the tall warrior beside her, dirtied from the day like everyone else, but with an alertness that nobody else seemed capable of. Tiernan didn't believe he was strong enough to be categorised with warriors like Set, but she did. He was strong, but his mind was the true weapon, and she was grateful for his presence.

Set kept a fast pace, while Maebh walked backwards, her dagger in constant sight. Ash would be impressed by her seamless march if she wasn't aiming a weapon at her. The look she gave both of them was clear; her loyalty lay with her brother and she would use deadly force if necessary. Her time with the Breen clan was over.

"He was just through here." Set came to a stop by another break off in their path and it took Ash a moment to realise that it was like the wind tunnel where symbols and an ancient language decorated its walls.

She pushed past everyone, ignoring both Tiernan's and then Maebh's warnings. When she glanced up at Set, he gave her that same look of pity before gesturing with his thick arm toward the bend. Ash willed her nerves to calm as she took the last step, but cried out as she caught sight of her brother. He sat against the wall just feet away, tightly hugging his legs.

"Con, are you okay?" Ash raced over, falling to her knees beside him.

He was dishevelled and she couldn't see his face, but he was breathing. He was alive. She looked up to her now approaching companions, a relieved smile on her lips, but when she noticed their horrified expressions, she glanced back down.

A grotesque mask lay at his side, and her breath caught as Tiernan approached with the torch, casting everything in a new, painful light. She imagined it was once white, but there were lumps of skin and tissue clinging to two long horns at the top. She recoiled from it on instinct. Conor didn't move as she peered at him and then the mask. Shaking her head, she let out a whimper. A headache formed as her mind fought for her to catch up. It wasn't a mask. It was an animal's skull made into some sort of helmet.

"Conor?" Ash didn't recognise her voice, but it seemed he did.

His head slowly rose from his knees, tear stains streaking through the mud and blood covering his face. "Ash?"

"Con, what did you do?" Tiernan's voice rose an octave, and he joined Ash's side on the ground as he gripped Conor's shoulder. "What did you do?"

She backed away, her legs shaking, only to be met by a wall of muscle. Set's hands clasped her shoulders as she fought to remain standing. "I'm sorry, Ash."

Footsteps looming behind them barely registered until highguards surrounded them on either side of the tunnel. Ash stared at her brother as Set spoke softly to the soldiers. The buzzing in her ears allowed little else to register, but she snapped out of her spell when a couple pushed past her, clasping Conor's hunched shoulders and hoisting him up. His long legs gave way as one guard picked up the horned mask.

"Where are you taking him?" she asked, trying to stand in the way as the soldier held Conor up by the arm and dragged him towards the gathered law enforcers. Their all-black armour was hard to distinguish, even after the added light they'd brought through lanterns.

"He will be brought to the castle to await trial," one guard said as he moved to the side, stopping Ash from following her brother. "Take the route you came, and head back to Tara Court."

Several highguard closed formation, hiding Conor from view.

"Stop. Let me speak to him first." Ash stumbled forward, but firm hands held her upright. Set didn't let go as she tried to follow the retreating guards. "Let me go! Conor!"

Her brother didn't answer. His unseen frame carried along with the marching men.

CHAPTER 41

AISLING

The stone castle loomed over Ash as she and her clansmen trudged up the steps and entered the cold foyer. She had tried to follow Conor, but two highguard had remained, blocking the tunnel. They had insisted she return to Tara Court in the other direction. When she'd asked how they'd known where to find her brother, they remained mute. The wall of silence had remained when she'd demanded to know where Ethne was; her brother's last words before he'd cut the rope ringing in her ears.

She also told me this next part must happen.

The druid had answers, and Ash would be damned before she'd let her brother rot in a cell for long.

Before they departed, Tiernan had informed the guards where Imogen McQuillan lay, and they followed them to her, assuring the twins they'd carry her back.

Both Maebh and Set remained quiet the entire journey, walking side by side, synchronised in their movements as much as their shared grief.

Her cousins, along with Emer and Niamh, had been waiting at the entrance of the Hill of Tara when they'd made it back. The moon had replaced the sun, but Ash had still needed time for her vision to adjust to the darkness she'd been entombed in. Upon seeing her clan, she demanded answers. Ciarán admitted to losing Conor soon after the rope was cut, so they'd informed the highguard of what had happened.

Ash swallowed her lump of frustration. Her clan had been the informers. She needed to speak to Conor. She couldn't believe he had anything to do with the murders. Fighting against the stack of evidence was like warring against a tide. No matter how much she fought to stay afloat, her brother's haunted face and the gruesome mask crashed over her, weighing her down.

Her clansmen flanked her as they wordlessly marched toward the castle, the McQuillans a few paces ahead, but she barely registered any of it. A numbness shrouded her, dimming every sound to an incessant hum.

"Matriarch, the High King wishes to speak with you," Ethne's voice sounded before the druid appeared in the lobby of the castle and the others collectively stepped back, but Ash stepped forward, teeth bared.

"Where is he? What did you do?"

Tiernan gripped her arm. "Easy."

The druid only angled her head, her sensuous mouth quirked in a small smile.

"I'm coming with you," Tiernan said, standing beside her.

Ethne's eternally youthful face smiled angelically, but those silver eyes simmered with an untapped wisdom that came from age. "The High King only wishes to speak with the matriarchs."

Ash followed Ethne's gaze as it landed on Maebh, who frowned, crossing her arms.

"I'm no matriarch." Maebh glared at the druid. "I left the McQuillan clan."

Ash wasn't sure if she realised she was gripping the hilt of her dagger.

Set placed his hand on his sister's shoulder, turning her towards him. "You are now, Mae. Brehon law dictates that the next female in line takes the role when the current matriarch dies. Mam . . ." His throat bobbed and it took a few attempts before he could finish. "She didn't publicly accept your departure."

"I don't give two flying fucks what the law states," Maebh's voice rose, and the once bustling lobby quietened to stare at her. If she noticed, she didn't care. "I'm not doing it."

"You have no choice, child." Ethne stood before the seething blonde. "Talk to your High King."

Even though Ash could barely keep up with what was happening, and wasn't sure how she felt about Maebh's actions in the tunnel, she stood beside her, reaching for her hand, still clenched around her weapon.

Their gazes met as she squeezed it within her own. "Come on, let's go."

"We'll be right here, Matriarch," Tiernan called as Ash followed the grey-clad druid to a set of winding marble stairs.

Before Ash could think of a response, Ethne turned. "Come along, children."

Ash clenched her jaw, hating how the druid seemed to want to remind them of their age difference, even if she appeared as young as them.

"I'm not your child." Maebh said, glaring at the druid's back.

Ethne didn't turn as she replied, "You are much more."

The women shared a look, but continued down a long hall that showcased plush carpets and opulent decor. Ash demanded answers from the ancient druid, but she continued to walk as if a torrent of questions weren't being flung at her back. She quickened her pace, intent on stopping the woman until she answered her, but a strange tingling sensation filled her mouth. Her tongue swelled, her throat tightening. With wide eyes, she gripped her throat just as Ethne glanced behind.

Still keeping her steady pace, the druid smiled at Ash. "Come along."

When she stopped trying to ask the druid questions, her tongue shrank. Through gritted teeth, she followed. Servants they passed nodded before continuing their duties. Dressed in long black tunics and pants, King Aedan's family coat of arms was stitched over their hearts.

In a large room they walked by, a group of Fianna warriors were convened, the doors open to showcase a roaring fire and velvet divans, tables filled with silver trays serving delicacies and decanters brimming with various amber and red liquor.

"I guess some clans enjoyed the luxuries of the castle rather than take part in the king's quest," Maebh murmured beside her.

Ash nodded before looking at the druid, who continued walking in front. She swallowed around the lump stealing her voice, but it didn't budge.

She glanced at her companion; the newly claimed matriarch. A title they'd both been groomed to take, but neither expected it would fall on their shoulders so soon. What did she think of Ash now? Knowing she was the sister of her mother's murderer? Her gut twisted as she fought back the tears she refused to shed. Not here. Not now. Later, when she had the comfort of falling apart in private, she would give in to the myriad of emotions battling their way through her. But now, she needed to focus on her meeting with the High King.

They stopped in front of an enormous set of iron doors with two guards standing to attention. Ethne remained facing the doors until Ash and Maebh stopped behind her, and then the grey lady nodded her head, signalling the guards to open. Once inside, Ash let out a sound of appreciation despite her troubled thoughts. The throne room was cavernous, with multiple archways holding up a painted ceiling, higher than any room she'd been in.

As they walked deeper into the room, she cast her gaze over the gilded frames along the walls depicting previous High Kings and legends of the past, until the scene above captivated her. It was like a fairy tale as they approached the throne. Towers, and rivers, Fianna warriors, and even the Fair Ones, filled every space. Twilight, starry nights and blazing suns bled together at a tale Ash wanted to be told. If she spent a month staring upwards in this room, she still wouldn't see every detail there was.

It was only when she bumped into the druid's back she realised they'd stopped at the steps leading up to a single carved wooden throne. Two long banners were suspended on either side, depicting the O'Dwyer crest, the most prominent feature of a lion at its centre. Unlike the first encounter of the High King, where he'd insisted she called him Aedan, he was sitting upright, a crown at the centre of his head, his dark curls orderly, and his attire clean. Ash bowed low in synchrony with Maebh and the druid. Once righted, Ethne climbed the steps to join his side while the two women stood before them.

Ash's throat thickened with dread. "High King, please listen, Con—"

Aedan raised his hand, and Ash stopped speaking. She wasn't sure what she was going to say. That Conor was innocent? That he hadn't killed Imogen or their own mother? He was her brother, of course he couldn't have done it. A wave of guilt crashed into her as she fought against her shaking limbs.

She cast a glance at Maebh, who remained rigid, her expression pinched. Not even her pungent perfume disguised her own scent of devastation.

The brother she'd known growing up had been joyful, loving, the most caring human she'd ever met. The man she'd been reunited with was withdrawn, tortured and Ash only realised now that she'd tapped into her gift, that his aura was . . . off. She wanted desperately to believe there was some other explanation, but could she?

Set turned into a literal monster, but she couldn't accept him as a killer either. The druid knew and perhaps the king did also, but she wouldn't share that information with them, anyway. Despite what happened underground, she couldn't betray the man she'd shared her secrets with under the stars.

She straightened her back and waited for the High King to speak, something she was surprised Maebh was doing. The blonde remained quiet and sombre, her head bowed and arms clasped in front and Ash noticed they shook, another sign she was hurting.

Gone was the fierce battle bitch who'd thrown her like a rag doll. Even though she'd taken her hand in the castle lobby, she wasn't sure if she could call Maebh a friend anymore. She wasn't even sure if she wanted to.

"Let me start by giving my deepest condolences to you, Maebh." Aedan's voice echoed throughout the room, empty except for the five of them, and guards scattered along the long walls. "She was a formidable woman, an influential leader of the McQuillan clan. May Imogen's soul continue on."

Maebh only nodded, her guarded expression unreadable as she refused to finish the blessing.

"And her love remain," Ash murmured. When the High King nodded with a tight-lipped smile, she rushed ahead before she could chicken out. "High King, may I speak?"

"You may."

"I need to see my brother." When Aedan only cocked his head to the side, Ash continued, "If I was permitted to—"

"No," The High King said. Ash couldn't make out his scent but she could have sworn he sounded almost disappointed she had asked. "You have been given a quest. Have you fulfilled it?"

"We were too busy stumbling upon mutilated bodies, Your Majesty," Maebh said, and although she still gripped her hands before her, a sneering smirk played on her lips.

Ash internally groaned, wishing the other matriarch's quietened demeanour had continued for a little longer.

Aedan cut the other woman with a look and, for the first time, Ash was afraid of him. Before now, she had thought he didn't seem kingly, but now, in his throne room, he looked every bit their ruler, demanding his subjects to obey.

Aedan gestured with a lazy hand and Ethne stepped forward, hands clasped primly in front. "Guards, you are dismissed."

In perfect synchronisation, they filed out of the room, some through the doors they arrived at, while others exited on either side of the back wall, behind the raised throne. Once the last door shut, Aedan spoke again. "Mourning the loss of your mothers will have to coincide with duty. As matriarchs, carrying out orders from your High King when called upon is part of that expectation. The Cath is an important opportunity for all Fianna. Are you so willing to deny your clansmen because you can't lead?"

For once, she wished Maebh would retaliate, but instead, they both fumed silently beside one another. Sulphur coated her tongue as she bit back a retort that would lead nowhere good. She had come here, dutifully, despite all the odds stacked against her. This king could take his opinion of how honoured they were and shove it up his gilded ass.

Maebh gripped her arm, as if in warning, but she shook her off. She would remain quiet. She wasn't a fool.

Aedan leaned forward in his throne and continued, "I would rather if you both could come to terms with all that has happened. But reality is far less kind than any good intention. The land has cried out for too long and we are duty-bound to answer."

"To answer what?" Ash looked between the High King and his druid, surprised at how calm she sounded when inside a storm was churning.

It was the female who spoke. "Find the first High King, and you will hear it answered."

The druid continued speaking, but Ash didn't hear any of it. Her eyes widened as she fought to steady her breathing. The first High King; 'TFHK'. Her mother had scribbled those initials all over her journal. Could she have been on the same quest?

Ash's head snapped to the king's as the druid told the tale of Fionn Mac Cumhaill. Her mother had clutched a letter in her dying fist stating Teamhair held the answer. The Hill of Tara. Her mother had known where to look.

"Your brother will be cared for under your High King's custody," the druid's voice finally filtered through to her and she forced herself to focus, "Until such a time when his hearing can take place, but for now, you must concentrate on your duty."

"So you think he's guilty?" Maebh asked, her voice loud in the cavernous room. "You think he killed our mothers?"

Ash's breath left her in a whoosh as a painful boulder landed on her chest. Her brother, the only one of her family who'd kept in touch after she'd abandoned him. For years, she thought it had been the other way around; that she'd been discarded. She had blamed her mother for not staying until Ash had finished her tantrum and deigned to return.

She knew what Fianna were. Land roamers, never staying in one place for longer than a few days. It was Ash who had left her family. Had left Conor. If she'd have stayed, would this have happened? The face he wore now was haunted; but was he a killer?

Ethne cocked her head to the side. "Yes, dear. The blood on his hands and the devil's horns would indicate so. You cannot let your grief cloud your judgement."

The world spun at her damning words.

"There must be an explanation. When will his trial be?" Ash fought the tremor in her voice. "Please let me see him?"

After a short pause, Aedan spoke, his elbow resting on the ornate armrest of the throne. "I will grant access once you have completed my quest."

Ash stared up at the king, her heart beating so hard she felt the pulse in her ears as loud as thunder. She could tell him what she found, but why was she stalling? He couldn't wake the first High King even if she led him to the cave with the statues. The legend said he could only be woken when Ireland called for him. There had been no call, she was sure of it. Aedan's issue with electronics was nowhere near a real problem. Technological advancements were always inevitable and truly, probably not the cause of the ashen forest. She sucked in a ragged breath, shivering despite the many lit fireplaces around the room.

Her mother had died, clutching clues that led to that cave. Ash needed time to think about what that meant. She turned to Maebh, who was looking at her with an unreadable expression. She could decide differently and tell them everything they'd found, taking the decision away from her.

"Why is it so important that we continue on this fool's errand?" Maebh asked, turning towards the throne, her voice raising. "What aren't you telling us?"

Silence filled the room as Aedan stood, stalking down the steps until he stood in front of Maebh. At her height, she was almost as tall as him, even though he was a step above her.

"On your knees."

The air thickened to the point Ash fought for breath and she waited to see what Maebh would do. It seemed she was taking too long as Ethne descended the last step, walking behind Maebh. The druid tapped the blonde's shoulder and a spark of light flashed, sending her to her knees. Even though it wasn't Ash, her own knees shook.

"If I tell you to bark like a dog, kiss my feet, sing me a song, kill for me, you do it. Do you understand?" Aedan's voice was low, lethal, his expression too calm.

Ash turned, not sure what she planned on doing, but the king glared at her and she froze.

"Do you understand, Maebh?" The druid bent low to whisper in Maebh's ear, but she was loud enough for Ash to hear.

Eventually, Maebh caved. "Yes, my king. As you wish."

Fighting against her upcoming breakdown, she tried to get a handle on what was happening. She could only see her brother if she brought the king what he wanted. "Can you give us time with our clan so we can continue our search?"

Aedan's face brightened with a smile that Ash would have found captivating, but now she only wanted to get away from this man. "Of course. You were underground for quite some time. Did you find anything promising?"

Ash hesitated, but Maebh spoke as she continued to kneel. "We split up, so we need to find out what our clansmen might have discovered. There are walls covered in an ancient language, but perhaps the others found more."

"Rise, Maebh," Aedan smiled again. When Ash met his gaze, his brows were creased, his lips puckered. After a pause, he spoke again. "As a show of my appreciation, and because I believe your clans will succeed in this quest above all others, I will confess something that both of you will be interested in."

Aedan descended the last step and directed them toward a curtained alcove. Ethne crossed first, opening the curtain to display a door that led into a large room, the most prominent feature a round marble table and shelves that housed hundreds of rolled scrolls. Aedan gestured for them to sit and as he did,

Ethne carried a silver tray from a side table with a decanter of dark berry wine and glasses. Ash accepted the glass but didn't drink, her stomach in a knot of nerves as she gripped the stem.

Aedan leaned against his chair, swirling his wine before taking a sip. "When I was much younger, a group of my friends and I were tired of performing in shows. We wanted nothing to do with the Gluttons, with ensuring the Fair Ones were kept hidden, and getting nothing in return but ridicule from both sides.

"The previous High King's only concern was to make himself richer by following everything the Tuatha Dé Danann demanded of him. The legends tell us that once Fionn wakes, we will restore Ireland."

Ash watched the High King as if he spoke of an old friend. Someone he greatly admired. He was obsessed; she realised. His shoulders sagged as he rubbed his hand along his jaw, his glass returning to the table.

"We searched for years, in both realms, finding nothing. After I became High King, I charged my most loyal warriors to continue searching. Your fathers, along with the Cassidy matriarch and a few others, came to me one night, excited beyond anything I'd seen. They were convinced they knew where to find him. Right here, under our noses this whole time."

He gestured around the room and chuckled, but there was no humour there. Ash's chest tightened as Aedan refilled his drink, sadness in his eyes as he downed the contents. "The caillte was created that night. They never returned."

The scraping of Maebh's seat was followed by an onslaught of curses as she seemed to fight for control. Ash stood too, afraid that she would do something to cause the king's wrath once more. As she watched for signs that Maebh was about to launch herself at the king, she thought about what he'd just revealed.

Her father had gone on the same quest she was now on. And hadn't returned.

"You are the reason my dad is missing?" Maebh began, her voice raising with every word. "You are the reason I was left to the fury of my mother, all for some fucking fairy tale?" Her hand clutched the hilt of her dagger as she stepped closer to Aedan. Ash pulled on Maebh's arm as she tracked the movement, but so did the druid.

Ethne was at the High King's side in an instant, her eyes clouded black and her hands creating a static lightning. The heat of it singed the air, and she pulled Maebh harder, afraid of what the druid's power might do. She knew of druids being able to manipulate the elements or cast spells, but Ethne's power seemed limitless. Every time she encountered the ancient woman, she revealed more than before.

Aedan shook his head, warning his druid not to intervene. He clasped Maebh's hands, releasing her grip on her weapon, and waited until she looked at him. "I'm truly sorry for the past, Maebh. I thought they would return. Know that I haven't stopped searching for them since."

Ash waited until Maebh eventually let go and they both righted their chairs and sat down.

"The two of you want something. And I can help you. Ash, you want to see your brother. Maebh, you want to find the caillte. Find the first High King, and you shall have both."

CHAPTER 42

AISLING

"So, let me get this right," Tiernan said from his seat around the table, an untouched glass of whiskey in front of him. "Those late night gatherings at my home when I was a child . . . the High King and all of our parents were discussing finding—and waking up—an ancient king based on a legend?"

Ash nodded as she looked out of the window. A maze of gardens crept as far as a lower wall than the one she could see even from this distance. The sun had set since they'd entered the castle, putting an end to this awful day. Not that the night would be any better. She hugged her arms closely around her, staring without truly seeing.

With a sigh she turned back, leaning against the wall. They were in a small room on the same floor as the High King's throne room. He'd dismissed them soon after it was clear Maebh wasn't about to attack him and end up in the same prison as her brother.

"You speak of legends like the Gluttons do, child." Ethne cocked her head from where she stood at the doorway. The Breen clan, along with the McQuillan twins, sat in uncomfortable silence, highguard stationed behind the druid.

She clasped her hands primly in front as she smiled angelically at Tiernan. "Your mind is so tied down by the limitations of technology that you have forgotten the full scale of magic at your fingertips."

"I'm aware of magic, but legends and lore are another matter."

Ethne's face seemed to glow in wicked delight. "I am a legend you have yet to discover."

She turned from the room, closing them in. As Maebh caught them up on what had happened, Ash wondered why the High King was putting his trust in two young matriarchs instead of the many other clans at his disposal. She knew the answer as soon as she'd formed the question. They both wanted something so badly he could manipulate them to get what he wanted.

And damn if it wasn't working.

"We have to tell him," Maebh said, her eyes flickering with fiery determination. "You see your brother, we find out where our parents are. We all walk away."

Ash squinted at the other matriarch. *Walk away*. As if her world wasn't hanging on by a thread. Where would she walk to?

"That's the only reason you came, isn't it?" Ash asked, her nails digging into her arms to stop herself from storming across the room. "You left your clan to come to mine so you could search for your father."

"Does it matter?"

Nobody else spoke as the women glared at each other.

"Have you always been this selfish?"

Set opened his mouth to speak, but his sister raised her hands to silence him. Her eyes never left Ash's as she smiled with one arched brow. Ash had seen this look before, the one before she launched into a series of insults. It had never been directed at her before.

"I need some air," Ash said softly before exiting the room. She didn't look back.

Ash blindly stumbled through the woods, fighting for a deep breath, but her lungs wouldn't allow her. What was she doing here? She didn't belong.

Everything she knew about this realm was because of her mother. She'd groomed her to take over, instructing her on how to strategise and lead her clan. Was it her mother's lessons that were faulty, or Ash's ineptitude? Everything Cara Breen had taught her felt like half truths and webs of deception.

Even Maebh, who she'd stupidly thought had become a friend, had used her. Turned on her at the first opportunity. She'd been about to discard her in the castle, in front of everyone. Even after everything, what had the other woman done since joining her other than cause trouble? She was always going to return to the McQuillans. How had she been so foolish not to see that? Why did she care?

She heard footsteps behind her, and didn't need to turn around to know who was following her.

"Go away, Tier."

Her own pace quickened, not hoping to outrun him, but with the realisation she was running out of time. She needed to get her shit together if she wanted to see her brother. It was clear that the only person who could give her the truth she so desperately needed was with Conor. She'd failed him. He'd asked her to return to their clan, and instead of protecting him, he'd become a murder suspect. A stitch formed in her side, but she grit her teeth, ignoring the pain.

"You can't get to my satellite without me."

She opened her mouth to speak, but closed it again. Not slowing her pace, she didn't argue as Tiernan fell into step beside her. When she turned in another direction, he grabbed her arm, jerking his chin straight ahead. "I will have to lead you the rest of the way."

As he pulled her forward, the feeling of wrongness seeped into her bones, reminding her of the cave full of statues, but she grit her teeth and let him tug her onward. As if she walked through an unseen sensor, her shoulders relaxed and her breathing slowed. A great big oak tree appeared before her, wires wrapping itself around it like coiled snakes and Ash craned her neck, barely able to see where a satellite dish was secured above them.

All she could think about as she sat in the meeting room was that she needed to speak to the only two constants in her life. Mary and Dom had been there for her since the day she met them. She needed just five minutes with people she truly felt were on her side.

She followed Tiernan as he hunkered to the base of the trunk where a waterproof bag lay. Unzipping it, he retrieved his laptop and turned it on.

"Here." Tiernan handed her the device before retreating a few paces, giving her privacy.

Ash let her eyes adjust to the screen, finding it alien in this twisted world. With shaking fingers, she logged into her account and connected to a video link. Dom's face filled the screen first, shortly followed by Mary, who had obviously grabbed the device from his hands.

"Is that you, Aisling?" Mary's voice came through broken, and Ash's throat closed momentarily as she wiped at her eyes. "I can't see you. The camera isn't working."

"It's me," Ash breathed, fighting against the tremor in her voice. "I can see you both."

Ash turned to Tiernan in question and he said, "That realm can only get sound, no visual, it seems."

Dom's voice was rough as he spoke. "Are you all right?"

"No." Ash burst into tears as she tried, but failed, to speak any further. When she realised she couldn't form coherent sentences, she wiped at her eyes and just stared at the couple. With some effort, she managed a few words. "I miss you."

"Darling, we miss you too," Mary said, wiping at her own eyes. The couple shared a look before Dom nodded and Mary continued. "Do you know how long you've been gone?"

Ash sat back on the damp earth with a shiver as she frowned. "It's been a couple of days here. Why?"

They shared another look before Dom answered. "It's been almost a month for us."

Ash cursed as she looked at Tiernan, whose eyebrows were raised. She knew time moved differently, but a whole month? He shrugged his shoulders but continued to look as if he was trying to solve a complex equation. It was Mary's voice that brought her back to the screen.

"There have been developments in your mother's case." She took a breath, fidgeting with the camera's angle, before sighing. "That awful detective who interviewed you. Detective . . . what's his name?"

"It doesn't matter," Ash said, fighting to keep her voice calm.

"Anyway. He came by about a week ago to ask where you were. We've been telling everyone that you've taken a trip with your brother and your . . . clan."

Ash pretended not to notice the disdain in Mary's voice. She had very strong opinions on what had happened between Ash and her family. She didn't have the energy to tell her she had it all wrong. Ash had always been the problem. The one who had abandoned them.

"Tell her about the evidence," Dom's gruff voice penetrated her thoughts, and she stared at the couple.

"What evidence?"

"They found DNA, Aisling. Other than your mother's at the crime scene."

It was only then that she realised Mary had called her by her full name; twice. It was something the older woman only did when Ash was in trouble or had bad news to deliver.

Dom said, "The DNA was a familial match."

"Meaning that it had to have come from someone related to your mother," Mary added, her face scrunched as if she was trying not to cry.

"I know what it means," Ash said. She'd read enough crime novels to know where this would lead.

Nowhere good.

This was proof that her brother was a murderer. Her stomach clenched with hopelessness. It was true, then. Was the evidence against Conor too hard even for her to deny?

"They also found a fingerprint." Mary leaned closer to the screen. "Are you still there?"

"Yes," Ash's voice came out in a whisper. The memory of seeing the bloodied fingerprint before she'd discovered how to use the portal forced its way in like a splinter twisting her gut. She had hoped the detective had seen it. Now she knew he had, and all along it had been Conor's. She knew the answer but asked, anyway. "Whose fingerprint?"

"Yours."

CHAPTER 43

AISLING

A sh had been a fool. Desperate to find her mother's killer, she'd placed her fingertip in the basin at Newgrange, sealing her fate as number one suspect.

"You tried your best, Aisling. It's time to put this behind us." Niamh's words barely registered as she sat on the log at the Breen campsite and watched the others pack.

How could she be so naïve? There was no way to explain the evidence. It's not like she could tell the detective the truth, that she needed a blood sacrifice in order to open the portal.

Emer hunkered beside her, pausing in her clearing of their camp. "You can still be part of the clan if you wish."

She looked up and noticed the wordless exchange between the wives. They were placating her; she wasn't welcome in their world. Not when Niamh would presumably take over as matriarch after the elders petitioned to the High King. It would be easy to highlight all of her failures.

What type of leader would Niamh make? As she hunched on the log, she realised she didn't know enough about her to guess. That was also her fault. Since taking the clan to Tír na nÓg, she'd been so overwhelmed by everything that she'd not taken the time to bond with her clansmen. Not really.

Tiernan sat cross-legged on the ground facing her, warming his hands to the flames, his face stony, as if trying to work out a complex coding system. Maybe he was. He'd been like this ever since her call with Mary and Dom.

She'd had a fitful night's sleep, and so had her clan. Ash could hear all of them shuffling in their bedrolls or murmuring to one another. The air felt charged, their combined anguish and despondency leaving a bitter tang. Tiernan had spoken little since they'd left the oak tree, other than to say they'd figure out a way to clear her name. He'd been the one she'd depended on most while here. If he were a woman, she'd have thought of him as a worthy contender as matriarch. He could rule Leinster, like his father, but women always ruled clans.

Glancing at the small group around her, she couldn't find her voice as they all cast wary glances her way while she pretended not to notice. Pressing her lips together as she stared at the firepit, she shivered, finding little warmth in it. The morning sun had heated the air in this fairy-tale world. She missed the bitter winter in the human realm. It felt real and raw. She'd been playing pretend for too long.

Had she ever really had a voice worthy of being heard? None strong enough to lead a clan. Tomás and Ciarán were at their bedrolls, but hadn't spoken to back up what Niamh and Emer had said as soon as everyone pretended they were sleeping. Not that they needed to. Packing was enough to show her they didn't see her as matriarch anymore either.

People milling around the green farmland along the castle wall surrounded her, but she'd never felt more alone.

She had no clan, her brother was imprisoned, and now she had no home to go to. If she went back to the cottage, they'd arrest her for murder. She'd missed a month of university, so had failed her classes. Not that it really mattered, anyway. Should she turn herself in? Try to show them she was innocent?

What would her life look like if she did? Even if charges were dropped, the rumours would haunt her for the rest of her life.

Could she go back to that life? Going to university, dating the wrong men, spending her time on social clubs and sports that filled her with a fraction of joy that being here did? Even under the circumstances, she'd never felt more herself. She hadn't missed her phone, the constant need to interact with a screen, to seek approval from strangers. It was liberating. Though the pressure as matriarch was a different level, it was a necessary and worthy one to have.

Watching her clan pack up to leave her, to leave this realm, made her jaw ache. She didn't want a normal life. The men she dated never saw the real her. She couldn't lie under the expanse of stars and share secrets. She didn't get butterflies with the possibility of seeing them. Having Faerie Sight meant she was constantly on edge, ready to pretend a púca was a cat, and the Fair Ones didn't exist. It was exhausting. She was Fianna. These were her people.

Men like Set were her people. He'd saved her from merrow-filled waters, carried her all the way to blood-filled Newgrange in a dangerous wood, and still admitted that Dom was scarier than any of that. She couldn't help but smile at how he looked in just a towel and too-tight top in her car. Her breath caught as she glanced to where the McQuillan clan's camp was. She could see their banner, but his tall frame wasn't visible, so instead she looked at his twin, who sat on a log beside hers.

Meabh hadn't explained why she'd returned to the Breen camp, even after what had occurred between them, and Ash was too bone-tired to ask. When she'd returned from the tree, the twins had been on the outskirts of camp, Set urging his sister to return with him. Whatever had transpired after the announcement of Imogen's death had left the usually fiery warrior defeated, her sombre presence a surprise. They hadn't spoken since Ash accused her of being selfish and she didn't feel the need to apologise, not when it had been true. Even so, she didn't want to fight with her about it.

Set had left last night, acknowledging no one else, and she couldn't deny the sting of that. Not that she blamed him. Gripping her hands together, she twisted her fingers until it hurt. She had thought he'd killed her mother and had been ready to act on the violence thrumming in her blood. When all evidence showed, it had been her own brother all along.

She needed to know why because nothing made sense.

The memory of the Newgrange portal invaded her mind and she shuddered. Her mother's blood had splayed the walls. Even in the human realm, there had been enough blood that Ash now wondered why she had needed to shed her own? What made that realm portal work? She sat upright, ignoring the looks around her. It called for a sacrifice. A shiver ran through her as she swallowed the sharp lump in her throat, and she winced as it went down into her stomach. Cara was used in a blood sacrifice. On Samhain. Every Fianna knew it was one of the Sacred Days.

"Ne'er shed a drop, or bubble's pop," she murmured, her voice gravelly from lack of use, remembering the saying her grandmother and clan elders said.

She had always known they meant bleeding, but the second part was a funny thing to say. When she was a child, she'd often made a popping sound using her forefinger and inner cheek when Granny said it, only to be chased and tickled and told she was as wild as a pixie. Her grandmother had been full of those sayings. Blessings and curses, and as their clan seanchaí, she'd known all the legends. If only she could ask her what any of this meant. Since her death, nobody had displayed that gift, so the Breen clan had been left without a true storyteller; the task rotating between the clansmen.

"My aunt Lorna says that all the time," Maebh said, and she turned to her. "She's a bitch; didn't take too kindly to the news her sister was dead. I had to come over here to get some peace." She gestured to their group. "Awkward silence is so much better."

Ash looked to the empty seat beside her and blinked back tears. They all knew who was to blame for Maebh having to deliver the news of her mother's death. He was somewhere within the castle. She looked at it now, cast in the early morning light. What was Conor doing right now? Were they hurting him? The dungeons were a notoriously cruel place.

A grief so fierce it stole her breath barrelled into her as she realised there was too much evidence to deny her brother's guilt. She had wanted to talk to him first, and she still would. But how could she deny the truth any longer? Should she be glad he was getting what he deserved? He'd killed not just her mother, but Maebh and Set's, too.

"Hey," Maebh murmured, waiting for Ash to look at her. "Don't take on his guilt. It's not your fault."

"But it is," she whispered, her voice croaking from pent up tears she'd refused to shed.

Tiernan's brown eyes met hers, his frown deepening. "It's not your fault."

She didn't answer, but looked across the grassland to where she could just make out Set with his clan. They were deep in a heated discussion. From this distance, she couldn't hear what was being said, but there were a lot of hand gestures being thrown around and at one stage, Set was restrained by their second. Would he turn at any moment? Did his clansmen know how dangerous he was?

"What does it mean?" Ash asked the new matriarch beside her, forcing herself to look away and think about anything else. "The saying."

Maebh poked at the fire and shrugged; she still wore her leather coat with the Breen coat of arms on it and Ash wondered if she was trying to make a statement or if it was an oversight. "You're not allowed to spill blood on Samhain."

"Yes, but why? What happens if you do?" She swallowed, trying not to think about her mother, but it was no use. Her gruesome body was an ever present torment in her mind. One Conor had placed there.

"I don't know. I spilled Set's blood after Samhain and look how great our lives have turned out since. I think it's a poor choice for any day."

She arched her dark brow, but Maebh continued to stoke the fire. Emer and Niamh stood huddled together, their bags on their shoulders, ready to leave. Should she apologise for failing the quest? She'd found Fionn Mac Cumhaill's cave, but it was easier to let them believe otherwise. She hadn't told the High King so she could just walk away.

Did losing mean the couple really won by getting rid of her? Perhaps she should congratulate them instead. Tiernan had told her that there were others within the clan who had wanted to take part, but the elders had refused to let them.

"This isn't right," Tiernan said, gesturing behind him to where his cousin was. Emer opened her mouth to speak, but he raised his hand. "Don't bother. I've heard enough of your bullshit. Ash is matriarch. You can't just take that away from her."

A sigh escaped her lips so deep she felt as if she could fall asleep for a month and still not feel rested. He was fighting for her when she wasn't. She caught Tomás's gaze and frowned when he didn't look away.

She tightened her jacket as she assessed her cousin. "Do you have something to say to me?"

Tomás opened his mouth to speak, but his brother pulled him away. They began murmuring to one another, so she watched the flames of their small fire, the pressure of a migraine forming. She needed sleep. Both of her cousins had seemed more receptive to her since they'd arrived. She knew now that Niamh had only been here to witness her demise, her wife here to support her.

No doubt Mrs O'Malley would push for Niamh to become matriarch when they returned to tell her how terrible a leader she was. Perhaps she was the right choice. Ash had done nothing right since she arrived.

Even now, she was choosing to lose. She could tell the High King about the wind tunnel and how to enter the ancient and scary drop. The memory of that replayed in her mind, and she frowned. Conor had led them to it, saying the druid had told him to. Why would Ethne do that and not tell Aedan about it? Her brother had tried to use his blood, and it hadn't worked. When he'd cut her, the passage opened, and Tiernan had used his blood to get them out.

Nothing is as it seems. His words to her at the cottage were a truth that hurt as sharp as the blade on her belt.

Something was niggling at her, but she was too exhausted to work it out. Perhaps she would ask Tiernan if that's why he looked so puzzled. He was smarter than all of them put together.

"Why did you use Granny's saying?" Tomás asked from his standing point beside the lanky hacker, his arms crossed over his broad chest.

Ash narrowed her eyes. "Do I need a reason?"

Ciarán came to stand beside his brother and she noticed their bedrolls were still out and neither of them had actually packed. "It means that if you spill blood on Samhain, you're opening both worlds."

A thumping began a steady beat in her head as her gaze flitted between the two brothers and she found herself whispering, "What did you say?"

Ciarán looked at his brother. They seemed to have a silent conversation playing out between them. She was about to ask again when the brothers sat on either side of Tiernan, joining their small camp.

Tomás looked into the flames as he said, "Everyone knows Samhain is the start of the darkest part of the year. Nights grow long and days grow cold. On this day, the veil between our world"—he cocked his head towards the Hill of Tara—"and this world is at its thinnest."

It was a moment of collective silence before anyone spoke. Her head was about to explode as she was on the verge of working something major out. She was usually good at figuring out puzzles, had been top at her university course, but she felt more lacking now than ever. Glancing at her surrounding group, she saw that the married couple were sitting behind Tiernan, bags at their feet, not joining in on their conversation but listening intently. She supposed it would be awkward to join her after declaring they no longer recognised her birthright as their matriarch.

"Are you saying that if you bleed on Samhain, you may somehow pierce the veil?" Tiernan asked, his eyebrows raised.

"Is that why my mother was murdered?" she asked, gripping her hands before the flames but not feeling the warmth.

Maebh sucked in a breath beside her and cursed quietly as both brothers nodded.

"That's what we think. But who would benefit from that? Conor has no reason for wanting that." Ciarán leaned forward, his usually emotionless expression filled with concern. "Cara asked us to monitor you after you left. You were never alone, Ash."

She stared at her cousin, and it was only after the third repeat in her mind that she reeled back as if she'd been slapped. "You were the ones to keep that surveillance book for her? You were stalking me?"

"We were keeping you safe," Tomás answered, and even though the fire was between them and others were around, she could smell that not one ounce of remorse came from him. He smelled like freshly laundered linen, and it reminded her of how she felt when she had all of her college assignments handed in and her weekly chores were done.

She could only conclude he believed what he had done, how he'd tracked her movements for her mother, had been justified. Right, even. She looked at her cousins, both sitting with their arms loosely hugging their muscular limbs. Raven, unruly hair, like all the Breens. She ran her fingers through her own knotted mess as she digested this. Besides her brother, and Cara, she had missed these men most after she'd left and it had hurt that there was a barrier between them since her return. They'd been keeping this from her when she'd thought they'd resented her for leaving.

Both had been like older brothers and best friends to her. Growing up in a travelling clan that performed shows night after night left little opportunity to make new friends, but she had never cared. Over the years, they'd got her into as much trouble as they'd helped her get out of.

Her throat felt coated with acid as she asked, "Why didn't you approach me?"

"Our instructions were to survey and protect from the shadows," Ciarán said, and for the first time, she thought she could sense regret. "Our orders remain, even after Cara's death, Matriarch. We will shadow you anywhere."

"You can't be serious," Emer said, standing, placing her hands on her hips. "Niamh should be matriarch. All Ash has done is cause more death."

Both Tiernan and Niamh stood simultaneously, the red-haired warrior standing in between him and her wife as he took a step too close.

"You're only interested in taking the clan for yourselves. You don't care about anything other than your rank," Tiernan said, voice filled with a fury she hadn't known was in him.

Everyone stood as Emer moved around her wife and shoved Tiernan. "And the only thing you've ever been interested in is finding your dead mother. Or now"—she jutted her chin towards where she and Maebh stood—"getting your dick wet. Don't think I haven't noticed."

The brothers held Tiernan back. Ash frowned, opening her mouth to argue that she and Tiernan were only friends, but Maebh stepped forward. "Em —"

"Save it, Maebh." Emer spat. "Is it just that you wanted any Cassidy? Didn't matter who?"

"That's not fair," Maebh said, her voice quiet as she looked at her feet.

Ash had never seen her look so unsure of herself as she stormed toward her brother.

"Maebh, wait," Tiernan called, but she didn't turn around. "You're out of order, Emer. You've always been a spoiled brat, but I thought you would have grown out of it by now."

"And I didn't know you wanted my sloppy seconds." Emer laughed, but it was off.

Angling herself between the two sides, Ash spread her arms wide. "Enough."

Emer argued, but she glared at her. "I said enough."

"Aisling, you will not speak to my wife —"

"You will address me as matriarch, or not at all." She stared Niamh down.

Niamh's blue eyes slitted, a flush darkening enough to conceal her freckles, but she stood back, gripping Emer's hand and pulling her to their discarded bags.

Waiting until everyone seemed to calm down, she said, "Sit. We have things to discuss."

As their attention landed on her, she made herself stand tall, refusing to fidget under their scrutiny.

There were only seven years she'd missed out on training from her mother. Every day before that, Cara had groomed her, taught her how to stand before her clan as matriarch. It was time to show them how much her birthright belonged to her alone.

"The only way we will get answers about the murders is to finish the High King's quest," Ash said to her clan, including Emer and Niamh. They all sat on logs around the fire as she paced, her mind reeling as quickly as her feet.

Her hurt had blinded her so much, holding on to it for so long, she'd never given herself fully to being matriarch. The elders couldn't strip her title so easily, not unless she allowed them. Now was not the time to run away. She had tried that and regretted it for every moment since. She hadn't given the Breen clan a chance to see her claim her birthright with gratitude and willingness. All they saw was a runaway brat who was unworthy. With the time she had left, she would show them not only that she wanted it, but she deserved it.

"What answers do you need? Your brother killed two matriarchs. The end," Emer said, ignoring the warning hand Niamh placed on her arm. She glared up as she paced behind Tiernan, who was currently seething at his cousin from across the firepit.

Ash gripped his shoulder as he was about to speak. Looking between Emer and Niamh, she smiled tightly. "You have only been part of the clan in my absence, Emer, but for seventeen years, I was there. Training, learning how to take over from Cara when the time"—she cut Emer's interruption with a sweep of her hand—"When the time came.

"I don't owe you anything. My birthright alone places me above you. My decisions are final and until we're told otherwise, you will listen and follow and do as you're told. I've been nice, I've been meek, but I'm over it. I am Aisling Breen, matriarch to my clan. If you don't like it, I hear the O'Neill clan is taking new members."

The others stared at her, stunned, and thankfully Emer kept her mouth shut. Niamh glared at her, but she ignored both of them, continuing her pacing. She couldn't help but glance at the McQuillan clan every few minutes. Both twins now stood, facing off in some argument between the rest of the clan. She frowned at Maebh's demeanour. Even from this distance, it was clear there was no usual air of defiance or playfulness.

The silence stretched on until she said, "We need answers. Why did Conor want to pierce the veil?"

Tiernan frowned. "That makes sense for Cara, but what about Imogen? She wasn't killed on Samhain."

Tomás added, "And why was Cara killed in Newgrange?"

"It's the largest and oldest portal to this world," Ciarán said, scratching his jaw where a few days of not shaving was showing. "It makes sense, Matriarch, but there's more to this than we know."

"And that's why we need answers."

"This is nonsense," Emer grumbled.

Niamh stood, tapping her wife on the shoulder and hoisting her bag. "Aisling, we are going back to the clan. If you plan to stay, know that you are doing so against the elders' wishes."

"You can't speak for the elders," Tiernan said, rising from his seat. Ash stood behind him, ready to intervene if needed. He continued, "Ash is matriarch, the High King recognises her alone. Go back to the elders with this warning. Stand against your matriarch and face the repercussions of Brehon law."

"Don't make threats with me, Tier," Emer said, gripping her bag. "Since Nessa disappeared, you've been blinded. You used to be fun, but now you're just a burden. You have been for years."

"I'm sure your wife isn't too happy to see how jealous you are at the thought that Maebh might have moved on."

"With you? You're both pathetic and deserve each other." Emer hoisted her bag and stormed towards the Hill of Tara, not looking back.

Niamh stood a moment longer, staring as if evaluating Ash. There was nothing left to say, so she stared back, her gaze unfaltering. With a sigh, Niamh wordlessly followed Emer. Watching them leave, she didn't really see, her mind trying to work out a puzzle she didn't have all the pieces to.

She turned to her cousins, still sitting on the log. "I need you two to go back to the clan while we go back to the wind tunnel."

"Not a chance," Ciarán said.

"We need to stay with you," Tomás demanded at the same time.

Ash looked between her cousins, and then back at the retreating figures in the distance. "Danger doesn't just lurk in dark tunnels. I need you to stop the clan elders from trying to take my birthright from me. They think they can easily discard me, but I'm the matriarch and I'm here to stay."

CHAPTER 44

TIERNAN

"We're not leaving you," Tomás said.

It would take more than Ash to convince them. She wanted to go back to the wind tunnel. Excitement brewed in Tiernan's blood; he could almost feel the thrumming vibrations of the underground cave. He would think it an impossible thought if it weren't for the ground he stood on. Tír na nÓg was a land of impossibilities.

"I need to go check on my satellite. Can Tomás and Ciarán come with me for that?" he asked Ash, who was in the middle of trying to convince the brothers they needed to follow his stubborn cousin. His jaw ticked at what Emer had said, but he swallowed down the bitterness. He wouldn't waste time on the negativity she spewed, but he couldn't help but glance at Maebh every chance he had.

Aisling sighed as the stand-off continued. "Sure. I'll pack and get breakfast ready. The other clans have already begun searching. Let's hope no one else finds the tunnel."

He watched as several groups trailed towards the high wall and out of the gate toward the woods in the distance, armed and ready for their quest. He looked at Ash and smiled. She was right about the tunnel. He could feel it in his blood. Answers lay there.

"Okay, I'll be back in a minute and then we'll go, okay?"

Tomás reluctantly nodded as Ciarán hunkered beside Ash, his tone urgent as he murmured to her.

Tiernan left the three remaining clansmen and turned toward the McQuillan camp. With every step, his heart rose higher until it was lodged in his throat. His newfound gift barrelled into him as he reached her clan. They were still in some sort of heated argument. Smells of sulphur and wet paint barrelled into him and he once again appreciated how difficult Maebh's life had been, smelling everyone's emotions for years. He'd only been subjected to it recently, but found it hard to concentrate. Mixed with all that negativity were wafts of Myrrh and tonka bean. No wonder she wore that perfume.

The clan didn't notice as he joined the outskirts behind where Set and Maebh stood. The tall, bulky second, Malachy, stood in the middle, the rest of the clan facing the twins. He was almost as tall as Set, but his closely cropped hair and clean-shaven face were odd among the hairy clan that looked like they needed several baths. He took a tentative sniff under his arms and grimaced, realising he too needed one.

Phrases like, 'you have no right', and 'you left us so can't take the role' drifted toward him and he quickly realised they were all directed at Maebh.

"Can I have a word, please?" he asked from behind, his voice quiet, but she heard him. Her shoulders stiffened as she turned. He'd never seen her so defeated before, and he frowned as he glared at the mob before them. "It'll only take a minute."

"Go on, Maebh. I'll talk sense into them," Set murmured as he twisted in his spot, nodding to Tiernan. He gently pushed her towards him, and she silently followed him out of the castle gate.

They headed to the outskirts of the forest, Tiernan fighting to find the words he wanted to say, and Maebh casting glances behind her as they went. He stopped after they passed the first line of trees and turned to her. "What's that about?"

Maebh startled as she looked at him, as if she'd forgotten she was with him. Her expression pinched, her once tanned face pale, she said, "They don't recognise me as matriarch." She laughed without humour. "Makes two of us."

Tiernan glared towards the gate, but he couldn't see them from this distance. "Brehon law—"

"What do you want, Tiernan?" Maebh asked, taking a step towards Tara Court again.

He ignored her brisk tone, even though it made his throat dry. He had been surprised by her regret after their time together, but her coldness now was hard to face. "I wanted to see how you are. Emer was out of order."

"Was she?" Maebh's full attention was on him now as her piercing blue eyes burned into him. "You know she's my ex-girlfriend. And your cousin. How fucked up is that?"

"It's not," Tiernan ground out. "She's married."

"You've had her sloppy seconds, and that doesn't bother you?" Maebh didn't sound like herself. Tiernan took a step forward, but halted when she threw her hands up to stop him.

"You are many things, but not that, Maebh." Tiernan crossed his arms and she turned, putting her back to him. "You regretted it as soon as it happened."

She didn't respond. His temper flared as he fought against standing in front of her, demanding her attention.

"Was it ever real?" he found himself asking. He didn't expect a response, but it still hurt when she didn't give one.

Visions of her between him and the oak tree swam in his head, taunting him. It had felt real to him. She had been just as intoxicated by him as he had her. His blood ran cold as he stared at her back. "You were only acting on the emotions I threw at you, weren't you? That's what you said happens. You're numb because others are so full. I made you feel those things for me, but it was never you."

Maebh walked to the edge of the woodland without looking at him. "I have to get back to my brother. He's trying to save me, as usual." She glanced backwards but didn't meet his gaze, instead looking at the ground. "What you both need to realise is I'm not worth the trouble."

"You're wrong," Tiernan said to her retreating figure, but he barely heard the words leave his mouth, so assumed she couldn't either.

Running his hands through his hair, he watched her for a moment longer, letting his feelings consume him before forcing them deep within. He would make her see, even if she wasn't interested in him. She would know her worth. But now was not the time. Storming back through the gate with his hands stuffed in his pockets, he forced his head forward, not allowing himself to feel the pain of being ignored by Maebh.

"Come on," Tiernan said to the brothers, not waiting for them to respond.

He heard Ash demand they follow and smiled as he heard footsteps behind him. She was finally acting like a true matriarch. At least, the other important woman in his life had recognised her worth.

Minutes of silence went by before anyone spoke.

"Why did you want us to go with you?" Tomás asked, weaving through the tree trunks.

"I need you to do something for me." He stopped and turned before the men, seeing the oak tree in the distance. "You'll have to let me guide you to the tree, as I've performed a spell so nobody can see it."

Both brothers scanned the area before looking back at him with a mixture of doubt and awe. Tiernan turned and extended his hands out. Ciarán held his right hand, and Tomás offered his forearm for Tiernan to grip. He smiled at the sight they must have been as he moved forward, both men tugging at different intervals to move in a different direction; the magic working against them. When he passed the threshold of the deterrent, they relaxed, and Tiernan released them, smiling at their wide eyes at the magnificent oak that, to them, had appeared out of nowhere.

He got to work, loading up his laptop and opening the software he'd created, as well as the secret bank account he'd set up for Ash. The two men hunkered beside him as he beckoned them. "When I searched Cara's room before we found her, I came across the clan's finance book. Things are bad." He glanced at each of them before continuing, "The elders have been pushing to reopen the fairground because it's the only way they know how to make money. I know a different way."

Turning the laptop to face the men, he waited for them to read the figure on the bank balance. Ciarán leaned forward as scents of peppermint filled Tiernan. Excitement, he realised. It was a mix of theirs and his. Their funds had doubled since the last time he checked.

"How did you make so much money?" Tomás asked. "Is it legal?"

"It actually is. Well, mostly. I've invested in online stocks with money I had saved. That's the legal part."

Ciarán leaned away from the screen, scrutinising Tiernan. "Do we want to know what the illegal part is?"

"I created a software that monitors everything that will affect the investments I'm in." Tiernan said, opening up the application and smiling as the strings of blue and green codes filled the screen. "It scans newspapers, companies, and major players in the investment world."

Tomás continued to scan the screen, his brown eyes zigzagging as the programme ran. "That doesn't sound illegal."

"I hack into company accounts and internal reports to find this info out. When the software detects a significant action that will affect stocks, it moves portions of her fund into the new stock." Tiernan sat back, leaning against the tree as he marvelled at his own creation.

"Okay, that part is definitely illegal." Tomás glanced up at him, his face illuminated by the screen light. "Her fund?"

"This money is solely for the use of our matriarch. It is not for the Breen clan to use until Ash returns and only when they sign this contract"—he clicked into a new tab—"that I took the liberty of drawing up. Only then will the fund be released for the Breen clan."

The men's eyes darted back and forth as they scanned the screen. Ciarán's smile widened with each line. He looked up at Tiernan. "They won't like this. We never use Glutton law to bind us."

"Desperate times," Tiernan said, raising his hand in a dismissive gesture, but his eyes shone with excitement. "I need you two to go back. No, listen for a second. Ash insists she needs you to stop them from doing anything foolish, and she's right. You both will have to fight against the elders because I'm sure they plan to leave the encampment and declare Niamh as their matriarch."

"She's no matriarch," Tomás growled, his jaw clenched.

"Exactly. I'm giving you the tools to stop them. The elders won't be able to fight against their need for money. Dangling this hefty carrot in front of them will do enough to delay them until we return."

Ciarán nodded, but then his face turned serious. "That tunnel is dangerous. Can you protect her if anything happens?"

"I would give my life if she needed me to. But..." Tiernan paused, turning the laptop towards him and closing it down. "She's able to protect herself."

The ceilings in the castle were too high, making him feel small for the first time since his last growth spurt at fifteen. He loomed over most people but never filled out, and no matter how much lean muscle he'd earned over his years of training, people still underestimated his strength. Even he did, he realised, but not Ash, or Maebh. His throat bobbed at the thought of her expression before she'd walked away from him. But now was not the time to dwell on Maebh McQuillan, the woman he'd never imagined would steal his thoughts.

Tomás and Ciarán had left in a hurry after he'd shown them his plan, but he hadn't returned to Ash. There was one more move to make before they returned to the cave.

He didn't know where his father's rooms were, but after finding a servant who then brought him to the castle steward, eventually, he was led to them. They didn't believe he was the son of the fearsome Rígfennid of Leinster, but after threatening his father's wrath at finding out they'd turned him away, the steward had finally relented. He didn't blame them. Other than their skin colour, there wasn't much similarity to the two men.

Bradan had no fixed abode, normally moving across the area he oversaw in both realms. It was a dangerous task; the Kingdom of Leinster was Fair One territory and being a human emissary in a land of deadly immortals was no easy task. He often wondered how his father could stand before them and not hate it. Perhaps he did. It wasn't as if he spoke about his interactions with them. He could see why King Aedan had chosen his father to act as emissary; of all the Fianna warriors, Bradan was one of the fiercest.

Having left the human realm six years ago, and not venturing back for longer than a few days at a time, he hadn't aged since. It made little difference yet, but Tiernan wondered how he would feel in twenty years when he looked the same age as his father. The servant let him into his father's chambers, signalling him to wait in the reception room, but he dismissed him, closing the doors abruptly behind him.

Taking a steadying breath, he headed toward the doors across the room, where he could hear voices. He'd come here to ask for something, and that only meant one thing for his dad. There was always a price. You received nothing from Bradan Cassidy without giving something in return.

Bradan was in a small sitting room, a gathering of guards and robed court members surrounding him, deep in discussion. When the leader saw Tiernan appear through the door, he raised his hand, the scars that criss crossed his skin visible even from this distance. They were a darker shade of brown, and Tiernan had never known his father without them, having traced them as a child while sitting on his lap. All chatter quietened as everyone turned to look at him. He refused to fidget; his few nights camping no doubt making his appearance less than appealing to these people.

"I need a word, Father," Tiernan said, not looking at the others.

"Everyone, please excuse me." Bradan's smile was solemn as he approached his son and gestured to the corridor that he'd just come through.

Bradan led him closer to the entranceway before choosing a door furthest from the room full of people. "I'm glad you sought me out, Son. I heard you found Imogen. Conor Breen is in the east tower and the king has tasked me with interrogation, seeing as he's under my jurisdiction."

"He's only eighteen. Don't hurt him." Tiernan's throat thickened as he warred with himself over his brother. He couldn't come to terms with seeing Conor with the antlered mask, bloodied and apologising to Ash. It didn't fit the man he knew. "Can I see him?"

Tiernan's hopes that Ash wouldn't need to go through the quest, and he wouldn't need to ask what he planned, were dashed when his father shook his head.

"You cared for him?" Bradan placed both of his shovel-sized hands on Tiernan's slumped shoulders. "I'm sorry for your loss, Son."

"He's not dead." Tiernan stepped away, gripping each of his elbows and hugging his torso. "Yet."

Brehon law was clear. The punishment, at a minimum, equated the act. If you stole, you had to pay with your time in the dungeons. If you assaulted another, you were beaten; sometimes the appendage you used to hurt would be amputated. If you killed . . . your life was forfeit.

"I'll make sure he is not harmed before the trial," Bradan promised. "What he did, though. Nobody can make head nor tail of it. Why would he do that? On Samhain, too."

"Has he talked yet?"

"He won't speak to anyone. He's not eating or drinking, and has barely moved from his bed in his cell." Bradan sighed. "There is no benefit from torturing a man who is already punishing himself."

"Why is he in a tower? I thought . . . criminals were brought to the dungeons."

"They usually are, but the High King's druid"—Bradan face twisted in disgust—"insisted he was placed up there. It's still a cell, with very little comfort, but I believe she has visited often."

Tiernan turned to the room they were in. Another sitting room with plush furnishings and a lit fire. He walked to the fireplace, needing to find warmth and fight against the images he had of Conor, curled into a ball in a dank cell. "I need your help."

Bradan took an armchair beside him, only nodding for Tiernan to continue when he turned.

"I need access to the ancient scrolls. Specifically, about Fionn Mac Cumhaill."

Bradan's dark eyes narrowed, and Tiernan instantly felt like a child asking for permission to get out of warrior training like he so often had in the past. He stood tall with his arms behind him; this was different, and he refused to leave with any other result than getting what he wanted. What his matriarch needed, if there was a way to wake up the first High King, would she still hand the location over to Aedan? He also wanted to find out what truly happened in a blood sacrifice on Samhain. That answer could explain why Cara was killed, and why Conor thought he'd done it. Until there was undeniable truth to the contrary, he refused to fully believe in his guilt.

A smoky odour filled his nostrils, and he tried to hide his surprise when he realised it wasn't coming from the fire. He didn't need to smell his father's anger, it was written across his face.

"Are you still playing foolish games? The High King is being disrespectful to all clans who have gathered here for the Cath. The honour of joining the highguard shouldn't be tainted with this quest."

"Have you spoken to the king?"

"No," Bradan said, cracking his knuckles as he sneered. "His witch refused my audience, saying His Majesty was busy."

"If I could just have some time with the scrolls, I want to find out more about the lore of Fionn Mac Cumhaill. What harm is there in research?" Tiernan shrugged a shoulder, hoping he came across mildly interested. He swallowed as he glanced about the room, willing his heart to beat less loudly.

"Do you really believe you can find his tomb?" His father was incredulous, and he couldn't blame him. He was normally a level-headed person, and Bradan knew how little he stored in Fianna superstitions and beliefs. What he didn't tell his father was that they'd already found it.

When he didn't respond, only raising his hands to warm them, his father sighed.

"The scrolls regarding the first High King are guarded by scribes."

"Are you saying you can't help me?" Tiernan fought against the weight of defeat, trying to press in on him.

They knew where the tomb was, and that was enough to win, but he wanted to find out as much as he could about the wind tunnel, and how to protect Ash if needed. He believed what he'd said to the Breen brothers; their matriarch could defend herself, and she'd finally seemed to realise that. Ancient magic and buried High Kings was something nobody knew how to fight against. Whatever lay in that tomb did not want to be disturbed.

"I can help you." Bradan stood, joining his son at the fireplace. The flames cast half of his face in shadow as he turned to face him. "But first I need you to agree to join me. Help me rule over Leinster."

"Under the High King's favour?" Tiernan asked, even though he knew there was more to what his father was not saying. The festival had planted seeds of doubt at his father's loyalty to Aedan, but now was not the time to worry about that.

"Aye," Bradan said with a tight smile. "While his reign remains."

He thought about what Tomás had said before they parted ways. He had called him Ash's second. It was a position of great power. One that normally went to another female, although it wasn't unheard of for it to be a male. Imogen McQuillan had chosen Malachy to be hers. If anything happened to a matriarch, a second would take her place if she were female. He would never have that role, nor did he want it. He also didn't want the position his father offered. Ash hadn't officially named him her second, but he felt duty-bound to serve her in that manner, regardless. And in that regard, he knew that the best way to serve was to agree to his father.

"I will."

CHAPTER 45

MAEBH

Her mother had never wanted her; why had Maebh thought her father would? Gripping the soft leather-bound journal she'd religiously clutched for countless nights, she wondered what the point of it was. Why had she wasted seven years looking for someone who probably didn't want to be found? Maybe Setanta was right and he was dead. She looked at her twin now, foolishly arguing with their clan over whether she should take over as their matriarch. She'd left their clan, but she was Imogen's daughter and the right to claim the role was hers.

She shivered in the midmorning air, a coldness to it that hadn't been present since they'd arrived in this realm. Shoving her journal inside her jacket, she zipped it up and glanced at the Breen emblem, a glaring insult to the McQuillans before her. She needed to walk away, get some fresh air, preferably nowhere near her kin, who seeped with an odour too close to rotten eggs. They were mourning a formidable leader she would never become.

Her mother was truly dead.

Without meeting Setanta's eye, she wordlessly turned and trotted through the soft mud of the farmland where all warriors had camped. Keeping her gaze down as the muck squelched and pulled her boots, she didn't acknowledge anyone she passed.

The market square was quiet today, the news of the fallen matriarch having undoubtedly spread by now. Two murdered leaders were as morbid as it was worrisome. But they'd caught the murderer. Hadn't they?

Aisling's brother had always seemed off, but she found it hard to imagine his pale, gaunt face and see it as a killer's. The castle loomed in the distance, and Maebh hugged her arms tighter around herself as she walked under its shadow.

Even in Imogen's dying breaths, she had only wanted her golden boy. Maebh grit her teeth at the reminder of how unwanted she had always been. At this rate, she'd crack a molar, her jaw screaming in protest at her constant abuse. The tavern they'd visited yesterday appeared around the corner of her aimless wandering, and she took it as a sign she needed a drink.

Reaching the door, she glanced upward, only registering the name above. 'Raven's Nest' was carved into a wooden post, suspended by wrought iron brackets, creaking in the light breeze that caused Maebh's unwashed hair to tickle her face. She grimaced as she sniffed; perhaps she'd finally learned the secret to avoiding the unpleasant smells of people's emotions.

Even in the early hour, the tavern had a crowd of patrons. Maebh waited at the entrance until her eyes adjusted to the darkness. Most ate breakfasts of fried meats and potato bread, but as she reached the bar, she noticed some were nursing pints of dark ale. There were no fae here today.

"What'll it be, wee girl?" the bartender asked, an oily cloth strung across his shoulder, his arms crossed as he stood in front of her.

He wore a simple tunic and trousers, like many of the locals. It seemed the odd mash of clothing worn at the festival was a rare treat for special occasions. She wondered how long he'd been in this realm. He looked like a man in his thirties, but that meant little here.

"Mead, please," Maebh said, perching on a seat farthest away from anyone. "And I'm not a wee girl."

His heavily hooded eyes narrowed as he placed both hands on the counter before her. "Not before I see coin. You modern warriors come in here expecting rectangle metal or paper as acceptable payment."

Sighing, Maebh slammed a few of her coins before him. "Now, pour."

Scooping up the loose change, he scrutinised them before pocketing with a nod. It was still the modern currency, but she'd known they only traded in coin or barter in Tara Court. Moments later, a thick wooden tankard was set before her, its contents steaming. Taking an appreciative inhale, she gulped down a generous mouthful. Lemon and honey hit her first, the warmth of the drink soothing as it trailed down her throat.

"This is delicious," Maebh murmured, taking another gulp.

"It's a family recipe," the bartender said, his gruff face unreadable but his tone friendly enough. "It's been passed down through this tavern since the beginning of Tara Court. We were the first tavern established."

Maebh only nodded while drinking, this time with smaller sips, as she could already feel the effects of the alcohol. Her stomach rumbled, and she wondered when she'd last eaten. The bartender disappeared into a curtained area at the back while she hugged her arms tightly, a weariness setting into her bones. Would anyone care if she rested her head on the table? Casting glances around the room, she appreciated the quiet reprieve. Most patrons were eating or drinking, too busy to talk, or like her, didn't want to.

A clatter sounded in front of her and she spun back around to find a breakfast plate before her.

"I don't want you falling asleep on my bar, or getting sick and giving my mead a bad reputation," the barman said while refilling another patron's drink.

"My coin didn't stretch this far," Maebh said, her stomach taking its cue to gurgle loudly.

"Prove you're not a wee girl and have some sense to shut up and eat."

Without another glance her way, he headed in the other direction, a tray full of drinks raised high. Smiling at his retreating figure, she appreciated his lack of customer service skills. He hadn't provided cutlery, but she took his advice and tucked in, relishing every sensation that hit her. Dipping a glazed pork and herb sausage into a fried egg, she munched into it while grabbing a triangular chunk of soda bread, ready to be consumed once her mouth was less full.

Halfway through eating like a savage and giving zero fucks about the glances coming her way, she was finally warm enough to relax her shoulders, her hands no longer stiff and sore. The comforting hum of the tavern, mixed with a proper meal, had eased a little of the building tension within her. Wiping the grease from her fingers on her combat trousers, she shirked out of her jacket, her journal falling to the beaten earth floor. Glancing at it once, she took another long sip from her lukewarm drink.

"You used to scream at me if I even so much as thought about dropping this journal," Set's voice was quiet behind her, but she didn't turn around.

"I thought you'd have found me long before now," Maebh replied around a mouthful of food.

Set's mess of curls came into view as he swooped down to pick up her book before perching on the high barstool beside her. Swiping a charred tomato from her plate and popping it into his mouth, he signalled to the barman he would have the same as her, placing more coins than she had in front of him. They didn't speak and Maebh had almost finished her meal by the time he received his.

"Well, go on, then. What was the verdict?" Maebh asked, shaking her head as the barman offered her another hot mead.

The sound of Setanta's chewing filled the space as he stooped over his plate, devouring the contents as eagerly as she had hers. Their twinship illustrated their need for sustenance while mourning. She snorted, realising she probably wasn't behaving the way her mother would have wanted. Even after Imogen's death, Maebh was failing her.

In between mouthfuls, Setanta said, "They're still unhappy with how you left, but the majority will accept you back and that's all that counts."

"Which side was Lorna on?" Maebh pictured her aunt's pinched face, an ever present scowl that surfaced every time she looked upon her niece.

"You know what she's like." Setana shrugged, keeping his focus on his plate. "It didn't help that you walked off without saying anything."

It was her turn to shrug, signalling to the barman that she would take that second drink, pushing Setanta's remaining coins closer to her as payment. When a fresh, steaming tankard arrived, she inhaled the citrus sweet concoction, letting it wash over her. Focusing solely on her beverage, she refused to think about anything else. There was too much to ignore, including her hulking brother, who had finished his breakfast and turned on his stool, surveying her.

He placed a hand on her shoulder. "Hey."

"Hey." Maebh set her drink down, tracing the wooden grooves of her mug.

"It's going to be okay," Setanta said, pulling her toward him so she was wedged between his arms. Her breath caught as the steady beat of his heart thrummed under her ear. "As long as we've got each other, we can get through anything, right?"

"Right," Maebh murmured, sniffing loudly before leaning away from him. "You stink."

Setanta's laughter filled the room as he playfully shoved her, knocking her from her seat. "I hate to break it to you, but so do you, Mae."

Waving at the barman, who dutifully ignored her, she grabbed her journal and jacket and followed her brother out of the cosy tavern. Casting a glance at the useless notebook, she'd debated leaving it behind. The spring air had returned and even though they walked in the shadows of the looming castle, it was warm. Tara Court had woken up since they'd entered the dim lights of Raven's Nest, the market in full swing as they walked side-by-side back to their clan. Maebh gripped the lapels of her jacket, glancing down at the Breen crest before grimacing.

Setanta tracked the movement. "We'll get you a new jacket."

She gave a noncommittal grunt in response and as they passed a large firepit already lit in preparation of roasting meats, she tossed her journal onto it, feeling lighter the moment it left her fingers. She already had one foolish quest looming over her. Giving up on the impossibility of finding her father was something she needed to do. Setanta stood beside her, not commenting on what she'd done, and they both stared at the open page it had landed on; the one it always seemed to open naturally to first. Their father's black-and-white image melted slowly as the flames licked the pages, and she fought against the irrational urge to grab the book back.

"That'll make the meat smell, you idiot." a woman approached her, apron stained with blood and who knew what else. "You could have easily bartered it."

"It was of no use to anyone," Maebh responded before digging into one of Setanta's combat pockets and handing a couple of coins into the woman's palm. "For your trouble."

"Really?" Setanta asked, taking his remaining coins and moving them to his other pocket, out of her reach.

"Really," she replied solemnly before bumping into his side.

He didn't budge, and she ignored his chuckle as she stumbled back a few steps on impact.

The McQuillan clan's large camp loomed as suffocating as the castle at her back, but Maebh steeled herself, only nodding at Setanta when he asked if she was ready. She was greeted with ridicule and openly hostile sneers as soon as she passed their self-claimed territory.

Setanta stood by her side as, one by one, the clan continued their debate about whether to recognise her as their leader. Despite her brother's assurances, she knew if they were to vote, Maebh wouldn't win.

Every time she opened her mouth to speak, they silenced her with harsh words and angry gestures. Sighing, she let it all wash over her. She wanted to tell them she would vote the same as them. Dancing in a tent full of five hundred groping stag parties would be preferable to leading this group of self-important assholes. No one passed their condolences on to her. Her mother had died, but their only concern was to ensure they cast her out of the clan.

Setanta was a torrent of words, arguing her birthright, and she fought the urge to roll her eyes. Malachy continued to stand between her and the others, facing neither but ensuring a semblance of peace. As long as Setanta kept his cool, she had no intention of fighting anyone. She smirked as she realised that may not be the case for the others, but let them try to swing at her.

"Look at her smiling, as if she doesn't have a care in the world," Lorna said, gesturing at her like she was an errant child. She was almost identical to her mother, but where Imogen had been beautiful, her aunt was unremarkable. Maebh had found it funny that Lorna could look so like her mother but have none of the charisma the matriarch had. "Do you have anything to say for yourself?"

"Not really."

"She's grieving." Setanta angled his body in front of her as he spoke. "We both are. You can't expect her to —"

"Behave like a matriarch?" Lorna seethed, pointing a bony finger in Maebh's direction. "She's McQuillan by name only. Her right to rule vanished when she left."

Drowning out the sounds of the murmurs of agreement, her thoughts drifted to Tiernan and her stomach twisted. She knew she should care about what was happening. Maybe she was in shock, or grieving, like Setanta had said, but she felt numb about everything other than the man she'd walked away from in the woods. He thought she'd only reacted to his attraction to her, and she was a coward because she couldn't tell him the truth. Sure, if they explored a relationship it would be awkward with Emer, but that had been a convenient shield to hide behind. They'd turned from rivals to allies, and while their flirtatious banter had been fun, she hadn't planned on exploring more with him. And then they'd experimented on that damned tree.

Seeing him storm towards his clan without glancing at her had hurt, but what had she expected? She'd made it that way.

Malachy was saying something, but she couldn't hear the second's words; it was as if she was underwater. The only thing she could hear was tones; he seemed to placate Lorna, but her aunt wasn't giving in. Maebh swept her gaze to the other faces behind her aunt, who were all seemingly in agreement with her.

"Like her surname, she will be matriarch in name only." Lorna's voice broke through and Maebh stared at her grey eyes, so similar and cold like Imogen's. "Setanta can rule."

"That's not how this works. The role can only be passed on to the next female." Setanta stated, his own eyes brewing into a thunderstorm with every suggestion made about overthrowing her.

"That works for me," Maebh said brightly, and all faces turned to her once more, so she smirked, winking at a few.

"You so readily agree to that?" Lorna asked, and Maebh didn't need her gift to know she was in disbelief.

"That's what you want. I agreed. Why is there a problem?" Maebh sighed, the weight of speaking becoming a burden.

Turning to the largest tent, she swiped the flap back to see her mother's unmistakable possessions. Before talking herself out of it, she stalked forward, closing herself in and plunking down on the bedroll. Everything was neat, as if Imogen hadn't slept here at all, and that somehow brought its own sadness.

Willing her breathing to slow into a steady rhythm, she lay fully dressed on the bed. She needed to sleep and dream of nothing. And what better place to accomplish that than in a dead woman's tent? The thought pulled her further into the pit she was falling into, much deeper than the cave where the first High King lay. The clan, or Setanta, thankfully didn't enter, leaving her in solitude to embrace her dark thoughts.

CHAPTER 46

AISLING

Ash could hear the McQuillan clans' raised voices from where she sat on her log. It had been an hour since Maebh had retreated into a tent, and Set had stormed off. She had been walking back from the market after bartering for some eggs and bread, intending to make breakfast for Tiernan and her. The Breen clan hadn't been big to begin with, but now there were only two of them.

Set hadn't seen her as they passed, or perhaps he'd been ignoring her, but she was too much of a coward to approach him. His stormy grey eyes had been focused straight ahead, the scent she associated with fury wafting as he charged through the busy street. She had been walking on the other side, but she could have easily darted across the narrow dirt road to talk to him. Instead, she'd continued to her empty camp.

She had finished breakfast, cleaned herself up with a bucket of ice cold water and determination, and was still waiting for Tiernan to return. What if he'd left, following Tomás and Ciarán? She shivered, even though the sun was blazing above. She'd go through the tunnels alone if she had to. Conor's haunted face as he sat slumped underground by the ghastly horned mask replayed in her mind. Glancing skyward, she promised herself that before the sunset, she would have answers to why her family was so torn apart.

Donning a low messy bun, she had put on her second set of Breen warrior clothes. If they stayed any longer, she would have to look into getting her first set cleaned, or barter for a change of clothes. As it was, she was one pair of socks down in order to pay for breakfast. Apparently, one downside of living in the Land of Eternal Youth was the lack of cotton foot coverings.

Where was Tiernan? She glanced toward the Hill of Tara, her heart skipping as she routed out their destination. Should she just go to the High King with the information she had now? What if he dismissed her when she couldn't prove what she'd seen? No, she would return and bring back evidence. There were plenty of stone white statues down there, although it would be impossible to carry one of those up, there had to be something she could bring. She also needed to ensure the black wall opened for them again.

A woman's high-pitched voice penetrated her thoughts and her eyes tracked Set's broad shoulders, standing before a shorter blonde. From this distance, she would have thought she was looking at Imogen McQuillan. As Maebh appeared from a tent and stood by her brother, the woman's voice rose even higher and more of the clan surrounded the twins.

She steeled herself before standing, ignoring the popping in her spine and the ache in her legs. With every step it felt like she was walking towards a battle rather than a clan.

"She agreed already, Setanta. Maebh will be matriarch in name only," the woman who looked strikingly like Imogen said, and as Ash reached the outskirts of their group, the woman's gaze pinned on Maebh. "You may be the head, but Setanta will be the neck."

"You have no right to decide that, Lorna," Set said while Maebh shrugged, looking off into the distance.

Ash approached, gripping her hand, startling her friend. And that's what they were, she realised. Despite everything, they had each other's backs. Maebh didn't let go, and she took that as a good sign, turning to the clan before her. "The High King called a meeting with your new matriarch and me, recognising both our birthrights. There is no discussion to be had."

"Go back to your own clan, girl," Lorna said, a sneer on her lips. Her hair was a shade darker than the twins', but up this close Ash could tell they were related. "I see you don't have many clansmen over there, so you can take my niece back with you; she likes clan hopping. Your brother killed our matriarch. How dare you step so close to us."

She spat on the ground, and Ash stared at the blob of saliva inches from her black boots. Glancing up, she arched her brow and studied the fuming woman, which only seemed to antagonise her further.

"Don't talk to her like that." Set stepped forward, placing himself to loom over the woman. She was wise enough to shrink back.

She fought against the fluttering in her stomach, stemming down the foolish hope that he may forgive her for her impulsive anger in the tunnel. Turning back to the group, ignoring Lorna at the front, she raised her voice. "I know how to succeed in the High King's quest."

Murmurs floated towards her, along with a tartness that reminded her of when she was about to sit an exam, and wondered if she had studied any of the right material. Swallowing down the excitement and disbelief surrounding her, she continued, standing tall and straight, projecting her voice so they could all hear her.

"I will share winning this quest with the McQuillan clan."

"You can't do that," Lorna seethed, crossing her arms and turning to the others. "Don't listen to this child."

"The High King said nothing about allying with other clans," Ash said dismissively before turning to Maebh, squeezing her hand. "I need you, Matriarch, to aid me in this quest. And Set." Ash tacked on, her voice coming out in a rush as she tried to remain authoritative.

Maebh squeezed her hand and then let go, facing her clan. "I'm going with Ash."

Her hair was still plaited, but unkempt, her clothes crumpled and Ash noticed she still wore the Breen crest on her jacket. But none of that mattered as Maebh marched toward the empty camp without another word to any of her own clan, seemingly uncaring of the tuts and insults that followed. Ash glanced backwards with a grimace. Maebh was going to have to work on her people skills.

Lorna glared after her niece before Malachy approached her, the burly second angling her away. Daring to glance at Set, her breath caught when she met his gaze, already on her. They regarded each other for a moment before he faced the clan. "I will help the Breen matriarch and with my sister ensure the McQuillans get through this quest. Only on the condition you accept Maebh."

Lorna opened her mouth to speak, but Malachy intervened. "Agreed." He raised his thick arms upright, silencing his clan. "We haven't been able to figure out this quest, and now we need time to plan for our fallen matriarch's funeral. The deal is struck."

He held his arm out and gripped Set's forearm. The two men nodded, and then Malachy motioned for his clan to disperse, leaving Ash to stand awkwardly behind the tall and clearly brooding warrior.

"Can I talk to you in private?" she asked, Set's back tensing as she spoke.

He didn't turn, but nodded, pointing toward the castle gate. "Let's take a walk."

Leaving the bustling market and wordlessly heading past the guards standing duty, the silence outside the walls was deafening as Ash struggled to keep up with Set's long strides. They drifted through copious trees, passing warriors who were scanning the area, presumably in search of Fionn Mac Cumhaill. As if he would be right outside Tara Court's walls. She almost felt sorry for them, but she couldn't help them. Not when it meant getting answers from her brother. The High King would have to allow her to visit him once she proved what she'd found underneath the Hill of Tara.

Ash swallowed the hard lump forming in her throat, only causing it to dry up as she turned to face Set once they'd reached a small clearing. He was once again already watching her.

"I'm sorry, Set," Ash began, her words coming out too quickly to be coherent. She paused, her heart thumping so loudly she was sure he could hear it. Taking a steadying breath, she tracked his unreadable expression as he leaned against a large trunk, his arms crossed. "My brother . . . I'm so sorry for what happened to Imogen. And"—she took a tentative step closer, ensnared by his grey eyes once more—"For what happened after we found you. I was blinded by rage and fear that something had happened to Conor. I shouldn't have even contemplated lifting my sword."

"Ash," he said, stepping forward only to hunker down to her eye-line. "You didn't do anything I hadn't asked of you. I wanted you to lift that sword. I thought . . . I'm a monster, so it was easy for me to believe I was the one to kill her. And Cara."

"But you didn't."

"No, but I could have." Set straightened, causing Ash to crane her neck to see his troubled expression. His savage beauty struck her all over again. It was enough to hurt her heart. A face that caused her to feel melancholy for something she'd never have.

407

She looked to the sky, only to find it obscured by leafed branches. The surrounding forest was alive with day creatures. The rustling of leaves on the ground mixed with the dewy scent of late afternoon created a peaceful scene, in contrast to where her thoughts were.

"Why didn't you tell me when we lay under the stars?" she blurted, her sorrow turning to anger. "Were you only getting to know me because you thought that you'd killed my mother? That's fucked up."

His throat bobbed, and Ash tracked the movement as confirmation. The pain in her chest turned up a dial as she nodded, looking at her feet. Kicking loose dirt and scuffing her black boots further, she chastised herself for being so foolish. What had she thought would happen? That they would have a special moment and suddenly ride into the sunset; happily ever after?

There were too many monsters in these woods, and one of them stood before her. Remembering his confession underground, she couldn't fathom it, even now. He may not have killed her mother, but he was capable of it. The man of her dreams was also one from her darkest nightmares. She was too afraid to ask what he shifted into, and a shudder ran through her as she tried to conjure an image of something that could tear someone apart and not remember afterwards. The shiver of fear slid down her spine as she hugged her arms close to her chest.

Ash didn't truly understand why she was so drawn to Set. Not until she broke it down and considered he was exactly the opposite of what she'd settled for in the past. He allowed himself to be vulnerable, though he was the strongest man she knew. He cared for others, his own difficult sister included. He was wounded and imperfect, but still here. Still standing right before her because something inside of him wanted her just as much as she wanted him. And she knew it.

Set wasn't a man she had to hide her true self from. He was a man she could be herself with. Set was difficult, but he was also easy. And she needed easy. If she was being honest with herself, she needed Set. But they had a mountain to climb together before that could ever be a reality.

"At first, yes," Set said before cupping her chin, his calluses grazing her skin as she willed her stupid heart to slow down. She wasn't afraid, not when he looked at her with such gentle confidence. He waited until she met his gaze. "I wanted to get to know you and find out if I'd been the one to ruin your world. But that changed soon after I met you. Ash, I couldn't tell you the truth until I knew.

"I was terrified that I'd somehow turned and got close to Cara. And then yesterday when I woke, covered in blood and remembering fragments of seeing my mother lying on the ground, I felt certain it'd been me."

Set let go of her when she stepped away, the phantom touch on her chin still tingling and the weight of his gaze leaving her nerves on edge.

She sighed. "I thought we'd become . . . friends. But that wasn't real."

Silence greeted her and those words hung in the air between them. Friends was the word she'd chosen, too afraid of showing her true feelings. Had it all been in her head? She heard him groan before stepping into her line of vision.

Gripping her shoulders, he stooped low again until they were eye level. "The time we shared under the stars was something I've never experienced before. I was more me than I ever could be. Few people know about my condition. You make me feel seen and accepted."

She swallowed a lump in her throat as she smiled, a tear sliding down her face. He tracked the tear before wiping it with his thumb.

"I feel the same about you," the words tumbled out of her mouth before she had time to stop them, but once they were out, she dared to look at him.

She was rewarded with a wide smile as he straightened. Winking at her, he said, "Technically, I told you I was a monster; you just didn't realise I was being literal."

Ash laughed despite her annoyance. Set sounded more like his twin than she'd realised. He shrugged his shoulders and she playfully pushed him, but of course, he didn't budge.

"That's still a pretty shitty excuse."

"You contemplated killing me, so I think we should forgive and forget."

"Please don't say it like that." Ash groaned, causing a chuckle from the tall warrior, so low and gravelly, causing her stomach to dip. She sighed. "Start over?"

"Deal."

They surveyed each other before Ash looked away, and she let out a nervous laugh.

"Friends?" Ash asked, offering her hand.

His smile was wide as he swallowed her hand in his. He didn't let go, and she didn't move away.

Swapping out his hand so they stood side by side, he linked their fingers together. "Friends."

Heat rose to her cheeks as she glanced between their joined hands and his face.

His grin was wolfish as he arched a brow. "Don't friends hold hands?"

Heavens. She was in trouble.

CHAPTER 47

AISLING

As they ambled toward the high walls, Ash stole glances at Set, tracking the feel of his rough palm against hers. She couldn't remember a time when her breath didn't catch as she looked at him. From the moment she first saw Setanta McQuillan she'd felt an attraction, even before her mother's funeral; but it had grown into something more for her.

Her stomach twisted as she fought the urge to pull her hand from his. He wanted friendship, and was clearly flirting, but she'd seen how hurt Orla had been. There was no denying the brunette warrior had been scorned by him. Chastising herself for ending whatever it was between them before it had begun, she forced herself to pay attention as he told her about life in the McQuillan clan, and how his performances had been a bone of contention between the twins.

Ash didn't highlight how awful his mother seemed to have been, forcing a wedge between the siblings, and it was as if Set needed to explain it, highlighting how tough life had been for both him and Maebh. She squeezed his hand in understanding, and he smiled.

Walking out of the forest beside a gorgeous man holding her hand, she could almost forget that she had a quest and an imprisoned brother to deal with. The problems in the human realm were another issue she didn't know how to solve, but she would have to deal with one impending threat at a time.

Entering Tara Court once more, they made their way to her campsite, Set keeping a comforting grip on her hand, and she couldn't remember the last time she'd actually held hands with someone. It was as thrilling as it was sweaty in the warm air. She didn't mind it, and he didn't seem to either. Coming close to the farmlands where most of the clan camps were empty, she spotted both Tiernan and Maebh sitting on the logs around the small campfire.

"Will Maebh be okay? Will your clan accept her?" Ash said, eyeing the twin's clan camp in the distance. Most of them had dispersed elsewhere, but a few, including Lorna, remained sullen-faced and glaring towards their matriarch. Lorna caught Ash's gaze and her scowl worsened as she tracked them, her eyes flicking to their joined hands.

"My aunt is worse than my mother ever was," Set said, waving with his free hand towards Lorna in a gesture so like Maebh's, Ash had to hide a smile. "One thing's for sure. I will not agree to stand in while they degrade my sister. Lorna thinks she can make me Maebh's neck, steering her rule. But they all should know my sister would only break it."

He didn't let go of her until they greeted the others. Maebh noticed their hands and smirked, raising her brows as she met her gaze. Ash's face heated, but ignored her clear provocation, gazing pointedly between the tall, dark hacker and her. Maebh glared back, but she shrugged.

"Fine," Maebh said, low enough for only her to hear as she sat in the log closest to her. "Point taken."

"Good," Ash replied with a grin.

They would both stay out of each other's love lives, if that's what any of it was.

"I've got some information that may be useful," Tiernan said, cleaning up his plates, oblivious to the women's quiet conversation. "Thanks for breakfast, by the way."

"No problem. It was a 'thanks for not abandoning me like the others' gesture," Ash said, trying for humour but failing miserably.

"You sent Tomás and Ciarán away," Tiernan replied, a small smile on his lips. "Don't worry about the other two."

Ash noticed he looked anywhere but Maebh, and she was also ignoring him.

"What did you find out?" Set asked, sitting on the log close to Ash. He took up all the room as he leaned forward, resting his elbows on his thighs.

Although they'd updated him at the castle, Ethne had been present, so they'd left out the most important part and it was no surprise he frowned at Tiernan's words.

"I went to see my father, who got me access to the castle library. We found the resting place, Ash, I know it."

Set opened his mouth, but Maebh cut in.

"We found a tunnel on the way here. Under the Hill of Tara," she said, pointing toward the tips of the mounds that could be seen above the roofs of the nearby village. "Yesterday, or the last sunrise—whatever timeframe you want to reference this warped place—we explored it."

"That's what you were doing before you found me?" Set looked to everyone as they each nodded, and Ash knew they were all quietly reliving what had happened after. "And what did you see? We searched a few of those tunnels too. What's so special about this one?"

Tiernan stoked the fire with a log before casting it in, the snapping of wood instant as sparks flew from the disturbed flames. "The sarcophagus."

Setanta gestured with his hand for someone to continue. They all looked at each other, the decision on what to do next sparking like the firepit.

"Conor . . ." Ash sucked in a shaking breath as everyone reacted to his name in winces or clenched jaws. "He knew how to gain access. For years nobody has been able to find Fionn's resting place, but we just stumbled upon it? It's too easy."

Set's eyes pierced her. "What are you saying?"

"He said the druid told him what to do," Ash murmured. "She has to know where the first High King is, but she didn't go herself. She directed us to it."

"But she's just as obsessed as Aedan is," Maebh ground out, no doubt remembering her ordeal in the throne room. "Do you know if Orla is okay? She's a bitch, but she didn't deserve whatever Ethne's spell was."

Set's face clouded over as he stared behind his sister and Ash tracked it to the McQuillan tents. "Orla's hand had to be bound, and her arm is tied behind her back. Malachy told me she keeps breaking through the ties and attacking herself. They gave her a tonic, but her hand constantly twitches, even as she sleeps."

Silence followed as they all stared toward the other clan camp. Ash tried to picture what Set had described and could only imagine the fear Orla must be in, not being in control of her own limb. A shiver ran through her and she remembered how she'd feared Ethne when they'd walked through the woods before meeting the High King. She had the face of an angel, but Ash feared she had the temperament of a demon.

What would she gain from Fionn Mac Cumhaill's awakening? She could only hope they weren't about to hand over a weapon of devastation if they really could wake up the sleeping king.

Ash's eyes darted to Tiernan as she licked her lips. She didn't know the answer, but there was something in that tunnel. A magic so strong it repelled them. If it truly was Fionn in that stone coffin, and she'd bet her freedom that it was, it was clear the magic protecting him meant he wanted to remain undisturbed.

Tiernan said, "The scrolls in the castle library account for several different times and dates to when Fionn Mac Cumhaill died. One scholar reluctantly told me about the scrolls the king is most interested in."

Ash leaned in, a thrill of excitement running through her. "Did you read them?"

He shook his head. "He wouldn't show me, but he recited the passages from memory. Fionn, before he drew his last breath, was cast deep underground. The scroll said that he slumbered underneath a great seat."

"That'd be uncomfortable," Maebh added, to which Set chuckled.

Tiernan continued after a beat, "Another described his resting place as a 'cauldron of plenty'."

Ash's gaze snapped to the Hill of Tara, her head buzzing. Years' worth of study in both history and lore ran at triple speed through her mind. "In the Iron Age, that hill was also known as the seat of the High Kings of Ireland."

Unable to contain her excitement, Ash stood, pacing a few feet toward the ancient hill and back. "We really found it."

"Okay, maybe you found it, maybe not." Set raised his hand when Ash frowned at him. "We searched those tunnels too, and so have many others before us. There are some crazy things down there, chests of cursed treasures and fae who relish in the dark for their wicked deeds. What makes you so sure your cave is the right one?"

"The druid," Ash said, her heart hammering against her ribcage. "For whatever reason, she led us there through my brother."

"He's in a tower," Tiernan's voice was soft, and Ash swallowed down her sorrow as she heard his plainly in those words, too. They had been as close as brothers and she felt a strange comfort in knowing they were mourning the loss of a man they thought they'd known. "My father told me he won't speak to anyone."

Ash only nodded before assessing the twins. She knew they had a right to feel whatever they did toward her brother, but a searing urge to protect him was still branded on her heart. She went from sure of his innocence to looking at the evidence stacked against him to feeling utterly defeated every few minutes. They didn't react to the change of topic and she pushed on, focusing on what she could control in this moment.

"Set, the tunnel both before the drop and after, pushes you with an unsourced wind, making it almost impossible to get through."

"Luckily, we're all stubborn bastards," Maebh added, a smile finally playing on her lips.

Ash grinned at her friend, relieved to hear the reliable, smart mouth she'd become fond of.

Tiernan smiled at Maebh too, but quickly seemed to remember who he looked at and returned to attending to the flames which were already too high. "Once inside the cavern, there are hundreds of stone statues stationed around the sarcophagus. There is only one entryway. The place is—"

"Off," Ash found herself saying, shivering at the memory of the deadened icy air as they manoeuvred around those statues.

Tiernan raised his brows. "I was going to say thrumming with an electric current."

When Set frowned, Ash added, "Tiernan has been getting this feeling underground, especially in that tunnel."

"It's like a force field." Tiernan shrugged. "I can't explain and nobody else notices."

They sat in silence. Unable to stand still, she retrieved their pot of water, angling it over the fire.

"So, for argument's sake," Set began, standing to take the pot from Ash. Maebh muttered something about feminism, but he ignored her as he continued, "what happens if this really is Fionn's tomb?"

Rummaging through their supply container, she hesitated before answering. "Do you believe the legend is real?"

Nobody answered and as she grabbed four tin mugs and added loose tea leaves into separate infusers, she noticed they all wore similar expressions of contemplation.

"If it is real," Ash said, gripping her mug and noting the edge of finality in her tone. "We do whatever it takes to win the quest."

CHAPTER 48

AISLING

The tunnels were as dark and cold as before. A dripping of unseen water echoed like a death knell, a reminder that not even the water sounded the same in this realm, deep underground. Ash's laboured breaths warmed her cheeks as she shivered in the chilled air. Each of them held a flashlight, Set having retrieved them from his own camp under the scrutiny of his aunt. Malachy had tried to convince the twins to allow him to come, and she was grateful they'd refused or she would have stepped in. She hadn't wanted to argue with them, but this was her quest and she was allowing them to come along.

Their heavy footsteps clanged in the dark passages as they wound through the first set. The task was easier with the assurance of where they were going, but the knowledge of their impending freefall had Ash's every fibre on high alert. They hadn't passed a soul other than the guards stationed at the entranceway to the caves, who had wordlessly let them pass, and she wondered who or what it was they were guarding against. Set had mentioned fae living underground, but she hadn't yet crossed one; something she was grateful for. The fae above ground were scary enough, and she didn't want to encounter any creatures that revelled in darkness.

Ash followed Tiernan's tall frame as he led the way, the twins taking the rear. She would name him her second, but wanted to wait until they had a moment alone. He had been a constant support from the moment they'd met. Although he'd hacked into her personal files online, she knew it had been done out of love. Maybe not for her at the start, but through loyalty to her mother, and she only hoped to earn that type of relationship with him, too. But if she ever found out he'd continued to invade her privacy, she would throw him into a cave where there was no magical substance to stop his fall.

In the normal world, stalking was a big no, but in their world—the one that bordered both realms—she'd learned that social etiquette was non-existent. They may play at court and High Kings, but it was a lie. They had always lived on the outskirts of society. Her time with Mary and Dom had made her forget that. They had opened her eyes to how normal humans lived. She appreciated that time, and them, but it wasn't for her anymore.

They arrived at the antechamber that held the seven tunnels. Murmurs from unseen voices carried in the air from other underpasses, and it was the first noise other than their movement and dripping water that had sounded since going underground. Even Maebh had been uncharacteristically quiet. She looked to the other woman now, who pressed a finger to her lips before pointing in the direction the voices were coming from.

Ash angled her torch to the tunnel mouth, beckoning the others to follow. Other Fianna were hunting for the king's treasure, but it looked as if their destination remained clear. The sense of 'off-ness' seeped from it, and she wondered if she only noticed it more now, or had it always been there. Her limbs stiffened as she forced herself to keep moving. Everything about it was unwelcoming; from its width to the wind, it was a place that repelled. And that, to her, was a sign she was right.

"Careful, Bro, it's a tight squeeze."

Ash angled her light backwards in time to see Set lodging himself in between a narrow part of the cave walls. She couldn't help her chuckle as Maebh pulled him through, even though she was also struggling.

"Why are we doing this again?" he grumbled, his forehead glistening with sweat.

"We're almost there," Tiernan said from directly behind her, and she let him pass to the approaching obsidian wall.

She angled her light to join where his own torch aimed at the marking. His long brown fingers circled the spiralling triskelion; and before she could offer her own blood, he'd already cut himself. Although she had expected it, the waft of cool air as the wall disintegrated, replaced by nothingness, made her breath catch in her throat.

"Matriarchs first," Tiernan said, and she smiled as their eyes met, remembering how he'd said the same thing the morning they'd entered the Hill of Tara in the human realm. How much time had passed from now and then still bewildered her. Although she felt like the days here had dragged, it was nothing to the month that had passed for Mary and Dom. If she stayed for a month's worth of time here, how long would it be for them? She shivered, and it had nothing to do with her impending jump into the abyss.

"Everyone, make sure your blades are secure so they don't nick you on the way down," Ash said as her hand gripped her mother's sword hilt. Looking down at it, she realised it was truly hers. It wasn't just a family heirloom forced upon her, she wanted this tangible reminder of where she belonged. Her throat tightened as she said, "We were lucky the last time, but at least we know what to expect."

"Not all of us," Set said, the obvious hint of worry in his voice.

Tucking her torch into her jacket, she cast a glance at him, a frown playing on his lips as she took a small step backward.

Winking with a smile, she jumped. His curse followed her as she plummeted into the darkness. The tears from the rapid speed she was picking up blinded her; not that it mattered. The darkness was too dense that even if she had held her torch; she doubted she could see anything. Trying to keep her arms tucked in tight was impossible as she twisted in the air, her cockiness disappearing with every breath. Afraid of how close she could be to unseen walls, she mimicked what skydivers did before they pulled their parachute cord.

On and on she fell, the terror engulfing her. The freefall was long enough that she doubted her willingness to jump. What if that magical drop only worked once and she was about to splatter herself at the bottom of the cave? Mary used to say, "If your friends jumped off a cliff, would you follow?" It had taken on a new meaning, but instead of her being the sheep, she'd been the idiot to jump first.

Before she hit the ground, her projection slowed by the invisible substance, stealing her breath. Blue hues of stone guided her way as she swam downward, her lungs burning as she met the film of resistance before sprawling ungracefully to the compact ground. Like before, she remained dry, but cold. Gasping for breath, she was only just able to compose herself enough before Maebh joined her, followed by Set and then finally Tiernan.

"Remind me never to do that again," Set said, as he stood beside Ash, his eyes scanning the long passage. His face was flushed and his long plaited hair had come loose, and Ash fought the urge to reach up and brush it out of his eyes. His gaze met hers as he frowned. "Do I want to know how we get out of here?"

"What goes down must come up," Maebh said, slapping her brother's shoulder as she ambled down the tunnel.

"That's not the saying," he said as he followed her, his hand landing on the handle of his curved sword.

"Are you ready for this?" Tiernan's voice was low, as if he didn't want the others to hear.

"Ready as I'll ever be," Ash said with a smile, pushing her hair from her face. "We don't know for sure if this is the first High King's resting place."

He looked at her with raised brows. "I think we do."

Her heartbeat skipped at the confirmation she knew to be true. "Come on."

Ash cast her light along the walls, the embedded blue gemstones glistening as she passed. The twins' figures disappeared through the narrow mouth of the tunnel and she steeled herself for what was to come. As soon as she stepped over the threshold, the same feeling of foreboding clogged her senses until she fought to breathe, the deafening sound of crashing rocks causing her to train her torch upwards. But again, there was no source to the noise.

When she passed the first two white stone statues, she jumped at the sudden presence of Set in front of her, who had turned back with a panicked expression. "We need to get out of here."

He grabbed her arm, tugging her toward the way they came, but Tiernan blocked the entranceway. Set looked ready to barrel into him, and Ash feared the damage the huge warrior could cause. "Set, it's okay. Once you get through a few feet, the feeling will pass."

Set's brows bunched together as he panted heavily, and she was sure he was about to argue or fling Tiernan out of his way. She tugged at his hand until his wide-set eyes met her own. She smiled reassuringly, even though she felt the same panic. "It's okay."

He resisted for a moment, gripping her hand to the point where she winced, but when he saw her grimace, he took a long breath and loosened his hold. Turning, with Tiernan taking the rear, Ash tugged him forward, but this time there was no thrill of the action as his almost vice-like grip was anything but sweet. Maebh stood in the distance, having passed the marker where the repellent magic lessened. Ash's own shoulders relaxed a fraction and her jaw hurt as she realised how much she had been clenching it. Letting go of Set once she was sure he would not bolt, she winced in pain before massaging her jaw.

"Sorry if I hurt you," Set said as he gingerly lifted her hand to see if there were any marks.

His warm breath tickled her forehead and she smiled up at him. "I'm fine."

"We should have warned you," Maebh said from behind her brother, a hint of amusement in her tone.

"You don't say?" Set grumbled, but Ash didn't turn around to watch the twins bicker as her focus trained on the stone coffin.

The brilliant white of the sarcophagus pulled her attention as the cacophony of rolling stones overwhelmed her once more. Frowning, she analysed the noise, tapping it against her arm. There was a steady beat, a rhythm that she knew but couldn't place. Was it really Fionn Mac Cumhaill that lay within? She didn't want to think of what came next if the answer was yes.

If she received confirmation it was truly him, could she give the High King his whereabouts knowing he intended to disturb this temple, with all the magic wards protecting it? But who was she to stand in the way of a king? If it meant she could see her brother and get some closure, why not?

Straightening, she marched forward, the rows of white statues a blur in her peripheral vision. Her mother had been killed on Samhain, and she needed to know why. If Conor had truly killed her and performed some dark magic on the night where the veil between both worlds was weak, it had to be reversed.

"Let's get this over with," Tiernan said from behind her, his presence startling her as she snapped out of her spiralling thoughts. Nodding, they both strode toward the sarcophagus.

"This place gives me the creeps," Set said as he rounded the stone coffin, his voice almost drowned out by that incessant beating.

She had to agree, her pulse thrumming in her ears as they each scanned the long slab of stone from top to bottom, circling it several times. She dared to trace her fingers along the various symbols; the stone was cold to the point it burned and she snatched her hand back. The top covering was the shape of a man, arms crossed over his chest, common to how the dead were often buried in the human realm.

Although it had most likely been down here for longer than she could fathom, it was blemish free. Not a crack or fracture could be seen in the artwork, and the white stone sparkled in the torchlight, much like the gemstones on the walls. The sides of the sarcophagus had markings of an ancient language. Her archaeological heart jumped with excitement, but before she could give in to her academic curiosity, Maebh called out to her.

"Ash, can you come here, please?" Her voice was laced with an edge that hurried her steps, halfway down the aisles of statues, her eyes scanning the area for any danger.

She frowned as she reached the tall warrior, who stood facing one statue, her brows bunched together, the beating louder here.

Breathless, Ash pressed her hand on her chest, willing her heart to slow. "What is it?"

She'd intended to take a better look at the strange art display, but now was not the time. She'd known of ancient customs from her studies, where societies placed statues made of prominent members; effigies to ward over the dead. There was only one tomb here and there were dozens of these stone statues. With her hand still pressed against her heart, she paused as the surrounding noise seemed to mimic her own heart. Scanning the area, she searched in vain for where the source was, so like the sound of multiple beating hearts.

The men's voices carried back to her, muted by the ceaseless drumming, and when it didn't seem like Maebh would answer, she stepped forward, intent on joining them again. The sooner they confirmed their findings, the quicker they could leave.

"Do you think this one looks familiar?" Maebh murmured, unmoving from in front of the statue she spoke of.

With a sigh, Ash peered closer, noticing the statue was made of the same white quartz as the coffin. She squinted, raising her torch higher. It was a man. Stepping back, she took in his body. The clothes looked military based. And even though it was just white stone, she could tell they were modern. The artwork was so well carved that when she cast her light from his feet upwards, she could make out laced boots, combats, and a jacket similar to what they all wore.

"Those are Fianna warrior clothes," Ash said. "There's even a coat of arms on the breast."

Maebh didn't move as she continued to gaze at the statue's face and Ash moved towards the next figure. Similarly dressed to the man, only this time it was a woman. Her hair was carved to make it look curled and full, her slender, tall frame set in a familiar stance. One she'd seen many times before. One that was currently stooped over a coffin.

The voices and grunts of Tiernan and Set barely registered as she studied the eerie likeness of Nessa Cassidy.

CHAPTER 49

AISLING

"It's not budging," Tiernan said, unaware that his mother's image had been immortalised through stone only feet away from him.

Ash's attention snapped to the men as they pushed the lid, but it didn't seem to move.

"Hold on." Set unsheathed his sword. "I'm going to use this as a lever."

As he prodded the dip between the lid and coffin, Ash rushed back to Maebh, realising she was still standing before the same figure.

"It looks just like him," Maebh murmured, reaching up to trace his mouth.

The drumming took on a frantic beat and Ash once again placed her hand across her chest, scanning the rows of statues as her own heart beat in time with it.

"I think I have it," Set called.

Tiernan rushed to his side again, pushing the lid, and Set continued to press down on the handle of his sword. She frowned as she stepped back from Maebh, and the stone that was carved into Gearoid McQuillan.

"This isn't right." Her throat constricted as a wash of panic flooded her, but this wasn't a magic-induced dread. Taking another step back, she scanned the rows of statues, blood pumping so loudly in her ears it almost drowned out that incessant noise. "We need to leave."

"It's not working." Tiernan grunted. "Switch positions."

If two of the caillte were carved into stone, would the others be here too? Her father's statue could be within reach. She swallowed down her ever-increasing dread and raced up the line of statues, looking for any similarities to the man who'd never treated her like a daughter, but had reared her anyway. She was still processing her mother's murder at the hand of her brother. Seeing her father's face in stone felt like too much.

Turning on her heel, she took two steps toward the coffin and the men still working on opening it, when an ear-piercing screech sounded. She could hear both men curse and grunt in synchrony as they inched the stone further, Set's strength winning against the ancient stone as the lid ground against its base.

The drumming stopped.

"What the . . ." Maebh said before stumbling away from Gearoid McQuillan's likeness. "I could have sworn it blinked."

Ash's heart beat in her throat as she raced back and focused her torch on the statue once more. Another screech of moving stone, but this time closer, and the statue's hand shot forward, Stone-Gearoid grabbing hold of Maebh's wrist in what looked like a bone crunching grip.

As Maebh cried out, Ash rushed forward, trying to loosen the grip, but it was unmoveable. She could hear the men shouting but couldn't figure out if they were still doing so out of excitement. Even more screeching of stone filled the space.

Maebh continued to curse and cry as the hand squeezed harder, darkening from brilliant white to a pallid flesh colour. Movement out of Ash's vision caused her to react before she could think, ducking out of the way as more of the statues rushed for them.

"Maebh!" Set cursed as he raced toward his sister. "Get off her!"

She hadn't stopped fighting to free herself, but she had slowed her movement. "Dad?"

Ash rolled away from a stone foot about to crack open her skull, losing her torch. The sparse lighting made the shadow stone beings even more frightening, but when she was on her feet once more, she had time to look at them, a curse flying from her lips. They were no longer made of stone. They were human, and coming for them.

"Ash, watch out!" Set's warning wasn't quick enough as a pair of arms circled her torso and hoisted her upwards.

She cried out, her years of training leaving at the feel of the cold stone wrapped around her. They may no longer look it, but whatever these things or people were, they still felt as cold as granite; as strong and immovable too. Raising her legs as high as they would go, she heaved downwards; the momentum propelling her forward enough to somersault out of her assailant's grip. The surprise on his face was enough to make her smirk before another stone being was upon her. With her cockiness short-lived, she assessed her opponents, nothing like she'd ever encountered before.

Her two attackers circled her and she couldn't focus on the others while a third joined them, even though she heard them fighting. Nobody came closer to her and in the dim lighting, she couldn't make out much of their features, other than their clothing, similar to the highguards. Long blades swung from their belts, which they hadn't unsheathed. Remembering her own sword, she went to her belt, but before she could grip the hilt, one of them barrelled toward her. She dodged his fist, bringing her elbow upwards, only to be met with stone. Crying out at the pain of essentially hitting rock, she stumbled backwards until she hit the craggy cave wall.

The stone men visibly relaxed, having surrounded her, penning her in. She glanced at the others to see how they were fairing as she clutched her elbow, fearing she may have shattered bone. Maebh had freed herself and was fighting against her father while pleading with him to recognise her. She couldn't see Tiernan, and her throat went dry. They were severely outnumbered. Set was the closest to her, fighting off five of the stone people as he tried to get to her. Their gazes met.

"Find Tiernan!" Ash ordered as she took on a fighting stance once more.

The three guards regarded her with expressionless faces. To them, the fight was over. Set called out to her, but she ignored him as she unsheathed her sword and thrust it forward. The blade hit the man's torso, and they both looked down at the blade, now bent. Her eyes met his before he smiled and swiped her blade from her hands, snapping it in half. Fury boiled her blood, the one piece she'd had of her mother, broken at her feet.

Without enough time to draw breath and roar like she wanted, he pinned her to the wall by the throat, inching forward so his icy breath was on her. He looked human, but there was no humanity staring back at her. Emotionless eyes met hers, pupils an obsidian darker than the abyss she had jumped through to get there. He leaned closer and inhaled deeply. She fought against him, but he was too strong. It wasn't a man that stood in front of her but a predator. He pulled back, raising his free hand and forming a fist.

A roaring sound like nothing she'd ever heard before erupted through the space. A shadowed beast rose from the ground behind the two stone men standing guard as the one holding her prepared to strike. The monster was twice the height of any man, its width wider than the guards stood together and as another earsplitting roar ripped from its unhinged jaw, they turned. She would have gasped if she could, but the stone man didn't seem to notice what stood only feet away; his gaze trained on her as he tightened his hold around her neck.

A clawed arm swiped sideways, and the guards flew off their feet, crashing to the wall beside her, the sound of stone cracking rang in her ears as they broke into rubble by her feet. The stone man finally loosened his grip, and she fell to her knees, gasping for air as her eyes watered. He took a step toward the beast, his hand unbuckling his scabbard, but not quick enough. A snarl vibrated the walls as the beast smashed him into the ground with one blow.

The monster's back was to her as it snarled and tore into any stone guard that attacked. A sob of relief stung her throat as she tracked familiar figures at the mouth of the tunnel where Maebh and Tiernan were fighting off several of the stone guards. Her breath caught as she rose to her feet, not finding Set where she'd last seen him, only a heap of rock. The monster roared again, and Maebh cried out.

"Set, remember yourself. Come back to us!"

Ash staggered back, once again pinned to the wall, but this time by her own shock. The monster roared and lifted one stone woman into the air above its head, tearing her in half and discarding the pieces to the ground.

"Set?" Ash heard herself saying, her voice low, but it heard her.

He heard her.

He twisted toward her, and Ash finally met the monster he'd been hiding within as his massive frame loomed above her. Clothes torn, she tracked his sinewy frame, no sign of his sun-kissed skin or savage beauty. His face was a grotesque version of what it once was, one eye lodged in a gaping hole at his throat, the exposed jaw gave the impression he was constantly grinning. His one remaining eye had stayed in its socket, and as she searched for any sign of the man she knew, the only thing that had remained was his mane of hair. Set took one step toward her and she pressed herself into the wall as if she could gouge her way to safety.

She watched, horrified, as he raised a hand, plucking out the eyeball in his throat. Before she could register what he was doing, he threw it. The eyeball flew through the air toward her and she tracked it with equal parts horror and fascination. She ducked low, trying to avoid it from hitting her, but it stopped mid-flight, inches from her. It remained stationary above her and she righted herself, staring back.

Her attention went back to Set when he roared again, and she noticed a stone woman had lodged her blade into his leg. He punched her, knocking her down, and then stood on her head, crushing it. Bellowing again, he grabbed her blade, tearing it from his leg, blood splaying the ground and once white rubble. Ash stepped as close as she dared to see if he was okay, but he snarled and she stopped.

"Set. It's me," Ash tried, but he barrelled forward, claws outstretched as if to grab her.

She waited until he was almost upon her and rolled, avoiding the pile of stone that was once a woman. She ran toward the exit but lost her footing, a blow to her side knocking the breath from her. Before she hit the ground, he snatched her around the waist and hoisted her high. Set snarled below her, his face close enough now that she saw fangs. His face had elongated to a sharp point, along with his ears. She clawed at his hand, large enough to hold her waist as he brought her close. The eye was now back in his throat and Ash found herself struck by the fact it was still the same stormy grey as before. She could see the human in it and tried to plead with the fragment still present.

"Set, you can fight this. You don't want to hurt me," Ash said, no longer trying to loosen his grip. She patted his thumb, wrapped around her front. "You held my hand in yours. We're friends. Remember?"

He seemed to hesitate, his furious expression becoming clouded. He lowered her but was jostled by another stone man. His tenuous grip on humanity vanished and he threw Ash at the stone man, causing both to fall to the ground and she gasped for breath. Before the stone guard could grab her, she jumped off of him and limped toward the exit, calling out to the others as Set barrelled through the guards in front. He stopped mid-stride, turning to face her once more, and she almost crashed into him before he disappeared in a plume of smoke. Blinking, she stared at the now empty space. Gone, just like the druid's trick.

"Quickly, Ash, move behind me," Maebh said, holding off two remaining stone guards with her sword as Ash stumbled forward.

Her breaths wheezed as she clutched her side, her elbow screaming with every movement she made. She was bruised and battered, but alive.

Tiernan hunkered by Maebh's feet, muttering as he pulled dried herbs from his various pockets. A terrible smell filled the air as he opened a vial.

"What—"

"Druid's repellent spell," Tiernan answered, gesturing for her to step back as he spilled the contents on the ground by the mouth of the narrow entryway.

Maebh kicked one soldier before swiping and pushing the other back. "That fucker broke my favourite sword," she said, using the bladeless sword hilt to punch a stone man. "Hold them off while Tiernan makes us invisible."

Ash took a deep breath but winced before grabbing a large piece of rock, thrusting it at the man closest to her. With a start she realised it was Gearoid.

"Try not to kill him, will you?" Maebh said between grunts. "And I'll do the same for yours."

Ash finally looked at the face of the man Maebh was fighting and let out a cry. Lorcan Breen raised his bare hand to stop Maebh's dagger, the sound of steel against stone vibrating through her ears. Movement caught her eye and she ducked in time to miss Gearoid's fist, the whoosh of air from where her head had been seconds ago. "Tiernan, any time now would be great."

He continued to ignore them, seemingly deep in whatever incantation he was reciting. She was no match for the strength of Maebh's father, and her only option was to duck and weave, hoping to keep him distracted while Tiernan worked. She tried to look behind the stone-men, their fathers, but through dim lighting and rubble everywhere, it was hard to make out if there were any others lurking.

"Ready." Tiernan jumped to his feet. "I need more room."

Maebh swivelled, one leg raised, kicking Ash's father so that he crashed into her own before shouting, "Hurry!"

Both men hit the ground and rolled into other guards, who had finally woken and were headed their way. Tiernan finished pouring the foul smelling potion at the mouth of the tunnel and looked up triumphantly before cursing. "Hold on, we need proof."

Ash's eyes widened as their fathers gained on them, faces contorted in rage. "Don't—"

He rushed forward, grabbing a broken piece of stone, throwing it to Ash. She glanced down to see a stone rendering of the O'Dwyer coat of arms, the same as what the High King's guardsmen wore on their uniforms.

"Tier!" Maebh's shout snapped Ash's attention to him.

He was a foot away when he jerked forward, falling against her. It was only when he was wrenched back that Ash saw Nessa

Cassidy standing before them, her wave of dark curls obscuring her face. When she looked up at Tiernan's face, his eyes were wide, his mouth forming an o.

"What . . ." Ash began but then she saw.

Nessa's fist had lodged into her son's chest.

The sound of his screams was muted by the blood pounding in her ears as she watched, horrified, as more stone warriors stood behind Nessa, and she raised him off the ground before pulling her hand free. In a numbed daze, she expected to see Tiernan's heart in his mother's retreating hand. But it was empty.

This wasn't happening. It couldn't.

Her mind wouldn't adjust to the sight of Tiernan stumbling forward. It was only Maebh's screams that woke her from her daze. He fell on his knees before he could make it to them. The walls pressed in until she couldn't breathe. A sob escaped her lips, raw with shock as devastation rippled through her, tearing her at the seams.

"I finished in time," Tiernan was saying, clutching his chest in a feeble attempt to stem the heavy flow of blood. "Stay behind the line."

She was undone, and there was nothing that could put her together again.

Ash caught Maebh's arm before she charged across the barrier he had created for them. To protect them. With one glance behind at her fallen friend, she could see the remaining stone warriors standing to attention, staring straight ahead, but making no move to attack.

"If you go across that line, Maebh, Tiernan's spell will be for nothing," Ash warned, even though she warred with herself.

Could they reach across and grab him?

"Don't," Tiernan grunted, reading on her face the plan she was formulating.

She knew Maebh understood, but she continued to scream as she pulled at Ash's arm. There was no way she could hold Maebh back, but she held on as they leaned on each other to stop one another from falling. Kneeling on the edge of an invisible line, Maebh sobbed as Tiernan lay on his back, his hand reaching forward. He murmured something incoherent and Ash strained forward too.

"You're my second, Tiernan," Ash whispered, too afraid to raise her voice.

Not for awakening those stone warriors again, but for the confirmation that death was near.

A fallen torch lay close by Tiernan's head, illuminating his sharply defined features as they contorted in spasms of pain. His eyes rolled backwards before meeting Ash's. "You've always been my first, Matriarch. I'm glad you can see that now."

Maebh reached across the line, grabbing his hand. She tugged him closer, but stopped when he cried out. "Don't."

Ash squeezed Maebh's shoulder in warning as the stone statues moved a step forward in unison. Their eyes couldn't seem to fall upon where the women were huddled in front of Tiernan's fallen body, but the movement had alerted them to their presence once more.

"Maebh." Tiernan coughed, his eyes closing as a tear fell on his flushed cheek. "Níl sé ach ina thús."

A beat of a second later, Maebh uttered the translation, her voice cracking. "It's only just begun."

"I've regretted many things." Tiernan smiled widely before it turned into a grimace and he panted before saying, "But getting matching tattoos isn't one of them."

"Tier," Maebh said, her words broken in between sobs. "I'm so sorry. I didn't mean . . ."

His body contorted in an impossible arch, the screeching sound of stone against stone deafening and out of place with his movement. His cry turned garbled, and then he went deathly still. Ash gripped Maebh's arm as they watched him stand, and the ground seemed to tilt as they followed suit, facing him as he stared past them with a detached look, his once brown skin turning ashen. She tracked his chest and although she didn't see blood flowing any longer, the amount already on his shirt was worrying. His chest didn't rise and fall. His eyes didn't blink. Ash lifted a discarded torch, bringing it closer to his now chalky complexion.

His eyes met hers at the same time his hand darted forward, grabbing the handle of her torch just above her own. His hand was ice cold.

"Go," Tiernan said, barely moving his lips. "Now."

The other statues stepped forward, and Nessa gripped her son's shoulder, tugging him back as he released his grip on the torch. His eyes pleaded with hers before glazing over, brown pupils dilating until they were nothing but black and then quartz-white. Clutching Maebh's arm, Ash swallowed against the painful lump in her throat, pulling her back with her. Heavy footsteps clunking along the ground as the statues retreated, guarding the stone coffin in the distance.

Ash's eyes blurred as Tiernan joined their formation, something she'd missed when they'd carelessly walked through to get to the sarcophagus. They were lined around the coffin, stone guardians to the sleeping High King. Ash raised her torch high, not daring to move any closer to waken the statues, even though her friend was now one of them. During the fight, whatever traction Set and Tiernan had made had now been righted. The tomb lid was in place once more.

"Set," Ash whispered, realising he might have disappeared and teleported to the tunnels like the last time. She gripped Maebh's arm tighter as she licked her chapped lips. "We have to find your brother."

Those words didn't rally Maebh, who jerked out of her grasp and continued to stare at the statues. Whether it was at her father or Tiernan—or both—Ash wasn't sure. She didn't have the courage to ask.

When they eventually turned to stumble through the tunnel, the sound of Maebh's feet dragging behind her the only sign she followed. They had no weapons. As Ash held the piece of rubble Tiernan had given his life for, careful to avoid contact with her injured elbow and scanning the area with her lone torch, she knew she would be no match to fight anyone. As they made it back into the smaller cavern where they could ascend, her feet faltered as the beam of light shone on Set, kneeling, utterly naked, with his back to them. His body was a work of art once more, his glistening skin over defined muscle, displaying a man who was stronger than most but also defeated.

Her pulse quickened as she surveyed his wounds; large gashes somehow stitching themselves shut before her eyes could track how severe they had been. She fought for breath as she watched his slumped shoulders; his head bowed so that his hair shielded his face. A fallen warrior.

"Set?" Ash whispered, wanting to alert him to their approach.

He made no move to acknowledge them, or to cover himself as they both stood before where he kneeled. Maebh held back, murmuring about finding the symbol to get them out of here while taking the torch and rock from Ash's hands, but she kneeled before him. Fighting the urge to lower her gaze below the panes of his chest, she reached for his hand. It was ice cold, but even as she squeezed, he didn't come out of his trance. Her eyes faltered, but only for half a moment, the guilt apparent on her flushed cheeks. She dared to gently graze his arm, tracing up his neck and then his bearded jaw, her other hand cupping his neck and feeling the reassuring pressure of his pulse underneath her fingertips.

"Set," she tried again, and this time his storm cloud eyes met hers.

"Ash." His voice was hoarse and his breathing jagged.

"It's okay," she reassured him, as she studied his pale, drawn lips and his widened eyes as they rolled before pinning her once more.

A shiver in the darkness caused Ash to grip him tightly before scrambling to her feet, only for Ethne to appear. Wordlessly, the druid removed her cloak, draping it around his slumped shoulders, displaying a simple silver dress that showed more creamy flesh and tattoos. Although the only light source was their lone torch, and the faint glow from the blue gemstones, the druid's skin seemed to radiate like the moonlight.

"Come with me," Ethne said, her smile as dangerous as a dearg due. "The High King wants to see you all."

Chapter 50

Aisling

"Tell me how you found the cave again." Aedan's dark eyes shone as he gripped the stone emblem of his family crest.

Ash fought against the nausea of loss, looking between the twins as both continued to stare at their feet. They'd stood before the High King's throne for over an hour, explaining everything they'd discovered about the resting place of Fionn Mac Cumhaill. Her legs shook, her breathing coming in weary sighs, and she winced whenever she moved her arm. Druid healers had been summoned, and although their potions were already taking effect, both in numbing the pain and speeding recovery, the phantoms of her wounds were still a niggling presence.

Ash had lost Tiernan. Another person she'd recognised as family. They hadn't spoken before Ethne brought them to the High King, but when she realised the twins wouldn't speak, she took the lead and told them what had happened, almost in full. She'd left the part about Tiernan turning into a stone guardian, one of many who stood between everyone and the first High King. Neither Maebh nor Set added to her tale, letting her decide what truths to share.

The lie of how Tiernan had become fatally injured felt sour on her tongue, and she wasn't fully sure why she hadn't told the truth. Ethne's expression was unreadable from her position beside the king, but every time Ash dared to glance her way, she was watching her, a smile on her plump lips. What if the druid had seen what really happened? The woman could appear and disappear in a heartbeat. There was no way to know if she'd witnessed anything, but she seemed content with the story Ash spun.

"It was Tiernan who saved us." Ash didn't fight the tremor in her voice. "He distracted the . . . beings while we fled."

She'd told him fae creatures had appeared on impulse and now she tried to sound convincing but feared she was already failing miserably.

As if beckoned by his son's name, Bradan Cassidy entered the throne room. After a swift bow, he stood with his back ramrod, one hand clasped casually around the hilt of his sword. "You summoned me, High King?"

"Yes, Bradan." Aedan sat forward. For the first time since their arrival, a sombre expression was on his face. "I'm afraid that I have difficult news to bear."

Bradan didn't react, only stood a little straighter, waiting for whatever revelation was about to befall him. Ash fought the sting of tears as she tried to pick out any similarity between father and son. From her brief exposure to this man, she had noticed none, and the pang of disappointment and relief rocked her.

"Your son was struck during the quest," Aedan said, taking the steps down to place his hand on Bradan's shoulder. "He didn't make it out. May his soul continue on."

The Leinster Rígfennid didn't recite the ending to the blessing of the dead, and it was Maebh's sob that broke the silence. She shook herself, resisting Set's attempt to console her.

"A fool's errand," Bradan's voice was little more than a growl as he slapped Aedan's hand from his shoulder. "You killed my boy for your warped belief."

"It is not warped. They found it," Ethne soothed, as if speaking to a temperamental toddler, and not referring to a young man's needless death. She ignored Bradan as he spat by her feet, only moving to stand closer.

"Bradan," The High King's voice was laced with warning, but it seemed the grieving father had no intention of heeding to it.

"Stay out of this, hag," Bradan spat again, raising his forefinger inches from her face. "You may scare everyone, and have enamoured the current High King, but you don't fool me."

"What do you mean by 'current', Rígfennid?" Ethne purred, silver eyes dancing with mischief. "Do you expect your High King won't remain so?"

Ash was struck by how much the woman seemed to relish all altercations. It was as if her skin glowed during any sort of malice or chaos in the air.

"Ethne, now is not the time for that," Aedan said, although a frown played on his lips, as if the barely veiled accusation hung heavy between the two men.

"Mr Cassidy, I'm so sorry," Ash began, but the rígfennid cut her off with a raise of his scarred palm.

"It is his fault, not yours, lass," Bradan said, his eyes turning to hers, and she felt the full force of the turmoil and wrath engulfing him.

She scented it from him, she realised, but instead of smells she had to guess at, the emotions came to her immediately, as if in a second language.

"We have called you here, Bradan," the druid said, as if he hadn't spoken. "To invite you with us."

Ash stared at Ethne, and then the High King, a frown forming on her own lips.

"The Breen matriarch will lead us to the cave where Fionn Mac Cumhaill slumbers."

The High King's words barrelled into her, and it took several moments before she grasped what he meant. She opened her mouth to protest, but Bradan beat her to it.

"You can't be serious." He laughed, turning to the twins. "You claim to have found his tomb? Do you buy into the madness of the High King?" He didn't wait for a response, or seem to notice the surrounding highguard collectively step forward when he glared at Ash. "Welcome to the realm of lore and lies, I hope my son's death was worth it."

"Tiernan died saving my sister and his matriarch." Set crossed his arms, and although it looked like an act of defiance, she could see the tight grip of his fingers digging into his loose borrowed shirt. Aedan had ordered clothes to be sent in when they arrived, and along with healers to mend their wounds, it was the only acts of humanity she'd noticed from the king since they'd returned.

"I'm not going back down there," Maebh's voice was an echo of what it once was.

She hadn't made eye contact with anyone since leaving the tunnels, but she met the High King's gaze now with a look that would cut through the largest gemstone in the cave below their feet.

"You said I could speak to Conor," Ash interjected, afraid of what her friend would say.

She knew by the set of his jaw that he would demand Maebh go, and even though he was king, Maebh was the sort of person who wouldn't hold back on giving him a vulgar hand gesture and telling him what he could do on it. The mood in the room had shifted drastically upon the arrival of Bradan, and he'd got away with the insults he'd thrown at a man he'd once called a friend. Maebh was not protected by years of fond memories and the status of grieving parent.

The High King eventually turned from Maebh. He angled his head toward Ash as if contemplating whether he had indeed made that promise.

"It is true, High King," Ethne added, smiling at Ash with a wink. "His guilt is written on his hands, just like the letter clutched in Cara's when she was found. But if Aisling needs closure, she should have it."

Seconds passed as her head buzzed at those words. Then the High King spoke, snapping her back into the room and from the bloodied chamber of Newgrange.

"Once you bring us back to Fionn's slumber cave, you may speak to your brother."

Ash willed her face to remain blank as her mind reeled. "May I speak with Maebh and Set in private?"

The High King dismissed them to a corner of the cavernous throne room with a wave of his hand, and Ash was relieved when they followed her. Fighting to control her erratic heart, she let out a whoosh of breath as the twins faced her. "Do you trust me?"

Maebh met her gaze but dropped it again, nodding. She knew it wasn't because she didn't, but it was more that her will to care was at its lowest. Ash wouldn't give in to her emotions like Maebh had; she needed to fight against the fog of grief a little longer in order to save her brother.

He was no killer.

Chastising herself now was useless, but she did it, anyway. She knew he couldn't have been, but had allowed the impossible evidence stacked against him to speak above reason. She, of all people, knew that evidence did not mean guilt. There was a detective in the human world clutching to the fingerprint he believed proved she was the murderer.

"I trust you," Set said, taking her hand and squeezing, bringing her back from her spiral. The healers had worked on him the most, but Ash still marvelled at how unaffected he seemed to be after what she saw him become. Other than dark circles under his eyes and a haunted expression, he was the unrivalled warrior once more. "What's your plan?"

Ash glanced across the room. While Bradan and the High King were deep in what was no doubt an argument, she tracked the movement of the ancient druid. The woman with untapped power, who emanated an ethereal glow. Ethne turned toward her and gave a knowing smile. It chilled Ash's blood to the bone.

"We have to bring them back to the cave," she said, trying to tell Set there was more to what she was saying through eye contact, but from the confused look on his face, she didn't think she was doing a good enough job at it. "It's the only way. Trust me, okay?"

Set's eyes bounced back and forth between her own. He gave her hand one more squeeze before letting go. "Okay."

Ash turned to Maebh, who was staring into nothing, her blue eyes glazed. She jumped when Ash placed her hand on her arm and leaned close. Whispering, but careful of what she said, "We'll figure a way to bring him back. Maybe not today. But we will."

They joined the centre of the room once more, where the High King stood with his druid and Bradan. A group of highguard were stationed to his left, armed and ready for his bidding.

King Aedan gestured with his hands toward the door, clear delight on his face. "Let's go."

Ash found herself at the group's front, the king and Ethne following directly behind her. From another glance behind,

Bradan was in what appeared to be a one-sided conversation with the twins, the guards' voiceless presence taking the rear. They passed court members and warriors during their exit from the castle, but didn't stop.

Although everyone had seemed to like Aedan at the festival, Ash noticed sideways glances and murmured exchanges from his clansmen as they passed by. Bradan, on the other hand, received nods and greetings. Tiernan had mentioned that his father was well liked by his Leinster clansmen, and Ash wondered if it extended to the other provinces, too. Perhaps the High King swapping the Cath to his quest had done little to hold favour with his people.

He didn't seem to care, and that was the problem.

The Hill of Tara loomed before them as they passed the stationed guards. Once in the darkness of the first tunnel, Ethne magicked lit torches and offered them to the group. Accepting hers, Ash put her theory to the test. She needed confirmation her brother was innocent and the woman walking behind her was the key.

"Tell me about blood sacrifices," Ash said, her voice stronger than her nerve.

Ethne chuckled. "What do you want to know, child?"

"Specifically about sacrifices made on Samhain."

There was a moment of silence, and as Ash raised her torch in front to direct her path, she wasn't sure if the woman would answer. The silence stretched on long enough that she dared to turn around, only to find the woman smiling and the High King staring at her. The darkness was too great to see whether Bradan or the others were close enough to hear their conversation.

"You know, don't you?" Ethne stated, sighing before continuing. "Blood sacrifices on Samhain are a way to pierce the veil between realms."

"Ethne," the High King began, but the woman raised her moonlit coloured hand and surprisingly, Aedan closed his mouth and waited for her to speak again.

"What happens when you pierce the veil?" Ash asked, instead of the question she really wanted to utter. She would ask it before they reached the cave.

They had entered the antechamber that linked all seven tunnels. No whispers carried toward them this time. They were alone, it seemed. The wind picked up as soon as they entered the tunnel, but Ethne walked close by, raising her voice to answer.

"The High King knows of my many . . . talents. I am old enough to know Fionn personally. Aedan believes the key to Ireland's salvation is by waking up the ancient magic within Fionn. I know that we also need to pierce the realms."

They weaved through the narrow gaps before reaching the triskelion key, and Ash noticed the shock on the High King's face as he too was realising what Ethne was saying.

"What do you mean by this, Ethne?" Aedan called out, his voice barely reaching her.

The druid seemed to slink past the narrow stones with little effort, while Ash and the High King fumbled through. The others were silently following behind, and Ash hoped they could hear their conversation.

"To answer your question first, Aisling, piercing the realm will bring back all manner of chaos. Even though humans do not realise, their world, and ours, is ruled by a race that cares little for their existence."

"The Fair Ones," Ash said.

"Yes." Ethne sneered, and it was the first time she'd looked ugly. "That's what they call themselves. The Tuatha Dé Danann is anything but a fair race. In order to bring down their power, we need to bring in destruction."

"Did you kill my mother?" Ash asked, hating the fact the woman, even now, was speaking in riddles.

"In a matter of words, no." Ethne said.

"Ethne, did you?" the High King pressed.

They were huddled around the symbol, but he didn't seem to notice, his eyes only on the druid.

"The boy killed her," Ethne said before adding, "All tools are sharpened and readied by the blacksmith. Does that make them complacent when they are used for battle?"

"You're lying," Ash seethed, gripping the woman's arm. "Did you make Conor kill her?"

"See you after the fall," Ethne said before shimmering out of existence.

Ash stared at the High King who was glaring at the space once occupied by his trusted advisor.

"Aisling," he began, but she cut him off.

"Do you know of anyone else who is powerful enough to control someone's mind? She did it to a woman in the McQuillan clan who lost control of her own hand. My brother is no killer."

The others had reached them by now, but the space was too small for them to join. She could hear soft murmurs from behind the last tight crevice, but her eyes remained on the High King.

"I'll speak to her about it," he said, his eyes fixated on the triskelion illuminated by the glowing blue gemstones. The flames from her torch made them look molten, as if they would burn to the touch. "There must be a reasonable explanation. Our plan was always to wake up Fionn, piercing the veil through blood was not part of it. On my word, Ash."

She continued to stare at him with a frown. What good was his word when all he cared about was himself?

"Why do you want to wake Fionn?" she pressed.

"You know why," he answered, reaching towards the symbol, but Ash stood in front of it, blocking his path.

She shook her head. "I'm not showing you how to use the symbol unless you tell me the truth."

"I am your High King."

"And I am daughter to a murdered mother, sister to an accused brother. I am matriarch of the Breen clan, and I demand answers on behalf of my kin."

The High King looked ready to argue, but he narrowed his eyes before responding. "You look so much like your mother right now."

She didn't respond, the flames from her torch dancing between them.

"Fionn Mac Cumhaill is of a time where Fianna and Fair Ones lived side by side, ruling over humans and having equal standing. The time has come to bring that back. We are rulers, not followers. The Tuatha Dé Dannan need to be reminded of that."

"Are you willing to give up your throne for Fionn?" Bradan asked from the unseen bend in the cave, his tone made it clear he was incredulous.

The High King smirked before answering. "Not quite."

"What about the Morrígan?" Ash asked, remembering how enamoured Aedan had been with the fae female.

"They are different to their species. The Morrígan is Tuatha Dé, but the sisters stand for something more."

"Can we get this over with?" Maebh's voice sounded from further away and Ash realised she was not getting any more answers out of the High King. It was the druid she needed, anyway.

Turning towards the spiralling symbol, she thrust the torch at Aedan and pricked her finger, opening the seal once more, mimicking Tiernan's movements. Her breath caught in her throat as she imagined he was standing beside her, instructing her on what to do.

The High King's earlier fascination came back twofold when the cave wall beside them vanished, much like the druid moments earlier. Without warning, she jumped, hoping Maebh would push the High King in. It wouldn't kill him, but it'd scare him. There was no rush of excitement this time, and she stood alone at the bottom of the cave until the others joined her. It was only when the last guard landed, Ethne reappeared closer to the cave mouth.

Ash rushed forward, ready to demand proper answers, but the woman shook her head. "Now is not the time. We will speak further, and soon. But now we must wake a slumbering king."

"There will be time to deal with her later." The High King eagerly stepped around them to enter the dark tunnel that led to the sarcophagus. Ethne ambled behind him, and if Set hadn't placed his hands on her shoulders, Ash would have struck her right there.

"Let's get this part over with," he whispered close to her ear, clearly having realised her plan.

After several long breaths, her temper cooled. He was right. Fighting the druid now wouldn't do them any favours. It would satisfy her thirst for vengeance, but they still had to deal with Aedan's obsession with this place. The guards pushed past, remaining close to their king. Ash grabbed Bradan's arm before he could follow. "No matter what you see, stay behind me. Understand?" Ash whispered to the rígfennid.

He looked at her with raised brows, but when she didn't release his arm, he nodded.

"No matter who you see," Maebh added, the obvious note of devastation in her voice.

Both Set and Maebh kept close behind as she led Bradan through to the mouth of the cave. Their footsteps echoed, but the rising noise of what Ash now knew were stone heartbeats reverberated throughout. Staying close to the mouth, knowing there was very little space after that, her eyes roamed on their own, knowing exactly where to look in order to break her heart.

Ethne and Aedan were already stooped over the coffin. The High King murmured to his advisor, but from this distance it was impossible to hear.

Ash angled her body toward Set, gripping his hand. "Make sure to keep calm."

He only nodded, his eyes tracking the statues.

"What are those?" Bradan asked, moving to step into the cave as he pointed at them.

Even from this distance, it was jarring to see the familiar faces of the caillte. Her vision blurred as she swallowed a sob when her gaze landed on Tiernan, stationed beside his mother. There weren't as many statues; Set's warp spasm had helped eradicate some of the stone guardians, the rubble the only sign they had ever existed. Had he killed any of the caillte? Who had the statues been before? Ash grabbed Bradan's arm, but he shook it off as he moved closer.

"Stand back, High King," the druid ordered, her voice magically carrying over the vat of noise surrounding them. She lifted her hands, displaying her pale tattooed arms. "And get your guards ready."

"If any fae enter, attack." Aedan turned to his men, gesturing them forward.

He was so consumed by his obsession to wake Fionn, he hadn't looked to notice that her small group had remained by the entryway. Ash's chest pounded as guilt washed over her for what was about to happen, but she couldn't see another way.

Ethne raised her hands, torches in every sconce lighting at once. Ash blinked at the sudden light and noticed a darkness still hung above her head where her hands were angled as if she was conjuring the darkness from somewhere else. Her palms, facing each other, pushed outwards, and the darkness surrounded the sarcophagus. Stone against stone ground together, the coffin lid vibrating as if the shadows seeped inside.

Maebh broke from Ash and Set, reaching Bradan as he stared up at his wife and son. Her speech was rushed as she begged him to return to safety. He shook his head, and as the noise in stone heartbeats became deafening, Ash nodded to Set who rushed forward, grabbing the rígfennid and effortlessly hoisting him over his shoulder. Maebh and her brother made it back across the invisible cloaking line just before the stone warriors opened their eyes.

Bradan cursed, his body angled awkwardly over Set's shoulders, but he momentarily stilled, no longer fighting to break free as the stone warriors took a step forward. Ash outstretched her hands, pushing her friends back. Had she misjudged the line to Tiernan's invisible spell? Had it already worn off against the powerful wards within this cavern?

She stumbled backwards as she stared at Tiernan, now immortalised in stone. All the other guardians turned to face Aedan and his highguard, who didn't wait to strike. Except Tiernan remained facing them, his expression blank, but his focus unwavering from where they stood as they watched his stone complexion darken to his deep brown skin once more.

"Tiernan?" Maebh asked, thankfully not moving past the line.

His gaze snapped to hers and he took another step closer.

"Are you okay?" Maebh asked, her words coming out in between sobs.

He took another step closer, now only feet apart from Maebh. If he wanted, he could reach forward and plunge his hand into her chest, just as his mother had done to him.

"Son?" Bradan said, fighting against Set once more.

Set grit his teeth as he held firmly onto the rígfennid, and Ash tried to pull Maebh back, but she didn't budge.

"Tiernan?" Maebh tried again, her voice stronger.

He angled his head to the side, the noise like boulders falling from a mountainside.

A guard rushed forward from behind and Maebh shouted in warning. Tiernan didn't turn as the knife cracked against his back, the blade bending. He grabbed the guard by the neck from behind, raising him high. His eyes never left Maebh as he crushed the guard's neck, tossing his body to the ground.

Maebh didn't speak as Tiernan leaned forward and Ash wanted to scream at her to move, but she found herself unable to. The noise coming from behind seemed to break the spell, and Tiernan turned and wordlessly joined the other stone warriors as they attacked the remaining guards. Aedan was fighting off three warriors, his guards all fallen. He was skilled, but not enough. As his swords were wrenched from his grip and he was seized by Nessa, Ash scanned the area, frowning when she couldn't find the druid.

She knew there was little chance of the woman sticking around after they were attacked. Her ability to vanish, saving her from the stone warriors was an infuriating reality Ash had to accept.

"We need to leave before Tiernan comes back over," Set warned. "He created the ward. He can see us."

Set waited until she nodded, but Maebh refused to move, even when her brother retreated with a struggling Bradan on his back.

Ash held Maebh's hand, squeezing. "We'll find a way."

The blonde nodded, not taking her eyes from Tiernan as she let Ash lead her through the mouth of the tunnel.

Aedan's shouts echoed around the cave walls, mixing with the growing boulder heartbeats as Fionn's stone guardians claimed more lives to join their watch.

CHAPTER 51

AISLING

"**O**ur High King is dead," Bradan said from his seat at the opulent marble table in one of the castle meeting rooms.

A collective outburst filled the large space and Ash winced as she breathed through the overload of mixed smells coming from the rígfennids. Her gift, if that's what it was supposed to be, hadn't been as overwhelming as it was in this room. The province leaders spoke over one another as they questioned what had happened, and she stared at the damned white table, following the lines of engraved symbols in between those seated. As she fought to keep her breathing steady, her eyes pricked, and she had to look away. It was much too similar to the sarcophagus belowground.

As she listened to Bradan's rehearsed speech, weaving semi truths with blatant lies, she tried to hide her discomfort as she avoided the many stares cast her way, no doubt wondering why they were there. Before calling the other leaders, he'd sworn them to secrecy, and although she agreed with his reasons, it didn't make it easy.

She stood by the wall with Maebh and Set, along with several highguard and she wondered if they knew how many of their fellow soldiers had been lost. What would they do if they found out she could have prevented it? Another wave of guilt washed over her; she could have warned them, but didn't. Bradan continued his tale, where his son was a hero who had saved them: truth. And they hadn't found the first High King, but a nest of fae: lie. She gripped her hands tightly to the point the pain matched the one in her heart.

"The druid has an order for arrest on her head," Bradan said and he raised his hand toward Ash and the twins. "The Breen and McQuillan leaders are witness to this. Ethne orchestrated the deaths of both Cara Breen and Imogen McQuillan."

"What about my grandson?" the Rígfennid of Munster, Fintan Breen, asked from his position beside Tiernan's father and Ash had to bite her tongue.

He was dressed in rich dark robes, the yellow and red Breen crest visible on his chest. His dark unruly hair matched hers, but it was the only similarity other than the coat of arms they shared on their chests. His gaze met hers as he spoke. "Conor is still imprisoned, yet you say Ethne was the murderer?"

Shame coiled in Ash's stomach at his words. He was right; she hadn't been able to convince Bradan to release her brother.

"Although Ethne confessed to orchestrating their murders, she was not the hand that bore the crime," Bradan said, a look of apology flashing in his eyes as he, too, looked at her. He straightened, clearing his throat. "He will receive a fair trial."

Murmurs followed. She refused to meet anyone's gaze as she glared at her scuffed boots. Her grandfather still wore a youthful man's face; one that hadn't stepped foot in the human realm in many years. She had never met him, and her mother hadn't spoken kindly about him. Since she'd arrived in Tír na nÓg, Fintan hadn't approached her, so why should she acknowledge him now? She grit her teeth. Let them remain strangers; his pretence in caring over the welfare of Conor did little to cool her temper. Ash was no longer the meek, unsure woman who'd entered this land. She had fire in her heart and a blade of reckoning by her side, and nobody would stop her from delivering it.

"The Tuatha Dé representatives will be here soon, so I want to wrap this up," Bradan announced, and all conversation stopped. "Brehon law must be upheld and I will inform them that our High King has fallen. As chief Rígfennid, I will represent the Fianna clans until the next king is chosen."

Ash barely listened to the rest of the meeting, wondering why they were still there. Glancing at the twins, she saw the same weariness she felt, along with tracks of dirt on their tired faces. She needed to clean up before visiting Conor, a promise Bradan made for her silence.

Maebh nudged her, murmuring, "Do you hear that?"

"What?" she whispered, rubbing her side and glaring at her.

"He's reneging on the quest."

Her attention snapped back to Bradan as her heartbeat quickened and she concentrated on his next words.

"The High King decided against our traditions," he was saying, followed by murmured agreements. "And that ends today. The Cath has always decided the honour of joining the highguard, and it was never turned into a quest at anyone's whim, High King or no."

Panic bloomed in her chest as she licked her dry lips, but it was Set who interrupted, his voice loud and sure. "We won."

"Aisling, Maebh and Setanta, I commend you for your bravery in seeking the first High King. It was Aedan's desire, but not ours. May his soul continue on," Bradan said as he turned to the three of them, clasping his hands in front. As the resounding 'and his love remain' followed, his smile was thin lipped when he added, "But your clans will fight in the trials like every other warrior."

Her breath caught in her throat as she replayed his words. Winning the quest meant she'd won the right to rule as matriarch, uncontested by the elders. It was no easy task removing a matriarch, but it wasn't impossible. Niamh and Emer were probably with Mrs O'Malley and the elders now, reporting on all of her failures. She thought she'd won at least one victory in all of this.

"No." Her voice carried over the seated leaders, and they all turned to look at her. She stood taller, moving her hand to her belt only to realise she no longer had her sword. It was left broken in the cave, like her patience. Hastily placing it on her hip, she continued, "We should be rewarded. For our sacrifices . . ." Her voice broke as she stared into Bradan's eyes, and once again she sought out similarities to her friend. To the man who should be standing beside her as second.

"You didn't succeed in the proper Cath, Aisling," Fintan replied coolly, and her attention snapped to her grandfather. "You will be tested for your worth as matriarch like everyone else."

The doors opened before she could retort and a familiar black haired fae ambled in, along with another of her kind. The Morrígan in her fae form stood in the centre of the room, but this time, thankfully, she wore clothing. It was a simple silken shift dress that did little more than allude to clothing, and as she moved closer to Bradan, all eyes were trained on her. Ash could taste the lust and hatred in the air, so thick it was suffocating. Maebh gagged beside her, and she gripped her forearm, applying gentle pressure in solidarity.

"Macha," Bradan said, standing before bowing low. Chairs scraped against the stone floor as everyone followed suit. As the highguard bowed, one tapped her shoulder, signalling for them to do so.

When everyone had righted themselves, Bradan turned to the other fae. "And Tara, what a surprise to see you."

The dark-brown skinned fae didn't move from the entryway, nor did he acknowledge the rígfennid, but everyone bowed once more.

"You sent a signal for our attention," Macha stated, the undertone of three voices echoing in their words, the ever-present reminder they were three beings in one body.

"High King Aedan O'Dwyer is dead." Bradan clasped his hands behind his back, not moving from his position in front of the female. "I have taken his place until the next High King is declared."

Macha cocked their head as they studied him, and Ash wondered how he didn't fidget under their scrutiny. "Has he, now?"

She could hear the hint of challenge in those words, but Bradan only nodded, his gaze never leaving their achingly beautiful face. They stood like that for an eternity and Ash's heart jumped when they finally broke eye contact, only for Macha's eyes to train on her with a soft smile before they winked. "What of his quest?"

"You knew of that?" Bradan's composure faltered before he recovered. "He was unsuccessful."

"Who are they?" Tara demanded, having appeared in front of Ash before she could draw another breath.

Set stepped forward, shielding half of Ash as he stared down the fae, but she pushed his arm until he moved back. She braved a look at Tara, trying to recall any scrolls that described him, but all thought scattered as her heart stopped. Beautiful, like every other fae, his skin had an ethereal golden hue. He'd pulled his black hair into a low bun and he wore clothes similar to the Court members, but his cream silken tunic and pants were far richer than anything she'd seen here. In stark contrast to the wild fae he'd entered with, he was sophisticated, poised, and furious.

His nostrils flared as his next question emerged like a growl from the back of his throat. "Who are your kin?"

Her stomach rolled under his scrutiny, but he glared at both Set and Maebh with equal disdain, which was time enough for her breath to return. She cleared her throat enough to whisper, "I'm of the Breen clan and they are McQuillans."

"Come now, Tara," Macha crooned, popping into existence beside their companion. Ash blinked, wondering if they'd teleported or their movements were that quick that her human eyes couldn't keep up. The female fae angled their head and Ash swore that her crow form flashed through for a second. The Morrígan's voices danced around her as the sisters added, "We must go to our High King."

Tara didn't move from his place in front of her, but she didn't dare to look at his face again. Swallowing a lump in her throat, she breathed out a sigh when he finally turned and stormed from the room. She bowed, realising everyone else had when Macha strutted to the exit, but not before adding in their horrible multi-layered voice, "*My* High King will be most interested to hear of this news. We will be in touch."

CHAPTER 52

AISLING

"Conor, please look at me," Ash pleaded, but the bars separating her from her brother were not the only barrier between them.

She'd taken enough time to clean up and change into the simple tunic and pants that had been delivered to her room, but had then raced to her brother's tower. Bradan had insisted she, Set and Maebh spend the night in the castle while they informed Tara Court and all the warriors of the news of Aedan's apparent death and of the reopening of the Cath. Imogen's funeral pyre would take place the following day, and then they were back to the beginning of the trials once more. But now was not the time to wallow in her inevitable demise.

The tower in the east wing of the castle was cold, but dry, and although prisoners were usually taken to the dungeons, Ethne had insisted Conor was brought here. She detested the druid, and knew there was no shred of kindness in her, but she was grateful for this small mercy.

Conor lay on his hay bed, huddled facing the wall as far away from the cell bars and her as possible. The wind howled outside, the starry night as unsettled as her brother, who tossed and shook, but would not speak.

"Has he talked yet?" Maebh murmured from the tower door.

Ash turned to find both her and Set entering, holding baskets of what looked like blankets and food.

"Bradan said we could give Conor these. Make his time more comfortable." Set reached where Ash was sitting in three strides and, as he set his basket down, gripped her shoulder.

"I don't deserve any comfort," Conor's soft voice sounded farther away than the end of his cell. He didn't turn. "I killed them."

"You didn't, Con. She did. Ethne made you," Ash tried again, but he refused to accept it. When he didn't acknowledge her, she sighed and leaned her back against the frigid bars. "Any sign of where the druid went?"

Maebh shook her head. "The highguards are looking, but she can vanish from thin air."

"Her rooms have been left untouched. It doesn't appear like she took anything and they are searching for any evidence of her plans," Set said beside her, taking her hands, his rough palms comforting. "I doubt they'll find anything."

"She came here," Conor whispered, but the quiet sound coming from him was enough to startle Ash.

"What? When?" She pivoted, scattering hay in the process, wrapping her fingers around the rusted iron bars.

"A few hours ago," Conor said. He eventually turned, but continued lying in a heap, hugging his knees against his chest. "She said that her time with you was at an interval. She would come back when you were ready to listen."

Ash leaned her forehead against the bars, trying to get a better look at her brother, but the space was filled with shadows and despair. "Her time with me?"

"With all of you." Conor sighed before rising unsteadily to a sitting position. His lips were chapped, and it looked like he hadn't slept since before being imprisoned.

"Please take this, Con," she whispered, not trusting her voice as she offered a cup of fresh water.

It looked like he would protest, but he crawled closer, just within reach of accepting the cup she'd angled through the bars. After he took a few mouthfuls, coughing in between, he accepted the blanket Set held out for him. Wrapping it closely around himself, he finally met her gaze. "I killed her."

"Con . . ."

"No, Ash. She controlled my body, but my mind was always awake. I saw everything. Felt it." Conor wept into the blanket, his words muted by fabric and heartache. "The things she made me do."

Wind whistled through the narrow slits of the window as Conor finally unburdened himself of the truth that had consumed his soul. Tarnished forever, but hopefully mendable. His words cut like blades of a confession he'd fought to get out but had been trapped inside of him. She'd used him. She wasn't finished using all of them for whatever end she'd planned.

Ash wanted desperately to go to him, but no matter how much she stretched, he was always out of reach.

"Let me," Set said, standing. He gripped two bars and pulled, bowing them into an arch.

Ash watched, wide-eyed, as the iron bent to his will. She knew he was strong, even more so when he was in ríastrad, but to see him bend something immovable with his bare hands was mesmerising.

She heard Maebh mutter, 'show off', as Ash thanked him and climbed through the opening to Conor. He jumped at her touch, his head appearing out of the blankets and the realisation she'd got into his cell. Eventually, he let her hold him, his head making its way to her lap as she stroked his matted curls. Dark circles rimmed his eyes, and his jaw was mottled with a beard. It was the first time she realised he was no longer a teenager, but a man. Burdened with unthinkable acts that had been cast on his back to carry for the rest of his life. Innocent, but riddled with guilt.

"She has plans for you," Conor said, his voice clearer than it had been. "Piercing the veil at Samhain was only the beginning. Something big is going to happen at Winter Solstice."

"Do you know what?" Ash murmured, continuing to stroke his head, afraid of breaking the spell of him finally talking.

He shook his head, shivering so much that Set silently threw another blanket on top of him. Both he and Maebh remained on the other side of the cell bars, but close enough to hear.

"Mam was trying to protect you from her."

Ash stopped working her fingers through his hair. "What do you mean?"

"I badgered Mam for years, begging her to tell me why she didn't ask you to come home. She eventually broke down after another visit from . . . her."

"Ethne used to visit our clan?"

"Yes, she and I were . . ." Conor stopped himself, taking an uneven breath. "Mam refused to let her see you. She was obsessed with you."

"But why?"

"It has something to do with your birth." Conor sat up, leaning over to a basket and plucking out a bread roll. He nibbled at it as he eyed the others. "You and your friends. She wants to collect you. It's why she needed to lead you to the cave. She said that she couldn't open the lock hiding the first High King without your blood."

Ash's heart thrummed wildly in her ribcage. Finding the tunnel wasn't as easy as it had seemed, she'd known that, but having it confirmed was another matter. The druid had always known where to look. She'd set them up.

Maebh sat at the edge of the cell opening. "I don't remember her visiting our camp."

Set frowned. "Neither do I."

Conor shrugged. "Imogen . . ."

He trailed off as if a horror had unfolded in his mind.

"Conor. Come back to me," Ash pleaded, gripping his knee.

He blinked a few times, before lurching to a bucket in the corner, emptying the contents of his barely filled stomach. After a few more dry heaves, he returned to where he sat, ignoring the bread roll at his side, but accepting the water Ash offered.

"Sorry," Conor murmured, not meeting anyone's eyes.

She could only imagine what mentioning Imogen's name conjured for him. To be out of control in his own body, but still awake. Ash looked between her brother and Set; both tormented by an uncontrollable force. She wasn't sure if Set was blessed with not being able to remember his deeds after turning.

"Don't say sorry for something you couldn't control," Set said earnestly, and she wondered if his thoughts had been in line with hers.

"Your mother probably protected you from her more than you know," Conor finally said.

They each sat in silence as the wind continued to howl through the slitted windows.

"Ethne found out I knew where you were and forced me to write that last letter to you," Conor whispered, his eyes glazed as he remembered a time before he'd had blood on his hands. "She wrote about your birthright. About how she was as much your mother, if not more than our own. It was all riddles and nonsense," Conor said, his tone aggravated. "But I fought against her hold on me enough to warn Mam what she'd sent."

"And that's why she stole the letter from the cafe and ended up in Newgrange," Ash finished the words she was sure were too hard for Conor to utter.

He nodded, tears flowing freely down his hollowed cheeks, leaving tracks on his unwashed skin. "Ethne brought me to the tomb, luring her there, too. Mam had met with her at the Hill of Tara earlier, threatening to expose Ethne for who she truly is."

Ash frowned at her brother, about to ask, but Maebh cut in. "Who is she?"

"Ancient," Conor said, shivering under his blankets. "A being more powerful than an average druid. Old enough to have met the first High King."

"A Fair One?" Set asked, his brows furrowed.

"She hates them," Ash answered, something not adding up. "Conor, if she isn't a druid, but isn't a Fair One, what could she be?"

"Something born to create chaos and destruction." Was the only answer he gave as he yawned, lying back on Ash's lap. "She never told me. Just used me."

His words hung in the dark cell and Ash fought to remain calm. He hadn't asked where Tiernan was, and she knew she should tell him, but . . . Looking down at Conor, it was clear he was only hanging on to his sanity by a thread. She wouldn't pluck it, only for him to unravel again.

"I need to sleep now. Could you stay with me awhile?"

"I'll stay with you for as long as I'm allowed," Ash answered, stroking her brother's head once more.

She looked at the others, who nodded before getting up to leave them. Set draped a blanket across Ash's shoulder, a sad smile on his lips. Angling herself to lean against the stone wall, she listened to the howling of the wind. If she could conjure calming thoughts for Conor, she would have, but her mind reeled and her own emotions fought for dominance.

Her mother had loved her and wanted to protect her from an ancient being more dangerous than a Fair One. Her brother was innocent, but blood was still on his hands.

Before she left her now slumbering brother, she placed a bundle by his head. Lovingly wrapped in a burlap ribbon, all of her response letters to him throughout the years. She'd thought maybe he wouldn't want them, but he needed to know she'd always replied, had kept them safe until they could be reunited once more.

It was not how she had envisaged finally giving them to her brother, but perhaps it would provide a small comfort while she fought for his freedom.

Heat radiated from Imogen's funeral pyre, and Ash stood amongst the other warriors. Surrounded by clansmen, but none were her own. She fought against the crashing waves of anguish. The room they had given her for the night was more luxurious than any she'd experienced before, but sleep hadn't come.

The names of who she'd lost replayed with every toss and turn in her feather-stuffed bed. Cara and Lorcan, Tiernan, and, in some ways, Conor.

Bradan stood with the other leaders as the fire blazed, Imogen's shrouded form no longer visible on the raft anchored on the river. The high walls of Tara Court were a backdrop and the sunset painted the sky in oranges, reds and purples, making it another perfect day in Tír na nÓg, despite the sombre affair.

News had spread of Aedan's death, and Bradan ensured his son's name was included in every tale. His heroism was painted in such a light, she was sure they would create a ballad in his name. He deserved it, but she wondered why his father wanted to make him a martyr instead of trying to find a way to save him.

Frustration festered in her stomach as the cracks and pops of the fire filled the air. They'd discovered where the caillte were, but weren't allowed to tell anyone. Although Ash and the twins knew about *their* father's outcomes, there were families left with unanswered questions. In fact, the caillte had grown.

King Aedan's quest was declared a practice run. All clans would be allowed to enter the real Cath taking place before Winter Solstice. Ash had spoken to Mary and Dom approximately three days ago, and they had told her that the solstice was days away in their realm. In Tír na nÓg, that meant it would happen at any moment.

The crowds dispersed, all filtering back through the walls of Tara Court and the feast laid out to honour the fallen matriarch. Ash wordlessly followed the crowds, avoiding anyone's attention as she shuffled to a table, unsure what her next move should be. Looking at the empty seats around her, she sighed. None of her clan were left, and she would have to travel to the human realm and convince the remaining warriors to follow her now. The elders had refused to allow her clansmen to join, and she'd been too meek to stand up for them then. She'd taken her birthright as matriarch for the wrong reasons, but it was hers now and she planned to fight for it and prove her worth to the Breen clan.

A dip in the bench to her left caused her to turn, finding Set had taken the seat beside. A plonk to her right, and the smell of strong perfume caused her to smile as the curly hair of Maebh slapped her as she turned.

Maebh took a long slug of her mead horn. "We're sick of our clan already. Can we join yours?"

"Party of one, I'm not sure I can squeeze you in." Ash laughed before remembering why they were gathered. "I'm sorry for your loss."

They both nodded before falling into a comfortable silence, watching the others enjoy the food and company. Unlike her mother's funeral, the night had a festive air to it, anticipation already mounting for the Cath.

She looked to the tower of the east wing, unable to resist doing so every few minutes. "I can't believe Bradan won't release him."

Set patted her hand before reaching across a passing server's tray and grabbing three more horns. He placed one in front of each of them. "Conor didn't want to leave his cell."

"But that's because he's so messed up with what happened," Ash began, but her shoulders dipped and she grabbed her drink. She'd fought about this with anyone who would listen, but it came down to the fact that even Conor still found himself guilty of the murders.

"Matriarch," a gruff voice sounded behind her, and Ash stilled. Before she turned, she noticed Maebh's wide smile, and met the gaze of Tomás, followed by Ciarán.

She jumped to her feet, embracing her cousins before noticing the large gathering of her clansmen wearing the Breen crest on their jackets.

"I called them through Tiernan's oak tree," Maebh explained, her words catching at the mention of their lost friend.

Not lost. Not forever.

Ash's eyes brimmed with tears of gratitude, and she fought to find her voice. "Thank you."

"You're going to need a clan to lead, Matriarch," Maebh said, shrugging.

Set stood, joining them. "Especially with what's coming."

To everyone around, they probably thought they meant the Cath. Ash let the shiver down her spine fuel her. That was only part of the trials she would soon face. She hadn't planned on staying on as matriarch past finding out who her mother's killer was. It had been a selfish decision, born from a place of hurt. Glancing at her surrounding kin, her fingers tingled with the knowledge of what she would do.

Her clan needed a better matriarch, and she would be that for them. She would prove Conor's innocence, and a key to that was finding the wretched druid. Ethne had plans, but so did she, and Ash would do everything in her power to stop whatever that woman had planned. A blood sacrifice had been made on Samhain, but so far nothing else had happened and she'd ensure her mother's death wasn't a catalyst to more devastation.

The lore of Fionn Mac Cumhaill was real, but that didn't mean the realms needed him to wake yet. Aedan had learnt that, now a statue guarding against the act of waking the first High King. Ash gestured for her clansmen to join them and stared into each one's eyes as they slotted around her, waiting for her lead. They would be ready for what was to come.

If she'd learnt anything, it was that fate often wielded a double-edged sword, and she would be ready to fight back with a fury born from destruction.

Epilogue

Tiernan

Tiernan's blood sludged through his veins like setting cement. He could feel it as clear as he once could a beating heart. Now the sound of rock chambers pumping deafened his inhuman ears, his new clan a constant presence in his mind. The clan he'd never wanted. The first High King's guardians were connected through stone, body and mind. *Stay*. Their thoughts flowed through him now, his to theirs, no matter how much he fought for control, for privacy. *Protect*.

Screaming through his prison, no sound escaped his frozen lips.

They heard everything, and so did he. *Ours*. Even now, the creature that had once been his mother tried to communicate with him. His head didn't move, but even if it could, he would not look at her. *Stay*. She'd stopped being his mother when her fist had torn through him, turning him into this thing. *Protect*.

He could recall that he'd wanted to live. He remembered what it was like to have a body made from flesh and bone. To breathe. To feel. To think.

More often than he'd ever admit, he'd thought of her. Maebh. A woman so fierce, she'd fought for him to return to his human form even when he'd stood before her, fighting against his arm.

From raising and plunging it into her chest. She'd have joined him forever, then. Like his mother, and the other caillte. *Protect.* They could have stood a metre apart for an eternity. But that's not a life he'd give her if he could help it.

Again, his mother and the other stone guardians talked into his head. *Stay. Protect. Fight.* They tried to push out his thoughts, so that he too would be as faithfully subservient to the slumbering king. He shut them out as best he could.

High King Aedan. Where had he gone? *Stay.* Searching through the tether linking all guardians, he found him. He'd already succumbed. *Protect.*

Even though he fought against it, he knew. Tiernan was no longer a man. He was something 'other' underneath the stone entombing him.

"There, child, do not fear your fate." A soft-spoken voice filled the black space, and he strained to see, frustration seeping out of his stone pores. He could not move his eyes. *Ours.*

A familiar face appeared inches from his own, but even now, his past life was fighting to fade as a new chant began. *Forget. Abandon. Break.* As slow as the cement flowing through his veins, his memories were harder to retrieve. If he could grit his teeth, he would. He'd fight this. Every damned day. They forced this fate on him, but he wouldn't allow them to steal who he truly was.

Ethne. The silver-haired druid smiled as if knowing he'd recognised her.

"You were never just a man," she said, rising on her toes to kiss his cheek.

He felt nothing.

She cupped his face before stepping back. He could see her better. Her smile was too wide, her teeth too sharp. Had she always looked this way, or had his memory already failed? She angled her head as she assessed his frozen state.

"Of my blood, but more. I will see you again. Soon."

Encyclopaedia

Pronunciation Guide

Aisling ASH-ling

    An Garda Síochána an guard-a she-a-kawn-a, meaning the Guardian of the Peace. The Irish police. Also known as gardai or the guards.

    Babd bau, baiv or bye-v. One of three sisters that makes up The Morrígan. Babd is their crow form. See also Macha and Nemain.

    Banshee A female spirit in Irish folklore who heralds the death of a family member, usually by wailing, shrieking, or keening.

    Bodhrán boh-rawn. An Irish frame drum consisting of a circular wooden frame covered with a goatskin head on one side. It is played by striking the skin with a small wooden stick known as a bodhrán beater, tipper or cipín.

    Brehon law Laws brought in place after the Peace Treaty between Tuatha Dé Danann and humankind. Most humans are unaware of these laws except for a small group of humans with Faerie Sight, known as fianna.

    Caillte call-cha. Meaning 'lost' in Gaeilge (Irish language). The caillte are a group of five individuals from different clans who went missing seven years ago. Rumours circulated around the time that two of the missing persons - Gearoid McQuillan, second to Imogen McQuillan's clan, and Nessa Cassidy, matriarch of the Cassidy clan - were having an affair. Another notable missing person during this time is Lorcan Breen, second to matriarch, Cara Breen.

Cath An important Fianna rite, where clan members may compete in a series of trials to win the High King's favour and be selected into a coveted position of highguard. If selected, warriors may live in Tír na nÓg.

Céilí kay-lee. A traditional Irish social gathering with a band of musicians and folk dancing takes place.

Changeling A baby or young child who has been secretly swapped by an ancient fairy who takes his or her place. The dying fairy tricks the infant's parents into caring for them until they die. It is unknown what happens to the human child afterwards. Some believe they are left to die, while others believe they are given as gifts to the fae in Tír na nÓg.

Ciarán keer-AWN

Cohuleen druith kaw-hool-een drew-ah. Red hat with turquoise feathers belonging to the merrow (male mermen). Magical qualities allowing the wearer to breathe underwater.

Cú Chulainn COO cullen. A legendary warrior hero and demigod in Irish mythology. Famous for single-handedly fighting an army during 'The Cattle Raid of Cooley', and for his ability to riastrád, or warp spasm, turning into a monstrous creature who knew neither friend nor foe during battle.

Dearg due dah-ruh-guh du-ah. Meaning 'red blood sucker'. The Irish version of a female vampire.

Diarmuid DEER-mid

Dowth DOW-th. One of three ancient monuments situated in Boyne Valley.

Druid A mix of Fianna (humans with Faerie Sight) and wiccans (humans with the power to manipulate the elements and perform magic).

Ethne eth-na

Faerie Sight The ability to see through fae glamour and therefore gaining the knowledge that fairies exist.

Fair Ones Fairies. There are two species of fae: Tuatha Dé Danann, the ruling class, and Fomorians, fae who are almost extinct in this realm, or banished to other realms.

Fianna fee-a-na. Humans with Faerie Sight. Fianna clans are made up of families who all serve under a matriarch, who in turn answer to a provincial leader known as a rígfennid. All fianna serve under one human High King.

Fionn Mac Cumhaill e-UHN mack-coo-ool. Also known as Finn MacCool. The first High King of Ireland and leader of Fianna warrior clans.

Fomorians or Fomori. Fair Ones. Thrive on chaos and destruction. Enemies to the Tuatha Dé Danann who defeated them during The Great Battle. Fomorians live in exile in the human realm.

Gardaí gaa-dai. Means guardians. Irish police.

Gearoid gar-owedge

Hill of Tara A hill and ancient ceremonial and burial site.

Knowth NOW-th. One of three ancient monuments situated in Boyne Valley.

Lia Fáil lee-a F-AW-l. Stone of Destiny

Macha One of three sisters that make up The Morrígan. Macha is their fae form. See also Babd and Nemain.

Maebh maeve

Manannán mac Lir man-ann-AWN mac leer. Ruler of the sea, grants beings passage to the afterlife.

Morrígán more-eh-GAWN. Sisters from the Tuatha Dé royal bloodline. Three female forms encompassed within their shared soul. Badb is the crow. Her fae form, Macha, is a fae and Nemain is a spirit warrior.

Nemain one of three sisters that makes up The Morrígan. Nemain is their warrior spirit form. See also Babd and Macha.

Newgrange Ancient monument located within Boyne Valley. Part of three monuments that make up Brú na Boinne - an archaeological landscape in county Meath.

Niamh Neeve

Níl sé ach ina thús. Kneel shay ach ina thus. It's only just begun.

Púca pooka. Fae creature that takes different forms. Known for mischievous behaviour.

Ríastrad reea-strad. Also known as warp spasm. Taking the form of a monstrous creature.

Rígfennid reeg-fen-ed.

Samhain sow-wen. Occurs October 31st. The veil between this world and Tír na nÓg—the Otherworld—is at its thinnest. Historically, people dressed up in order to trick harmful spirits into leaving them alone. Hence the tradition of dressing up as witches and ghouls at Halloween.

Seanchai Shan-e-khee. A traditional Gaelic storyteller/historian.

Slainte slawn-chte. Means cheers in Gaeilge (Irish language).

Teamhair cha-wur. The ancient name given to the Hill of Tara.

Tiernan tier-nan

Tír na nÓg Tier-nah-nogue. Land of Eternal Youth. Alternate realm where time moves slowly. Humans can live there almost as immortals as long as they never touch the human realm soil again. They can still die here.

Tomás toh-moss

Tuatha Dé Danann tooah-je-danann. Fair Ones. Known for their beauty. Children of the goddess Danu. Also known as Tuath Dé which means 'tribe of the gods'.

Warp Spasm also known as ríastrad. Taking the form of a monstrous creature.

Will O' The Wisp Sprites who lead travellers through the woods at night.

Please note there are several dialects within Gaelic, so readers familiar with the Irish language should use what they are comfortable with.

Acknowledgments

Thank you, lovely reader, for reaching this part, which means you stuck it out. I hope you'll stick around to find out what I put my misfits through next time. Speaking of sticky situations, I'm sorry for leaving things that way. They are tough cookies, they'll hopefully figure it out . . .

Acknowledgements are hard to write, and it's not because I'm ungrateful. There are so many people who've helped me make this book a reality. These words are hard because I want to get it perfect. To convey how much each of you means to me. Even if it's not perfect, I'll settle for heartfelt. So here it goes.

I dedicated this book to Michaela because without her, it quite honestly wouldn't exist. As only sisters can do, she badgered me. Constantly. I had to endure, 'Did you write that book yet?', as a greeting for so long, I finally caved. And here we are. Thank you, Sister, for not tolerating my excuses and pushing me to pursue my dream. Maebh is for you.

My husband Lee is a patient man. He has listened to my complaints for many years, and although he has no idea what I'm talking about, he listened. Thank you, my love. Here's to more moments where I describe my half-baked ideas and you encourage me to go for it.

Being a mother means I could not have an acknowledgment section without naming my gorgeous human beings. Ethan, Alison and Eve. May you never read this, but know that I love you with every heartbeat and beyond.

Being a mother also means I know how badass mine is. I love you, Mam, even if you don't understand why I need to write about "such dark topics". You're the only person who could tell me they didn't finish the book and my response is to laugh. I told you so. Dad, I think you'd be able to handle the contents of this book better, but I'm also sorry if it's now weird . . . We can pretend it never happened, and I know you're proud of me anyway. Brendan, thanks for educating me on all those sayings. If only I could come up with something as ingenious as Blackadder's, 'Needs must when the devil vomits in your kettle'.

To Darby and Miranda. How do I thank you without the use of GIFs or emojis? You pulled me along this journey with your vast knowledge, enthusiasm, and tolerating my 5%. For your advice and encouragement, thank you, friends. To highlighting repeated words, and asking wtf do I actually mean here? To being in love with my characters and issuing threats on their behalf. You both better stick around forever because I can't do this without you.

To my F&BHB's. Twenty-plus years of friendship under our belts means a lot of my character inspiration comes from you . . . only the good parts, of course. To all the memories we have that can never be told . . . Aoife A, Aoife C, Catherine, Clare, Leah, Mary, Paula and Sarah. I love you girls.

Chloe, Kelsey and Nichole. You are an incredible bunch of individuals. Keep living your best lives and crushing it like you do.

Thank you Karley for beta reading. Your DM reactions and theories throughout brought so many smiles to my face.

My street team is made up of an amazing bunch of readers and dreamers. Your support will forever be immeasurable. Thanks for coming on this crazy journey with me.

Sara Starbuck, thank you for casting your keen eye over these words. You don't know this, but when I approached you with that other story years ago, I was deciding whether the writing business was truly for me. Without your positive and helpful feedback, I may not have continued writing. You will always be my banshee.

Taire, thank you for designing my cover and making it even better than I imagined. Tony Viento, thank you for bringing my characters to life through your art. Thank you, Adriano Bezerra, for creating my map.

I come back again to you, my lovely readers. This is my debut novel and I'm extremely proud to have gotten to this stage. It's been a long road and one of the biggest stumbling blocks was me! Having three kids, a husband, and a job has meant many early mornings and late nights, and a lot of daydreaming of characters and scenes when I should have been concentrating on something else (most likely laundry). It took more perseverance than I thought I had to see this through, and I finally made it happen. Ignoring chores helps.

Did you enjoy this book? I'd love to hear about it. Honest reviews help readers find the books they love, so please consider dropping a few lines on Amazon or the retailer of your choice. You'll forever be a legend in my eyes if you do.

About Author

Realm of Lore and Lies is the debut novel by Claire Wright. She currently lives in Ireland with her husband, three children and one eccentric dog.

When she's not reading or writing, you may find her thinking about all the things she should be doing, or driving her kids to their many, many activities.

Claire pulls her inspiration from the rolling mountains to her left, the crashing waves of the sea to her right, and a small town steeped in Irish lore.

The second book in the Fair Ones trilogy will be coming 2023.

Follow her at authorclairewright.com or @clairewright.author on Instagram & TikTok.

Also By Author

Fair Ones Book 2 coming 2023